TAYLOR

# REAL LIFE

# REAL LIFE

## D. J. TAYLOR

The author and publishers wish to emphasise that all characters in this book are entirely fictitious. Any similarity of names, physical characteristics and any other features as between the characters and any living person is purely coincidental, and the activities and events depicted are solely the product of the author's imagination.

The author and publishers wish to stress that the character described as Morty Kronenburg does not refer and is not intended to refer to any living person of that name.

Chatto & Windus
London

# Rachel's

Published in 1992 by
Chatto & Windus Ltd
20 Vauxhall Bridge Road
London SW1V 2SA

This novel is a work of fiction.
All the events and characters
depicted are entirely fictitious.

A CIP catalogue record for this book is available from the
British Library.

ISBN 0 7011 3888 2

Lyrics from 'Definitive Gaze' by Devoto/McGeogh
© 1978 Virgin Music (Publishers) Ltd
reproduced by kind permission of Virgin Music (Publishers) Ltd.

Photoset by Intype, London

Printed and bound in Great Britain by
Mackays of Chatham PLC, Chatham, Kent

So this is real life
you're telling me
and everything
is where it ought to be
Howard Devoto, Definitive Gaze


In real life, things are much worse than as represented in books. In books, you love somebody and want them, win them or lose them. In real life, so often, you love them and don't want them, or want them and don't love them.
Anthony Powell, The Kindly Ones


. . . the still eternal light through which we see the infinite unchanging vistas we make, from the height of one year old, out of suburban gardens or municipal parks in summer, endless grassy horizons and alleys which we always hope to revisit, inhabit in real life, whatever that is.
A.S. Byatt, The Virgin In The Garden

# Part 1

EARLY ONE AFTERNOON in the late January of 1974 a young woman set out to walk the short distance from Piccadilly Circus underground station to the National Gallery in Trafalgar Square. Although her journey was in a certain sense premeditated she moved slowly and hesitantly, sauntering diagonally along Coventry Street and waiting for nearly a minute under the Swiss Centre clock on the outlying flank of Leicester Square. Later she could be seen drifting in the same strangely reluctant way along the square's western approach, pausing to stare at the cinema advertisements and the gaping tourist boutiques.

The young woman's name, for the purposes of this particular fiction, was Caroline. She was perhaps twenty-two or twenty-three, with square, regular features and shoulder-length blonde hair. In the fashion of the time she wore a short, belted coat and shiny, high-heeled boots, the latter impeding her progress even further and causing her to waver timorously on the icy pavements. At regular intervals she would stop and kick the toe of each boot rigorously against the kerbside to dislodge the particles of snow that had collected beneath.

Early afternoon in Leicester Square. Snow, fallen two days previously, lies banked up in off-white drifts. An opaque sky gives promise of more. A whirl of distant voices, given sudden coherence as from the south end of the square a procession of young men, shaven-headed and dressed in billowing robes, their vanguard chanting and banging small drums, comes clanking into view. Walking towards them the girl briefly disappears, caught up in the flow of shuffling movement and outstretched arms, re-emerges and turns hard right into a side alley.

In Panton Street, past a newsvendor's table and a cinema showing pornographic films, the girl's pace increases. The pavement is more crowded here – a traffic warden, a file of school-children lofting satchels at one another – but she presses forward, stumbling occasionally when her feet catch on the impediments of kerb or paving stone. Two workmen's braziers, glowing against the grey frontage of shops and the muted light, give her passage into Whitcomb Street a faintly numinous quality: the hurrying figure at first dissolving into a haze of shaky air, then seen striding purposefully on past pale, empty windows towards the distant traffic.

The man stands waiting on the gallery steps. Women with heavily laden baskets, foreign students with clipboard files clamped under their arms, surge about him. Miraculously, as she approaches they clear and there is only the single dark figure, the shoulders hunched higher in the overcoat, the eyes nervous and intent. The man is in his early forties. He has sparse, receding hair which has been slicked back over his scalp with oil or grease. The girl divines that he has shaved recently – there are rough, red patches on his neck – but imperfectly, so that a small coin-sized blob of bristles sits on the point of his chin. As he sees her he flicks down a cigarette and grinds it with his heel. The eyes stray, down across the crowded pavement, upwards into the dense air, back to the girl. He says, 'I didn't think you'd come.'

'You thought wrong.' The tone is – artless? Obedient? Its precise nuance fails to register with the man. He goes on, 'It's not far. We could take a cab.'

'If you like.' The girl pauses, a look of intense concentration passing over her face. 'What sort of place is it?'

'Just fine,' the man says. 'For what you and me've got in mind, just fine.'

In the taxi – a dark, lurching vehicle allowing occasional close-ups of the passing street – the man says urgently, 'When we get back to my place I'm going to fuck your brains out.'

The girl leans back in her seat, legs splayed. She sticks out her tongue and lets it rest on her lower lip. 'I know,' she says, 'I know all about that.' She pauses again. 'Let's hope you're as good as you say you are.'

Charing Cross Road. Cambridge Circus. Past overbright shop-fronts. A brief glimpse of the lowering sky. Shaftesbury Avenue.

The man, eyes staring blindly in front of him, takes the girl's hand and places it in his lap.

The flat is small, sparsely furnished. A bed. A chair. Pictures cut out of magazines taped randomly to the walls. The electric fire glows. Standing in front of it the man casts long, angular shadows. From the window behind there are views of huddled rooftops. In the distance the Post Office Tower. 'Let's talk business,' he says. 'How much is this going to cost me?'

The girl leans negligently against the door, arms folded across her chest. 'Twenty. Thirty. It depends what you want.'

'Whatever you've got. That's what I want.'

Naked, their clothes flung in serpentine coils around the room, they examine one another. It is an unfortunate contrast: the man's scrawny torso, grey haunches, white, tapering legs; the girl's plump, rosy contours, fresh dappled skin. Her right flank, edging nearer to the fire, is scarlet from the heat. Together they might form part of some medieval figurative painting: Spring and Autumn, say, or Maidenhood Sold into Bondage. The girl raises her hands above her stomach and begins to massage herself. By this stage, as the man lopes hungrily towards her, their conversation is barely intelligible, a series of muttered, raunchy monologues, spoken over each other's shoulders.

*. . . You London bitches just fuckin' ask for it. Think you're so flash . . .*

*. . . I want a man who can give me a good time. Are you going to give me a good time? Are you?*

*. . . So fuckin' flash. I could hurt you if you wanted me to. I could hurt you so bad that I . . .*

*. . . A good time. A good time. A wonderful time.*

*. . . Fuck your brains out.*

Once in the course of these poorly choreographed preliminaries, as the man lies prone on the cheerless bed, the girl sprawled across him, something unlooked for happens, something unplanned. 'Look at it,' the girl says, sinking back momentarily on her haunches. 'Look out of the window.' The man stares intently, his eyes registering both panic and bewilderment, until he sees the first restless flurry of snowflakes. 'Snow,' he says woodenly. 'Sure,' the girl says. 'It's starting to snow. Look at it.' They pause for a moment as the flakes drift down over the huddled Soho rooftops, pink and luminous in the glare of the lamp. The man smiles. 'I'm going to fuck your brains out,' he says with a touch of sadness.

Finally the act is completed, there on the narrow bed, a bizarre, self-conscious spectacle in which limbs are weirdly deployed across the white sheets, where there are strange tensings and pauses, inexplicable confusions and variations to the routine of push and shove, the warp and weft. Such is the intent synchronisation of gesture, the stylised breaking apart and coming together, that one might almost think there was a third presence in the room, staring out over the writhing bed towards the dark wall of glass. Beyond, the snow continues to fall.


*Capital Pick-up*, Leisurevision's first major feature, was filmed on location in central London and at the loft in Dean Street. The principal actors – two hard-up and unmemorable associates of Morty's named Jake Gordon and Irma La Douche – were paid fifty pounds apiece. I did the lighting: a row of raw bulbs placed a yard or two above the protagonists' heads. Morty directed. An afternoon's work, the editing completed two or three hours after Jake and Irma's departure, sweating and glassy-eyed, from the premises, the product transferred to an eight-reel later that night. Sound: Crazy Rodney. Camera: another of Morty's stringers. Executive producer: Terry Chimes.

Inevitably for a first feature shot on a shoestring there were problems. Chief among these was Irma La Douche's inability to learn her lines. The intent look, the grimaces of urgent concentration on which so many subsequent observers remarked, were the product not of mild over-acting but simple amnesia. Later when we had dialogue coaches, printed scripts – all the careful paraphernalia that came to characterise Morty's operations – such deficiencies were grandly overcome. As it was, the game amateurism of these early forays was thought to suggest a certain ready verisimilitude, an authenticity which later productions with their practised starlets and easy dialogue were presumed to lack. Then there was Jake's inability to respond to any word or gesture not in the script. The exchange about the snow, for example, was entirely spontaneous, a consequence of Irma rais-

6

ing her head from Jake's puny torso at the exact moment when the first flakes began to fall, in sheer over-excitement with scene: a random, fleeting quirk which was to invest *Capital Pick-up* with its single moment of charm.

Inexplicably, several of Morty's early films were to possess this odd, elegiac quality, a characteristic which set them apart from other more clinical ventures, undertaken by other Mortys in other, similar studios peopled by other Jake Gordons and Irma La Douches, attended by other tensions and anxieties. There is the moment in *Doctors' Wives* in which Sheri La Grange, stepping out of the pile of hastily divested clothing, ignores the beckoning figure on the couch to turn and smile briefly at the onlooker, a mysterious Delphic smile, having no relation to any event taking place on screen or off. There is, again, the scene in *Possession*, with its country-house vistas of blazing log fires and coy maidservants, in which the camera moves falteringly beyond the savage coupling on the rug to record the spatter of rain on glass, a glimpse of dense, untended foliage. In his way Morty had some claims to being an artist. A vulgarian would have given these episodes an unmistakeable ironic force, had Sheri La Grange deliver only a mournful pout, timed the slap of water on glass to coincide with another more obvious conjunction. With Morty there was a sense in which these minor detours in the forward march of the plot existed wholly in isolation, played no part in the wider development of theme or content. I recall in particular *Latchkey Kid*, another Leisurevision effort from about this time, filmed once more in the loft in Dean Street, the familiar outlines disguised with heavy curtains and hired furniture. Its plot again was rudimentary. A lissom schoolgirl (gym-slip, hockey stick, straw hat – Morty liked this sort of *haute* stylisation) is presented by her mother with a door key on the understanding that the mother will be delayed that evening. The daughter subsequently returns to the house accompanied by a brawny youth in a leather jacket. An inevitable sequence of events then follows, broken only – both parties by this stage maximally aroused – by the early arrival of the mother. Seen a decade later *Latchkey Kid* has little to recommend it, apart from a curious moment when the camera, ignoring the sight of Candy Barr sleekly unrolling fishnet stockings, swivels to take in the framed photograph which rests on a side table next to the sofa. It shows a wedding couple from a period perhaps thirty or forty years before, arm-in-arm, smiling fixed, snaggle-toothed smiles, ducking instinctively as a whirl of confetti descends upon their heads. The camera lingers, trawls slowly over the archaic hairstyles and the dilated eyes, and for a moment Candy Barr and her consort are forgotten, a blur of limbs dimly descried in the distance, a swish of abandoned clothing on the crackling soundtrack: a fugitive moment, suffused with poignancy.

More moments from these early days: Morty auditioning a pool-side scene in front of a line of thatch-haired girls in swimsuits; scripting *Doctors' Wives* in a rented Harley Street consulting room half an hour before filming ('Make it tasteful,' Morty said, 'and cut the crap.'); the Dean Street loft awash in coruscating artificial light. Twitches on the thread. Rushes from the endless tape. Watching the rough cut of *Possession* at the preview cinema in Wardour Street with Terry Chimes asleep in his chair. Fiery dawns, intent and red-eyed on the cutting room floor. And the girls: Sheri La Grange, Irma La Douche and Lila St Claire, Terri da Motta, Berkeley Lush and Corona d'Amour. Impossible complexions, improbable names. They came in waves. When we started they were all Sixties cast-offs, ageing waifs who'd had walk-ons in films about Swinging London called Keki or Boo or Jade. A little later they began to be named after hotels: Tiffany, Berkeley, Ritzy. A bit later still they had men's names: Sam and Joe and Jake. Only towards the end when everybody – producers, directors, actors – were casting envious glances towards America did they assume that three-pronged, EEC-diluted uniformity: Martina La Chasse, Gaby du Pont, Cornelia del Hacienda. As the names changed so did the attitudes. At the start the girls were naive, generous and trusting ('Listen love,' I can remember Morty instructing some pouting ingénue, 'this is a *pornographic* movie, right? You take *all* your clothes off and get on the bed,'), gamely tolerant of the indignities visited upon them. Subsequently amateur warmth gave way to wary professionalism: girls with agents, contracts, artistic integrity, scruples, percentages; girls who emerged frostily from bed, shower, embrace or pose to examine small print, call for a telephone, an understudy,

8

a renegotiation. The scenes move sharply into focus now, lose the ethereal gloss imposed by distance. Filming *Plasma Party* in bare, angular chambers streaked with artificial gore. The prodigies of costume design demanded by *Nazi Death Camp*. That grim procession of sex, money and lies, lies, money and sex. Studio lights pulse through the fog of cigarette smoke. Morty smiles his mad, off-centre smile. The cameraman grins. The figures recede and fade away. At these times Irma and her rhapsodies over the snow remain only as a faint memory, a fading tint of romanticism in a picture since given over to harsh, brutal colours.

Nearly dark up here in the study. Outside the window and its vista of identikit terraced houses the streetlamps have begun to go on in that mellow, autumnal way they have. In the remoter distance over towards Heigham Park, a frail pinkish glow. A second, keener light shines up from under the door. From below there are odd, fractured sounds as Suzi roams noisily around the kitchen. Gusts of air blow in through the half-open window.

Sometimes I listen to the sounds people make as they walk by outside. You get to know them all: the fugitive clatter of high heels – they still wear high heels round here – the slurp of trainers as some lurching oaf shuffles past on his way to the pub, the whisper of the sandals the old women wear. The noises are rarely confined to footwear. Children slither by in the gloaming, a salvo of chatter that vanishes instantly on the wind; teenagers slink past to rustle the leaves of the hedge with their shoulders; burly women loiter for a moment on the pavement by T. Coulthard's grocery shop, leaving behind a snatch of gnomic repartee. I looked out once at two a.m. on an airy summer's night, alerted by vigorous rustlings borne on the breeze, and found Fat Eric from two doors down practically giving his girlfriend one in the front garden.

Such bucolic licence is long past now. From below there is another random crash of crockery. The radio rasps on, then off. Outside the cars purr by in the murk: sleek roadsters with wound-down sun roofs, nippy Minis driven at speed. Astonishing vehicles. Fat Eric from two doors down has a squat, hump-backed conveyance which, fleeting memory assures me, is a 1966 Hillman Husky. I listen to another gutsy squeal of rubber on tarmac, peer outside. There are lights going on all along the street now; the myriad flicker of the television sets. I light a cigarette and stand at the window considering the wide portholes into narrow, bookless rooms, the restless, screen-tethered heads. Downstairs the noises from beyond the kitchen door have quietened down to the staccato clink of Suzi chopping vegetables and Suzi singing disagreeably along to the radio. In the gloom of the hallway the telephone message pad gleams palely. Elaine rang yesterday. The message is still there, written in Suzi's Marion Richardson copperplate. 'A woman rang. Said she'd ring back.' Elaine, without a doubt. After all, what other woman would ring me up unbidden? Emma? Wouldn't have the number. One of Morty's actresses? Disappeared, disappeared into the random clutter of time. No, it had to be Elaine.

Amid the passage of a crowded life, you forget things . . . It must be two years since I last set eyes on Elaine. Not much less, for that matter, since I last set eyes on all of them, on Morty, Terry Chimes, Crazy Rodney or whoever. Two years of silent, self-imposed sequestration, broken only now by this ominous twitch on the thread. If it *is* her, that is . . . Wondering uneasily about this I pull a coat over my shoulders, step out into the cheerless streets.

Fine spray mists over the glass of the streetlamps. A bicycle weaves past. The muffled thud of flesh on metal discloses that Fat Eric from two doors down is out there doing his car. Fat Eric does this quite a lot, usually at the most unpromising hours of the day or night. Dawn on a vicious December morning finds him, an otiose scarf wrapped over his tee-shirt, full-length on the pavement guiding his freezing hands towards the chassis. Noon on an eighty-degree August scorcher reveals him splayed over the bonnet, glistening in his sawn-off jeans, morosely polishing the windscreen. As I lope by, gratefully feeling the cigarette smoke crackling in my lungs, he straightens up from his engrossed rear-wheel crouch and nods.

'Hi.'

Clad in a sweatshirt and a wantonly tight pair of tracksuit bottoms, Fat Eric is a tremendous spectacle: unbeautiful hands, face a wedge of reddening flesh. He has one of those awesome professional footballer's haircuts that resemble a bunch of grapes laid lengthways across the scalp.

'How's it going, Fat Eric?'

Fat Eric and I talk about football. I read about it in the *Eastern Evening News* and tell him whether I think Darryl McKenzie will make the city team next week and what the news is on Kevin Flack's groin strain. The result of this elementary exercise in news-gathering is that Fat Eric imagines me to be absurdly knowledgeable on the soccer scene. One of these days, he grandly intimates, we might even go and see a game together. Now he merely looks thoughtful, sets off immediately on one of his random monologues.

'You see the highlights the other night? I thought it was fucking diabolical. That ref . . . I mean,' says Fat Eric, 'I saw him when we played the Arsenal last year. Two penalties in the first half, right? And then, when Flacky gets one in the head right on the edge of the six-yard box, what does he do? Gives a fucking goal kick.'

'But Fat Eric,' I chip in earnestly, 'they reckoned he wasn't fit, you know.'

Kevin Flack is Norwich City's latest discovery: a tiny, rock-headed Scot who fled over the border at the end of last season with a couple of paternity suits and an alcohol problem that they didn't find out about until after the transfer forms had been signed. Local opinion is divided about Kevin Flack. The *Eastern Evening News*, having hailed him initially as a 'soccer sensation', devotes pointed headlines to his failure to score in the last eleven matches. But Fat Eric has other, mutinous ideas.

'Fit? Wouldn't matter if the kid was fit, would it? Papers have got it in for him, haven't they?'

'I suppose they have. Well, see you around.'

'See you around.'

I leave Fat Eric back by the rear wheel, where he looks suddenly immutable, a vast, unhappy mammoth anchored eternally by folds of permafrost. And so: on. Past the dogleg alley that leads you back into a maze of side streets and lock-up garages where tethered Alsatians whine balefully at the sky. Past the hole in the road with its arc of winking lights. Past the City Gates on the corner, where the door swings open for an instant and there is a sudden confused impression of smoke, light shining off glass, mute, aquarium faces.

The western side of Norwich was built on hills. The wide arterial roads that snake out to the suburbs – Newmarket, Unthank, Jessop, Earlham – run through valleys. Between them the side streets rise, undulate and fall: College Road. Recreation Road. Christchurch Road. Teeming terraces, away from the thunder of the traffic and the taxi roar, a discombobulated world. You can tarmac over the hills, you can turn a wilderness into an asphalt floor, but you cannot tame what lies beneath. Under the West Norwich streets there are old chalk workings, refuse pits full of vanished Saxon dung. They open up occasionally and a bus disappears, lists comfortably into a funnel of cascading earth, a tree totters inexorably to one side, a house is scythed neatly in two by the shifting void below. The past refuses to lie down here. It will not go away. Sometimes, prompted by chance malfunctions of gas and electricity, they dig up the grey streets and find Nazi bombs, or parched skeletons grown white and friable beneath the sandstone grit. The bombs come from a Baedeker raid in 1942 when Goering tried to erase Norwich Cathedral; the bones are from centuries back, from Danish burial grounds, from Angevin plague pits: a cavalcade of grim history sealed up in the wet earth, ripped open by prying fingers of iron and steel.

Up College Road. Left along the dense outline of the park. The spectral hand of a more personal heritage looms up here, the twitch upon the thread grows insistent. Each stroll through the back streets of Norwich has become a tightrope walk over a frothing cauldron of reminiscence. The house on the corner? That was where you attempted to put your arm round a girl called Alexandra Dodd fifteen years ago. The wide concrete lead-in to the park gates? Where your friend flipped lazily off his scooter and snapped a wrist. You can hear the bone crack now, screaming back across time.

I halt on the corner of The Avenues and Christchurch Road and light another cigarette, watch as two spiky-tops, a boy and a girl in the standard leather and bondage gear, saunter by. In my absence, inexplicably, Norwich has become a place of

violence. Fat Eric tells me about it sometimes, waxing philo-
sophical over his can of Strongbow: 'Fucking diabolical it is too.
This old woman, friend of me mum's, comes home and finds
her door's been kicked in. And then when she looks in the
kitchen . . .' Fat Eric is a walking, recitative case book of the
lore of local horror. 'So then they tied the kid to a tree and . . .
Beat up his mother and then . . . Waited until he'd unlocked the
back door and . . .' The gangs, the lads you see looking sullen
and anxious outside the park gates, have designer names these
days: the Steins, the Dawn Patrol, the North Park Avengers. The
Steins got hold of a police Alsatian out on Eaton Park last week.
According to Fat Eric's admiring testimony, it came back in
fillets.

This is what they've done to my city, where I sowed my
youthful dreams . . . Back outside the house there is an odd,
untenanted darkness detectable in the front room. Suzi has disappeared. I admit myself cautiously, careful not to rattle the key
in the lock, inch silently across the musty carpet. Here Suzi has
printed a note on top of the message pad. 'Elaine rang. Will call
back.'

What do you know? It was her. Unbidden, half-remembered
images crackle in my head: Elaine decked out in a wedding dress,
hair *à l'impératrice* for the preliminary scenes of *Virgin Bride*;
Elaine romping through thigh-high bracken, stalked by three
slavering, Amazonian pursuers, in a spoof Morty once made
called *Daughters of Giant Hulk*; I halt on the stairs for a
moment, seeing her face with its queer, intense look emerging
out of a backdrop of unknown physiognomies and random paraphernalia, clamber upstairs into the raging darkness.


Later I ask Suzi, 'The girl who rang, Elaine. What did she sound
like?'

'Which girl?'

'The girl who rang called Elaine. The girl who rang and you
took the message. What did she sound like?'

Suzi turns from the television set where she is adjusting the
video to record a snooker final. There are files of unmarked
examination scripts strewn over the carpet.

'I don't know. I wasn't listening.'

'Did she sound cheerful? Angry? Preoccupied?'

'I don't remember.'

'Did she have an Irish accent?'

There is a tinge of scarlet seeping into Suzi's flabby and generally marmoreal cheeks. She says, 'You just don't have any tact at all, do you? Some ex-girlfriend of yours you've never told me about rings up and I have to answer the telephone, and all you can do is ask me, "What does she sound like?" and "Does she have an Irish accent?" '

'Did she?'

'I don't remember,' Suzi says. She slams the tape viciously into its slot. 'I just don't remember. And if she rings again do you know what I'm going to do?'

'No.'

'I'm going to slam the phone down,' Suzi says. 'I'm just going to slam the phone down.'

There is a brief, puzzling moment before I gather her up in a neutral, compensatory embrace. She cries quietly for a moment. 'You should have told me about her,' she says.

The room falls quiet again. In the distance, towards Unthank Road, the traffic hums.


I still have the photographs. They fell out of a drawer the other day and came tumbling down over the carpet: parti-coloured leaves on the dead forest floor, glistening evidence. Scuffed now, stained and split by half-a-dozen hurried removals and uneasy resting places, they have their own patterns. Contrived, formal portraits: Morty, Terry Chimes and I pictured behind desks, posed with flustered starlets at industry launches, lined up outside the office door at Dean Street; stills from the major Leisurevision productions, full of bobbing breasts and wanton undress; odd, miscellaneous shots taken in the studio, in pubs, in the Grunt Records foyer. Elaine stares intently out of a frame of cameras and lighting equipment; Morty, frozen in mid-gesture, hovers in the centre of an arc of bright, inexplicable light; a joke portrait of Terry Chimes asleep on a sofa, eyes keeled crazily to one side. There is a flawless, perfect photograph taken by David

Bailey which appeared at the height of our fame: we sit stonily, side by side, behind a glossy oak table strewn with discarded film reels. Somebody – not myself – has captioned it '*Sunday Times*, November 1977'.

Other pictures. Morty and Terry Chimes shot in the Bethnal Green Road, around 1975. Crazy Rodney stands a pace or two behind them, eyes lowered, hands stuffed into his East End frightener's overcoat. Terry Chimes pictured with some of the Grunt Records roster: with the Glasgow Express, a panorama of tartan flares, macaw haircuts, bony, Scottish faces; with Bobby Dazz, the latter encased in a white tuxedo. Countless portraits of Elaine: Elaine in black fishnets and satin camisole lying on a bed of white roses (the promotional shot for *Virgin Bride*, I recall), Elaine in a girl-guide uniform standing before a full-length mirror, shot in shadow so that her pale face stares up out of the murk. What strikes me most in retrospect is the consistency of the expressions. Morty looks nervous, uncertain, head turned half to one side, eyes permanently distracted by something beyond the camera. Terry Chimes, in contrast, is the epitome of self-possession, grinning, ironic, contemptuous. Elaine seems remote, preoccupied. There is a single photograph of the four of us taken on a boat on the Thames which neatly encapsulates these attitudes. Morty's face is averted, gathered up in shadow, the rest of his body slung to one side. Terry Chimes stares straight ahead, one hand clasped round a pint glass, hair streaming in the wind. I have my arms folded high up my chest, an odd, knowing look. Elaine is disagreeably amused. 'I am here too,' her expression seems to say. 'I am part of this, but I wouldn't want you to think that I was in any way enjoying myself.' Behind us the choppy water stretches away to a back-drop of rotting wharves and tumbledown warehouses.

Suzi's attitude to this portrait gallery is revealing. I watch her sometimes as she turns the pictures over, critically, but with cautious interest. Her comments are careful, designed in however small a way to connect her to the pantomime of face and gesture rather than to establish distance. 'I knew a woman who looked like that,' she says, examining a print of some forgotten starlet, or 'There was a girl at school who did her hair that way.' Seeing the picture of Elaine and the roses she said once, 'Wasn't that a poster? I'm sure I saw it in a magazine somebody had at school.' Her comments on my own appearance are, I suspect, purposefully mundane. 'You look ill there,' she says. 'Ill. And you haven't shaved.' The wider implications, of livelihood and past association, are set prudently to one side.

There is a faint wistfulness about these excavations. On one occasion she said, 'I was on TV once.'

'When was that?'

'At school. Every year in the week before Christmas, Anglia TV used to choose someone from one of the local schools to read from the nativity story and one year it was me.'

'Did you enjoy it?'

'They said I had very expressive diction,' Suzi says primly, 'and that I responded well to the camera.'

Later on, several stills photographs of this performance were brought out and arranged before me. They showed a small, plump schoolgirl, abundant hair falling over green blazer, reading from a heavy prayerbook. There were glimpses of festive scenery: snow-covered logs, a lavish crib, a henge of beribboned parcels, a file of choristers processing across the stage, ersatz snow pouring down above them. They seemed as remote and unreal as anything Morty and I had ever contrived.

'I was quite famous for a bit,' Suzi said. 'People used to stop me in the street and say they'd seen me.'

Only one of the photographs causes me anxiety, and that not on account of cast or circumstance. Taken in Venice, where Morty and I had gone on business, at the height of *Carnivale*, it supplies an immense, fantastic panorama. Pierrot, Harlequin, other figures out of the *commedia dell'arte*, stylised Venetian noblemen, are performing an intricate and expressive dance, their faces, white-painted, hidden behind black eyemasks, wholly absorbed. Morty and I, tourists bidden to the ball by one of Morty's associates, stand in the centre of this assembly, uncertain and somehow ill at ease. Many of the dancers wear animal masks: bear, eagle, panther, zebra. There is something mildly sinister, certainly, in the precision of their grouping around me, but the disquiet is that of association. Looking at them you think, inevitably, of fog over the Piazza San Marco, water lapping across the grey flagstones, light shining from high, desolate windows. The picture, with its hints of entrapment, the suspicion of evil disguised within a cloak of frivolity, has always unnerved me, but I have never been able to throw it away.

Suzi approved the photograph. 'Nice costumes,' she has said on more than one occasion. 'You must have enjoyed yourselves.'

Early in the morning, two days after Elaine's call, Suzi advances on me bearing something small and flimsy between her fingers. 'I found this stuck down the side of the radiator in the dining room. I thought you might want to see it.'

A photograph, yellowing at the edges and blurred by years of heat. I twitch it out of her hands, flip it face upwards on to the desk and my father stares up at me, a single figure posed beneath a tree, shading his eyes against the sun. I turn it over. There is a date pencilled onto the hard, shiny paper: 'June 1957'.

Suzi hovers expectantly. 'Do you know who it is?'

'Just my dad,' I tell her noncommittally. 'Just my dad when he used to live here.'

This seems to satisfy her. When I look up from the desk a moment later she has disappeared. In the distance I can hear her feet moving rapidly down the narrow staircase.

Although my father invariably referred to himself as a 'native' and had been known in his more elevated moments to talk about 'ancestry', his arrival in Norfolk had been of recent date: it was not until the beginning of the 1960s, with various professional commitments fulfilled and personal obligations decisively severed, that he had finally settled himself at the house in Norwich. Once installed he had lost little time in erasing those traces of his previous life which might have been thought to compromise newer affiliations. There had been a flat Midlands accent once and occasional half-affectionate references to 'Brum'. Neither of these survived the transit east. Subsequently he gave the impression of a man unreasonably absorbed in milieu, the possessor of a fund of specialised information which could be used to eke out conversations with more knowledgeable acquaintances. Precarious at first, this thin coating of local lore soon hardened into an impenetrable carapace. Though he might show mild uncertainty in dealing with more obscure areas of Norfolk life – National Hunt racing courses, say, or the history of Norwich City Football Club – he rarely allowed himself to be caught out.

This abrupt transformation – from vagrant to habitué – was typical of my father's character. Set down in an unfamiliar environment, shunted off into fresh spheres of influence and intrigue, he set to work immediately to reinvent himself, to take on some inconspicuous but recognisable shape that would be acceptable to the people around him. The new job, the chance encounter, the unfamiliar face seen across the garden fence: no introduction of this sort could proceed very far before my father had first emerged to reconnoitre, sniff the air and establish what was required of him and his ability to supply it. At the time I assumed, uncharitably, that this caution arose out of sheer deference, social uncertainty, simple fear, that the bewildering shifts of opinion which it demanded reflected nothing so much as an engrained lack of resolve. Only later was it possible to establish that they grew out of a profound desire for assimilation. My father wanted people to like him, wanted it very much, and to this end was prepared to conciliate almost any foible in the people he ran up against. While this characteristic implied deep-rooted insecurity, there was also in it the suggestion of the actor, someone happy to exchange the blander aspects of his own personality for a feigned but potentially more engrossing role. In this sloughing-off of one temporary skin and its replacement with another there lurked, not infrequently, an appreciation of comic possibilities.

My father's relationship with Morty Kronenburg was invested with something of this air. They had come across each other in the early 1960s in the course of some long-forgotten business transaction: a relationship kept up on my father's side by a willingness to please and considerable amusement. In this respect, at least, the connection did my father credit. An intransigent conservative of a kind rarely found even at that time he might have been expected thoroughly to disapprove of Morty, his race, his trade and his morality. My father's opinion of the Jews was wholly untenable. 'Look at the Middle East,' he would say. 'A perfectly decent set of people, all going about their business and perfectly amenable to British influence. And then suddenly the Jews decided to come interfering and ruin everything for forty years.' Curiously this blanket condemnation did not extend to Morty Kronenburg. 'No doubt Mr Kronenburg makes his money in ways which moralists would find obnoxious,' he would say. 'That is beside the point. He has never, so far as I know, committed a crime. Consequently he is entitled to any professional service I am able to provide him with that he cares to pay for. You will only find me complaining of him at such times as my bank refuses to honour his cheques, and that occasion, I am pleased to say, has not yet occurred.'

My father was a chartered accountant, specifically an insolvency practitioner concerned with the winding-up of small businesses and the reclamation of debt. It was the only subject on which he spoke with any bitterness. 'When I was a young man I had a number of talents. At school I won prizes for composition. I had a passable tenor voice. I was not unaccomplished. But they made a chartered accountant out of me. Consequently I have spent my life evaluating the contents of sweetshops and arguing with creditors over ten-pound notes.' Some hint of these early attachments still lingered: he approached the *Insolvency Practitioner's Gazette* with the air of a man determined to find fault, not so much with its professional lore as with its defective grammar; he sang in the chorus of the Norwich Philharmonic Society for twenty years. At the same time, there was something mildly defiant in the way he pulled on his dinner jacket, or lamented a faulty subjunctive: an impudent and derisive gesture to an unseen audience.

As a parent he was unapproachable. To have waylaid him on one of his journeys to or from the house, to have interrupted him in conversation, to have proposed alterations to his routine – each would have been unforgivable. It was my father who sought me out, who discussed or directed. At these times, and with affected reluctance, he would talk about his clients: 'I went to see a man today who sells vacuum cleaners in Heigham Street. Five thousand pounds owing and dropping stumer cheques all over the place. I told him,' my father would say, pausing for emphasis, 'that he was *properly in queer street* and no mistake.' The out-of-date commercial slang was characteristic. My father brought to any discussion of business an unmistakeable aura of the past, the suggestion that he moved amid a world of silk-hatted clerks at their stools, financiers in Astrakhan coats and Threadneedle Street fogs. In this, as in so much else, he seemed a deliberately archaic figure.

But perhaps in this brief account I have wholly misjudged my father. Perhaps, in retrospect, there were times when the mask dropped, when the carapace of suavity and self-possession fell away and a more recognisable human face emerged. If so I do not remember them. Purposeful, intent, absorbed, he gave the impression of existing inside some remote, high-walled palisade, the key thrown away, the door indistinguishable amid the yards of fencing, the process of forcing an entry requiring a greater resolve than I possessed. Or perhaps this too is simply an illusion of hindsight and there were great tracts of my father's character that I failed to investigate, great open-cast mines simply requiring the coal to be lifted from their surface. Perhaps too the incidental remarks with which my father strewed his conversation – the hints about his ancestry, the half-revelations about his early life – were simply lures designed to draw me into a web of shared knowledge and easy familiarity. If so, the bait remained untasted. I liked my father and I think he liked me, but the gap between us was as bare and arid as any desert.

Though all this might suggest that my father neglected his duties as a parent, that he abdicated the many responsibilities conventionally assumed under this role, this was not the case. He was, for example, unreasonably exercised by my choice of career, linking it to other similar decisions of which he had some knowledge, using it as an excuse to impart a great deal of lapidary advice. Curiously, the degree of personal interference which he brought to most aspects of my life was here wholly set aside, buttressed by alleged powerlessness. 'It is a *great mistake* to expect children to imitate their parents,' he would say. 'Take Parsons,' – Parsons was a crony from the Philharmonic – 'a surgeon at the West Norwich Hospital and wants his boy to go into medicine. The boy's a cretin, of course, but Parsons will fix it. You'll see. He'll write to his old friends and get the boy into medical school. Where he'll come a cropper, I shouldn't wonder,' said my father innocuously. 'Now, if I wanted to get you articled as a chartered accountant, it *simply couldn't be done.*' The glint in his eye suggested that it was my capacity rather than his own which lay in doubt.

But he approved my choice of journalism. 'It is an honourable calling. In fact where would we be without newspapers? I have often thought that the degree of coordination required to produce a single issue of the *Daily Telegraph* must be quite remarkable. No doubt at some future point you will be able to tell me how it is done.'

Later he said, 'Your cousin James had some ambitions in that direction. I believe he aspired to be the sports editor of a newspaper in Sunderland. But it came to nothing, alas. It came to nothing.'

It was here in these preparations for a new life that would be lived out far away from Norfolk, beyond immediate surveillance and recall, that my father's detachment from reality became complete. He was put out to discover that the course took place in London. 'But my dear boy, where do you intend to lay your head? I should be very sorry to think' – a rustle of the newspaper – 'that you should be reduced to the position of one of those unfortunate young people' – another rustle of the newspaper – 'who are, I believe, forced to sleep on the Embankment.' It was useless to explain about government grants, about halls of residence and accommodation agencies; ideas of this sort, once fixed in my father's head, were not readily dislodged. He cheered up, however, in a discussion of my likely colleagues. 'There is, I gather, a category of journalist known as the hard-nosed investigative reporter, who occupies his time drinking gin and peering at unsuspecting politicians through the windows of what I believe are known as love-nests. I trust that you, at any rate, will aim slightly higher.'

Time passed. I went away to London, rarely to return. My father gave up his insolvency practice and sank into retirement. The housekeeper who had looked after me and attended to his own limited wants was dismissed. Curiously, absence wrought a change in our relationship, in my father's conception of himself and the duty he might be thought to owe to his dependant. He wrote regularly in a thin, clerkly hand and there was about these letters a tinge not so much of affability – my father was always affable – but of revelation. He spoke mostly of his acquaintances, the cronies of the Philharmonic or the masonic lodge, but seldom to the exclusion of his own personal concerns. 'Parsons is having great trouble with his son. The boy has been expelled from medical school and wants to go on the stage. I was able to assure him that I had no worries in that direction.' I was touched by the compliment, if compliment it was, the more so in that it seemed to elevate me into a new frame of reference. Compared to Parsons' delinquent son I had taken my place among the various mechanisms with which my father regulated his life.

In retirement my father was not without resource. He had certain little antiquarian hobbies which he continued to work up: the antiquities of Norfolk, the route and dimensions of the old City Wall. There is a photograph of him taken at about this time, reprinted from the *Eastern Evening News*, standing beneath the walls of Norwich Castle, his eye fixed rigidly on the distant battlements. It was at this stage in his life, too, that he began to cultivate the society of his neighbours. This was an unexpected departure. Dislike of neighbouring families, of their children, personal habits and social status, was one of my father's most marked characteristics. He had an exaggerated notion of respectability, of appropriateness to milieu, vague attributes subsumed under the convenient shorthand of 'class'. It was rare for any newcomer to the neighbourhood to match up to these exacting standards. Predictably the neighbour whom my father selected for his overtures of friendship was of a more acceptable type. 'Perkins is a decent little man,' he informed me. 'Sat upon by his wife, of course, but we can't mind that at his age.' The reference to age was consciously fantastic. Perkins was a retired insurance clerk a year or two younger than himself, but it amused my father to pretend that he was a much older man, to suggest, in fact, that Perkins' continued existence was a matter for wonder and congratulation. 'It is a marvel how much Perkins gets about,' he would say. Or, 'Perkins astonishes me with his vigour.' It was a deliberate fantasy, which lent colour to an otherwise prosaic relationship, but my father kept it up. He took an obtrusive interest in Perkins' hobbies and immediate family. 'I spent an agreeable afternoon looking at Perkins' collection of cigarette cards,' he wrote at about this time. 'Apparently he shows them at exhibitions and is offered large sums of money for them by American collectors.' What Perkins made of this gentle patronage was anyone's guess. I saw them together only once, in the mid-1970s, setting out to attend a cricket match at the county ground at Lakenham, and he had the puzzled look of the man who feels, amid much ancillary politeness, that he is being made a fool of. Shortly afterwards came another letter. 'You have made a fine impression on Perkins,' my father wrote. 'He enquires after you constantly.'

And then something went wrong between them. Whether it was that Perkins grew finally to resent my father's patronage, that my father became bored with his creation, or that some other agency intervened, I never discovered. But there were no more references to cricket, to cigarette cards, or life insurance. To my father such severances were quite irrevocable. Once thrown down, the frail pontoon bridges that joined him to the rest of humanity could not be restored.

I saw my father for the last time in the summer of 1976. He had lost none of his old vigour. Oblivious to the heat he led me into the back garden, where a hosepipe lay leaking water on to the parched grass, and criticised the drought regulations. 'A ridiculous intrusion. I have had a man here from the council actually insisting that I cease to water my lawn,' he said, giving the hose a little kick with his foot. 'Naturally I told him that it was his duty to supply me with water and that I should view any interruption with extreme gravity.' I had not seen my father so gleeful since a rival for masonic high office had fallen down drunk at the festive board in front of the Senior Provincial Grand Warden. Later, as we sat drinking tea beneath the cloudless sky, he revealed a new and consuming interest.

'What do you think of that tree?'

There was an old lime tree which grew a yard inside the neighbouring garden. Long unpruned, its yellow foliage fell low over my father's rose bushes; sweetish scent hung in the dead air.

'It does seem rather overgrown.'

'*Exactly*. That is exactly what I said to the man from the council when he came to inspect it. Overgrown. Neglected. A health hazard too, I shouldn't wonder. Naturally, I am taking legal action.'

The neighbouring property was owned by a bedridden spinster. 'Couldn't you ask her to prune it?'

'I should have thought that you at least might have supported me in this,' said my father mildly.

Clearly in the matter of the tree my father had become rejuvenated. At dinner that night he was more animated than I had seen him for years. We ate in the kitchen, as the shadows fell over the gloomy garden and the smoke from his cigar rolled against the windows and lay curled there like grey cotton wool. In this final encounter his conversation was a simulacrum of the prejudice of the last twenty years. Later when, searching for memories of my father, I came to reflect on the scene, it seemed to me that there was a suspicious fluency about these remarks, that they existed, albeit unconsciously, as a kind of apologia, patiently rehearsed over many years and only now thought suitable for display. In their triumphalism – the triumph of one who had survived, endured, maintained rigid principles in an age of dissolution – there was an unmistakeable note of elegy, tempered by complete isolation from the ordinary processes of life. 'Do you know,' my father said, 'those people I see at the club, Parsons and that sort. All they ever talk about is the past. You know, the women they had thirty years ago and how happy they were. I never heard anything so deplorably sentimental. I have lived for seventy years, followed a more or less respectable calling and, I trust, behaved adequately to my fellow men, and do you know I never stopped to consider whether I was happy. In fact,' said my father, '*happiness never came into it.*'

I had a sudden glimpse then of bright, flawless machinery put to some ugly purpose, of a rare and subtle mechanism grinding inexorably on out of trim.

Later, we walked out once again into the garden and the tree wrought a final, magical effect. 'Do you know,' said my father, 'I shouldn't wonder if it was a very long dispute.'

It was his final victory. By a curious stroke of fate the solicitor's letter informing my father of his neighbour's capitulation arrived on the day of his death. It was returned to me amongst a pile of unopened post: masonic communications, requests for unpaid subscriptions, the paraphernalia of comfortable old age. He was found collapsed in his bedroom, having failed to keep a lunch appointment in the city. 'I should like to die in my chair,' he had often said, 'like an old Viking. Not in hospital being chaffed by a lot of silly nurses.' In this as in other areas of his life my father was narrowly triumphant.

In the week after his death I received two letters which shed some light on my father's character. The first was from the elderly lady who lived next door. Its tone was conciliatory. She explained that while she had not spoken to my father for some years, she was 'inexpressibly pained' by the news of his death, which might be construed as 'a warning to us all'. As a mark of respect she had given instructions that the tree should immediately be cut down.

The second letter was from Mr Perkins.

It was a diffuse, rambling document, clearly written under some constraint, concluding with a request that I should call at the Perkins' house to receive various 'items' – the word was underscored – lent to Mr Perkins by my father and never returned. I called at the Perkins' by appointment some days later to be handed, without explanation, a large brown-paper parcel. It contained several hardback books with titles such as *The Jewish Conspiracy: and what can be done about it*. I remembered a remark of my father's early on in their relationship. 'Perkins is very strong on the Jews,' he had said. 'It is one of his many agreeable features.'

My father had left a thousand pounds; a handful of trifling debts. The whole realised a sum in three figures. I was his sole legatee. There remained the question of the house. At an early stage I had felt confident in disposing of my father's estate. The property would be sold, I thought. Children would come and run over its musty staircases and despoil the regularity of its well-kept lawn. The estate agent, a jaunty young man whose brother I remembered from school, had another suggestion.

'You want to rent it,' he advised. 'People coming into the city these days, they're schoolteachers, students. They can't afford to buy property – letting's what they want. A bedsitter or a flat. You could make a hundred a month from this place if you went about it in the right way.'

I took him at his word. A contracting firm gutted the downstairs rooms, stuck Fablon on the kitchen walls and painted over the cracked ceiling. I spent a day in the city buying cheap, serviceable furniture for the three bedsitting rooms. A second contracting firm came to install coin-operated gas and electricity meters, and finally the business was done. I left the letting arrangements in the hands of the solicitor, who promised to acquire 'a good class of tenant'. I can remember thinking, as I signed the necessary documents, that my father would have approved the sentiment.

All this took place in the long summer of 1976. At first Morty had grown nervous at the prospect of my long absence and for a time I received sharp, admonitory reminders of the world I had left behind me. 'The least you can do while you're down there is to read a few scripts,' he remarked a day or so after my departure.

One day in early September, having collected a set of keys from the solicitor, I paid a final visit to the house. Six weeks had elapsed since my father's death and already all trace of him seemed to have been expelled from the bright, nondescript rooms. There was a television set occupying the far end of the lounge – something he would have abominated – and a long angular sofa had replaced the narrow chintzes. Only in the dining room, with its cluster of mahogany chairs and the framed sporting prints out of Surtees, was there any hint of his departing spoor. Curiously it was here in this meagre, ill-furnished space, motes of dust dancing in the flood of sunlight, that the memory of my father, long kept at bay, rose up finally to disturb me. For a moment it seemed to me that in refurbishing his house along these bland, anonymous lines I had destroyed him far more effectively than any stroke. Subsequently, such was my distress, I went rapidly from room to room in a search for other tangible reminders of his presence. Little had survived the enthusiasm of the contractor's men. A cupboard on the landing disclosed a dusty edition of the works of Sir Walter Scott, each volume firmly inscribed on the flyleaf with my father's initials; there were patent medicine bottles collected in the bathroom cabinet. Back numbers of *Accountancy* still lay piled up in the spare bedroom. But these were insubstantial ghosts. I went downstairs and stepped into the garden.

Here everything was much as I remembered it. In my absence the solicitor had sent round a jobbing gardener and the square lawn and the gravelly walks retained their original character. There had in any case been little for him to do. The drought had lingered on into September and the grass was white and friable. At its fringe a few plantains grew to knee height. Beyond, the summer's rose heads lay mouldering. I had never liked the garden, which from an early stage in his occupancy my father had appropriated entirely for his own use. It was here that he had sat on summer evenings reading newspapers or listening to classical concerts on the radio, here that he had stood gossiping with his odd, anonymous acquaintance. To have played football on it or skirmished through its borders would have been an act of despoliation. There was something neat and pedantic in its arrangement – a whiff of the fussy, authoritarian side of my father's nature which required the symmetrical draping of table-cloths, the measured stacking of newly dried crockery. I would have preferred a wilderness. As it was, the garden in its later incarnation had always reminded me of a girlfriend from the early days with Morty, a woman of such spectacular beauty that its maintenance seemed to preclude any form of intimacy, flaw-less yet inhuman.

Moving on over the dusty grass it was possible to detect the first hint of autumn. Dry leaves crackled underfoot. A faint breeze blew in from across the park, bringing with it the scent of smoke. It would rain soon, I thought, that relentless Norfolk rain which sweeps in from Jutland to saturate the landscape and provide the characteristic smell of wet compost and extinguished bonfires. Older memories crowded in now, of an attempt to dine outside cut short by thunder, of the scurry to convey food, tables and chairs hurriedly inside, of my father's panama hat left alone and unclaimed amid the downpour. Dead, I thought. Gone. Rising up before me with its high, lonely windows, brickwork dark in the faltering light, the house seemed as remote and tenantless as any desert island. I went indoors.

*

I saw my father twice after his death. On the first occasion he walked into the cutting room at Dean Street late one evening as I sat talking to Morty and stood just inside the doorway, his shoulder pressed against the wall. I have no idea how long he remained there: in the half-light, the neon gleaming above us, it took some time for me to establish that the accretion of lines and shadows was a human form, still longer to establish that the form was my father's. In the brief instant before he disappeared I had time to register only an impression of mild bewilderment, as if he had strayed into a long-remembered room whose furniture had now been changed out of all recognition. Indeed, such was the speed with which the sensation passed that I was not completely sure that it was my father. Tired, preoccupied, I would have dismissed it as a trick of the light had it not been for the smell: that odd compound of tobacco, tweeds and chalk, as distinctive as musk.

The second occasion was on an underground train at the end of the Metropolitan line near Uxbridge, late one winter's afternoon when the fog lay over Watford and the distant spread of Metroland. Again recognition came late. It was not until the short figure in the mackintosh had stepped off the train and stood uncertainly in the frame of the closing doors that I realised who it was. He was gone in an instant, leaving me half out of my seat staring at the empty platform.

Morty took a great interest in these visitations. He said, 'You saw your old man? Here in the studio and then again on the tube? That's really unusual. Once I can understand, but twice, that's really spooky.'

'It was disagreeable, I'll give you that.'

This was intended to stop the conversation, but Morty went on, 'What did he look like? Would you say he looked unhappy?'

'Not unhappy. Preoccupied, perhaps.'

'Uh huh. Usually they look unhappy. Did I ever tell you about the time I saw a ghost? Girl called Angela who used to work here, but then she died. Drugs or something. It was before your time. I saw her in Leicester Square and she looked *deathless*.'

Later he said, 'You see him again, I want to hear about it. And this time look into his eyes. That's a sure sign.'

It was an unnecessary injunction. I knew I would never see him again.


Once, out of curiosity, late one night at the loft in Dean Street, I asked Morty, 'Tell me about my father.'

Morty looked surprised. 'Your old dad?'

'My old dad. Tell me about him.'

For a while Morty thumbed dejectedly through the clumps of shiny models' portfolios that lay strewn over his desk. Then he said, 'I dunno, Martin . . . What do you want to know?'

'Well, where did you meet him for a start?'

'Where did I meet him? Jesus, Martin, it was a long time ago. 'Sixty-two, 'sixty-three maybe. Time some nudie magazine wholesaler went bust: he had to liquidate the stock. Which was a laugh, when you think about it, getting someone to liquidate eight tons of fanny mags. But he did me a favour, your old dad did. Let me take a whole run of *Cleavage* out of the warehouse and no questions asked. You remember *Cleavage*?'

'Before my time, Morty.'

'I suppose it was . . . Well in those days the only way you could get away with nude shots was to call it art. You know, you have a row of strippers waltzing round in bits of gauze, but you have a caption that says, "East Sussex Ladies' Greek Danc-ing Championships", that sort of thing . . .'

'But what about my old dad?'

'Your old dad? Your old dad did me a favour once in a while. Any time a wholesaler called in the receiver I'd give him a call.'

'Just that? Nothing else?'

'Like I said, Martin,' Morty said vaguely. 'It was a long time ago.'

THE FIRST TIME that I saw Elaine she was lying face down beneath the male lead of a pornographic film called, if memory serves me, *Girlschool Janitor* during a shooting session at the upstairs loft of the studio in Dean Street. Bright days, gems amid the confusing clutter of the years, not beyond recall. Morty Kronenburg's studio . . . I can see it now. Ten a.m. on a basting July morning with the windows open to admit the scents of the clotted streets below. Morty's film crew, intent veterans of *Manhunter* and *Innocence*, loitering around a tray of sandwiches, plastic bags of ice which were applied every five minutes or so to the nipples of the female lead, the piles of scabrous paraphernalia: there was a school uniform hanging on the wall in its neat dry-cleaner's sachet. I was moving determinedly on towards the office when Morty grasped my arm.

'No, Martin, you have to see this. One of Frank's best. And the chick.'

They still called them chicks in those days. I glanced over at the set where a gaunt, unhappy-looking actor named Frank Fellatio was positioning himself meticulously between the legs of a tall, busty girl with abundant dark hair. In these early days the physique of pornographic film actors still seemed worthy of remark. Even the American ones, the surging hunks with names like Pete The Prong and agents and six-figure salaries, sported beer bellies and toupees. Frank Fellatio was a terrible specimen of humanity: lank, receding hair, badly chewed nails, a few feeble hairs rising from the marbled drum of his chest.

'Are you sure he won't drop dead from exhaustion?'

'He's a good boy, Frank is,' Morty said without much conviction. 'One of the best. Okay he may not look much, but the punters like that. Say you were going to a dirty movie, right? Who would you want to see up there on the screen giving it to

Talia Silk or Nancy Slick? Ask yourself, Martin. Someone who looked like Mr Universe or someone who looked like you? Viewer identification, that's what I'm after.'

'What about the girl?'

'Opposite rule applies. Obviously the girl's got to be the best that money can buy.'

'I meant this girl.'

'Elaine or Eileen or something. Another one who wants to do fucking *Hamlet* at the RSC. The agency sent her along. Look, just watch, will you. It's quite a turn-on.'

It was, as Morty maintained, quite a turn-on. Back on the set Frank Fellatio and Elaine or Eileen or something were in the middle of an athletic routine which involved Elaine or Eileen splaying her muscular legs on either side of Frank's puny torso while Frank attempted to burrow gamely into her midriff. I caught a glimpse of the girl's face as Frank flipped her over on to her front and skated airily over her buttocks. Not a happy face: resentful and remote. But – and this is the remarkable thing – the film crew were raptly attentive, bug-eyed faces bent low over the zoom lens. Now, adult movie film crews are a silent, indifferent breed. I was in a studio once when an actor named Hank Mohair led Lynsey Laguna through a devious food-and-drink routine, ending up by munching *pâté de foie gras* out of her navel, without so much as a raised eyebrow. Not here. When Frank got to the part where he had to roll his eyes and carol with fictitious lust there were whoops of encouragement and handclapping. Redfaced and perspiring, the bodies rolled apart.

'It's a wrap,' Morty Kronenburg said. 'Give it ten minutes, will you, and then try the scene where Frank finds the gym mistress in the shower.' He draped his arm over my shoulder in a gesture that was meant to convey brotherly affection. '*Hey.* Come into the office, will you?'

I followed him warily over the set, nearly colliding with a burly scene shifter carrying a lacrosse stick. This was the mid-1970s. Now at that time in pornographic films, or in the sort of pornographic films that Morty Kronenburg shot, or in the sort of pornographic films that Morty Kronenburg shot in London, the characters did not have sex. Soft-core. It was only in the early Eighties that the studios became full of straining members and gynaecological close-ups. Still, Morty was doing his best to nudge forward the frontiers of his art. A chain of adult cinemas on the south coast had even sent back a recent Leisurevision production – a thirty-minute tape called *Thrash* – on the grounds that it offended public decency. These were proud scars.

Morty's office: a lurid booth decked out in red plush. On the wall hung a framed photograph of Morty's son being bar mitzvah'd. Morty waved me into a chair, a grim, eager chipmunk searching amid the detritus of his desk for a cigarette lighter.

'Fuck, am I glad to see you. I've got problems like you wouldn't believe.'

'The agency again?'

'Uh huh. You wouldn't believe the sort of thing they're sending me, you wouldn't.' For a moment Morty looked as if he could cry. 'Thirty-five-year-olds with outsize tits. Fourteen-year-olds with no tits at all. Plus *Milkmaids* got taken out of Smiths again.'

'No?'

*Milkmaids* was one of Morty's milder men's magazines, of the sort that more or less got sold legally. It got taken out of Smiths every three or four weeks. 'We're going to have to redesign the cover,' Morty said cheerlessly, 'and take out a whole four-page spread.'

'That's too bad, Morty.'

A telephone rasped from the desk. 'Yeah,' Morty said wearily into it. 'No. The fuck? Tell me about it.' I watched him interestedly as he hunched himself back into his chair and cradled the receiver around his neck. Occasionally when a Sunday newspaper runs a vice exposé you get to see pictures of pornographers captured in all their meretricious glory: greying grandfather types with bouffant hairdos and roguish glints in their eyes. Morty did not correspond to this stereotype. Morty, it is fair to say, looked like a chartered accountant. In fact, Morty *was* a chartered accountant: at any rate there was a framed certificate on the wall made out to 'Mortimer Kronenburg FCA'. Morty found these letters magically efficacious in his occasional dealings with the Inland Revenue.

Morty's history. The *News of the World*, when they did the series, maintained that he had been to Harrow. In this particular, though not in others, the *News of the World* was wrong. Morty attended Rotherhithe Council School, which he left at sixteen with an open scholarship in Mathematics to Magdalen College, Oxford. Which he left at seventeen after a slight misunderstanding. Apprenticeship served as clapperboy in his uncle's back garden in Poplar making shorts with a hand-held Rolleflex. At eighteen he was art director on *Cutie*. The rest is history. Scary history. It was a fact, for instance, that Morty knew the Krays.

'Ron and Reggie? Reggie was a gentleman. Very polite. You know, always used to hold the door open if you were walking into a pub or anywhere.'

'What about Ron?'

'Ron? Well now, Ron . . .'

Scary history. Once when he was drunk Morty told me about a famous fight in which the Krays had neutralised a Maltese pornographer who had tried to muscle in on the youthful Morty's patch in Dalston ('And then Ron got this cutlass . . .'). You didn't want to listen. Back at the desk Morty had finished his telephone call and was staring morosely into space again. Out of the tail of my eye I could see the tall girl being togged up in a plastic mackintosh.

'That was Baff Thackeray,' – nearly all Morty's friends in the adult cinema trade had names like Baff or Griff – 'owns the Regal in Brighton. Said ever since we sent the tape of *Thrash* the council have been sending inspectors round to see the reels. Says he can't do *Girlschool Janitor*. Says it's too much of a risk.'

'What's so bad about *Girlschool*?'

Morty sighed. 'Nothing. We've done worse than that, *much* worse. I did a count on the scenes. Twelve straight hits. Some messing about with shaving cream. And the bit in the changing rooms where the lacrosse team finds the vibrator. Christ, you don't even get to see Frank full-frontal. But Baff reckons the Festival of Light are really big down there. One sniff of *Girlschool Janitor* and there'd be a demo outside the cinema, that sort of thing.'

'I've done the rewrites on *Prime Time* plus I called Starfinder, and they think they can get us Minty Greenbaum.'

'Great.' Morty slapped his fist down on the cluttered table. His eyes glinted with pleasure. 'Now, would you mind excusing me? I have to make a phone call.'

I nodded. Whenever Morty made a particularly chanceless killing, it was his innocent habit to telephone his wife – a refined little woman who lived in Ongar with Morty's three children – and tell her about it. I remembered other such calls. 'Honey, I got the UK rights to *Sweet Body of Bianca* . . . Baby, you'll never guess, I just managed to sign up Lynsey Laguna.' I left him crookbacked and intent over the receiver and wandered outside into the airless studio.

They were still filming. Bright, merciless lights. Cigarette smoke rising in dense, vertical lines to the leprous ceiling. Occasionally a bulb popped with an edgy, fragmenting noise like an egg being smashed. Elaine was standing mid-set, wearing a plastic mackintosh, beneath a shower arrangement of serpentine hoses and see-through curtains. As I approached, Morty's director, a cerise-shirted homunculus with tattooed forearms, was saying sternly to the sound man, 'Look, if we drop the fucking mackintosh we don't have anything for her to take off, right?'

'You ever know a chick who went into a shower with a mackintosh on?'

'I fucking do as well, if it comes to that.'

A few threatening gestures later and a reminder from the sound man that Morty would be along in a minute or two to see how things were progressing and they get the cameras rolling. Elaine whisks the curtain back to its fullest extent and begins languorously to finger a bar of soap, inching the raincoat off her shoulders as she does so. I smoke a cigarette and look nonchalant, as if I've seen it all (I have, I've seen it *all*). Meanwhile furtive Frank, clad in mechanic's overalls, stalks leerily round the back of the shower. Elaine arches the raincoat over her midriff. Frank lays a furry paw tentatively on her shoulder. And then, 'There isn't any water.'

The director and the sound man exchange weary, incredulous glances.

'Sure there's no water. This is a film. That's a set. You're supposed to pretend.'

Elaine shoots out one of those intransigent looks I will come to know so well. 'Look, how am I supposed to do a shower scene without water?'

There are some goblin chuckles at this. Morty's crew can

do without the Gielgud dramatic verisimilitude bit. Who needs accessories? I once heard a director called Andy Scrod maintain that you could shoot *War and Peace* using a bed and a couple of shotguns. Elaine starts to button up the mackintosh.

'Forget it. I quit.'

The onlookers stare. A whinnying intervention from the director is brushed aside. I pause to take in the scene: the sound man is wheezing over a cigarette; Frank Fellatio emerges trouserless from behind the shower curtain and starts to examine a vivid red weal on his thigh. Another bulb pops.

And then, imperceptibly, I knew that this was the start of something, that some queer, ineluctable mechanism had cranked noisily into gear, seizing me up and bearing me away into unfathomable distance. As in some crowded Elizabethan drama, the incidental characters — cooks, scullions and gentleman attendants — had faded away, moved back into the surrounding tableau, allowing hero and heroine to step forward and transact their business.

I stood up as Elaine swooped purposefully towards the doorway where Morty and I loitered, her charcoal hair sweeping in the breeze of the fans.

'Now you listen to me, Mr fucking *Kronenburg*, or whatever your name is. This was supposed to be a proper *film*, that's what you said. None of this, "I'm sorry, darling, we're economising, so the set for the next scene is this bed here," none of these fucking actors who have to get finished by four so they can get back to their fucking *milk-rounds* . . .'

'But baby . . .' Morty began brokenly.

'. . . Who're practically *bald*. "Oh baby, you have to work in this new feature I'm planning," ' – the mimicry of Morty's nasal East-End drawl was surprisingly accurate – ' "with all these *major stars* and this *big-time director*." '

'Listen, Eileen . . .'

'It's Elaine, actually. Elaine. But I don't suppose you noticed that, did you, when you were staring at my tits in the audition, Mr *Big-time Producer*?' She turned to me for the first time. 'Have you ever been to one of his auditions? You say a couple of lines and then he goes, "Perfect baby, just perfect. Now go ahead and take your clothes off." '

'Listen, Elaine, we can work this one out, okay? We can just . . .'

And then, quite unexpectedly, she burst into tears. Morty shrugged, hunched his shoulders into his jacket and backed away. I said, 'You mustn't mind him.'

'What do you know about it? Who the fuck are you, anyway?'

'Oh, I just work here. But you mustn't mind Morty.'

'No?'

'No. Why don't you put some clothes on and we can talk about it?'

She looked up suspiciously. There was an ancient director's deckchair a few feet away with a dressing gown hanging over the back. With this wrapped around her gleaming shoulders, shielded from the gaze of prurient onlookers by my cautious arm, with Morty staring resentfully from the doorway, Elaine allowed herself to be led away.

'He's not really called Frank Fellatio,' Elaine said later.

'He isn't?'

'He's called Frank Bence-Jones. He's got a wife and two children and he lives in Walthamstow.'

'He does?'

We were having dinner in a restaurant on the Bow Road, a favourite resort of Leisurevision staff after filming sessions in Docklands, urinous studios down by the river in Millwall and Cubitt Town where guard dogs prowled restlessly over the asphalt floor. For Morty, now vanished on some mysterious errand up west, this was a venue of impressive personal significance. It was here, according to legend, that a sixteen-year-old Morty had run messages for gangsters, sold stolen number plates and burnished counterfeit jewellery.

'How do you know he's called Frank Bence-Jones?'

'He told me. In the coffee break. He told me some other things. Like he owes Morty five thousand pounds. And Morty has the deeds to his house.'

'That as well?'

'He's only got one lung,' Elaine said reprovingly. 'And he has to do the next two films for free to pay back the money Morty lent him for the operation.'

36

I was used to hearing these stories. Whereas about Morty's actresses there hung a faint, intangible glamour, over Morty's actors there rose only the fetid stink of desperation. They came from places like Forest Gate and Chingford. They moonlighted from day jobs as taxi drivers, fruit-stall barkers, ambulance men. Ambition, alone, marked them out as components of Morty's improbable, ramshackle cortège. Late one night in Dean Street, while Morty frowned over a defective storyboard, I once questioned a harassed, balding father of three who appeared under the stage name of Johnny The Wad over his motives. 'I want to be a *star*,' he said simply.

'And you,' Elaine said, 'what do you do?'

'I'm the writer.'

'The *writer*?' I stole a look as she applied herself busily to the contents of her plate: charcoal hair emerging out of her scalp like a giant furzebush, wide, sloping chin, tilted nose, an air of massive, deep-rooted intransigence only narrowly appeased. Beyond, Terry Chimes appeared in the doorway, dressed in a mauve suit, stared pruriently towards us and then departed noisily in search of a table.

'Who's that?'

'He's called Terry Chimes. He works with Morty.' It seemed a prudent description.

'That figures. He was there at the audition.'

'What made you choose Morty?'

'The agency. They said it would be good experience.'

'Good experience for what?'

'*For being an actress.*'

You got a lot of this. Burly twenty-year-olds with appendix scars who'd failed for RADA anxious to 'broaden their perspective', game veterans of provincial rep naively bewildered by the sight of a cine camera. Elaine seemed a novel addition to their ranks.

There was a loud interruption from an adjacent table as Terry Chimes, now grown innocently boisterous, flipped a wine glass on to the floor. 'Listen,' Elaine said. 'I'll tell you about it if you like.'

And so, as the dusk began to fade over the striped plastic tablecloths and the lights of the Bow Road flashed up furiously behind us, disturbed only by the blare of the police sirens and the raucous interventions of Terry Chimes, Elaine explained. It was a considerable monologue, taking in her parents' removal from Cork twenty years before, grey North London Irish childhood, the linoleumed floors of the convent school, a philosophy degree at Birkbeck, the general effect oddly unrevealing. When we emerged at length into the dense streets of the East End it was as if I somehow knew less about her, that the result of this rambling autobiography was to conceal rather than to disclose.

Time telescopes now, emerges from the scrambler in random, piecemeal fragments. Elaine turning up at the flat in Hammersmith a month later with a suitcase; her mother's rich Kerry brogue echoing down the wire; waking up once in the small hours and finding her sitting crosslegged in the front room, white face staring through the gloom, expressionless as a sphinx; effortful, energetic sex. What do I remember about her? The usual things, I suppose. *Anger. Irishness. Unpredictability* (not turning up when expected, turning up when not expected). Seeing her at work once in Morty's studio and thinking fitfully of the unreality of it all, as if we were merely children at play, and that our real lives were being lived out somewhere else, far away from the tapering snout of the zoom lens, in echoing space and silence.


Pornography. These days, of course, I can no longer rely on the magazines and the impedimenta of the film studio. These days, I have to make my own.

'Tell me about those boyfriends of yours.'

'I already told you.'

'Tell me again.'

'If you want. First time when I was fourteen. It was after a party. I didn't know what I was doing. I thought it was going to be just kissing and so on. Then there was Adrian, about the time I was doing my O-levels. I was serious about him: I'd have married him if he'd asked me, given up school and everything.'

'Then there was Keith, and the one who worked in the bank?'

'Steve?' Suzi's face assumes a look of dreamy reminiscence. This, after all, is her past being unfurled. When she considers the bleak expanse of her life to date, these are the meteors which spring up to irradiate it with their phantom light. Adrian, Keith and Steve. 'He was sweet. He used to take me to school on his motorbike.'

'And after that?'

Slowly Suzi ticks off the names on her fingers. 'Mike. Robert. Anthony. He was the one who got upset when I went to college. He said it was going to break his heart.'

Mike, Robert and Anthony work for the Norwich Union now, or at the big garden centre up the Daniels Road, or in the jewellery shops along Gentleman's Walk. Suzi sees them with their families sometimes when she goes shopping at Sainsbury's and they stare gamely at her.

'Then when I went to college there was Ashok. I was really serious about him.'

Ashok was the son of a Nigerian chieftain, sent out on a Commonwealth scholarship, who on the first occasion they went to bed together presented Suzi with a dozen fifty-pound notes. The relationship foundered when she discovered the existence of three other wives back in Lagos.

'. . . Bob, Marcus, Justin . . .'

Suzi, of course, would greatly resent the suggestion that she is promiscuous. She is a modern girl, taking her pleasure as modern girls do, but each of her relationships is invested with a patina of moral seriousness. She has been engaged three times – short, tense engagements foundering on ill-will and uncertainty – nearly engaged another four times. Moreover the whole progress, this modern Wife of Bath's tale without the marriage, has been framed from the outset within strictly defined limits. When she was sixteen, Suzi told me, she set down a catalogue of the men who existed beyond this pale: men who were married, men who were more than five years older or five years younger, men of whom her parents might be expected to disapprove. This last category I found touching.

I look at Suzi for a moment as she reaches the end of the story of her last engagement ('Everybody there at the party and we were in separate rooms not speaking to each other'). It broke down a month before the wedding and the engagement presents lie gathering dust in her parents' loft. There is about her a fundamental self-possession, a hard inner coating, a disconcerting refusal to be drawn. Mike, Robert and Anthony and the dusty file of fellow-conspirators had been no match for this pitiless intelligence, I thought.

'Seventeen. That's quite a lot.'

'I was *serious*,' says Suzi firmly. Nothing infuriates her more than the imputation of light-mindedness. 'I've always been serious.'

The faint hint of ulterior motive drifts over the conversation, loiters for a moment, goes away.


Some memories of Elaine:

*Unpunctuality*

In the early days of our relationship Elaine elevated unpunctuality, formerly a traditional female wile accepted with a good-natured shrug of the shoulders, into a rare and devastating weapon in the sex war. Invited to dine at eight, she compromised on nine-thirty. Asked to be at a theatre half an hour before the performance, she might saunter in mid-way through the second act. Her record was one of Morty's supper parties, convened in honour of a beetle-browed American hardcore director named Scazz Fogelburg, when – the company bidden to assemble in Ongar at 7.30 – Elaine arrived at a quarter to eleven. Insouciance, cultivated negligence, might have made these failings narrowly tolerable, but in fairness Elaine always volunteered perfectly plausible explanations for her tardiness. For example, the excuse for arriving late at Morty's party involved two defective underground trains, an epileptic mini-cab driver and a bomb scare closing the A12.


*Indifference*

Related, I suppose, to the foregoing. Once, exasperated beyond measure by some chance delinquency, I asked, 'Why do you behave like this?'

'Behave like what?'

'Who do you turn up late to places? If I tell you the table's booked for eight, why do you always get there at nine?'

She thinks about this for a bit. Then she says, 'Listen Martin, why don't you find someone who'll do what you want?'

'What do you mean, "What I want"?'

'Someone who'll turn up at places by the time you want them to. Someone who'll go to bed with you at the time you want them to. In the way you want them to. Why don't you find someone like that?'

Elaine specialised in unanswerable questions of this sort. Eventually I said, 'Will you have dinner with me tonight?'

'A girl's got to eat.'

'Will you make a special effort and turn up at eight?'

'All right.'

I cheated, of course: I booked the restaurant for nine. It was a futile gesture. Elaine arrived at thirteen minutes past ten.

### The Rose of Tralee

Have you ever heard of a magazine called *Ireland's Own*? They sell it at London mainline stations and you can occasionally see fuddled Irish labourers poring over it in pubs. The subtitle – *A Little Piece of Ireland* – is printed in outsize capitals on the cover, generally beneath a black-and-white drawing of Parnell or O'Connell, and the inside is devoted to potted biographies of nuns, viscidly sentimental short stories and pictures of gap-toothed children captioned 'A fine young man from Leinster'. Well, Elaine's family subscribed to *Ireland's Own*: 'Every year when I was a kid Dad used to take a picture of me in my party dress and sent it in. You used to have to say how old you were, where you went to school and what your favourite article in the magazine was. There was a series about an old lady who was a private eye – "Ireland's twinkliest detective" – so I always chose that. Every year Dad used to send it in and we'd get the paper and see if they'd printed it, but they never did. In the end, when I was about fifteen, Dad was going to give up – he thought it was a fix, you see, and they just printed pictures of people they knew or who'd sent them money – but then he thought he'd give it one last try. Only this time he made me write down that I came from Tralee, because they liked captioning girls' photographs "The Rose of Tralee", and sure enough they printed it: "Elaine Keenan, the Rose of Tralee". I got people writing to me after that, terribly polite letters from boys at Irish private schools who wanted a penfriend from England. And a dirty letter – from a priest it was as well – who said I was a pure vision of Irish loveliness, and a lot of other things too. Dad took that one to Father Michael, who said it was very shocking and he had a good mind to write to the other priest's bishop . . .'

I saw the 'Rose of Tralee' shot once. A face of sharp, extraordinary beauty, like a cross between a Kate Greenaway girl and something out of Alma-Tadema, and, in its intimations of future obduracy, quite terrifying.

### Her manifold suitors

The distinguishing mark of Elaine's allure was the number of people who wanted to marry her. Not to sleep with her, more or less obligatory in circles where not wanting to sleep with a woman was near proof of inversion, but to marry her. The serious thing. Morty asked her. Terry Chimes asked her. Even Crazy Rodney, late one night in an otherwise deserted studio, shuffled across with unignorable evidence of his regard. This last request fascinated me above all.

'What did he say?'

'He was very formal. He said he wanted me to know that he'd always liked and respected me.'

'Anything else?'

'He said his old mother in Romford would die happy if I said yes.'

'What happened when you said no? You did say no?'

'I thought he was going to get nasty. But in the end he just looked sort of sad and backed away.'

There were other, equally unlikely, aspirants to Elaine's hand. Frank Fellatio. Bobby Dazz. Two members of the Glasgow Express. Her manifold suitors included a Conservative M.P., an American porn tycoon and the merchant banker who inhabited the flat downstairs from us in Bishop's Park.

'What do you tell them?' I asked once, a lunch date with the proprietor of a West End model agency having ended in the inevitable declaration.

'I just say I'm sorry but it's impossible, and in any case there's someone else.'

'And what do they say?'

'They just look upset. Sometimes they start crying. Hugo' – Hugo was the Conservative MP – 'said he was going to kill himself.'

Late one night in a taxi coming back from Morty's place in Ongar, drink and intimacy having wrought a conducive atmosphere, I asked her. Elaine shook herself slowly awake out of the nest of furs.

'You want me to do *what*?'

One eye fixed nervously on the black conveyor belt of the road, I repeated the request.

'You want me to *what*? Well I'll tell you what you can do for a start, Martin, you can get the fuck out of this car. Right now. Go on, just get the fuck out.'

What do you do in such circumstances, with the fog rising up over the Mile End Road and the taxi-driver chortling over the intercom? I smiled. I got the fuck out.


And where are they now?

In Dean Street Morty works on into the darkness. It is past midnight and the tribe of PAs and art directors has disappeared, gone away to the Zoom Club or Tokyo Joe's, but Morty labours on. It will be two or three before he drives back through the dead streets, off through the East End and along the A12 towards the Essex rabbit-run. It is quiet in the studio, quiet but not inert. There are three video screens running simultaneously and Morty watches them all, head bent low down over the desk, framed in the beam of the anglepoise. Sometimes he flicks a switch and the screens stop while he examines the frozen images with their improbable conjunctions of human flesh. Morty is busy censoring hard-core movies for an American cable network, wiping out the appalling close-ups and the jittery climaxes – two seconds here, ten seconds there – running the resulting gaps and sound-breaks effortlessly into one another until all that remains is a seamless web of anodyne soft-core. The task is to his taste. It is, after all, the pornographer's abiding challenge – establishing what you can get away with. Beside him on the desk there is a checklist sent by the American cable network marking out forbidden areas, but Morty rarely consults it: his intuition is an infinitely superior guide. Onscreen a burly, tumescent actor breaks out of a clinch and turns briefly towards the camera. Morty flicks another switch and winds the reel forward, ponders for a moment, winds the reel back again and scrubs the offending exposure. Later the trained eye will detect a tiny hiatus in the action, a momentary wavering of tangled limbs, but how many trained eyes watch American cable networks late at night? Morty lets the blemish pass. Somewhere in the outer office a telephone rings; Morty ignores it. He works on amid the flickering light.

In Suffolk Terry Chimes wanders back from the fish farm with a brace of rainbow trout swinging fatly on his arm. The farmhouse yard is empty, as well it might be, for this is not a proper farmhouse yard but a show country gentleman's estate and there is a suspicious regularity to the piles of baled straw and the row of shiny agricultural implements. In the kitchen a great deal of gleaming pine, a counterfeit kitchen range and a blonde woman in her thirties drying dishes. Terry Chimes says disconsolately, 'I got these. The rest of the fuckers are dying. I fished a dozen out of the overflow pipe just now. Covered in gunge and stuff.' He sits down heavily on a pine armchair, hoists one Wellington over his knee and lights a cigar.

'I told you those fish were a mistake,' the woman says neutrally. She has a peculiar, stylised hairdo, like a parrot's, the fringe teased up in spikes over her forehead, the rest curling down over the nape of her neck.

'Not my fault,' Terry Chimes says listlessly. 'Fucking nitrate in the water, isn't it? Fucking farmers pumping it into the river.' He brightens. 'Why don't we get the car a bit later and go into town? Go to a club or something?' The woman nods. They stare at each other, two people massively out of place and out of time, achingly bemused by their unfamiliar milieu, the sensation oddly disagreeable.

In the flat in Romford Crazy Rodney says, 'Turn over.' Outside a watery November sun shines over the roofs of council houses disappearing up the hill. On the bedside chair a radio rasps football results.

'What do you want me to turn over for?' the girl asks. She

has pale, dirty features and there are odd purple bruises on the skin of her inner arm.

'That's a bloody stupid question,' Crazy Rodney tells her tolerantly. 'So I can stick it in you from behind, of course.'

At least that is how I imagine it.

But of course the chief ornament in this ghostly picture gallery eludes me. Morty and Terry Chimes are at the end of telephones somewhere. Even Crazy Rodney I could track down if I had the time and the interest. But Elaine. I don't know. I ceased knowing two or three years ago. And now that I want to talk to her again, now that I have this urge to find out what she wants, the trail is cold. Curious, isn't it? After the crash, when Morty panicked and Terry Chimes stopped answering the phone and barricaded himself into his office, I didn't hear from her in a long while. Just rumours, vague, absurdist rumours pulled out of thin air. In Paris with money. In London without money. In New York with a recording contract and a duplex. Rumours of that sort. Then, when Morty and I nervously re-established contact a year or so later, her name began to flit warily again across the wires, a sharp parenthesis in the bland recitation of sleaze and sensuality.

'So how was the launch, Morty?'

'It was a scene. Scazz Fogelburg had these chicks flown in on a Lear jet . . . Yeah, and that Elaine was there.'

'She was?'

'Sure, with some record producer I never heard of. She said to say hi.'

A few months later the postcards began to arrive, undated, unsigned, the only clue to provenance contained in the postmarks and the vivid pictures on the front. Postcards from New York, from Venice, from Reykjavik. Postcards from exotic or strange locations: from Tunis, bless you, from Tromso, from Consett, County Durham once with a picture of a derelict steelworks. And always from these furtive, cosmopolitan outposts the same laconic messages: 'Here for a couple of days. . . . a couple of weeks . . . a couple of months . . . weather good . . . weather bad . . . weather mixed', the same familiar handwriting.

The postcards continued to come. One a week on average, corresponding to no known geographical trajectory or series of flightpaths. From Rome, then Delhi, then Tokyo. From Albuquerque, then Rio, then Fiji. Eventually after two dozen or so of these I made a brief, rescipicient effort to track Elaine down. I spent a day over it. I telephoned people I hadn't spoken to in three years, people who slammed down the telephone as soon as they heard my name, people who babbled threateningly about forgotten debts and ancient scores until I too slammed down the telephone, people who couldn't or wouldn't remember me, people whom I couldn't remember. I phoned Morty. I phoned Terry Chimes. I phoned booking agents all over Europe. I phoned record company A&R men. I phoned Elaine's parents in Wembley Park. At one point I even acquired an Irish telephone directory and phoned some people with Elaine's surname in County Cork. It was all to no avail. The frail alliances of the past lay endlessly exposed. Morty thought that he might have seen her at a party in San Francisco a year since. Terry Chimes thought she might have got a part in a film called *Lick My Decals Off, Baby*. One or two of the A&R men recollected fuddled encounters in the grim days after the crash. Elaine's parents accused me of corrupting their innocent child. It was a relief, in these circumstances, to turn to the Keenans of County Cork and their voluble relish of unknown callers.

So where did she go? I like to think of a life of low-key exile; a deracinated Becky Sharp yawning sadly over the cocktail glasses and the ashtrays while Rod or Mack or whoever it was attended screen tests or record studios, a ghostly revenant to the great cities of Europe. I like to imagine that her first flight wasn't far, to Paris perhaps, or Frankfurt, where she could read the English newspapers and meet queer half-acquaintances in the record company offices. And I can see her smiling over the defeat of it all, the defeat of watching Rod or Mack or whoever making his third-rate films or records, of Sunday mornings in hotel bedrooms far away – but I don't think she can have liked it. I don't think she can have liked Rod or Mack or whoever, I don't think she can have liked the hotel bedrooms, or the queer company. Every city in Europe has its contingent of English exiles – the foreign correspondents who no longer correspond, the demure chanteuses who had a hit in 1972 and have just emerged from ten years' litigation, the bit-part actors who appear in films that even Morty Kronenburg wouldn't care to know about. A reckless, rackety life, this attendance at studios in Munich or Hamburg or Amsterdam for previews or press launches or parties, but I don't think she can have taken to it.

She did not quite disappear, of course. People never do. Later I discovered that Elaine had left her own unreasoning footprints through several of the capitals of Europe. A promoter claimed to have seen her backstage at a concert in Lille. Somebody said that they saw her in a preview cinema at the 1982 Berlin film festival. But then the trail went dead. A number I had in Hamburg said she had left six months previously. A letter I sent to an address in Cologne came back unopened. And so Elaine slipped away, a faint, negligible scent, leading off into rocky, unpromising terrain, kept alive only by memory and rumour.


There's something else, though, that has to be dealt with first. The photographs come in a sagging brown envelope, bunched in half and squeezed within a coil of Sellotape. Name and address handwritten in frail, spinsterish scrawl. A half-inch pile of Polaroids, the work of someone with scant chance of a future in this line of business. However, on this occasion the form interests me rather less than the content. There are twenty-four pictures, consecutive. In frame one the hero and heroine sit on a sofa in some cluttered, featureless room, he in a suit, she in one of the joke tart get-ups in which people attend fancy dress parties. Identifiable items amongst the debris at their feet include a Marlboro cigarette packet, the *Daily Mail* and a copy of Keith Thomas's *Religion and the Decline of Magic*. Frame two is broadly identical, except that a packet of Polos has appeared mysteriously in the region of the *Daily Mail*. And then, as in all decently constituted narratives, sequentially and with consecutive revelations, things start to happen. By frame four there is a definite loosening of clothing. Yet this is not your standard hot-action stuff. Increasingly, as frame succeeds frame, it becomes clear that whoever perpetrated this horror is something of an artist in his or her way: frame seven, for example, consists simply of the suit, hung cursorily over the back of the sofa, while frame eleven involves sundry manoeuvrings with lofted limbs and

47

mirrors. Later on things become quite strenuously athletic, but there's some droll, off-camera symbolism, frame eighteen ignoring the on-sofa frenzy altogether to linger over a phallic, table-bound cactus.

Except that there are two reasons why this isn't funny. First, towards the end, things turn nasty. In frame twenty the man in the suit – who isn't wearing the suit by now – has just smacked a hefty backhander into his accomplice's face. Frame twenty-three is a nightmarish thrash of frozen, jerking limbs. I steal a single glance at the last shot and then tear it shamefacedly in two.

There is another reason why it isn't funny. The man in the suit is me.


As the hours pass, the photographs become a pivot on which the day turns. Left on a desk-end, lodged two feet down in a choked cardboard box, hidden under a carpet, they are a magnet drawing me back, through the dense, headachy air. *I didn't do this*, I say to myself at intervals during the mesmerised contemplation of these shiny, perfidious rectangles, *I wasn't there*. There is a faint – a very faint – comfort in the knowledge that I have nothing to do with this *at all*. And yet in minor, muted ways this sort of thing has happened before. I remember . . . I remember five years back, one autumn, strolling out of the Grunt Records vestibule towards the murk of Oxford Street and walking into an actor called Jim Woodward. You will not, perhaps, have heard of Jim Woodward. He played bit-parts in films ten years ago that perhaps you didn't see: the stolid chauffeur in *Driven to Lust*, the leery headmaster in *Spank Academy*. The encounter took approximately half a minute. A second or two for Jim to wheel into view, a further five for me to detect a vengeful glint of recognition in his vague but unpromising eyes. The rest consisted of Jim's fist flapping weakly against my chest once or twice, a little badly staged grappling, and me giving him a double-fister in the throat that made him burst into tears. I left him sitting cheerlessly on the pavement and thought no more of the episode – after all, actors are violent people, they frequently accost you in the street without warning. Two days later at one of Morty's parties in the loft at Dean Street something equally queer and inexplicable happened. Picture the scene: Morty and I in our shiny leather jackets exchanging confidences, an ellipse of attendant women, a rough cut of *Man-eater* showing on the wide screen in the viewing room, when suddenly one of the women craned forward and attempted to jab a champagne glass in my face. Have you ever had a champagne glass pushed into your face? The trick is to deflect, thus, meanwhile doing as much damage as possible to your opponent. I remembered this and did quite a lot of damage. While they were cleaning her up I had a word with Morty.

'Who's the girl?'

'Who's the girl? You tell me who's the girl. I thought she came with you.'

'I thought she came with Vanessa and Scazz and that lot.'

'Vanessa and Scazz thought she was with *Adult Video World*.'

Morty made enquiries: Jim Woodward's girlfriend. But this, it transpired, was a mild preliminary. Two days later someone hurled a postcard reading 'Martin Benson must die' through the window of the flat in Bishop's Park, attached to a brick. Twenty-four hours after that I took delivery from a messenger boy of a registered letter containing a dozen razor blades. 'Maybe you upset him or something,' Morty suggested, when pressed for explanations, 'how the fuck should I know anyway?' Jim Woodward turned up frequently over the next few days: on the far side of street corners feigning an interest in window displays, a lurking troglodyte presence on the edge of parties, late at night on the end of telephones. I couldn't establish what it was that I was supposed to have done to him, or what it was that I was supposed to do in recompense. On the day after two undertakers had rung, unbidden, to offer sympathy and discuss my funeral arrangements, I decided on the magniloquent gesture and sent a thousand pounds in ten-pound notes on a bike to Jim Woodward's flat in Leytonstone. They came back the next morning in fragments. After that Morty sent Crazy Rodney round in a minicab. I don't think he hurt him much.

Amid the passage of a cluttered and eventful life you forget things.

Later on, in the soft, misty twilight, I make a closer inspection of the photographs. I deal the pack out card by card on the kitchen table and search anxiously for the inevitable clues of time, location and identity. The room? The room is the sort of room in which these sort of pictures get taken: minimally accoutred, devoid of those revelatory knick-knacks. Frame nine gives a hint of French windows somewhere in the background. Frame thirteen, shot at floor-level, discloses a vista of white, rolling carpet. It could be anywhere. Time? A magnifying glass applied to the copy of the *Daily Mail* reveals a date sometime in March 1978. What was I doing in March 1978? I don't recall. It might have been the time we did *Girls On Top* with Talia Silk, but it might not have been. The girl? Five nine. Maximally endowed. Morty had a file of them half a foot thick. This one didn't work for a month or two afterwards though, that's for sure.

Unless, unless . . . In pornographic cinema, as in more rarefied art-forms, artifice is all. Towards the end of the 1970s Morty got into making splatter movies: *Slash*, *Mad Surgeons*, *Plasma Party*. Given the low budgets and the prognathous actors Morty was forced to employ, they were narrowly realistic. Thus in *Cannibal Island* a man and a woman arrive in tropical paradise, frolic for a while in bounty hunter fashion, only to be caught, molested and eaten by the randy, starving inhabitants. It was, for a late-period Leisurevision film brilliantly executed. Morty shot it at low tide on Sheringham beach, the cannibals were all extras blacked up with boot polish, and the horrific finale – in which everyone chews daintily on splayed human limbs – involved some dextrous sleight-of-hand with cocktail sausages. And yet *Cannibal Island* was nervously declined by four German hard-core importers on the grounds of taste.

Dissimulation. Illusion. You can do anything with pornography. You can prune away puny genitalia and paste in hulking substitutes. You can graft on bogus torsos, turn that rictus of rheumy disgust into a calm, gratified smile. Wise to these tricks I ran the magnifying glass over that taut, pitiless body looking for signs: the tiny blemishes a shade or so darker than flesh which show that someone has been tampering, the faint blur of retouching at neck level. It was to no avail. There was one particular shot of me in close-up, the girl clasped disinterestedly over my lap. Quite flawless. You can even see a grainy, pointillist swirl of dust on the girl's shoulder. You can't fake a shot like that. Even Morty, I reason, couldn't fake a shot like that.

After that I scoop up the photographs and put them back in the box.

BACK IN EARLY '82 when I finally came back here, it was the snow that I remembered, just as I had remembered other snows falling in other cities long ago: in Paris late one night in the parks by the *École Militaire*, in Venice where it descended softly and fruitlessly out over the windy lagoon, more mundanely over thronged Midland rooftops in a silent dawn, snow falling gracefully through the thin air. Now as the train rattled eastward over low, flat countryside it brought back other memories, some recent – a white carpet stretched over Kensington Gardens stained by a single trail of footprints, others more remote, connected indelibly with childhood. Oddly these recollections were linked with landscape rather than emotion. Taken as a child to the high expanse of Mousehold and invited to look out over the wintry city, its spires and office buildings rising up out of the pale dusk, one remembered only detail: the square outlines of Norwich Castle, light neatly constrained to reveal the glowing banks of the city hall. Whatever profounder sensations might have been stirred now lay dormant.

The train out of Liverpool Street was crowded. Generally at such times – Thursday, late in the afternoon – one counted on a degree of uniformity: business people, City men in dark suits with copies of the London evening paper going back to commuter stations down the line, a rare seagoing tourist bound via Harwich for the Hook. Now something had weakened this homogeneity. Students, ticketless and self-absorbed, sat on their bolster-shaped rucksacks ready to scurry off at the guard's approach. Elderly chattering ladies with mysterious parcels. A rugby team back from the Continent, their luggage stacked in doorways and under seats, skirmished fitfully in the bar. Later as the train passed Colchester they would divide and dwindle, leaving only a handful of long-distance commuters, but for the moment their effect was to impose a spirit of willed raucousness upon the teeming carriages, a capacity for collective action. Alone in their seats, bent over coffee cups, books or crosswords, the passengers nonetheless displayed a definite unity: an announcement crackling over the Tannoy causing them to stir like troubled dreamers, a rugby ball sailing overhead producing shy, fugitive smiles.

Colchester. Manningtree. Ipswich. Stowmarket. Diss. The familiar names ran in my head. Recalling ancient, deep-rooted associations, suggestive of other, more innocent days, they combined with current doubts and anxieties to produce a context in which the past took precedence over the present, in which latent uncertainties were replaced by a hardening of resolve. This was unusual. Previously I had found myself resisting any deliberate step, gaining comfort from the dense hinterland which exists between thought and action, fascinated simply by my own inanition. Now I found that I no longer cared what Morty Kronenburg might say or what Terry Chimes might do, what the consequences of this escape (for that is what it amounted to) might be, no longer cared about future reckonings or contingencies. As the train rattled on through the damp Norfolk landscape, past the shrouded churches and the dark, endless fields, as the remaining passengers – the old lady with her circle of cases, the sallow schoolgirl – slept noiselessly on, I found myself gripped not by doubt but by a queer exhilaration. As the outlines of Norwich station slid into view, awash suddenly in blinding light, a glimpse of distant, scurrying figures, I registered neither fear nor anxiety, only the satisfaction of a successful retreat.

I left London in winter; returning to Norwich I found spring. There were crocuses out in the briny fields on either side of the Wensum; beyond them small river craft lay at anchor, motionless beneath clear grey sky. Next morning the sun was shining and I walked through damp, airy streets to the Cathedral Close.

In the past six years I had had little contact with the solicitors. They wrote occasionally giving details of new and departing tenants and forwarding rent cheques. In recent years these had declined to the point where the house barely covered its expenses: the result, successive letters had explained, of a glut in the local rental market. At the same time the number of tenants had markedly fallen off. At first the property had attracted a steady stream of lodgers: students from the local university had lived for years at a time in the small bedsitting rooms, hung Indian broadcloths across the doorframes and decorated the landing with Athena posters: unmarried schoolmistresses had arrived to fill the lounge with bowls of potpourri and hold housewarming parties in the draughty kitchen, but over the years they had fallen away. Now only a single tenant remained: a single woman who, six months before, had been allowed to take over the entire house. It was this arrangement that I wished to disturb.

The solicitors' premises lay in the oldest part of the Close, their frontage directly opposite the west door of the cathedral. Episcopal coats of arms rose over the brass plate of its entrance: and within there was a short, tiled passage with a glass roof where ferns grew in buckets and queer clumps of foliage curled up towards the light. The reception area, unlit, containing quantities of musty furniture, preserved this air of grave, clerical gloom.

It was the same solicitor whom I had dealt with six years before. He greeted me effusively. 'Hullo. How are you? I was wondering when you'd look in. Have a seat, won't you?'

'I take it you received my letter?'

'I did. About the property in Unthank Road?'

'Glebe Road.'

'The property in Glebe Road. And you want planning permission, that's right?'

'On the contrary. I want to live in it.'

He was older now, in his early thirties, and there were family portraits clustered at one end of his desk. Beneath the bonhomie I detected deep, unconquerable reservoirs of disquiet. Eventually he produced from his desk a statement of account covering the previous three months: the amount owing was inconsiderable.

The solicitor watched nervously as I read.

'You'll see there have been one or two extras in the past few months. Repairs to the property and so on.'

I ran my eye over the closely typed columns. 'Item: replacement of roof tile; item: renewal of door frame; item: replacement of panes in greenhouse.'

'Who authorised all this?'

'Well, the tenant – a Miss Richards – gave the actual instructions. Naturally the bills were settled by us.'

The solicitor hesitated. Clearly I had touched some tender nerve of reminiscence. 'Between you and me we find this Miss Richards a bit of a trial. Always on the telephone asking for this and that to be done. Writes letters too. You see, there is a clause in the tenancy agreement about maintaining the fabric.'

I felt a momentary stab of irritation at this fussy, sensible spinster and at the complicity which abetted her.

'You might have spared me the greenhouse.'

The solicitor laughed. For a second I caught a glimpse of that bright, hard sheen of professional detachment. It was the client, I thought, having the client's little joke. But there were other, more pressing, matters at hand.

'When can I expect to move in?'

'Let's see. It's the end of February, isn't it? We do six-month tenancy agreements. The current one expires March thirty-first. I think you might expect a month.'

Later I walked out into the Cathedral Close. It was midday now and small files of schoolboys were passing on their way to the Norwich School refectory at the back of the old bishop's palace. Beyond them towards the Ethelbert gateway besuited figures from accountants' offices proceeded to lunch. On impulse I turned into the cathedral and jostled for a moment with the early tourists collected before Bishop de Losinga's tomb and the Lady Chapel, but it was to no purpose. A shadow had fallen over the day and I had no place here among the grey stones and the demure memorials to a thousand-year, ecclesiastical past. I went back to the small hotel on the west of the city near Chapel Field and slept until dusk.

The days passed swiftly. I set out to explore the city of my childhood. I wandered over Mousehold Heath. I ate lunch under the high Georgian chandeliers of the Assembly House and browsed in the secondhand bookshops of St Benedict's. Norwich was much as I remembered it. Here and there new buildings had risen above the ancient thoroughfares and passageways, there was builders' rubble piled up over the cattle market, but the bones of the old city shone through, a bright, gleaming skeleton impervious to this modern camouflage.

At an early stage I returned to the office in the Close. In the interval the solicitor's enthusiasm – his name, I remembered, was Robey – had waned.

'There seems to have been some mistake. Apparently the tenacy agreement runs annually from New Year's Day.'

'The tenant knows about this?'

Mr Robey handed me a typewritten letter. Its purport was unambiguous. It contained, additionally, a request that the solicitors should install a cat-flap 'as a matter of urgency'.

'Have I any legal rights at all?'

'Not really,' said Mr Robey cheerfully. 'You could try offering her money, of course, but it would look very bad if the case ever came to court. In any case you'll be in by Christmas.'

It wanted a few days to the end of March.

'Let me get this clear. I am expected to spend nine months living in a hotel as a result of some legal oversight?'

For the first time in our dealings, Mr Robey looked pained. 'I wouldn't put it like that.' He seemed for the first time a less solid figure. 'Of course I can write to Miss Richards and explain the situation in any way you think suitable.'

I said, 'At any rate you can tell Miss Richards that there is not the slightest chance that I will consent to pay for her cat-flap.'

I resolved to take matters into my own hands. I wrote to Miss Richards the same afternoon, informing her of my intention to inspect the property. Then, two evenings later, as the light faded in little crimson streaks over the western edge of the city, I left the hotel and walked purposefully through the narrow streets towards Glebe Road. The route lay southwards, past the Chapel Fields and the Roman Catholic cathedral. Here, at last, I found evidence of the changes of the past six years. There were hotels now in Unthank Road, crowding out the private houses with their wild little gardens, turbulent roadhouses ablaze with light. Traffic thundered past in the direction of Cringleford and the Ipswich Road. I had an exact notion of what I might find. Miss Richards' letters with their careful language and their intimations of cats and greenhouses told a familiar story. I imagined a middle-aged woman with a choice vocabulary and distinct political opinions, her evenings devoted to frugal suppers and conscientious housework. There would be ironing going on, I thought, the room draped with white, austere garments which would be hurriedly removed from my sight. But there was no way of proving this hypothesis. Though lights shone at the house in Glebe Road and noise resounded from within, no one answered the doorbell. I stood waiting for several minutes and then went disconsolately away.

In despair I returned to Mr Robey.

'I simply do not believe that she has a right to deny me access to the property. Surely as her landlord I am allowed to carry out an inspection?'

'That depends on your motive. She could argue, you see, that your intent is a hostile one and not in the spirit of the agreement.'

'And is that what she does argue?'

'I've had a letter,' Mr Robey said indifferently, 'which accuses you of harassment. If I might say so, you really are putting yourself in an unfortunate legal position.'

I saw how it was. Mr Robey had grown bored with my predicament. He saw me as an annoyance, motivated only by an unreasonable, personal anxiety, dug into a pit of my own making.

'Is there any other solicitor in your firm who could help me with this situation?'

It was a fatal remark. 'The law is the law, Mr Benson,' Mr Robey said stiffly. It was as if I had begun to cross-examine him on some delicate aspect of his private life. There was nothing more to be said. I walked out into the close, leaving him amid the damask draperies and the mouldering ferns.

On the next morning I wrote to Miss Richards offering her five hundred pounds for immediate repossession. She replied by return of post, enclosing a copy of the tenancy agreement with the crucial clause underlined in red. I wrote again, doubling the amount. This time there was no response.

And then, curiously, fate lent a hand. Quite by chance, having tea one afternoon in the Assembly House, I met an old friend of my father named Mrs Stephens. My father had possessed few female friends, tending to regard even the wives of his acquaintances as exercising a wholly doubtful influence, but he had made an exception of Mrs Stephens who taught French and had been expelled from the local Conservative Association for undemocratic views. We had a long, reminiscent conversation about the circumstances of my father's death.

'I thought it such a shame,' Mrs Stephens remarked, 'that even when he was ill he should be harassed by the business of that tree. In fact, after the funeral I wrote to that dreadful old woman and told her so.'

Here, plainly, the flame of remembrance still burned. But there was another surprise. When I mentioned the problem of the house, Mrs Stephens grew thoughtful.

'Dear me. I have a feeling I know this person. I believe she teaches in our junior department.'

'It's a common enough name.'

'No, this one lives in Glebe Road, I feel certain. *Such* a pretty girl and so delightful with the children.'

For the first time, obscurely, I had an ally. Mrs Stephens promised to make enquiries and, if necessary, to intercede. 'Your father was a very dear friend of mine,' she explained as we said goodbye beneath the city hall clock.

With the vision of the punctilious spinster fading rapidly I wrote again to Miss Richards proposing a compromise. I had no wish to disturb her arrangements. It would be sufficient, I suggested, if we could merely occupy the house together. Two days later another letter arrived. It said simply: 'I don't mind, Suzi.' I sent Mrs Stephens a bunch of flowers. It seemed the least I could do.

Mr Robey provided me with the keys to my father's house. Now that a compromise had been found he seemed strangely animated, as if, I thought, he had played some subtle role in the negotiations of which I had previously been unaware. He insisted on standing me what he called a 'celebratory drink', so I allowed him to take me to a small pub near the cathedral gates and buy two glasses of bitter sherry. Once installed in the meagre bar-room he grew confidential.

'Of course, I remember you from school. You were in Nelson, weren't you?'

'Parker.'

'Parker, was it? Odd how your memory can play tricks on you. I still keep up with some of the old gang, you know. You ought to come along and say hello to us one evening.'

'I should like that *very much*.'

Presently he was joined by a couple of lawyer cronies; I slipped away and took a taxi to the house. In daylight it seemed a frail and insubstantial edifice. There were sprigged lace curtains that had not been there before. Within, the hallway disclosed a number of unfamiliar furnishings. Letters lay on the mat – Miss S. Richards, Susan Richards, Miss Suzi Richards. Obeying some proprietorial instinct I picked them up and arranged them on a small occasional table. Here, in addition to the telephone, was a pile of neatly snipped-out soap-powder coupons. The house no longer retained its own smell, an odd, musty compound of pipe smoke, chalk and tea. In its place was an artificial, feminine odour of air-freshener and the hint of perfume.

For a while I roamed around the downstairs rooms, matching the contents against their imagined former state. There was little I remembered. Cheap, unfamiliar pictures hung on the walls. The kitchen had been repainted, badly, so that feathery brush strokes strayed downwards on to the wainscoting. The place had that generalised, impermanent look that I knew from my own days as a student – neutral, unloved, a receptacle – but here and there were signs that a single personality had attempted to impose order: jars of herbs, neatly labelled, stacked up in the kitchen, a file of glass animals – cats, mice – that ran crazily across the mantelpiece in the lounge. Two or three invitation cards rested against the back of this carnival procession: an old girls' reunion, a tennis club supper, a parent-teachers'-associ-ation ceilidh. They seemed grim entertainments.

In the ramshackle porch that separated the kitchen from the back door there were tennis rackets, discarded tracksuits, a smell of sweat. I opened the door and stepped out into the garden. Whatever memories I might have preserved of it received no answering call: there was a mound of bare earth where the lime tree had been; the rose bushes were wild and unkempt.

Later, as the light began to fade and footsteps resounded on the pavement outside, I wandered through the upstairs rooms. Here the trail was firmer. There were Monet posters on the landing, chiaroscuros of blue hills beneath mounting shade; the second of the two smaller bedrooms had been converted into a makeshift study with a desk, a chair and a typewriter. The door of the third room, my father's bedroom, now appropriated, was slightly ajar. I found nothing I recognised. A single bed, its pink coverlet folded back, took up the far side. There were flowers in the ancient fireplace. A line of toy animals – bears, hippopotami, raccoons in day-glo yellow – marched along the dressing table. It was a schoolgirl's room, I thought, wanting only the pony club rosettes, the posters cut from *Jackie* and *Just Seventeen* to produce a final, authenticating touch.

A female voice said sharply from the doorway: 'Do you always snoop around in people's bedrooms?'

Turning back I saw a small, plump, sulky-looking girl regarding me balefully. In her late twenties, perhaps, dressed in a bulky tracksuit, her face pink from recent exercise, the effect was not prepossessing. She gave the impression of some small but rapacious creature of the field, cornered in its lair and liable to turn nasty.

'Suzi,' she said, advancing briskly into the room. 'Suzi Richards.'

'I didn't mean to take you by surprise.'

'It's all right. The solicitor told me you were coming.' She gave me a cross look. 'I just didn't expect you till later.'

There was a large basket-chair in the corner of the room. She sat in this, still frowning, and began to unlace her tennis shoes. 'Look. I know you're the landlord and there're all sorts of questions you probably want to ask me, but I have to get changed and go out. Tuesdays are one of my busy nights. So perhaps you'd be kind enough to just go away and let me get myself together.'

I had come badly out of that. From the doorway I looked back, but she was already seated in front of the dressing table, head lowered intently over the mirror.

I spent the evening contriving a bed in the second spare room, occasionally returning downstairs to search for blankets or pillowcases. Once the telephone buzzed; I let it ring on unanswered. Later I sat in front of the television and drank gin out of a bottle I found in the kitchen; at eleven I went to bed. She came back, noisily, at midnight. Lying in the darkness I heard her moving about in the bathroom. There was the occasional slamming of a door. At eight I awoke to find the house empty.

It was the first of many similar evenings. Miss Richards kept odd hours, I discovered. Often I would return to the house late in the afternoon to find that she had been and gone, that the remains of a frugal supper already lay on the kitchen table. She rarely came back before eleven. At weekends, the time at which the denizens of lodging houses traditionally emerge to sniff the air, she became still more elusive, often disappearing altogether to return late on Sunday night, flustered but unforthcoming. From an early stage I was intrigued by these absences. Did she visit her parents or relatives? Did she have some boyfriend many miles distant? There was a pile of Duke of Edinburgh Award Scheme literature on the coffee table in the lounge. From it I devised an elaborate fantasy in which she led groups of romping schoolgirls along mountain paths or pitched tents amid lakeland scenery. There would be mugs of cocoa around the camp fire, I thought, and prurient discussion of sex. Such visions had no grounding in reality and were soon abandoned. Miss Richards remained as an intermittent, vagrant presence, reluctant to be drawn into wider orbits of conversation or complicity, like some child on the edge of a crowded playground, happily intent on a game of its own invention.

Slowly and imperceptibly fractures emerged in the ice.

'I should hate to think that you were avoiding me,' I said one evening, meeting her on the stairs.

'I'm not avoiding you. I just happen to be very busy at the moment.'

'Too busy to set foot in the lounge?'

'Much too busy.'

Later that evening she appeared in the front room with a basketful of washing and an ironing board.

'Will I be disturbing you? By doing this, I mean?'

'No.'

She ironed studiously for an hour and then went away. The clothes lay in a pile on the sofa. They were utilitarian garments: pairs of plain white briefs, Aertex shirts woven in the spongy, punctured cloth that I remembered from my childhood, a dirndl skirt or two. I had a working knowledge of women's clothing – the rucks of discarded underthings which the models left in the changing room at Dean Street, the fanciful camisoles that Elaine wore around the flat – but these struck an unfamiliar note. They combined with the glass animals and the girlish bed to suggest a recognisably older world – homely, economic and inviolate.

I set about subjecting Miss Richards to deliberate study. As a palaeontologist takes a fragment of bone or a scrap of fossilised vegetation and extrapolates from it some cumbersome beast roaming in a primeval swamp, so I assembled a gesture, a look, an intonation, and construed a personality. Tiny accretions of detail – an overheard conversation, a chance remark – each played some part in this grand but notional design, like a vase reconstituted out of shards so tiny that only the glue gives it pattern and coherence. The archaeological metaphor was, I found, appropriate to a process of re-creation demanding the weighing-up of evidence, the dismissal of untenable early theories. In particular, I thought, I had been mistaken about her appearance. She was a short, well-built girl – no more than five feet high, perhaps – but there was a definition about her features which set her apart from the plump Glebe Road housewives. Her most original feature was her hair – copious and corn-coloured – which when treated with the appropriate lotions and mousses fell in rippling cascades on to her shoulders. I suspected artifice, but its shade never varied and there was upstairs no trace of incriminating bottles. She was vain of this adornment, settled it occasionally against her neck with a complacent gesture and spent long periods combing it out in front of the mirror. It had particularly impressed the Nigerian prince, she told me.

There were other reassessments, other readjustments to this frail early prognosis. She was erudite in a small way, the possessor of a stock of specialist lore that enabled her to name an obscure foreign capital or a chemical symbol. It was a false erudition, I thought, born of the general knowledge required to excel in after-dinner games and television quizzes: it was, I suspected, from the files of MasterBrain cards that most of her information was derived.

What she did at the school I never wholly determined. Cars, presumably driven by colleagues, occasionally called for her early in the morning or returned her late in the afternoon; their owners remained unseen. There were stray references – it was a small independent school, precariously financed – to the headmaster and matron. She taught for the most part small boys, nine- and ten-year-olds, and was oddly well-informed about their personal circumstances – which had parents who were divorced, for instance, or were being pressed to fulfil vicarious parental ambitions. Beyond this tightly coralled arena the landscape of her private life stretched out into shadow. She had no women friends, I concluded. Her interests, such as they were, were entirely masculine. She watched sport on the television in an absorbed, critical way. There was a snooker player named John Marshall whose progress she followed around the professional tournaments and whose performances I was occasionally asked to video. Her social life seemed mapped out by the invitation cards on the mantelpiece, but there were hints of wider affiliations beyond the tennis club dances and the old girls' reunions. In the fortnight after my arrival a man named Christopher telephoned repeatedly. It became a kind of ritual between us. 'Christopher rang,' I would say as we met on the stair. 'Did he? Thank you.' 'Who is this Christopher?' I asked once. 'He seems very anxious to speak to you.' She shrugged. 'Oh, just someone I know.' It was, in its way, a rebuke. The small barrier that we had imposed on our dealings had been breached and she resented it.

Once, passing outside her room late at night, I heard the unmistakeable sounds of sexual activity. The noises went on for a long time: strange heavings and ululations, pantings and grunts, a man's voice raised in recrimination. To one who had presided over so many simulated expressions of ecstasy, wheeled microphones close in to get what Morty called a 'killer soundtrack', it seemed vaguely indecent, a sharp gust of realism blowing over Morty's bland, tidy dreamscape. I listened for a while and then, ashamed of my own voyeurism, went away.

It was another tiny dent in the barrier. Next morning Suzi said, 'Do you know, I sometimes think that the worst thing about men is that they make assumptions about women that they'd never dream of making about a car or an electric drill.'

I had heard this sort of remark before. It had not seemed to

63

bear repetition. 'Not quite as mistaken as the assumptions women make about men.'

'I hadn't thought of it that way.'

'Women never do.'

Looking back I can detect a sense of shared confidence that almost certainly did not exist. Hindsight imparts complicity. At the time, I am sure, we saw ourselves as nothing more than two ill-assorted people whom chance had thrown together in circumstances beyond our control, uneasily determined to make the best of things. Meanwhile there was news from other quarters, flickers of continuity burning beneath this slow, disjointed progress. Postcards came from London, Rome, Los Angeles, postcards from Morty, Terry Chimes, Crazy Rodney, messages from other queer denizens of the world I had left behind. I took them into the kitchen and read them looking out over the bleak garden – bleak even in spring – with unmitigated wonder. They had no place, I thought, in the placid low-key landscape I was fashioning for myself, were no more than dispatches out of a battlefield from which I had long since retreated. Afterwards, out trawling the wet Norwich streets with their quotas of dull Norfolk faces, they lost even their zestful, energetic quality and became only memorabilia, regimental buttons wrested from decaying cloth, spent cartridges pulled out of the mud. Eventually I lost interest in these mementoes, leaving Suzi to collect them from the mat and arrange them without comment on the mantelpiece.

Summer came. The wind blowing in from the sea lost its sharpness and there were ice-cream vans in the streets. Suzi believed in the restorative powers of sunshine. On Sunday afternoons she put on odd, formalised bathing costumes – relics, I correctly diagnosed, of her schooldays – and reclined decorously on a garden chair, her face raised towards the heat. There was a painful innocuousness about these performances: no artifice attended the arrangement of limbs or the choice of pose. It was, I saw, a routine, something that one did in Norwich at certain times of the year when the temperature had reached a certain point, regardless of personal consequence, like my father's compulsion to eat outdoors at any date after May Day. Suzi burned in the sun. An hour in the garden chair left her skin red and angry, her face contorted in a mass of fat scarlet flesh, her fine hair bleached out of recognition, but she persevered gamely. Watching her from the kitchen window through the glaze of reflected sunshine, one was aware only of an intent, silent figure, motionless amid the heat.

Once around this time she said, 'I could cook you supper tonight if you like.'

'I should like it very much.'

'It wouldn't be anything very special.'

'I should still like it.'

So she cooked me supper: a substantial meal as it turned out, eaten formally around my father's dining table with place mats produced from the kitchen cabinet and previously unseen china. She ate copiously. In the intervals between courses she told me about Christopher. 'It was just one of those things that you do,' she explained, 'just one of those people that you meet. But I could see it wasn't working out.' Later she said, 'He was very demanding. He always expected me to be there, round at his house, going over to see his mum and dad, and he used to get angry when I had to do marking or go to something at school, so in the end I finished it.' The vague, talismanic phrases were familiar. It was how people talked, I remembered, about cast-off lovers, bogus affiliations finally given the lie. '*Just one of those things . . . could see that it wasn't working out . . . so in the end I finished it.*' So Morty, abandoning one of his improbable mistresses, would talk of 'knocking it on the head'. I had a glimpse of a brief, arid courtship, cut short by cynicism and good sense. It was a new phase in our association.

Our relationship prospered. We ate long, scrappy meals together on summer evenings, emerging from the wreckage of plates and tattered cellophane to wander through the streets to pubs on the edge of the city, in sight of the wheat fields and the water meadows. Suzi was knowledgeable about pubs. She knew which served Adnams Ale, the treacly local beer, at which of them you were likely to find a Norwich City footballer smoking furtively at the bar. Such knowledge was oddly agreeable, a proof that one had deciphered the abstruse codes by which the city was governed, that one was somehow as representative of milieu as the white-flannelled bowls players with their tankards, or the crophaired students from the Norwich School of Art. Later we ventured further afield to Mulbarton, Hempnall and Brooke, tiny villages in the southern half of the county, each with their symbols of neat, regimented rural life: church spire, war memorial, green, occasionally a cricket pitch. No wild country existed now in Norfolk. There was a hint of display in these excursions. Suzi was not in any strict sense a local girl – her parents lived in Bungay on the Suffolk border – but she had been to school in Norwich and taught there since her graduation. In her unveiling of out-of-the-way beauty spots and rare lych gates I detected the authoritative note of the tourist guide.

Suzi did not talk much about her parents, whom she referred to as 'Mother and Father'. There was a photograph of them on her bedside table: the man's face weatherbeaten, canny, obstinate; the woman's bland, emollient, grey hair cut on roundhead principles. She said once, 'Mother and Father didn't hold with university. They wanted me to work in a shop and get married.' There was no trace of bitterness in this, rather one of pride. It suggested that she admired her parents, respected even the more questionable among their beliefs, and yet admired most of all herself for her ability to flout the conventions they had imposed upon her.

At the beginning of August Suzi took a fortnight's holiday. In the interval beforehand I found myself speculating on her choice of venue. It would be Corfu, I thought, or Mykonos, French provincial church architecture or Rhine castles: that was where these single, independent-minded schoolmistresses went of a summer vacation. I had not reckoned on a streak of insularity. It was the Lake District. She went with a schoolfriend named Lucy, a girl who had hitherto existed simply as a voice on the telephone, but who was, I gathered, frequently brought out and put to service in this way. There was the additional fact that Lucy required consolation. 'Lucy's been badly let down by a man,' Suzi explained. She wrote postcards from the guest-house on Lake Windermere in a crisp, girlish hand. It had rained. It had not rained. Lucy had been ill. Lucy had recovered. They were brief, characterless messages, giving no hint of the sharp, self-contained intelligence which had indited them.

In her absence I grew restless. Solitude, long anticipated, swiftly became irksome. At night I prowled through the empty house, or sat watching the blaring television. Once, in desperation, I sought out Mr Robey and spent an evening with him and his friends in the Maid's Head Hotel. They were professional men, assistant solicitors, junior partners in accountancy firms: heavy-set thirty-year-olds who laughed boisterously at their own jokes. Several of them had vague memories of me from adolescence. They said, 'Weren't you in old so-and-so's house? Didn't you play in the fifteen?' A dozen years on, the school still exercised an unreasonable hold over their personal lives. They wore its old boy's ties and looked forward eagerly to its reunion dinners. But amid this opulent nostalgia I detected a faint air of unease. 'Of course it isn't the same,' they said, 'not any more. They've closed down the boarding house and they say the new head's keen on soccer.' I listened to them with amusement. I was detached from their world, I thought, I could leave it at will. Their ties were physical: they had jobs, wives, children. Mine were abstract, I thought complacently, the ties of memory, instinct, association; they could be lived out wherever I chose. The ten thousand pounds I had brought from London lay gathering interest in the building society.

Mid-August came and Suzi returned. I saw immediately that absence had wrought a decisive shift in the way that she regarded me. The holiday had not gone well. 'Lucy got cystitis and had to stay inside a lot,' she explained. 'I spent most of my time bringing her cups of tea.' 'What else did you do?' 'I went for walks,' she said, '*lots* of walks. Or I listened to Lucy telling me about what she does in bed.' I saw how it was. Intimacy to her meant roguishness, innuendo, the exchange of slightly lurid confidences. She had brought me back a comic postcard, bought on a daytrip to Barrow-in-Furness. It showed a tiny, pallid cleric escorted, or rather propelled by a voluptuous woman in a tight skirt. Two crones looked on. 'Does that vicar have any children?' 'No. They say his stipend's too small.' There were other signs of our changed relationship. She came down to breakfast in a dressing gown, or walked around the house in her nightdress searching for a handbag, a mislaid newspaper. Once I surprised her sunbathing topless in the garden: she was unabashed. This newfound role did not suit her, I thought. Flooziedom, with its range of gesture and response, its comedy of titillation, seemed alien and inappropriate. The short, plump girl turning on the garden mat, the white breast, the sloping grin: none was in the least erotic.

As a signal, however, it was unmistakeable. Later that evening she appeared in the lounge, clad in her nightdress, and grasped my hand. 'I want it done,' she said, 'I want it done now.' I followed her upstairs along the lightless passage. In bed she was brisk and commanding. 'Wait,' she said at one point. 'Now . . . and then wait again.' There was calculation, I thought, in the practised arrangement of her limbs. Afterwards she gave a short, commendatory sigh, like a small child who has completed a not very enjoyable task to the best of its abilities.

'How do I match up to Christopher?'

'Pretty good. Christopher was always very concerned about Christopher.'

I let the matter lie. There would be other revelations, I knew, other disclosures from the dark catalogue of past intimacies that would come my way. Lying there on the narrow bed, the ridged sheet stiff and uncomfortable, the air heavy with musk and sweat, I though inexplicably and yet with infinite longing of Elaine.


'The thing to do if you're drinking pints, is not to hang about.'

'Too right it is.'

'After three then. One, two . . .'

'One, two . . .'

It's Saturday night and I stand in the front bar of the City Gates with Fat Eric from two doors down. Several other of Fat Eric's *convives* are posed negligently about the place – a character called Woody, who I think sells Fat Eric misappropriated car spares, and an exophthalmic teenager called Mad Trevor, and through the shifting, smoky air I can make out the figure of Kay, Fat Eric's girlfriend, buying another round of crisps at the bar.

'Bloody hell.' Fat Eric slaps down the glass, a fragile goblet in the dense wrapping of his fist. 'Your round.'

'Adnams?'

'Adnams it is.'

I saunter off to the bar and purchase another four pints of the local beer, while Fat Eric renews a menacing conversation with Woody about a flat car battery. I like it here. I feel at home here with Fat Eric in the bar of the City Gates, drinking pints of Adnams and watching people who resemble Fat Eric's younger brother playing snooker. A little later, if I feel so disposed, I may have a game of darts, or join Kay over by the jukebox and see what they have in the Sixties and nostalgia section. These are simple pleasures. I relish them.

Back at the table – anxious onlookers deferentially making way as I wander past – Fat Eric hoists a pint glass expertly off the tray.

'After three then. One, two . . .'

'One, two . . .'

We have been in here half an hour and Fat Eric is on to his fifth pint of Adnams. Me, I've had three and I'm already noticing that the cigarettes are becoming harder to light and that I've joined in a raucous singalong to 'Hi Ho, Silver Lining' on the jukebox. Now, Fat Eric can *drink*. I'd put him into the Terry Chimes class, without question. I once saw him and Mad Trevor stage a drinking contest in here one evening after a horse named Dandruff, the repository of much local goodwill, had splayed itself nonchalantly over the final fence in the National, twenty lengths clear of a receding field. They began by drinking six pints of Adnams each, Fat Eric helping his down with sundry handfuls of pickled gherkins, cheesy snacks and whatnot. They then had a couple of gins apiece, Fat Eric in the meantime sending out to the takeaway for a brace of cheeseburgers. After this they went on to snappers, a high-octane cocktail composed of lager and brandy, exclusive to the locality. They stopped after seven of these, when Mad Trevor passed out, whereupon Fat Eric went off for a curry and an informed discussion of whether Kevin Flack could shoot with his left foot.

Saturday night in the City Gates. Occasionally Fat Eric takes me to other places – to the Romany Rye up by Bunnett Square or the Farmhouse in Colman Road, but predominantly we come here. Fat Eric likes a quiet pub. The City Gates is a quiet pub: full of silent, slimmed-down versions of Fat Eric and their mournful, hilarious women. Fat Eric is a species of god here, a molten monarch. People get out of his way when he lumbers up to the bar: the tough boys with the lacquered hair queue up to buy him drinks.

Fat Eric and Woody have now left the subject of the flat car battery in favour of Norwich City's craven performance a few hours previously against some bunch of northern cloggers. I shift gallantly to one side as Kay, Fat Eric's girlfriend, steams back from the bar with her cargo of crisp packets. Kay. About fifteen years ago in this part of the world I used to know girls like Kay. Kay is perhaps twenty-one or twenty-two, but looks older, much older. As it happens, Kay isn't from round here. They come in from the country, people like Kay, from godforsaken hamlets like Holt and Fakenham, tiny towns on the bare Norfolk plains where the wind sweeps in from the sea and you spend your teens in the market square smoking cigarettes and waiting for something to happen. At seventeen or eighteen you leave that job in the wool shop or the chicken-packing factory, say goodbye to your parents' bungalow on the squeaky clean estate where the air always smells of salt and the gulls hover endlessly, and head towards the grey bedsitterland of the city. Norwich is full of people who come from somewhere else, from Lynn or Thetford or one of the dead towns on the coast. Kay comes from Framlingham, twenty miles over the Suffolk border, and you can tell it in the way she speaks, clipping the vowels to say 'hev' instead of 'have', 'rud' instead of 'road'. Fat Eric, alternatively, is stage Norvicensian. If he admires something it's 'reely nice'. He doesn't ask me what I think of something, he says, 'What you reckon?'

It grows pleasantly comfortable here, pleasantly blurred, as Kay jams her pit-prop calves against mine beneath the table, steals a look at her mutinous complexion in a hand-mirror, monitors Fat Eric who is flexing his wrists in preparation for an arm-wrestling bout with Mad Trevor. Fat Eric nods benignly and tells me that City have an evening match on Wednesday and do I fancy coming. I nod back as Kay and I start one of our regular conversations about music. Ever since she found out about my former career, Kay has treated me with beguiling deference. I could tell her anything. Tonight, flapping stubby, carmined fingers over the Babycham, she wants to know, of all people, about Bobby Dazz.

'And did he really . . . do what they said in the papers? Found a deer sanctuary and give all that money to charity?'

'We all liked Bobby.'

'And Barbie. I read an interview where he said that even after twenty years the first thing he did every night when he came off stage was to phone her.'

'She's a great girl, Barbie.'

'And do they, you know, *keep in touch*?'

'I get a Christmas card. A telephone call every now and then.'

Bobby Dazz. I could tell Kay one or two things about Bobby Dazz. Imprimis, the deer sanctuary was actually a venison farm. Even when I knew him, which was in the mid-Seventies, he hadn't spoken to Barbie (real name, Edna) for five years. The one thing you could say in Bobby Dazz's favour was that he had a good PR man. Whenever he cracked up it was always in the papers as 'overwork', and even when a tabloid newspaper grew fractious once about the drink Barbie weighed in with a felicitous mastectomy.

'I joined his fan club when I was a kid,' Kay says moistly. 'He sent me a signed photograph once.'

No he didn't. I happen to know that all the photos were signed by Bobby's agent, but this is not the time to despoil childish illusions. Instead I call over to Fat Eric, who has just finished grinding his opponent's fingers into the table top.

'So who are we playing on Wednesday, Fat Eric?'

'Fucking *Newcastle*. Beat us in the Cup last year.'

'Any good?'

'Fucking soft cunts,' says Fat Eric. 'No trouble.'

Another thing about Kay: Fat Eric hits her. I once heard him do it, round at Fat Eric's house, two doors down, where we had retired for coffee and a browse through Fat Eric's video collection (there was a tape of *Girlschool Janitor*, which levied a faint, Proustian smile). I was in the lounge when it happened, staring at the record rack and darkly conscious that the raised voices in the kitchen were some way beyond the customary lickerish banter. They were arguing about . . . I forget what they were arguing about. Arguing with Kay, along with Norwich City FC and drinking, constitutes Fat Eric's principal hobby. It is his habit to argue with her about things she doesn't actually know about: about how you revived a defunct car battery, whether Manchester United had won the FA Cup in 1971, that sort of thing. On this occasion, however, they were arguing about something on which Kay did have some, admittedly tenuous, view: Kay's mother.

'I suppose you want the old girl to live here?'

Kay made some muffled rejoinder. I recollected that her mother lay bedbound in a council bungalow outside Saxlingham. The volume of noise increased.

'I suppose you want the old girl living here and telling me off about *drinking* and *smoking*, then?'

Silence. I could imagine Kay's dull realisation that, yes, he wasn't joking and, no, there wasn't anything she could do and, yes, there wasn't any point in appealing to me and, no, there was no obvious course to pursue except to wait for something to happen, that something which would hurt but take the fear away.

'I suppose you want the old girl ringing me up every day and telling me to get a *proper fucking job*?'

More silence. Meanwhile the air had grown tense and headachy. I remember taking a purposeful interest in a framed photograph that hung askew on the wall, finally recognising the Norwich team from four years back. The blow, when it came, was nothing: no explosion of sound, no clamour of voices, merely a soft twinge of bone on flesh, followed, a little later, by an encore of furtive scuffling. Two minutes later Fat Eric came and lowered a cup of tea nonchalantly into my lap.

'Girl's a bit upset,' he said. 'Gone upstairs for a bit.'

That nonchalance. I remember Terry Chimes once coming to blows in a pub in Shaftesbury Avenue with some failed rock dinosaur he had recently erased from the Grunt Records roster. It took precisely half a minute. Half a minute later while they were sweeping up the broken glass and retrieving the two halves of the pool cue which had been smashed over his opponent's head, Terry Chimes was back in his chair nursing a large brandy.

Such disagreements are in abeyance this evening, however, here in the City Gates where the air grows thicker and the women ever more tired. Each female face conceals, narrowly, its own quiet resentment, its own desire for solitude, the absence of the raucous, convivial partner. Each would rather be with its children, asleep, in front of the television, anywhere. There is a faint, ominous pressure on my shoulder as Kay begins her slow, somnambulistic slide. Seeing this Fat Eric lurches across and slaps her jovially.

'Carm on, girl. Can't have you falling asleep. Not in here. Not in front of everybody and that.'

For a moment Kay's head rolls, glassy-eyed, until she remembers where she is and that the prospect of sleep is at least three hours distant.

'Sorry,' she giggles weakly. 'Must be the gin.'

Or the Pernod. Or the Bacardi. Kay drinks enormous amounts in a wry, disinterested way. 'A real *alki*,' Fat Eric will say proudly, 'a real *boozer*,' when this fact is drawn to his attention. He plods away again to conduct some vague superintendence of a pool game in which Woody and Mad Trevor are now engaged. There is a brief exchange of chatter. He saunters back. 'Why not come back to my place?' he suggests. 'Come and have a talk?'

On these occasions Fat Eric is very keen that I should come back to his place, come back and have a talk. The reasons for this are almost exclusively financial. Fat Eric thinks I have money. Further, Fat Eric thinks I have money which could be harnessed to the lurching tumbril of his own commercial ambition. For oddly enough, despite the hours tethered to the bar-stool, Fat Eric is a businessman at heart, part owner of a minicab and a stall on Norwich market, hitherto trammelled only by want of capital. At an early stage in our relationship he began to hint outrageously that I might make up this deficiency. He did this, subtly enough, by means of newspaper headlines. The libel award, the out-of-court settlement to the discarded girlfriend, the damages paid to the Joan Collins lookalike with the champagne-bottle shoulders – Fat Eric uses them all for the purposes of invidious comparison. 'Course,' he says. 'Wouldn't mean anything, would it, to a man in your position?' There are more of these genteel clichés: 'Someone of your standing', 'A man with your resources', more phrases from the soaps and the tabloid court reports. Once I came clean. 'Look, Fat Eric,' I told him. 'I've got no money at all. Just forty quid a week I get out of the building society and what Suzi pays me in rent. What about that? Will that do?' Unfortunately, or perhaps fortunately, Fat Eric treated this as an enormous joke.

'Why not come back to my place?' he suggests again. 'Come and have a talk?' He stands over me, a brooding, solicitous giant. There is no alternative but to acquiesce. Kay, prodded, poked and propelled by Fat Eric's saveloy fingers, shambles before us to the door. Fat Eric turns, modestly adjusts his jeans, waves – there are nods of recognition from the boys at the snooker table, a smile from mine host – and we move out into the night air.

Outside the street is damp: a gust of fine rain. An infant whirls by on a skateboard ('Watch where you're *fucking going*!' Fat Eric yells goodhumouredly after him.) Passing the house I wonder if I can hear a telephone ringing. Nothing. A week has passed now since Elaine rang. Wedged in his doorway Fat Eric is suddenly stricken by atavistic proletarian formality, ushers me in, sweeps a strew of cans from the sofa, plumps cushions, installs me by the glowing gas fire, plods to the kitchen. Kay disappears up the narrow staircase. I watch the dispirited droop of her shoulders. Doors slam. Taps go on. In the distance, through the adjoining wall, the buzz of television.

The decor of Fat Eric's house is oddly familiar. I remember ten years back watching *Coronation Street* and marvelling at the flight of ducks which adorned Hilda Ogden's wall. Fat Eric has an identical set, a dart pinioning the head of the leading bird. There are splayed record covers: *Now That's What I Call Music Vol. 23*, Bobby Dazz's greatest hits. Alone, in an alcove, four books: *The Rothmans' Football Yearbook*, *On The Ball City*, *Norwich City: The Divison One Story*, *Flying High With The Canaries*. Inspection reveals that the latter has been autographed by the entire Norwich team. A square foot of cigarette packets stacked neatly like bricks against the far wall recalls the two thousand Benson & Hedges that were Fat Eric's price for silence after one of Woody's recent escapades. Fat Eric trips back into the room with a tray to disturb their symmetry, fingering the corner packet and searing the cellophane with his thumbnail. I draw his attention to *Flying High With The Canaries*.

74

'All eleven of them, Fat Eric. Plus the substitutes. How did you do it?'

Fat Eric looks modestly around him. 'End of last season. They came down the Gates. Some charity do or something. So I said, if you want me to give a fiver for crippled kids, you got to sign this. They *signed*,' says Fat Eric truculently, 'they *signed*.'

Smoke rises. Fat Eric flicks the television on, coaxes Bobby Dazz's greatest hits out of their sleeve and puts them on the turntable. From above, the sound of footsteps. Fat Eric moves his head upwards with unfeigned disgust.

'Listen,' he says. 'Let's talk *business*.' Without encouragement Fat Eric talks business for the next fifteen minutes to the accompaniment of a police serial and Bobby Dazz intoning a series of ballads of glutinous sentimentality. The gist of it appears to be that Fat Eric's plans for his market stall are being sorely frustrated by his timid partner. At present they don't possess a van, which means that the produce, which comes in every morning from New Covent Garden, has to be purchased at extortionate rates from a local supplier. Fat Eric wants to cut out the middleman and have his own truck sweeping up and down the A12 six days a week. Then there is the tame farmer in Lincolnshire from whom Fat Eric maintains he can extract a concession for beetroot and curly kale. Then there are the exotics. At present, he claims, Norwich market furnishes a subsistence diet of fruit and root vegetables: swedes, turnips, parsnips – the queer ethnic fodder of Norfolk. Fat Eric wants to bring in yams, mangoes, passion fruit, nectarines. There is poetry in the way he talks about them.

Naturally, all this will cost money. How much money? I fear that Fat Eric doesn't know. There are contemptuous references to someone called Ron, presumably Fat Eric's partner, and to the City Hall, which won't let them put up a neon sign. Our avid colloquy is cut short by the re-emergence of Kay wearing a pastel-pink dressing gown and drying her hair with a portable dryer. Without her make-up, seen in the haggard late-night glare, Kay looks pale and white, very pale and white. A dropsical calf peeps momentarily through the folds of her gown. Fat Eric regards her with distaste, examines his watch and mutters something about wanting to see Woody before the pub closes. I watch him prowl off, the cigarette a tiny, glowing stub in his mottled fist.

Kay says, 'You don't want to listen to what he tells you about that market stall.'

'I don't?'

'Him and that Ron. Couple of crooks they are.'

'Yes, well . . .'

'No. Couple of crooks they are. I been out with them on Sunday afternoons. Out in the country. Out near Wroxham. Digging up cabbages and that out of people's fields.'

Kay pauses, as if to let this entirely predictable piece of intelligence sink in. Flopped down on the sofa she looks sad, tired, exasperated. These East Anglian girls lose their looks very quickly. Twenty-one, twenty-two, and the subcutaneous fat rises up to fill in their cheekbones, puff out the skin around torpid eyes. Wet, torpid eyes.

'Kay . . . Don't . . . Please, don't *cry*.'

'I'm sorry.' She snuffles for a while, face averted. 'Listen,' she says. 'Would you . . . Would you tell me some more about those people you know. About, well, Bobby Dazz and the others.'

'Sure, Kay. Anything you want. Who would you like to hear about?'

Kay lights a cigarette, the tears already a fleeting memory. 'Did you ever know Lulu Sinde?'

As it happens I did know Lulu Sinde. I came across her in the mid-1970s, when we were on the way up. Lulu Sinde, predictably, was on the way down. 'These old women,' Morty remarked, having briefly considered her for a part in *Indiscreet*, 'incredible the way they keep going. Just incredible.' I sense Kay's questioning stare.

'Sure. I knew Lulu. A real trouper.'

'That's what my dad used to say. In those *Carry On* films.'

'That's right. She's a great girl, Lulu.'

We look at one another in that helpless, inarticulate way. 'Oh Martin,' Kay begins and I tense myself for some epic revelation about Fat Eric, about how he wants it eight times a night and threatened her mother with a chainsaw. It never happens. Instead a moment of confidence is shattered by the crash of the front door and the return of Fat Eric, monstrous and triumphant, clutching a bottle of whisky.

'Later,' I say, patting Kay's dormant hand. 'Tell me later.'

An hour later everyone is drunk. I am drunk. Kay is drunk. Fat Eric is drunk. Here, however, the resemblance between us ends, for while I am drunk and exhausted, Kay is drunk and sad and Fat Eric is drunk and boisterous. In this condition we have watched a video Fat Eric has recently acquired of a badger-baiting excursion, sung along to Side One of Bobby Dazz's greatest hits, and discussed Norwich City's abject mid-week performance against Sunderland in the Littlewoods Cup. To the accompaniment of raucous laughter – his own – Fat Eric has ferreted gamely inside his beloved's dressing gown and Kay has fainted gracelessly on to the sofa, only to be revived by a jug of water poured over her face. At midnight, as I stumble through the doorway I can hear Fat Eric bawling with a complete absence of self-consciousness into the dead air:

> On the ball, City.
> Never mind the danger.
> Steady on, now's your chance . . .
> Hurrah, we've scored a goal!

Outside the street is moist and silent. The lights flash and boomerang around my head as I move on into the pressing darkness.

Back at the house, chaos threatens: in the front room a sprawl of billowed sofa cushions; in the kitchen a stack of ancient, unwashed crockery. I loiter in the kitchen, which has somehow taken on vast, Brobdingnagian proportions; nervously I totter past huge footstools, stretch yearning hands up at remote, unreachable cupboards, negotiate the monstrous obstacle course of chairs and tables. It scares me, this giant's clutter. Knives and forks, stacked on the draining board, are obscure implements of war, the saucepans gaping cauldrons. Grappling with a remorseless, unwieldy blanket – a tea-towel probably – I come upon the morning's post, concealed there by Suzi. Two items. A postcard and a large, squarish parcel. The card is post-marked 'St Tropez'.

On its cover two bare-breasted beauties sit at the poolside drinking from frosted glasses. On the back are the words, 'Unfortunately Brigitte and Dolores already have agents.' The writing, that pinched, doubtful hand, is unmistakeably Elaine's.

The kitchen continues to enlarge: each fork a barbed infantryman's pike, each plate a gleaming spacecraft. The parcel, bound with string, with thongs, with electric cables, with tentacles, contains . . . an obelisk? A mattress? A block of concrete? Eventually, undone and placed on the kitchen table, it discloses a small plastic container. I stare at it for a moment and then at the piles of leftovers, the festering coffee cups, trying to find some explanation for the rank, heavy odour. I prise open the gaping maw of the oven: empty. Realisation dawning, I look half-heartedly at the soles of my shoes. Nothing. Despairingly I move closer and, three feet distant, take a sniff at the container. After this I don't bother to open it. Gingerly I convey box and wrappings to the dustbin and loft them inside. On the way back I find a black-bordered card which must have fluttered to the floor during my transit. It says, 'To Martin Benson, from an admirer.' I cry silently now, face down on the kitchen table, as the Queen of Brobdingnag cackles airily above my head.

IN THE AUTUMN of 1969 I went to London to train to be a journalist.

My father came of a generation which emphasised the significance of partings, seeing them as a finite, concrete barrier beyond which lay only uncertainty, and the excuse for a great deal of lapidary advice. 'I daresay,' he said, as we assembled my baggage on the platform, 'that you'll find London much as I found it. A lot of queer people living an ever queerer lot of lives.' It was a prophetic remark. As the tide of passengers began to move purposefully towards the waiting train another thought seemed to strike him. 'You must write to me,' he said. 'You must write to me *often*. Don't do what Craddock's boy did. He didn't write to his father for over a year and finally when they decided to investigate they found him in a squat in Camden Town with a lot of Buddhists.' As the train pulled out through grey, desolate sidings and on into the wet Norfolk countryside the image of him, intent and waving from the platform, persisted, until at last, at Diss or Stowmarket, it faded away and there were only the fields, the distant church spires and the angry skies. Later on, in the ensuing months, fragments of this homily would occasionally settle in my head. 'There is a class of undergraduate known, I believe, as professional agitators. Stay out of their clutches.' Their influence was negligible. To me they seemed as remote and insubstantial as cracker mottoes.

I remember London, this early innocent London, as a series of textures, a city given definition by colour: the dark earth thrown up by the road diggers near Waterloo – they were building the office blocks above Lambeth then – over-bright buses trawling the streets near Oxford Circus, the russet expanse of treetops seen from Hampstead Heath. Textures, colour and names.

I had enrolled myself at Goldsmiths' College, a choice deplored by my father on geographical grounds. 'South of the river,' he had observed. 'You'll end up spending all your money on taxi fares, I shouldn't wonder, and find yourself having to leave concerts before the end to catch the last bus.' But he would have approved of the college and its unassuming premises in Lewisham. Barely a year had passed since the turmoil of 1968, its influence still traceable in the whitewashed graffiti on the concrete walkways and bellicose articles in the student newspapers, but little sign remained of the bruising encounters of the previous autumn. On my second day, I recall, we were addressed by a bearded postgraduate in a Lenin jacket who informed us that further education was an instrument of social control and that examinations were socially divisive. We paid him no heed. 'That sort of thing,' as Roger Garfitt remarked with prescience, 'had rather had its day.' In contrast we were a studious group, already much exercised by the thought of sub-editorships and outplacement schemes. Two or three students who had already served a year on provincial newspapers were regarded with awe. We wrote passable imitations of *The Times* leaders, read *The Economist*, then regarded as the acme of journalistic style, from cover to cover and on two evenings a week were instructed by our professor, a courteous middle-aged man who had once been literary editor of the *New Statesman*, on the importance of the point of view.

The time passed quickly: an intense, hermetic life lived out largely beyond the college borders. Of all the people with whom I came into contact in these early years, it was Roger Garfitt who exercised the most profound influence. He was a tall, ambitious boy from a Yorkshire grammar school and, at nineteen, a figure of enviable sophistication. With him I roamed around south-east London. We lived in Brixton, Brockwell Park, Hither Green, queer suburbs known only from the street maps, rented furnished flats in decayed mansion blocks in Streatham Hill and Penge. We ate in Chinese restaurants in Half Moon Lane and Denmark Hill with occasional forays further afield to Nunhead and Peckham Rye. On Sunday afternoons we took buses to Richmond and Hampton Court Park, or loitered by the river at Mortlake. It was not, I am happy to admit, a relationship of equals. It was to Roger, for example, that I owe my first experience of women. His own attitude to the girls we met at Goldsmiths' or encountered in the course of our travels was unfathomable. He liked women, he was happy to be seen with them, to take them out and spend money on them, but he shrank from any deeper involvement; an involvement that most of them were anxious to prosecute. The result was that at any given time there existed a gaggle of admirers simultaneously attracted by Roger's inscrutability, marked down in the phrase of the time as 'lack of introspection', but puzzled by his indifference. Though they could occasionally be detached from this grouping – 'Roger's harem', not entirely a joke – and offered consolation, the original impetus still lingered. 'Doesn't he *like* women?' a girl called Alice once asked me late at night in Streatham. 'I mean, he knows I'd take my clothes off now, right here on the spot, if he wanted me to.' I had no answer.

But in any case our paths had begun to diverge. There was nothing obvious about this, no violent disagreement or deliberate treachery, simply a slow, spreading fracture that grew a little wider on each occasion that we met. He had changed, I thought, in some subtle, ineluctable way; his ambitions now social rather than academic. The Alices and the Julias gave way to the Camillas and the Jennifers, braying upper-class girls from secretarial colleges or the Lucie Clayton, who smoothed their skirts carefully over the battered sofa of the Streatham Hill flat and declined the pungent cups of tea. There was an eager, wholly unselfconscious pride in the way Roger showed off these acquisitions, as if they were exotic, brightly plumaged birds brought down by skill and cunning. What game he was playing, what snare he had laid down to entrap Camilla and her kind, what great prize he hoped to emerge with, I did not discover until later. Shortly afterwards, at the beginning of our third year, Roger moved out of the flat. I did not regret his passing. There was something unreasoning about him, I decided, a self-possession unwarranted by the facts. Like a nervous small boy on a games field he had assumed a superiority over his peers which did not exist; the next scrum, the next tangle of arms and boots, I thought, would see him exposed and derided. In his absence Streatham Hill became a place of ghosts.

*

Though our professional lives took separate paths, Roger and I kept up in a small way. We met infrequently in the corridors of newspaper offices, in pubs near the old *Daily Mail* building in Carmelite Square. It was a relationship founded on telephone calls, sightings across crowded rooms and imperfect memory. 'Martin is one of my oldest friends,' Roger would say if any third person happened to intrude into one of those brief reunions. If that person happened to be a woman he would go on to say, 'Martin knows secrets about me. You see, at one point he was my father confessor.' This canvassing of past intimacy in a way designed to leave the listener at once bemused and intrigued never failed to annoy me. I supposed it a consequence of his job, in which these small revelations and greater mysteries seemed to cohabit in a rather uncomfortable way. Roger was a gossip-columnist on a London evening newspaper – a considerable position for someone of his age and background; it seemed reasonable to suppose that this talent for public mischief-making should infect his private life. He spoke knowledgeably about 'Paddy' Litchfield and 'George' Weidenfeld. The photograph of him which appeared above the column – black-tied, hair swept back and looking rather like Ronald Firbank – seemed to confirm his elevation into rarified circles where I could not hope to penetrate. There was something about Roger in these days, something hard, shiny and engrossed, which had not been there before. Like the carnival reveller who places a white, sculpted mask over his face as a prelude to saturnalia, he had whirled off, disguised and ungovernable, into a landscape of private fantasy.

Meanwhile I set to work, laboriously, at the job of becoming a freelance journalist, a task not without its satisfactions. I wrote feature articles for trade journals – *The Retailer, Haberdashers' World* – sober chronicles with large circulations. I wrote book reviews for the *New Statesman* in the brief, rancorous period under Crossman's editorship. For a bizarre six-month period I acted as resident sub-editor on a magazine devoted to the construction of plastic aeroplanes. Later, during the years with Morty, souvenirs of this time would surface to embarrass me.

A year or so passed. Looking back I can already discern the first faint outlines of the world that would rise up to claim me.

I went out for a time with a girl who worked as a glamour model and was occasionally photographed for the Sunday newspapers. Later, under the auspices of a satirical weekly, I was sent to interview the publisher of a range of what were then known as 'male interest' magazines. Each of these encounters impressed me less by their exoticism than by the sense of ordinary people making do in the face of unpromising circumstance. The glamour model with her lavish bathroom rituals and her sturdy self-possession, the pornographer, found in his office eating sandwiches amid bundles of page proofs, neither seemed to me more than casual vagrants picked randomly from a debris of similar flotsam, uncertain of motivation or destiny.

One day late in 1973 when I was at work on an article called 'Why stay-at-home housewives may soon be a thing of the past' the telephone rang. It was Roger. He said, rather wearily, 'I *insist* you come to dinner next Friday.'

I knew from the tone of his voice what had happened. A string of other acquaintances had let him down.

'Anyone interesting coming?'

'Lots. Caroline Mallender.'

'Who's she?'

'Writes children's books. Rather good children's books.' Roger's attitude to his dinner guests was that of a loyal flat-racing trainer, anxious to defend his stable against imagined slights. 'And Keith Harrison.'

Keith Harrison was a recently retired first division footballer whose memoirs Roger was supposed to have had a hand in ghosting.

'I nearly forgot,' Roger went on. 'It's rather exciting. There's a pornographer coming. Morty Kronenburg.'

Roger found all his dinner guests, these minor novelists and strident television producers, 'exciting'. For a moment I wondered what Morty Kronenburg had done to commend himself to this all-seeing intelligence. Then I remembered a newspaper report about the prosecution of a newsagent under the Obscene Publications Act. A magazine Morty produced had been mentioned in court.

Roger interpreted the silence as indecision. 'Come on,' he said heavily, 'do me a favour. Say you'll come.'

'All right,' I said, with equal heaviness. 'I'll come.'

In the week before Roger's dinner party, events of wider significance intervened. It was the time of Mr Heath's confrontation with the mineworkers, of the national overtime ban and the three-day week. Looking back it is hard to assimilate the passions that were roused in that silent English winter of 1973–4, a time when phrases like 'collapse of government' and 'breakdown of law and order' were bandied about and the scent of anarchy hung in the air. It was the time, too, when my father finally achieved a certain immortality on the occasion when he wrote and had published in the *Daily Telegraph* a letter beginning with the words, 'Dear Sir, Writing by candlelight . . .'. The phrase, appropriated by a socialist historian and used as the title of a famous essay, resonated through the later 1970s as a byword for bourgeois hysteria in the face of minor inconvenience.

I began the evening of Roger's dinner at a publisher's launch party in Bedford Square. Here the atmosphere was grimly festive. Arc lights and a generator had been procured in case of power failure. People – publicists, book trade habitués, literary agents – stood in twos and threes discussing the prospects for a settlement of the dispute. 'It can't last,' they said gloomily. 'Heath will have to settle.' 'It can't last,' they said later, after the room was suddenly plunged into darkness. 'Gormley's a reasonable man. They'll have to settle.' I exchanged a few words with the author in whose honour the party was being held, a small, shy American academic. 'I didn't realise things were so bad as all this,' he said. 'I suppose it must have been this way in the Blitz. Now they tell me there's a real prospect of the government being overthrown.' Later the lights came on again. Optimism, like some long-neglected plant suddenly allowed to luxuriate in sunshine, was briefly renewed.

'They'll have to settle. They say the money's leaving the country and at this rate it might not come back . . .'

'I know a man who knows Heath, and he said . . .'

'I know a man who knows Wilson, and he said . . .'

'Back where I come from we have recognised procedures for dealing with this sort of thing: declare a state of emergency and call out the National Guard.'

'It was a mistake ever to expect the miners to be reasonable . . .'

'It was a mistake ever to nationalise the mines in the first place . . .'

Later I walked out into the Tottenham Court Road and took a bus through the empty streets to Kentish Town. Here both electricity and gas had failed at a crucial stage in the preparation of Roger's elaborate menu. We ate out of tins in Roger's cramped kitchen, at a table lit by strategically hung torches.

It was not a successful meal. In later years those people who dined out in the winter of 1973–4 were eager to devise tales of straitened conviviality and unexpected pleasures. The reality was less appealing. Miss Mallender and the professional footballer arrived late and regarded each other with barely concealed distaste. Roger, depressed by culinary disaster, scarcely spoke. Morty, alone amongst the row of minor celebrities, seemed to be able to take events in his stride. He ate a large meal of beans on toast. When in Roger's sitting room, fortified by brandy and cocoa, some sort of conversation began it was his voice which rose decisively above Miss Mallender's remarks about her Carnegie Award and Keith Harrison's homely interjections, an intent monologue whose substance I can remember even now.

The provocation was Miss Mallender's account of *Last Tango in Paris* – now a rather elderly scandal – to which she had been accompanied by her literary agent.

'I suppose it was his way of making a proposition,' she said, 'sitting there for two hours in a darkened cinema – and do you know it really was *very* dark – watching people crawl all over each other and catching his breath, poor man, when anything particularly objectionable happened.'

'It sounds horrid,' said an epicene young man who worked on Roger's newspaper.

'Cut to ribbons,' Morty said suddenly. It was the first time I remembered hearing him speak. 'Guy I know works for the editing company told me about it. Forests of pubic hair all over the cutting room floor, Brando's cock, everything. Just popcorn. You could take your grandmother to see it.'

'Well, I don't know that I'd want to take my grandmother to

85

see it,' said Miss Mallender skittishly. 'In fact I don't think I could ever look a knob of butter in the face again.'

Morty made a small growling noise, suggesting a sedate yet rackety motor vehicle brought rapidly into gear.

'Let's talk,' he said, 'about pornography. Now, you mightn't think that pornography concerns you. Forget it. Pornography concerns every one of us, every one of us down throughout time. You've seen those Roman frescos, the stuff you get in the Pompeii exhibition? Pornography, every inch of it. Go back a couple of thousand years and ask the man in the street what turns him on and he'll tell you: pictures of people fucking. Or rather, not people fucking, but people looking as if they're about to fuck. Because pornography,' Morty said, 'is about delayed gratification. A girl who's taking her clothes off is more exciting than a girl who's taken her clothes off, right? A naked girl sitting there on a chair showing you her tits is *beautiful*, okay? A girl who's just taking her top off and doesn't know if she'll let you see what's underneath is *erotic* . . .'

Miss Mallender muttered something about titillation. Morty ignored her. 'Let's talk,' he continued, 'about the varieties of pornography. There's the pictures you see in the newspapers, the page three girls. That's not pornography, that's just a picture. Let's consider pornography as a social force. All those guys sitting there in their bedsitters beating off over *Penthouse* and *Men Only*. Power. Unusual power. Bring it together and it would terrify you . . .

'I'm not a sexual libertarian, I'm a businessman. And an artist. I'm not telling people to have sex. Jesus, fourteen-year-old girls coming home and telling their mothers they've just fucked for the first time and what's going to happen! Disgusting, just disgusting. I'm telling people to look at sex. Safety valve, social control, whatever you like to call it. People would be fucking in the streets if it wasn't for me . . . Books, music, pictures hanging up in fucking stately homes. You can forget about all that. Well let's just say pornography, *pornography is the new art form* . . .'

It was an impressive performance. Even now, ten years later, I can see Morty hunched in his chair, the pale light gleaming on his bald head, declaiming his text with the fervour of some medieval hedge-priest. But it had an ironic fervour, a series of complex codes given unity and design by sheer force of delivery. Like the amateur debater who proposes fascism or compulsory euthanasia as a way of exercising his rhetorical skills, his was a triumph of simple oratory.

The party broke up early: Miss Mallender and Keith Harrison in search of taxis, Morty and I to walk the few hundred yards or so to the tube station. As we lingered on the empty staircase he said, 'You're a writer, aren't you? Always looking for writers. Come and see me tomorrow. Come and see me and we'll have a talk.'

Our trains arrived simultaneously, his to go northward, mine to go south. Through the opening that divided the two platforms I watched him for a moment, face pushed down into his collar, jammed between the tall, leather-jacketed youths and the Irish navvies with their knapsacks: he was wholly absorbed. Then there was a grinding of gears, a slow, painful rattle of far-off machinery and the train bore him away.


I went and saw Morty: we had our talk. The studio at Dean Street was at this time half-built: decorators moved carefully around the piles of sawdust and exposed woodwork, studiously avoiding the three or four girls who had assembled for what Morty described as 'a screen test'. Seen in this environment, blinking in the haggard morning light, he seemed a diminished figure, anxious over minor alterations to schedule, tiny setbacks. 'That cameraman's on double time,' he said more than once, 'so where the fuck is he?' It was only then that the splendid battlements of the previous night swung aside to reveal a frailer edifice. We went into Morty's office where there were glistening ozalids lying over the desk and a pile of empty cigarette packets.

'A lot of people in this business can't write a script,' Morty said. 'They think it has to be like a sitcom, like something on the BBC. And lots of nudge-nudge dialogue. This is an outline.' He threw me a plastic wallet containing two sheets of paper stapled together. 'I want to make a twenty-minute film. Take it away and see what you can do.'

I spent a week on *Hookers in Hampstead*, a short feature which in the event never progressed beyond the big storyboard in Morty's office. The plot was of slight dimensions: a young man picks up a prostitute outside Hampstead tube station. They go to a house in the High Street. There in mid-coitus the man remembers a vital appointment. The remainder of the story concerns his frenzied efforts to extricate himself both from the girl and a bevy of playmates who inhabit the floor below. I gave it minor strokes of irony – the man nearsighted, unable to move without his glasses, the prostitute given the same name as his wife, their dalliance continually interrupted by the ringing of the telephone. I imagined the dialogue to be hard-boiled but with occasional touches of comedy, although in fact, it achieved neither of these aims. Oddly Morty approved.

'Not bad,' he said. 'Not bad for a first go. But what the punter wants is action. Or at any rate he wants to think there's going to be action, and that it's going to happen soon. And don't take the piss out of sex too much. Last thing a guy who pays money to see a pornographic film wants to think is that you're taking the piss out of sex.'

I persevered. For a month I declined all other commissions and sat in my room devising scripts from the storylines Morty supplied. I wrote another twenty-minute feature called *Stately Lust* in which a group of elderly libertines, each dying of some unspecified complaint, arrive at a country house for a last, epochal orgy, and a longer piece, a costume drama centring on a Victorian cleric's futile attempt to reform a woman of the night. Oddly the task was to my taste. I became adept at refining dialogue, at allowing the plot to advance by means of gesture or intonation, at inserting punchlines, at conferring rhythm and pattern on to the chatter about sex. As the power cuts grew longer in duration, as Mr Wilson succeeded Mr Heath – the only image I remember, curiously, that of Mr Heath's piano being removed from Downing Street – I persevered. At the time there seemed no more enviable destiny than to sit in a room in a city, alone and unregarded, and to write.

At the beginning of March Roger telephoned. I had not spoken to him since the evening of the dinner party. He said in a subdued way, 'Are you going to Morty Kronenburg's party tonight?'

The invitation, florid and embossed on manila paper, had lain on my mantelpiece for a fortnight. I had planned to spend a

hard evening working on a script called *Mandy Does Mayfair*
which had arrived that morning, but somehow I did not feel like
telling Roger this. 'I don't think so.'

'I'm going. There may be a story in it for the paper and I need
someone to show me round. Say you'll come.'

The subterfuge, I realised, was wasted. Roger knew all about
my association with Morty.

'All right. I'll come.'

And so we went to Morty's party, held on the very evening
when Harold Wilson accepted Her Majesty's request to form his
third administration. At the loft in Dean Street the atmosphere
was chaotic, the heavy press of people made indiscriminate by
music and flashing lights. I knew a few of the guests by sight.
None was known to Roger. At first this detachment seemed
not to trouble him and he roamed happily enough around the
curtained rooms, peering into doorways and examining the
garish decor. Later, when the volume of the music lessened and
various exotic dancers began to perform on a raised dais at the
rear, he grew restive.

'Do you think it would be a good idea to call the police?'

'Why should you want to do that?'

By this time Roger was very drunk. 'This is practically an
orgy. And it would make a good story, don't you think?'

Roger went outside to a telephone box and called the police.
They came almost immediately, a harassed-looking sergeant and
a brace of constables from West End Central. The music stopped,
the lights came on and there was general consternation. The
policemen knew Morty of old. 'Sorry to trouble you, Mr Kronenburg,' they said. 'Complaint received from a member of the
public and we had to investigate.' They made a cursory inspection of the premises, after which the party resumed. I caught
sight of Roger smiling inanely. At least, I thought, he had got
his story.

A little later Roger said, 'Do you suppose those policemen are
corrupt?'

'I shouldn't wonder.'

'That's a pity. The editor doesn't like attacks on the police. I
suppose I shall have to keep that side out of it.'

A few days later a short item about the party did surface in

Roger's column. It bore no relation to any event that either of us had witnessed. But a week after this his portrait ceased to appear above the page devoted to society goings-on and metropolitan gossip. Morty, as Roger discovered to his cost, had powerful friends. He hung on for a year or so – he wrote for one of the London listings magazines, a genre then in its infancy, I heard his voice one or twice early in the morning on a commercial radio station – but it was to no avail. From time to time, loitering in the Fleet Street pubs and drinking dens, I came across his old colleagues and acquaintances; their silence was an eloquent testimony to what had happened. Roger continued to telephone me sporadically, the gaps increasingly drawn out, so that, hearing his voice, I would have to concentrate for a moment before I remembered who he was. When he rang for the last time, early in 1975, I failed to recognise him. Shortly afterwards he left London to work on a provincial newspaper and our relationship, such as it was, came to an end. Later, when some odd juxtaposition of memory and circumstance brought him back to mind – walking past Goldsmiths' College, an afternoon in the late Seventies spent with Elaine at Hampton Court – it was hard to believe that Roger had ever existed. He seemed to belong to an older, less concrete world whose boundaries and prohibitions I had long since left behind. Occasionally when some rare acquaintance who had known us both, some woman met years later at a party, asked, 'Do you remember Roger Garfitt?' I would have to pause a moment before answering: a cruel memorial, perhaps, but one which I was not inclined to alter or dispute.

EARLY EVENING, TWO days after Fat Eric's *soirée* and the Tupperware box full of shit. Waking up this morning, late, in bright sunshine, with Suzi already departed to school, I had one of those glorious daybreak amnesia sessions. I came down the stairs whistling, I scanned the post with guiltless interest and I was halfway through breakfast before my eye fell inexorably on a shred of wrapping paper lying in the wastepaper basket. Instantly, like iron filings obeying the call of a magnet, everything fell back into place again – the pictures, the stinking parcel, Elaine – and, no, it wasn't something I could just write off, wasn't something I could file cheerily under Life's Little Ironies. *I have to find out who's doing this to me.* And I have to find Elaine, because I want to know about this sudden interest in my whereabouts and why it stops short of actual contact, and whether she knows anything about the photos and the parcel. Which, knowing Elaine, she will.

I lock into a round of phone calls. Suzi is at the parent-teachers' association. The odd car shudders past outside. First I try Morty. I try Morty a number of times. I try him at his house in Ongar and get an answer phone telling me that Mortimer Kronenburg is not presently available. I try the studio at Dean Street and get nothing at all. I try the timeshare cottage in Devon and get a piece of posh trash who claims never to have heard of him. Then I remember the flat in Greek Street. The phone rings for quite a long time before Morty picks it up.

'Martin. Good to hear from you. How are things?'

'Fine, Morty. Just fine. What about you?'

'I can't complain. *Jungle Lovers* went in the adult video ratings at number two.'

'That's great, Morty . . . You ever hear of Jim Woodward these days, Morty?'

'Jim Woodward? Sorry, Martin.'

'Jim Woodward, the actor.'

'The one who was in *Spank Academy*? Haven't seen him in two years, not since he married the bimbo who threw the glass at you that time . . . Something worrying you, Martin?'

I tell Morty a bit about the photographs. Morty whistles through his teeth down the line.

'And you're sure it's you? That's bad, Martin.' There is a swirl of random gusty movement somewhere. Morty's voice edges back into focus. 'Sorry about that, Mart. I have someone here right now . . . Listen, you have anyone you owe money to?'

That's a laugh. The bastards all owe me money. Morty. Terry Chimes. Elaine . . . 'No.'

'Not Eddie Lyle? Frank Rosati?' – Morty mentions a brace of time-honoured Soho frighteners. 'No one like that?'

'No.'

'No bimbo after a pension?'

'Not that I can think of.'

There is a silence, followed by a faint scuffling noise in the remoter distance.

'Are you there, Morty?'

'Sure, Martin. It's just that I have someone with me right now. Look, if I hear anything off the wall I'll let you know. Okay?'

I cradle the phone handset for a while against my shoulder, hoist it reluctantly back on to the table. The silence echoes.


Eight a.m., two days later. Mist coming close up to the window. The garden is half obscured by queer, vaporous trails. Suzi, cross, whey-faced, hair tied back with a sliver of ribbon, bustles noisily around the kitchen in her dressing gown. At one point she says, 'I'll be late back tonight.'

'How late?'

'Eleven. Twelve. I don't know. It's the school concert.'

Later I watch her reversing the car out of its parking space in that neat, fussy way she has, each precaution, each cautious manoeuvre and glance in the mirror wholly exaggerated. Suzi is immensely proud of her driving. The car moves off and Fat Eric lounges past, head nuzzled into his collar against the cold. He does not look up.

Yesterday another batch of photographs arrived, neatly done up in cellophane and packed tightly into a padded bag. I didn't bother to take them out and look at them. There is a drain twenty yards down the street opposite T. Coulthard's grocery shop. I waited until the pavement was empty and T. Coulthard, seen through the plateglass window, had disappeared into his storeroom before posting them eagerly through the grating.

Shortly after this I have an idea. A good way of finding out if Elaine is still around, is still in the business, say, would be to phone one of the Soho model agencies Morty used to deal with. There were numbers of these sad, dead-eyed procurers sitting in endless repose in flyblown offices at the top of staircases in Wardour Street or Golden Square: Starfinder, Movie Girl, Screen Talent. In the guise of a Social Security *fonctionnaire* I do the rounds of telephoning. Movie Girl and Screen Talent have never heard of her, but at Starfinder I get a bored-sounding American who preserves some faint recollection of Elaine's accomplishments.

'Elaine Keenan? Yeah, I remember her. Irish chick who frowned all the time. Used to be in *Driven to Lust, Spank Academy*, all that early Leisurevision stuff Morty Kronenburg used to put out.'

I murmur something about being more interested in Miss Keenan's whereabouts than in a résumé of her career.

'Okay. I get the picture. Haven't seen her for a while, but she's probably still on the books. You want me to go take a look?'

He returns with a phone number. Unfamiliar. I make a great show of thanking the American for his assistance.

'Glad to help,' he says. 'Who'd you say you were calling from?'

'Department of Health and Social Security.'

'Uh huh. Nothing to do with the IRS?'

'Nothing at all.'

'Glad to hear it. I hate those fuckers.'

Later on I ring the phone number. A man's voice, incomprehensible amid a blare of noise. I try again until, halfway through the second attempt, realisation dawns. West End Central Police Station. You have to hand it to those Americans.

A bit later the implications of the West End Central joke begin to dawn on me. The phone number is a plant. Question: who planted it there? The American or someone else? Having brooded about this for an hour or so, I ring Starfinder again. The same bored-sounding voice.

'Hi, man.'

'This is the Department of Health and Social Security. I believe we spoke before.'

'Sure. The guy who said he wasn't from the IRS, I remember. What can I do for you?'

'Well, the thing is that we're having a slight problem contacting this Miss Keenan on the number you gave us and I, that is my colleagues and I, were wondering if you could give us any further information.'

'What sort of information?'

'Have you spoken to Miss Keenan recently?'

'I got forty girls on the books here. I don't make a ledger note every time one of them rings up to tell me she's putting on weight. Wait a moment, though. I got a feeling she rang in last month, to tell me she was on a new number.'

'Elaine . . . Miss Keenan telephoned you?'

'Could have been her. Could have been some guy. Sometimes they get their boyfriends or their managers to phone in. I don't remember.'

'Last month?'

'Last month. Two months ago. Who knows? Hey, I've got plenty of other girls here. Sure you don't want one of them instead?'

'I don't think that will be necessary, Mr . . .'

'Zappa,' intones the voice. 'Francis Vincent Zappa.'

As I said, you have to hand it to those Americans.


More artefacts from the Kronenburg years. A stack of Grunt Records press releases advertising Terry Chimes' progeny to the world: the Glasgow Express on tour; Bobby Dazz coaxed out of retirement. A Leisurevision illustrated calendar from 1978, of the sort which Morty sent out to the trade, featuring Miss Lila St Claire and 'Legs' Alice La Faye. A photograph of Morty lugubriously eating *paella* in a Spanish restaurant in Maddox Street. A frail, crumbling copy of *Pages*, Mr Tovacs' literary annual, with contributions from Garcia Marquez and Kundera. Press cuttings from the *People, Daily Mirror, News of the World*. A shot of Terry, Morty and me at the poolside, relaxed, quizzical, the prone bikinied body behind us probably Elaine's, difficult to tell. Pictures of Morty with various East End frighteners, with Charlie Kray, the Major, Mad Jimmy Parsons. One of Morty's election bills. Elaine in an SS officer's greatcoat at the head of a file of stormtroopers. Dead things, out of a dead world. It has never occurred to me to throw them away.

The stormtroopers I can date with some precision. Towards the close of Morty's late-Seventies period, the period of *Plasma Party* and *Body Snatchers*, there was a mild vogue at the smart end of the hard-core market for war and sex films. They bore titles such as *SS Experiment Camp* and *Unmarked Grave* (there was even a gay one, I seem to recall, full of thrashing young members of the Hitler Youth movement, called *Nazi Lust*). The high street cinemas were chary, naturally enough, but the bleary video shops were interested, and one or two of the continental distributors. Emboldened, Morty hired two dozen Nazi uniforms from a theatrical outfitter's, acquired a number of dummy stenguns and persuaded a friend to lend him a remote island off the Hebridean coast for a week's shooting.

The film was called *Blitzkrieg Bondage*. The treatment, which I devised during the course of the rail-trip to Stranraer, was unexpectedly imaginative. A crack SS unit arrives stealthily on the Isle of Muck late in 1942, cleverly forestalling the efforts of a handful of bewildered crofters to raise the alarm. The local laird, a monocled fifth columnist, gleefully makes over his ancestral house as headquarters. Holed up in Castle McIntosh and amusing themselves with the local womenfolk, the SS men unveil the purpose of their mission: a bacterial rocket loaded with a deadly virus trained on Glasgow. All would be lost, were not busty Flora McKillop able to persuade the treacherous laird of the error of his ways . . .

It was a disaster. Late November, a pale, watery sun scuttling across the crags and blasted cliff tops. It rained continuously for seven days. Hunter Stagg, the American hard-core star imported at vast expense to play the part of the SS *Gruppenführer*, came down with pneumonia. Half the cast were nearly drowned attempting to film the landing scene. Eventually, frustrated by the crepuscular light and the onset of darkness shortly after lunch, Morty decided to film most of it inside the castle. An all-action scene in which Flora McKillop, played by Elaine, abseils to safety from a top-floor window was aborted when a sound man fell to his death from the slippery ramparts. In the end Morty decided to cut his losses and had me rewrite the script to accommodate a rugby team arriving by mistake for an evening at a Scots health farm.

Morty and I had a serious ethical chat about *Blitzkrieg Bondage*. Our first.

'Doesn't all this bother you?' I asked, early one morning as we stood on the battlements staring unhappily at the rain.

'No.' Morty peered down to the spot where half a dozen of the extras were rehearsing their initial molestation of Flora McKillop. 'It doesn't bother me.'

'But what about the Jews, Morty?'

'What about the Jews? Martin, you don't want to worry yourself about the Jews. Listen, I'll tell you a joke. It was my father told it to me. They're herding this pile of Jews into a gas chamber, right, and because it's the camp commandant's birthday every prisoner is allowed one last request. For some it's a cigarette, for others it's an extra five minutes alive. But one little guy wants a piano, that's right, a piano, and the sheet music to Beethoven's Fifth. So they set the piano up in the corner of the gas chamber, close the door, switch on the taps, and that's that. Quarter of an hour later they open up again. Everybody's dead except the little guy who's playing away like there's no tomorrow. "So what's all this?" asks the commandant. "How did you do it?" "Well," explains the little guy, "I guess tunes help you breathe more easily".'

As I said, a serious ethical chat.

Some more history: Morty's fledgling career as an entrepreneur during the early 1960s had been blessed with certain advantages. Not least among these was the location of the Kronenburg senior dwelling at 174 Vallance Road, E2, two doors down from homely Mrs Kray. Then there was the *éclat* of the Kronenburgs themselves. This derived not so much from Councillor Kronenburg's political affiliations, substantial though they were, as from sheer weight of numbers. There were a lot of Kronenburgs, variously at large in the thoroughfares of local commerce. They kept pubs, sold radios, worked as kosher butchers and used-car dealers. Collectively their numbers were sufficient to populate Morty's adolescence with a series of lurid exemplars, a pageant of weird uncles, mad aunts and desiccated cousins. Periodically in the early Seventies they re-emerged, surfaced like bloated, long-forgotten fish above the waters of some stagnant pond, and then were gone. Oddly bejewelled women waving to Morty across Oxford Street, gnarled elderly men nodding from shop doorways; nervous at first of these tangible reminders of his past, Morty swiftly anaesthetised such wraiths by means of anecdote, each revelation firmly checked by the barrier of family solidarity. 'My Uncle Hymie,' Morty would begin reminiscently, 'now take it from me, Martin, it just wasn't true about the . . .' About the used car racket, the leant-on shopkeepers and all the rest.

Crazy Rodney enlightened me about the Kronenburgs once. There were a lot of Kronenburgs, a few too many for comfort. They beat people up, intimidated their children and – a traditional East End expedient – threw paraffin heaters through the windows of rival shopkeepers. According to Crazy Rodney's appreciative testimony any threat of competition – a new used car lot, shutters taken down from some long moribund grocery – sparked a paranoid campaign of clan activity, meticulously planned, extending across three or four generations.

In the early 1960s a small shopkeeper was unwise enough to set up a modest emporium across the street from Uncle Hymie's extravagantly decorated Food Mart in the Bethnal Green Road. He lasted a fortnight. On the opening day Uncle Hymie established two of his nephews, armed with air rifles, in an upstairs window of a house across the road. Undeterred, a few customers dodged past the spray of pellets to negotiate the fragmenting doorway. When the shopkeeper replaced his windows with heavy-duty shatterproof plate glass Uncle Hymie sent gangs of juvenile Kronenburgs in to pilfer from the bags of stacked confectionery and mouldering fruit. Denied access by sternly worded signs they gave way to intent Kronenburg pensioners who roamed noiselessly through the silent corridors, blundered innocently into the neat, geometric stacks of tins and left vast orders which they then declined to collect. Midway through the second week, none of these expedients having proved immediately effective, Uncle Hymie persuaded Morty's father to exert some influence on the council works department. Subsequently two workmen with pneumatic drills and a heavily bribed road-digger operative spent two days and nights breaking up the adjoining pavement. Miraculously the shop struggled on. A lesser man might at this stage have permitted his opponents some modest respite, but Uncle Hymie, animated at first by this new diversion, had now grown bored. Late at night two days later he stole an elderly Landrover, drove it at speed in the direction of the shop's frontage and jumped out seconds before impact.

It was an impressive heritage. These were proud exemplars.


A characteristic sight in late-Sixties Norwich was the fat girl skipping. Threading your way through the dead Sunday-morning council estates, a trail of scuffed verges and burly middle-aged men washing their cars, you could be confident of seeing them: at the edge of the roadside, in somebody's driveway wedged between a juddering pram and a wrecked Mini. There would generally be three of them: two to hoist the rope, one, the fat girl, heaving herself over it in that shambling, splay-footed way they have. The fat girl. Twelve or thirteen. Torso, stomach quite undifferentiated, the whole like a large flat bolster crammed into the print dress, the too-small frock. The red face. The helmet of dun hair bouncing from side to side. The *intentness*. Always the fat girl: the two spindly rope-turners simply stooges, accessories to the fact. Sometimes there would be two or three to a street, the only movement beside the loafing car-washers, the only sound except the faint rasp of a radio somewhere beyond the yellowed hedge. And always the fat girl, pausing a moment perhaps outside the rope's arc to regain her rhythm, engrossed in her hop-skip-and-jump routine, immobilised on tiptoe by some ill-judged twist.

Those fat girls. I fear they don't exist now, that they get put on diets at birth. I went looking for them once. I loitered around outside school playgrounds. I spent an afternoon trawling Eaton Park, I even followed the old Sunday-morning paper-round route through the West Earlham estate, past the ragged grass and the glittering cars. There was no sign of them. I looked in vain for those anaconda legs labouring grimly over the zebra crossing, the drowsy, lymphatic smiles, the neutral, filled-in features, looked in vain for those brooding puffball families – fat, youngish mother, butterball four-year-old, pudgy baby. Those fat girls.

Suzi is a fat girl. Sometimes, watching her arrive from the upstairs window, noting the cautious decanting from the car, I speculate about Suzi's early life, wonder about that lost, alien girlhood. They have tough childhoods, those fat girls: the snickering cronies in the changing room, the chalked outrages on the bike-shed wall. Later, in the tense huddles of adolescence, the fat girl is fair game. An unwritten law of courtship. Everyone knows you can do what you like with a fat girl, pull her hair, chew on her breasts, lose your fingers in the folds of her rump. They have to tolerate it. Later they marry thin, sullen men who hit them.

I watch Suzi now as she extricates herself from the worrying harness of the car, pauses uncertainly before the gatepost, contemplates the troublesome two-yard dash to the door. Suzi is one of those fat girls to whom life is a strenuous denial of unshakeable evidence. Like the murderer found carrying the blood-stained bundle she coaxes a whole style out of her phantom blamelessness. And she's *not* fat, because the scales said nine stone three this morning and considering her height and . . . Suzi is five feet tall, and edging towards stoutness. The flaming cheeks. The heavyset tread. The thick high heels. Various aspects of the traditional fat girl routine are starting to descend upon her. As she bustles towards the door I look at the car, the cluttered Renault with its hapless paraphernalia of tennis rackets, badminton gear and bunched swimsuits (sport, that useless fat girl panacea) and smile.

*

For one with such a precise appreciation of the public taste, or of the avenues down which the public taste might be induced to wander, Morty was surprisingly slow to investigate the potential of what were at the end of the Seventies coyly known as 'special interest publications'. Such diffidence was all the more curious in that Leisurevision prided itself on attention to market research, customer relations, consumer attitudes – all the wool-pulling, hoodwinking phrases that Morty gleaned from his occasional trawlings through shiny American management magazines. At the time, subtlety having come late to the backward UK pornography market, such an attitude smacked of novelty. Deep into the mid-Seventies there lurked the conviction that pornography was *easy*, that all one needed was a woman taking her clothes off in suitable surroundings and a minimally proficient cameraman. The girl, the bed, the slow divestiture – anything more, any variant on this elementary narrative theory, and the purchaser rebelled, switched his allegiance back to staider certainties. Morty didn't think this. Morty thought pornography was *difficult*, that it needed to be worked out, that there were complex laws by which it functioned and flourished. A characteristic sight at this time was the spectacle of Morty leafing respectfully through some Scandinavian import, some bristling display of Technicolor pudenda, and adducing sophistication from the artful conjunction of limbs and the tricksy plotlines. It was about this time, too, that he began to consult books with titles like *Strategies of Eroticism* and conduct deep, theoretical discussions with baffled art directors.

'. . . You see, Martin, there's what they call "a *trajectory of desire*" in all this . . . I mean, I don't want to get heavy, but okay, the chick comes into the room, right, and looks at you. When's the time you start fancying her?'

'That depends, Morty. It depends on what she looks like.'

'Okay. She's a looker, we'll take that for granted . . . But tell me the point at which you actually *desire* her?'

'That depends as well. It depends on what she does.'

'Look . . . I realise this isn't an easy concept to handle, but . . . What I mean is, there's a sort of what they call *erotic grammar* working here, right? Say you're in a pub watching a stripper. Now the turn-on, the real turn-on is not when the chick's taken her top off, it's the split-second before she's taken it off. It's the *suggestion* of what she's got underneath.'

'You're saying that we ought to print pictures of girls just before they take their clothes off?'

'No. All I'm saying, Martin, is that we're underestimating the punters. There's ten, fifteen other fanny mags out there in the paper shops and we ought . . . we ought to be *educating* them.'

The upshot of this was a surfeit of reader questionnaires in *Bouncers*, *Upfront* and the rest of the Leisurevision stable, a file of returnable coupons, a mounting two-way traffic of editorial canvassing and reader response. Reader response. As occasional editor of the correspondence sections I was familiar with the unquantifiable varieties of reader response. 'Dear Sir,' writes N. G. of Huddersfield, 'I was fascinated to examine your picture spread of Miss Lila St Claire in the recent issue. Does Miss St Claire ever have cause to visit the West Lancashire region? I can assure her of a hearty welcome at 17 Acacia Avenue should she ever chance to pass this way.' That was in the mid-Seventies, the old, polite days of genteel locution and elegant italic script. The 'bountiful charms' of Miss Aimée Ortez, the 'girlish sensuality' of Corona d'Amour, the 'pouting insouciance' of Martika: all were hymned, not unmovingly, in such terms by C. J. of Ewell, Surrey, M. B. of Highgate N6 and 'Your faithful reader' of Skegness. Only later did the tone turn nasty, the intimations become less veiled. 'Tell Terri da Motta if she wants a fucking good time to ring Lowestoft 57002 and ask for Rod.'

The worst transformation took place in the 'Readers' Wives' section, where the coy photographs of plump housewives – middle-aged women waving from bathtubs, spreadeagled on pastel eiderdowns, emerging from grubby kimonos – gave way to nightmares, to scarred waifs bent over sex toys, to frightened, gaping teenagers. I remember one picture from these earlier times. A lurid, overlit room, in the background a rumpled, unmade bed. The woman – well into her forties, feigning a game smile – stood sideways on to the camera, one haunch jutting forward. Balancing on her hip, tethered by means of a flowery garter belt, was a rosette with the number '1' stencilled on to it. A feeling of infinite sadness enveloped the moment in which hubby put down his lager and his cigarette to brood over the tapering zoom lens.

The questionnaires were printed, returned, examined and collated. Hitherto the readers of the Leisurevision stable had subsisted on a steady diet of blondes, brunettes and redheads, tall, small, fat and thin. Invited to state their preferences, to select some garish exemplar, they chose redheads, brunettes and blondes. They wanted them small, tall, meagre and plump. They wanted homely scenes and exotic scenes, they wanted girls on hearthrugs and desert islands, in the backs of cars and on the backs of motorbikes, singly and severally. Confronted by such a roster of heterodox opinion, Morty was frankly perturbed. Casting his eye over the neatly tabulated statistics ('large breasts, twenty-seven per cent') he could find no clue as to his customers' salient desires, no hint – in a phrase suggested by his business magazines – of a reader profile. At the conference staged to discuss the findings such confusion plainly disturbed him.

'Okay, Martin. We print fifty thousand copies of *Bouncers* every month. We send them out and the newsagents sell them. Who reads them?'

'Christ, Morty . . . people like you. People like me.' The fixed gaze instructed me to elaborate. '. . . Schoolkids. Men on building sites. High Court judges.'

'Uh huh. I'll run with that. But what distinguishes them? What sets them apart from other people?'

'They're men, Morty. That's what sets them apart from other people.'

In conversation, Morty and irony existed in remote, watertight compartments. He went on, 'It might surprise you to know, Martin, that I took a pretty good look at that last bunch of readers' letters, a pretty good look. I think I have an idea of the sort of person who reads the stuff we put out.'

'You do?'

'Sure. If you asked me to describe our typical reader I'd say this: I'd say he was a married man, in his thirties maybe, with a couple of kids. I'd say he was successful, attractive to women. An educated man – some of those letters were well-written – but dissatisfied, wanting more. And that's why he comes to us.'

If you had asked me to describe our typical reader I would

have said that he was an unmarried man, in his twenties or his teens, unsuccessful and unattractive to women, and thick as a plank. Just an ordinarily furtive masturbator, in fact.

Morty continued, 'But what excites them? What is it they want?'

'Blondes, brunettes, redheads . . .'

'These are sophisticated men, Martin. Men of the world. Not kids with their tongues hanging out because they've just seen a stripper in a pub. What sort of trajectory of desire is that . . . ? Did you look at that stuff Terry brought back from Sweden last week?'

'We couldn't sell it here, Morty. It's not legal. Not in England.'

'I know, Martin. I know that. But did you look at it?'

As a matter of fact I had leafed cursorily through the copies of *Scandi-Sex* and *Erotomania*. They depicted fresh-faced Swedish women staring at bananas or daintily urinating into glass jugs. 'Pervert corner, Martin,' Terry Chimes had said. 'Just pervert fucking corner.'

'It's a bit . . . specialised, Morty.'

'A hundred thousand copies a month, Martin. That's how specialised it is.'

'You mean we ought to sell pictures of girls with bananas?'

'No, Martin, I'm just saying that there are other things, that there are other types of woman. Look, they did a survey at the National Gallery the other month – I read about it in the paper – and do you know who was the favourite painter of male visitors under the age of forty-five?'

'Rembrandt?'

'Try again.'

'Cézanne?'

'And again.'

'Rubens?'

'Correct,' said Morty. 'Absolutely correct.'

The upshot of this was an addition to the Leisurevision stables, the first of Morty's special interest magazines. Slight initial conflict over the title having been resolved – base Terry Chimes wanted to call it *Wobblers* or *Double Helping* – Morty eventually compromised on *Outsize*. Fat girls, thirty-two pages of them. Girls with vast, distended breasts gazing up out of cascading bath foam, girls with wanton, dewlap haunches crawling distractedly on all fours, engaged in nude mud-wrestling sessions or frenzied netball games. Even here in a medium encouraging the blatant and the overblown Morty's sense of artistry did not wholly desert him. His favourite trick was juxtaposition, the establishment of a context which was then mocked and deflated, a reality undercut by crass yet unsuspected illusion. Thus two monstrous female twins, clad in the regulation schoolgirl gear, are pictured side by side in the act of undressing. It is, to the fascinated observer, an identical divestiture: the same otiose skirts removed to uncover bolster thighs, the same blouses unpeeled to disclose identical pudgy forearms. Only in the final frame does the joke emerge, as the second girl tugs free of her undergarments to reveal a pair of inflated balloons. Another of Morty's variations on the stream of adipose female tissue was the introduction of a male element, a male element at once cowed, puny and ambiguous. Flushed out effortlessly from places of concealment, tiny, insignificant men with meagre torsos and harassed expressions were driven hither and thither by these bulging Amazons, were balanced across stalwart knees and callously thrashed, pinned down beneath the rolling flesh and endlessly humiliated. Sad, pitiable dwarfs in boxer shorts were confronted by mountainous dames bearing hockey sticks, wistful homunculi with washboard ribcages craned over by eldritch rolypolies. In a small, insidious way *Outsize* impinged on the public consciousness. Its pages were robbed to supply calendar illustrations, or the frontispieces of novelty greetings cards. You will remember the picture, so many times reproduced now that it must be famous, in which – the environment a bedroom and a gaping hearth – a wizened Father Christmas is shown pinned to the ground by his tormentor. Morty's memorials were many. Trailed over the dense, unpromising terrain of the 1970s, his footprints strayed over several minor pathways and marginal defiles before returning to broader routes and sturdier destinies.

More memorabilia from the early years with Morty: some rejected designs for the Grunt Records logo; a frayed, stretched tartan scarf; a picture of Terry Chimes standing next to a Radio

One disc jockey; a *Music Week* singles chart from late 1975. Having left them scattered on the kitchen table I return to find Suzi turning them over. She seems oddly animated.

'Isn't that the Glasgow Express?'

Four cowed-looking Scottish teenagers, unhappily marshalled in their suits, staring at a framed replica of a silver disc.

'Don't tell me you were a fan of the Express?'

'My sister was. She even joined the fan club and bought a pair of tartan jeans. Father used to try and stop her wearing them.'

The picture stays on the table for a day or two before I take it away again.

Grunt Records, formed by Terry Chimes late in 1974, maintained a heterodox roster of artistes. There were all-girl groups with names like Candyfloss and Pussycat, ageing male vocalists encountered by Terry Chimes in his old Sixties Tin Pan Alley days, bands of plausible-looking boys next door put into suits and given arresting soubriquets such as Kenny or Biff. 'Music,' Terry Chimes used to say at around this time, 'music is about *gimmicks*.' The Express's gimmick was tartan and sawn-off jeans, together with stylised North-of-the-Border names like Rory and Kelvin. They were huge, no question. When they arrived at Selfridges once for a guest appearance a thousand adolescent girls rioted in the street outside. When Wee Jimmie the midget drummer appeared on a television chat show to announce his engagement the studio got burned down and there was an actual suicide. They sold two million copies of a record called *Pillow Talk*. Yet the Express's ascent to stardom was not without its problems. For a start they couldn't play their instruments, they really couldn't, and the bass player was a mental defective, but it was nothing that Terry couldn't fix, nothing that couldn't be glozed over by his tender ministrations. Session men were imported to make the records, the band went nowhere where somebody might casually ask them to sing or pick up a guitar and Kelvin the bass player stayed safely locked in his hotel room. All went well – sales, acclaim, television – until the day on which their manager sidled shamefacedly in to see Terry Chimes and confided that the boys had been thinking very seriously about their careers, very seriously indeed, and the upshot of this deliberation was that they wanted to play live. In fact they wanted to play live so badly that they had, on their own initiative, booked themselves into a week at the Apollo Theatre, Glasgow, and the ticket details had already gone out. Terry Chimes tried to talk them out of it, of course. He told them that it would be bad for their careers, he assured them (less plausibly) that no one would come. Their manager was offered a quarter of a million pounds to stop being their manager (he declined). But the music papers were already running 'EXPRESS TO TOUR' headlines, the tickets sold out in a day, and then there was nothing for it but to go ahead.

It was, naturally enough, a disaster. Grade A. Amid conditions of lavish security Terry had employed a session band to play behind curtains at the back of the stage and spent a week giving the boys intensive mime coaching. What could go wrong? In the event Tam the lead singer tripped over a microphone wire half-way through the opening number, flopped off the stage into the orchestra pit and sprained his ankle. As the band craned anxiously out into darkness the music blared on, almost drowned, fortuitously enough, by the noise of the screaming girls. Eventually, when they had dragged Tam out of the orchestra pit, given him emergency first aid and sent him back on stage, things got worse. Unbeknown to the backstage minders Wee Jimmie had packed his drum kit with flash powder. It went off three bars into *Lassie I Love You*, sending Wee Jimmie head first in the air, deafening the first six rows and blowing a small hole in the roof. As the band reeled dazedly around the vibrating stage, Kelvin the bass player began to have an epileptic fit. Finally the curtain fell away at the back of the theatre and the session men were revealed in all their embarrassed glory.

A day or so later Suzi says, 'What happened to the Glasgow Express?'

Broke up. Re-formed. Broke up again. I can remember asking the same question of Terry Chimes, six months after the concert.

'So how are you doing with the Express, Terry?'

'Bloody bad. I thought I'd fixed Wee Jimmie up to do a series on Scottish TV. You know, *Edinburgh Rock*, something like that. It turns out the cunt can't read the autocue.'

'What about Tam?'

'Haven't seen Tam for a month or so, now you mention it.'

'And Kelvin?'

'Kelvin's dead . . . At least I *think* Kelvin's dead.'

What happened to the Glasgow Express? Died, disappeared, went the way of all flesh. Vanished into that lost, boreal world of betting shops, dole queues and remembered, evanescent glory. What happened to all of us, for that matter? Morty goes on making his films in a muted, low-key way. Terry Chimes, that monstrous epitome of twentieth-century urban man, retired to the country. Crazy Rodney? Lost in the random clutter of our times. Elaine, alone amongst these shadowy wraiths, these gaunt reminders of another world, continues to haunt me.


Another thing about Elaine: I hit her once. Quite hard, in fact, my only excuse extreme provocation. It was at a dinner party given by some friends of hers whose names might have been Jason and Amanda, who might have lived in Holland Park. Elaine's friends occupied no recognisable social category and performed no obvious function in her life. Stray, incidental baggage, picked up in the course of foreign holidays or retained from her university days, they appeared to have been chosen on an entirely random basis or to fulfil obscure criteria of which they themselves could hardly have been aware. Jason and Amanda were wholly representative of this tendency, happy to entertain us, but conspicuously baffled by the way Elaine spoke to them and her complete inability to distinguish them from other similar friends met in other and apparently indistinguishable circumstances.

I hit her quite early on in the proceedings, just as the prawn cocktail had given way to the veal escalope ('They're vegetarians, by the way,' Elaine had said in the cab), when she turned to me and said, 'One of the troubles with you, Martin, is that you're such a wimp.'

'Oh, I am, am I?'

'Yes,' (meditatively), 'a real wimp. Has anyone ever told you that before, Martin?'

'As a matter of fact, no.'

At this point Jason made some cautious deposition about the food getting cold. I gave him one of my God-isn't-she-a-scream looks. 'Listen,' I said, still keeping it joky, 'if I'm such a wimp, how come I could render you immobile in five seconds flat if I tried to?'

'Go on then. Try.'

It took, as I had suggested, approximately five seconds. Pulling the chair carefully to one side I yanked her to her feet, twisted both arms behind her back and applied a double Nelson.

'Point taken?'

'Point taken.'

Pausing only to note Jason and Amanda's smiles of relief, I relaxed my grip. Next minute I was bent double and retching on the carpet, marvelling simultaneously at the pain and the fact that I'd managed to miss such a carefully signalled express-train knee in the groin.

I hit her after that. Just a single backhander across the face. Nothing you could erect a court case around. We left soon afterwards.


One a.m. Three days after the round of phone calls to the model agencies. Suzi comes slowly awake, eyes blinking furiously in the relentless light. The side of her face is creased from the sheet. I watch her as she shakes her head bewilderedly from side to side, slides over on to her hands and knees and rambles clumsily over the pillows. Naked, there is a squatness about her that I try not to notice.

'Why's the light on?'

'I don't like the dark. Don't like it at all.'

Later, somewhere in the early dawn when there is pale sky lurking outside the window, the phone rings in the hall.

'Martin? Sorry to get you so late.'

'Morty. It's four a.m.'

'Is that so? Well, I'm sorry. Only I had these Americans here and they only just left. They said to say hi.'

Morty's Americans. I remember Morty's Americans from the distant days. I suppose it's good that they still remember me. The line crackles: I hear a siren go by a hundred and twenty miles away.

'. . . Anyway, I asked around like you said. For a start, you can forget about Jim Woodward.'

'I can?'

'You can forget about Jim Woodward because I talked to him last week. He's retired; hasn't made a movie in years. He didn't even remember you.'

I slide a fingernail down that mental check list of suspects.

'What about Frank Rosati?'

'Hey, where've you been? Frank went down to Brighton a year ago with his wife and kid. Last thing I heard he was opening an antique shop.'

'Anyone else?'

'Act your age, Martin. Act it. You know the business. People move on. People pull out. People die. It's all over now. Nobody remembers. Nobody cares.'

For some reason I start crying at this. I don't know why. Perhaps it's something to do with the thought of the look on Elaine's face when I hit her, or the memory of Suzi's coltish smile, that tensed anticipation. I cry silently, staring out into the haggard dawn, the street with its rows of bunched cars, unyielding curtains. After a moment or two I say, 'So who is it, Morty? Nobody remembers. Nobody cares. So who's sending me this stuff? Who's doing this to me?'

A pause. Suddenly I wish I were a hundred miles away, sitting in Morty's office, as in the old days when we returned from a jag and couldn't be bothered to go to bed, talking on into the morning or heading for an early breakfast in the all night café in Dean Street. Or . . . forget it. Dead. Gone. I look down at the street again and see, of all people, Fat Eric loafing round a gatepost, bent on some mysterious matutinal errand.

'I don't know,' Morty says coldly, 'I just don't know.'


Where have I been? I've been sitting on my backside here in Norfolk for the past two years, that's where I've been. You lose touch. You forget things. At first I tried to maintain some neat, peripheral vantage point on all this. I subscribed to *Adult Video World*. I worked up a few tired scripts. I even had Morty send me copies of his show-reels. And from afar I watched the spectacle of

Morty picking up and disentangling the cats-cradled threads of his career.

People moved on, pulled out, died. Lila St Claire became a straight actress. Johnny The Wad ended up as a prison warder. Frank Fellatio became a traffic warden. I know because he once tried to give me a parking ticket in Wigmore Street. Parched, resentful faces. I grew used to seeing them in unpropitious circumstances, in underwear catalogues, in furtive pubs south of the river, in another world.

I once asked Morty about his retirement. He became prodigiously animated. 'Retire? Listen, Martin, if there's one thing I can tell you about my retirement it's that it's going to be perfect.'

'Tell me about it. Describe a typical day to me.'

Morty's face creased over. 'You aren't kidding me? Okay, I wake up and I'm in bed with Cindy Lu Win. Or better still, Cindy Lu Win and her daughter. We fool around for an hour or so and then it's breakfast. Fruit juice. Bacon. Eggs . . .'

'*Bacon?*'

'Sure. I'll have dropped all that Orthodox stuff by then. After breakfast I have another session with Cindy Lu Win, only this time she goes on top. Then I get the car to take me to whatever race meeting happens to be on that afternoon. I'll stay to the end of the card. I'll always win.'

'How come?'

Morty was shouting now. 'Because I'll back every horse . . . Back to London – I'll have Cindy Lu Win with me in the car, of course – and tea at my club. White's. The Athenaeum. I'm not fussy. Maybe then a little roulette, or Cindy Lu Win. Depends on how I feel.'

'Won't you ever get bored? Doing all that, I mean.'

'No.' Morty shook his head emphatically. 'I won't get bored. Ever.'


Pornography has its own codes, its own subterfuges, its own way of doing things, its own paradoxes. It is not a matter of revelation but concealment, not of gratification but denial. Morty, in particular, was obsessed by the suggestive nature of his art. 'Tease them,' he would say. 'Tease them right up to the end.' Each of his films followed the path suggested by this maxim: a slow progress of tiny advances and smaller retreats, the construction of vast exotic panoramas which were subtly defused and undermined, the whole easily reinterpreted as a complex ironic device. Students of the Leisurevision *oeuvre* grew used to characteristic tricks, the thumbprints he appended to standard scenarios of window-cleaner, pick-up and virgin bride. A favourite Kronenburg stratagem was moving scenery, the incidental effect at first glimpsed from afar, but later usurping the dramatics of the centre stage. A young woman stands undressing before the saloon-bar doors of an opulent shower-room. The doors, animated by some spectral breeze, blow back and forth as she completes her preparations. She is seen, in a split-second collision of frames, first, clad in a towel outside the door, second, naked but partly concealed, from within. On another occasion, at the high point of a film called *Al Fresco Lust*, shot in the New Forest, Morty hired a road digger to traverse slowly across the set as the film's climax was played out. It is an impressive yet confusing finale. In a woodland glade ten yards distant a young couple remove each other's clothes: an alluring spectacle this, the occasional glimpse of breast and buttock, the frequent exhalation of breath, but all the while the viewer is conscious of the momentous distraction moving into vision on the edge of the screen. At first it is simply a matter of noise: the hissing of steam, a grinding of gears, mechanical screeching, but even this, curiously, is enough to distract attention from the mounting frenzy beyond. By the time the digger appears the onlooker is completely absorbed, indifferent to anything but the inch-by-inch progress of this lumbering juggernaut across the clearing. Perhaps three minutes elapse before its hindmost part disappears. The couple lie decorously in each other's arms, spent and exhausted.

Censorship accounted for much of this evasion, but there was a sense in which Morty relished the prohibition of the classification boards and the ukases of the industry watchdogs. They gave him scope, he said, they furnished a framework for the particular conceits he wished to nurture. I asked him once to describe an ideal screenplay. He thought for a moment and said, 'A guy's wandering about at night in this old castle in the woods, through these passageways lit with flaring torches. All the rooms are like cells, barred up, but with spy-holes so you can see what's going on inside. He looks into one of them and sees this girl taking her clothes off, very slowly, button by button. He shouts at her, but she doesn't hear, just goes on taking her clothes off. So he starts breaking down the door. By the time he makes it inside the girl's disappeared. So he walks off down the corridor, looks through another spy-hole and there's the girl again doing the same thing. The door's even more barred up with locks and bolts, but he goes and gets a power drill and busts his way in. No sign of the girl again. And so it goes on: six or seven different rooms. And each time it's more difficult to get in, and each time the girl's coming on stronger, waving her fanny at him and feeling herself. One time she's even got another guy in there with her. And so finally he makes it in there for the last time and what does he find? I'll tell you. He finds an inflatable doll shrivelled up on the floor and hissing away as the air falls out of it.'

The Kafkaesque imagery, the predicament of the hero – baffled, confused, unappeased – were typical. So was the setting, the vistas of stone and firelight, the Rackham-like interior. Morty disliked 'realistic' pornography on aesthetic grounds. I remember in the early Seventies watching with him a hardcore German tape, the first either of us had seen for that matter, bought by Terry Chimes in one of the Beate Uhse shops and smuggled home on the cross-channel ferry. It went on for thirty minutes and consisted simply of a man and a woman in a room on a bed having sex. Morty was scandalised. 'It was just so . . . so fucking boring. I mean, nothing happened, nothing at all. You mean to tell me, Martin, that in Germany there are poor, cabbage-eating, Teutonic fuckers paying money for this?' Morty wanted costume, he wanted spectacle, dark forests, vagrant, scurrying humanity. There was a baroque air to his productions in later days, a deliberate cultivation of artifice. At one point he did indeed make a film very like the imagined screenplay. It was a costume drama called *Codpiece* (ironist though he was, Morty never scrimped on the titles) set in fifteenth-century Sweden and almost obstinate in its refusal to let the hero approach the

heroine. Its highpoint came midway through the second half
when, in a tunnel beneath the mountain fortress, two lovers
standing five feet apart appraise each other's naked bodies.
Moving forward, the hero's foot activates a hidden switch,
whereupon a massive iron gate crashes down between them.
*Codpiece* did badly at the box office.

And of course it isn't funny. In its broader implications it isn't
funny at all. I once saw a film, or perhaps I should say part of
a film, in which a woman was beaten with baseball bats. I
watched it at the screening room at Dean Street along with
Morty and the obscure, wretched acquaintance of Terry Chimes
who thought that Morty might be able to help him distribute it.
He was a small, badly shaven man with red eyes and a flat
Northern accent. As we watched he apologised nervously for the
poor quality of the print – it was in black and white with
scratches on the surface, for the absence of a soundtrack. 'Easy
dub one on later,' I remember him saying, 'if you like it, that is.'
Transfixed by the slow arc that the bats made as they descended,
neither of us paid him any attention. It seemed realistic, which
is to say, there were bruises where previously there had been
only pale unblemished skin, and the choreography was amateurish, with the people who were doing the beating knocking into
one another or occasionally stumbling over furniture. There was
a terrible moment when the girl, naked now and dragging one
leg awkwardly behind her, got as far as the door only to find it
locked, a sudden lurch of camera angles suggesting sharp, intrusive movement behind her. We watched for about ten minutes,
until Morty said very quietly, 'No. Yeah, turn it off.' The small
seedy man stared uncertainly as I flicked the cassette out of the
machine and handed it back to him. Morty said, 'Look, there's
no market for this stuff, this S&M freakshow stuff. You might
sell it abroad. Amsterdam. Berlin. You might sell it there. But
not here.' The small man shrugged, unabashed, gathered up his
case of tapes – he even had a business card, I remember, which
he pressed upon us – and went out.

Later Morty said, 'You think all that happened?'

'What do you think?'

'I don't know . . . Jesus, you can do anything these days with
films. I've been on sets in the States where they cut chicks' heads

off and ran them over with motorbikes, and then seen them come up smiling in the hospitality lounge half an hour later.'

I remembered the look on the girl's face as she clutched for the door handle. 'You'd have to be a pretty good actress to pretend all that was happening.'

'I don't know, Martin, I just don't know. There's some queer cunts Terry knows, some real filth. *Real* filth. All right, I'd slap a chick around once in a while – who wouldn't? – but I wouldn't have somebody standing behind me with an eight-reel for ten minutes while I was doing it.'

'Neither would I.'

Morty gave me that indulgent, Jewish paterfamilias grin. 'No, you wouldn't, would you? No, of course, you couldn't, could you?'


Here in Norfolk people have their own nomenclatures, their own ways of doing things, their own subterfuges. Fat Eric has names for cars, names dependent on the circumstances, on the value, on the ownership, names finely judged and capable of endless shifts and tergiversations. Wagons. Machines. Grids. Jalopies. Each carries its hint of disparagement or approbation, each, more to the point, depends for its effect on the intonation Fat Eric chooses to give it. 'Like the motor,' he will say with genuine admiration as some turbo-charged Metro passes us on the ring road. Set against this was the occasion when Woody from the City Gates acquired a fifth-hand purple Ford Capri with stripes and a spoiler. 'Like the *motor*,' Fat Eric told him with thinly veiled contempt. With particularly exalted or desperate vehicles his names leave the realm of actual description – registering something in terms of its characteristics and resemblances – and become purely emblematic. A super-charged Bentley to Fat Eric is 'class' ('class coming up on the outside lane . . . class reckons he can overtake us'). Minis and baby Fiats, for some reason, are 'bastards' ('cut up a couple of *bastards* coming down Newmarket Road tonight').

When I came back here I assumed, wrongly, that the Norfolk people had no irony. They would have descriptions for things, I thought, that actually described; they would have words for objects, people, words even for states of mind, that saw these artefacts or conditions for what they were. Above all, I assumed, they would see things without artifice: their reactions would not be filtered through any stream of over-conditioned self-consciousness, but simply emerge out of an authentic perception. It would be the difference, I assumed, between actuality and metaphor. And yet I was wholly in error. To Fat Eric language is a finely honed instrument, a subtle code of communication, awash in barely uncoverable nuance. He has a way, for example, when asked if he is going to do something, or if he has done something, of replying, 'Reckon I will,' or 'Reckon I did.' This is ironic, but it is not simply ironic; it has its own twists and ambiguities, it is not merely the opposite of what is implied. It does not mean, 'I will not do what you have suggested.' It does not even go one stage further and indicate the inadequacy of the question; it does not mean, 'You must be very stupid if you assume I will do what you have suggested.' It admits a relationship. What 'Reckon I will' means, approximately, is, 'Our intimacy is such that you know already that I will not do what you have suggested. Therefore, by suggesting it, you have given me the opportunity of making a joke at my expense – as it discloses my own incapacity – but also at your expense, because it indicates the futility of your asking me to do anything which I do not want to do.' At the same time it is more even than this. It is evidence of a power struggle in which Fat Eric, from the outset, has the upper hand. For by asking Fat Eric to do something which you know he will not do, and even, as Kay does and I do, asking it simply in furtherance of an ironic ritual, is to acknowledge your own inferiority in the relationship. It is the relationship which exists between the stand-up comic and his feed: a series of dialogues, fair enough on the surface, which will always end in effortless victory.

Suzi has this characteristic. From time to time in our relationship, people – colleagues from work, wistful men – would telephone her and suggest that she accompany them to cinemas, football matches or restaurants. 'I might do,' Suzi would say, 'I might do.' 'I might do' in this context did not mean 'I might not'. It meant 'I am in charge here.' It meant 'By making this request you have placed yourself in a position of extreme vulnerability. I may choose to do what you request, on my terms and in accordance with my stipulations, in which case you will have allowed yourself to become a victim of my condescension, or I may choose not to do it, in which case my indifference will render you foolish and resentful.' A less subtle thraldom, perhaps, than that practised by Fat Eric, but no less powerful.

When I came back here I assumed, again wrongly, that I would find directness, a way of life that was unfeigned, a manner of doing things that was in some way authentic. Instead I found Suzi and Fat Eric, with their evasions and their unwritten charters of superiority. I found the Norwich shop assistants who, if you miscount the money you hand to them, say, 'Whatever are you like?' which means, paradoxically, 'I know exactly what you are like.' I came looking for what I conceived of as real life, for some definitive gaze on these shifting landscapes, and found only subterfuge, illusion, a persistent refusal to be drawn. Like some soldier, the veteran of months of jungle warfare, who moves on gratefully to open country, I had discovered only the same camouflage, the same bunkers concealed beneath fronds of ersatz foliage, the same howitzers grouped menacingly together behind unbending, painted trees.


If there was one cinematic technique which Morty distrusted above all others it was realism. The commodity in which he dealt was, as I have indicated, in his eyes the least straightforward of functions. To have reduced it to an elemental basis – the man, the woman, the bed – would have been to him a betrayal of the imaginative faculty. This assumption – that one needed trappings, incidentals, continual embroidery – had deep roots. He was, for example, one of the few people I have met who found the sexual act, or at any rate its depiction on film, uninteresting. Sex to Morty figured as a slightly unappetising and somewhat frugal meal, requiring endless titivation and decoration to render it palatable. To film it he needed above all room for manoeuvre, ideally some greater knowledge that he could spring on an unsuspecting cast. A typical Kronenburg trick was to impose some extra dimension on to the filming of a screenplay, some unthought-of contingency to which the actors themselves had not been made party. In the late Seventies, for example, I was present at the filming of *Mayfair Orgy*, a project which represented the high point of this approach. The plot was straightforward – suspiciously so for anyone acquainted with Morty's techniques – involving no more than the convening of a group of libertines at a mews house in Berkeley Square (specially rented for the purpose). Halfway through the proceedings the sound of sirens could be heard in the street outside, to be followed a few moments later by the breaking down of the door and a full-scale police raid, its conclusion the herding of the cast, most of them half-clad or draped in blankets, into waiting vans. Only I, Morty and the cameraman knew that the dozen or so policemen were in fact extras, hired from a theatrical agency which specialised in such deceptions. It was perhaps Morty's finest hour. To the sound of police whistles, amid rapid, obtrusive movement, as terrified actors fled hastily to places of concealment, he continued to film. The result is an impressive piece of verisimilitude: moments of genuine antagonism, the camera occasionally dislodged to provide unexpected angles, a final shot of abject terror on the face of Cindy Lu Win as she is led away protesting. Several of the actors refused to work for Morty again, yet he remained triumphant. He had created something novel, he thought, something splendid and coherent from the unpromising chaos around him. When I protested that his creation was realistic – actual surprise, authentic terror – he disagreed. To Morty one level of unreality had been strengthened by a second. The emotion might have been genuine, but the circumstance trailed gossamer threads of fancy and that, for him, was enough.

For a brief period Morty caught the spirit of the times. The pornography of the late Seventies cultivated an attachment to fantasy. It was the time of the *Emmanuelle* films, of which Morty made several low-budget spin-offs, the time of *Mitteleuropa* costume dramas, of erotic parodies of the famous and innocuous. Leisurevision's adult versions of *The Sound Of Music*, featuring a nymphomaniac Julie Andrews lookalike, and *Chitty Chitty Bang Bang* date from around this time. He shot desert epics, sex dramas acted out on Swiss ski-slopes, spoof Westerns: lavish productions with extensive casts. Later on, when the chill, elemental winds blew in from the Continent, he was dismayed. You could buy German sex videos on the underground market by the late Seventies, Swedish sex soap-operas, gory works of realism in which grim Scandinavian businessmen could be seen paying energetic court to their secretaries before proceeding homeward to perform the same efficient service for their wives. It should be said, in his defence, that Morty's distress was genuine. He was appalled not by the crudity, by the tendon-grinding close-ups, but by the underlying assumption, the thought that the pattern of everyday life, however highly charged the sexual atmosphere, should be considered a fit subject for cinema. 'Real life,' he used to say around 1980, 1981, whenever some foreign salesman caught him unawares, 'real life is for people with no imagination.'

The fat girl was generic. There were other figures that I remembered from the Norwich past, specific figures, framed in their own peculiar landscapes. There was, for example, the man with the dog. At a remove of twenty years I cannot recall precisely when it was that the man with the dog first strayed into my consciousness, but it must have been sometime in the mid-1960s. Certainly by 1967 or 1968 he was as fixed and immoveable a part of the local terrain as the Carrow ironworks or the lofty tessellations of the City Hall. As a fixture on the Norwich streets the man with the dog was not unique. There were others like him, other faces with whom one became familiar – flustered women in mackintoshes, broods of noisy children – but somehow they lacked the man-with-the-dog's staying power, his regularity, his range, fell away until they became vague attendants in a tableau where the central part had already been cast: it was the man with the dog who rose above them, who, by means of his continual presence, confirmed the narrower patterns of their lives. At the time I was scarcely conscious of the fascination which he exercised. It was only later, when I left Norwich, that I realised how central he had become to any re-creation of these fading landscapes, how consistently he emerged to inhabit the memories of familiar streets and parklands. This role was all the more puzzling in that I could remember nothing concrete about him – what he wore, what, specifically, he looked like – only the fact of his presence. It was, I supposed, simply that he was always there, marginal but unshakeable from the corners of this mental picture, down there on the edge of things, inviolable.

The man with the dog had the advantage of longevity. But there were other characters, less prominent perhaps, but capable of exercising an equally potent spell. Chief among these was the man with the shoes. The man with the shoes first appeared in the Christchurch Road area of Norwich in perhaps early 1968. Whereas I recall nothing about the man with the dog other than the fact that he was there, I remember the man with the shoes precisely. He was young, a year or two into his twenties, with tousled hair and a put-upon expression, and with a fat woman whom we supposed to be his wife, and with his shoes he began to walk past our house on perhaps three or four afternoons a week. I often speculated about those shoes: stack-heeled boots in vivid colours, a pair of scarlet sports bootees with grandiloquent, guttering laces. Where did he buy them, I wondered? What shop or salesman had been prepared to sell them to him? The highlight of his wardrobe, a sight so incongruous that it would bring my father hurrying joyfully to the window, was a pair of curving, canary-yellow moccasins. The effect was as if the man with the shoes had acquired two outsize bananas, hollowed out a portion of the pulp and simply placed his feet in the gaps.

The man with the dog. The man with the shoes. Even when I left the city in 1969 I had managed in a small way to keep up with them, to maintain some hold on their remorseless trajectories. My father referred to them in his letters. Then, on my visits home, I would assure myself of a sighting or two: the man with the dog seen late on a winter's afternoon crossing the westernmost corner of Eaton Park, the man with the shoes prancing once again at breakneck speed past the house. Each survived deep into the 1970s. I saw the man with the dog as late as 1975 on the corner where Christchurch Road meets The Avenues, and as the car taking me to my father's funeral moved away from the house the first person whom we met was the man with the shoes. Each, I thought, was immortal. And yet coming back to Norwich in the early 1980s I discovered that neither had survived my departure. They had gone, disappeared, and I had returned to a city devoid of human landmarks.

Of the two it was the man with the dog whose absence I most regretted, so much so that in time I began to haunt parts of Norwich where I thought I might encounter him: by the river near Earlham, out in the Cringleford marshes, nearer at hand down the long sweep of the Newmarket Road. It was no use. I never found him. But even then the suspicion lingered in my mind that he was still there, that his absence was merely a puzzle deliberately imposed upon me, wanting only my own ingenuity to solve it. For this reason, even until quite late on, when all reasonable hope had passed, I walked the Norwich streets with the hope, the very faint hope, that here in the dogleg leading across from Meadow Rise to Colman Road, there at the point where Earlham Park meets the university, I might find him, that this vital piece of the jigsaw might be restored.

And then, nearly a year after I returned, I did find something: something only marginally connected to the man with the dog, but enough to convince me of the folly of my search. In the centre of Norwich, a good mile or so out of his natural orbit, I met the man with the shoes. It was early in the morning, raw and damp, and he stood in the doorway of a supermarket with the collar of his jacket hunched up to his chin. Though I had not seen him for six or seven years it was unquestionably the same man: the same tousled hair, the same half-nervous, half-insouciant look. He even gave me a faint quarter-glance of recognition, the scintilla of a nod, as if he remembered me, but could not quite locate me in his own mental landscape. And yet, staring at his feet, at the white baseball boots, mildly outlandish, certainly, but in no way as bizarre as the stacked heels or the platform soles of long ago, I realised that he was no longer the man with the shoes, but simply an ordinary middle-aged man glimpsed in a shop doorway. Like the man with the dog he had lost his glamour, the one through absence, the other through removal of that single defining quality. Like the Gaumont Cinema or the old thoroughfares of London Street, each had either disappeared or been changed out of recognition by the intervening years, and I had sought refuge in a past that no longer existed.

IN THE LATE Seventies Morty got ambitious. It was a gradual process, so gradual that medium-term associates like myself and Terry Chimes scarcely noticed, a process made manifest in tiny changes to routine and procedure. Crazy Rodney, who had once had the unhappy privilege of delivering Morty to his meetings in a superannuated post-office van, was given a chauffeur's uniform and a Lagonda. Morty's accountant, who had worked first above and latterly in a pub in Maddox Street, was dismissed in favour of a Big Eight firm in the City. Stray touches, minor adjustments to the smooth trajectory of Morty's career. There was one lawyer who vetted the magazines and films Morty put out on the legal market and another lawyer who advised him unofficially what he could get away with in the illegal trade. The primitive distribution system – Crazy Rodney and the van – was replaced by a svelte firm in Twickenham. A little later I began to wear suits to meetings and was referred to as 'our creative director'.

Cautious, watchful, but ambitious. By 1975 Morty had a stockbroker. A year later he had finessed an entrée into one of the City livery companies – it might have been the Worshipful Company of Dyers – and was parcelling the money together for an American distribution deal. Slowly, subtly, imperceptibly there emerged a new resplendence to Morty's operations, an annual sheaf of pointers to these shifting horizons and beckoning goals. It was at about this time that he began to place what were for Morty crazily unprecedented sums of money on horses with fanciful Jewish names that were brought out for weekly humiliation at minor race-courses in the north of England. It became an engrossing daily ritual: the flustered exit from a shoot in one of the warehouses down by the river at Bow or Poplar, the scurry through the mist, the late afternoon phone call to the on-course correspondent at Doncaster, Towcester, York, the unfailing intelligence that Solomon's Fancy or Star of David had fallen at the third or thrown its rider at the seventh, emerging with Morty into the pale autumn light of the East End to hunt for a pub. Matters came to a head when a horse named Samson's Delight, on which Morty had staked a thousand pounds at 13–1, failed to emerge from its stall in the Cesarewitch and was summarily disqualified. 'It dies, Martin,' Morty told me subsequently. 'For that it just fucking dies.' I hadn't realised that he'd owned it. Neither, it transpired, had anyone else.

The secrecy was characteristic. Not overtly clandestine, it proceeded out of Morty's conviction that you kept the various parts of your life in individual compartments. Only later when the journalists got to work did anyone realise just what Morty was up to in the 1970s, how truly circumspect he was, the types of people he hung around with. The people Morty hung around with had names like Bald Ernie and Terry the Blade, had pale, mad eyes and wore suits that were twenty years out of date. Morty knew them from way back, back from the old Bethnal days. I was once clambering up the stairs to the loft at Dean Street when an unassuming man in a brown suit, the sort of man you see sitting on his own in the corner of a pub nursing a half-pint glass, ambled by.

'That was Charlie,' Morty said, shuffling the papers on his desk intently. 'Haven't seen him for a while.'

'Charlie?'

'Charlie Scaduto.'

Charlie Scaduto. Mad Jimmy Parsons. The Major. Morty knew them all. Morty's ambition? It was, it is fair to say, colossal. It was unrelenting. It hovered high above the slot-machine arcades and the bookshops that he bought his way into in '76, '77, the desolate frontages in Greek Street and Brewer; underpinned the criminally favourable deals he did with the Maltese club owners and the nervous two-man printing outfits in Commercial Road. It embraced plans for floating Leisurevision on the unlisted securities market. More narrowly it brooked no opposition. By the late 1970s you didn't mess about with Morty Kronenburg, you just didn't. A series of less than trustworthy associates limped off into penurious retirement. A bookshop proprietor in

Frith Street sustained a fractured skull. Did Morty do that? I don't know. I know only that he bought the lease when it came up for sale a fortnight later.

Trammelled by law, weakened perhaps by the disadvantages of background and profession, Morty's ambition was capable of fitting into more conventional patterns. Respectability, held at bay by the bread-and-butter necessities, by the films, the magazines and the escort service in Nottingham Place, was never far distant from his more grandiose schemes. Morty's business cards, updated every year, now in embossed black type, then with *Mortimer J. Kronenburg* engraved in trellises of gold leaf, underpinned this sense of continuous refinement. In the mid-Seventies the inscription ran simply 'MORTY: MAGAZINES AND FILMS' and the telephone number belonged to Morty's solicitor. A year later it was '*Mortimer J. Kronenburg FCA & Associates Printing Consultants*'. By 1978 it was 'Leisurevision', an actual company with paid-up share capital and a tame peer who owed Morty money sitting on the board, and one of its subsidiaries made up the plates for the *Radio Times*. That was how far Morty had progressed by the late 1970s. There was, to be sure, the comic paraphernalia – the grim vans full of pallets of *Bouncers* and *Upfront*, the swivel-eyed gentlemen on the pavement in Meard Street ready to inveigle you down the tapering steps – but the accountants were Messrs Saffery Champness of Gutter Lane and the fixed assets included two drinking clubs and a wholly legitimate warehousing business in Deal.

And what about Morty? Morty didn't change. Morty sat tight. Morty burrowed on relentlessly through these dense, populous years, an intense, guttering light, never wholly extinguished, always capable of flaring dramatically upward. Often towards the end of the Seventies he was abroad: in America with Terry Chimes, in Europe where he had connections with one of the big German porn houses. Returned to London he grew restless, dissatisfied, a sullen figure decanted from a taxi to complain about airport delays or roadside litter. 'What this country needs, Martin, is a good shaking up,' he said once or twice on these occasions, an ominous remark, forgotten at the time, but remembered in the light of what came later. Abroad had a galvanising effect on Morty: most of his foreign excursions were followed by some unrelated business coup, some gross extension of his sphere of influence. Early in 1979, recalled from Hamburg to an England of piled snowdrifts and industrial unrest, he unveiled his most ambitious scheme to date.

Morty's office in Dean Street. Outside thin rain was falling over the grey rooftops. In the aftermath of a power cut the lights had fused: from the studio beyond the doorway electricians murmured softly to one another. Morty said, 'I didn't think things were this bad. You should have rung me up and told me.'

'We didn't know where you were.'

There were galley proofs lying on the desk in untidy coils, the first fruits of a plan to produce an intimate-contact magazine. Morty flicked through them unhappily for a moment and then held one up a foot or so in front of his face.

'Adult male, 42, well-built, seeks afternoon playmates . . . Do you think this stuff is going to sell?'

'Circulation thinks it will. There's a big order from the Midlands.'

Above Morty's head a lightbulb fizzed for a moment and then went dead. He frowned at the greying sheets again and went on, 'It's all right, Martin, I'm not getting at you. It's just . . . Do you realise this morning the power went halfway through a shoot? There're three actresses sitting down there wrapped in blankets freezing themselves to death. Scazz left in a taxi half an hour ago. He says he won't come back unless I can lay on heating. What am I supposed to do about that?'

Dressed in a fur coat, thinning hair brushed low over the front of his head, Morty looked more than usually depressed. He said, 'You know, Martin, would it surprise you to know that I was thinking of going into politics?'

I had grown used to these bizarre revelations. There was a fantastic side to Morty's make-up composed entirely of ungovernable whims. Periodically there emerged the idea that he should start a national newspaper, or buy a football club. Nothing ever came of them. I shook my head.

'What sort of politics?'

Outside the tempo of the rain had increased. Morty picked up a copy of a model directory that was lying on the corner of the desk and began to leaf through it. He said evasively, 'These girls ought to be more truthful. It says here that Candy Ingrams is twenty-four and has starred in several full-length feature films. Now, I know for a fact that she's thirty-one.'

'Do you want me to go and see how the actresses are?'

'She was in those black and white shorts that Frank Rosati used to make and that was ten years ago. No,' Morty said decisively. 'I want you to stay and listen to me. Seriously, Martin, I'm thinking of going into politics. Proper politics. Not pissing around on some town council with a lot of old women in twinsets. The real thing.'

'The real thing?'

'Sure. All right, Martin, I admit that I may not give the impression of being a serious person. I can see that. But I've been doing a lot of thinking about the way this country gets run. A lot of serious thinking. On the plane coming back from Hamburg I . . . Jesus, Martin, that fucking Labour party. I mean, do you know there are people dying out there because the ambulances won't take them to hospital? And when some ambulanceman stops playing cards long enough to take them to casualty, ten to one a goon turns up with a placard and tells him to go away again.'

'It's a disgrace, certainly.'

'*Exactly*. A disgrace is exactly what it is. And you know, Martin, it breaks my heart to say this because, well, I don't know if I've told you this before but my father used to be big in the local Labour party. In fact, you know the Kronenburg Daycentre off Bethnal Green Road? Well, it was my father that raised the money. They had Aneurin Bevan down for the opening ceremony. And, well, it breaks my heart to see the fucking *Labour* party responsible for all this.'

In fact I knew about Morty's dad from Crazy Rodney, whose own father was an embittered veteran of the Bethnal Green Labour Party. A colourful grocer with premises off the Bow Road, Councillor Kronenburg had gone down before one of the great town hall corruption scandals of the late 1950s, when he was found to be supplying all eight local old people's homes under a complex system of aliases. A little later his chairmanship of the local schools board had coincided with all six Kronenburg progeny passing the 11-Plus. I knew all about Councillor Kronenburg.

'. . . Anyway,' Morty went on, 'I've been talking to one or two business contacts – you know, Charlie Scaduto and Bald Ernie – and they've convinced me that I ought to stand.'

Unbelievably he was serious. He was, I later discovered, so serious that all previous undertakings became invested with the retrospective taint of lightmindedness. In fact, investigation revealed that the plan to become a Conservative MP was already well in hand, attended with all Morty's characteristic foresight and attention to detail. At the time Trotskyist entryism into the Labour party was a subject much in vogue for newspaper exposés. Morty's takeover of his chosen constituency would have done credit to the wiliest revolutionary cadre. The moribund Conservative association in the carefully selected East End seat – Labour majority 14,000 – stood scant chance. Within a month of Morty's decision to take over the seat – this was late 1978 – membership mysteriously doubled. Within three months Morty had Charlie Scaduto, a horrifying figure who sold secondhand TV sets somewhere in Forest Gate, installed as party chairman. Crazy Rodney, voted in as constituency secretary at an extraordinary general meeting attended by nineteen of Charlie Scaduto's drinking companions and eleven appalled members of the local bourgeoisie, helped by throwing the filing cabinet containing the membership lists into the Thames.

Inevitably there were problems. Chief among these was the prior existence of a prospective parliamentary candidate, a motherly woman who sat on Newham Council. Charlie Scaduto cultivated her assiduously in the bar of the constituency association headquarters after meetings. I record an early dialogue.

'The problem about the Labour Party, right, is that they're a *load of fuckers*.'

'Well, I . . .'

'A load of fuckers. Take my business, right? Two years I've been trying to extend down the street, put in a showroom with a couple of neon signs, something tasteful. Can I get planning permission? No. And all because the fucking Paki in the sweetshop over the road keeps complaining.'

'It does seem a little unfair . . .'

'*Unfair?* One of these days I'm going to get hold of Mr fucking Aroni, Mr fucking Aroni with his fucking *turban*, and jam one of his sticks of fucking London rock right up his . . .'

The prospective parliamentary candidate's resignation, for reasons which she would sooner not disclose, having arrived fortuitously at Conservative Central Office on the day before the fall of the Callaghan government, the field was clear. Morty won the hastily convened selection conference at a canter.

There were some other problems. Most obviously there was the question of what Morty did for a living. At first he featured in the local press as 'businessman Mortimer Kronenburg'. A little later he was being referred to as 'businessman Mortimer Kronenburg with his interests in the adult entertainment market'. Two weeks into the campaign the *Daily Mirror* ran a story headed 'PORN KING'S BID FOR PARLIAMENT'. Then there was Charlie Scaduto and what he did for a living. Charlie Scaduto specialised in long-firm companies, an auspicious piece of fraudulence popularised by the Krays. The theory is time-honoured. You buy up some likely-looking high-street site, stock it with a shelf-full of pricey electrical goods (all legitimately acquired from suppliers) and put in a manager to run it. The manager signs the cheques and deals with the suppliers, and nobody knows you exist. For the first six months you administer the shop like an ordinary business. Every week or so you place an order with the suppliers (you deal with lots of different suppliers) and you pay them on the nail. The manager ingratiates himself with the local bank, talks plausibly about expansion and cashflow, and negotiates a loan. Finally you send in a large order to all your suppliers, take delivery of piles of stock and preside over a grand sale at knockdown prices. The manager disappears to Switzerland with a percentage and the suppliers, when they come to investigate, find only a boarded-up shopfront concealing a pile of mildewed invoices. This is the theory. Charlie Scaduto's practice of it, characterised by meanness and the tendency of his stooges to relocate in places like Upminster, ran sadly adrift. Barely had Morty got his libel writ in at the *Mirror* than Charlie Scaduto appeared on the front page of the *Star* under the caption 'TORY CHIEF IN ELECTRICS SWINDLE'.

In the teeth of these difficulties Morty fought a lively campaign, finely attuned to the locale and its traditions. He had himself photographed eating whelks in the Bow Road. He went to his public meetings in a brewer's dray attended by Pearly Kings. When the local Labour Party headquarters got firebombed – the publicity happily obscuring the simultaneous arrest of Charlie Scaduto – he sent a widely quoted message of sympathy. Bright, tense days; in commotion. Once or twice I went canvassing with him down in the dark tenements of the East End. At night, trawling the gloomy corridors of the towerblocks in Rotherhithe, negotiating the urinous staircases, monitoring the thump of hectic jungle jive, Morty became an uncertain, deracinated figure, someone out of his milieu, out of his time, out of his mind. We took Crazy Rodney with us on these occasions, Crazy Rodney with a baseball bat stuffed inside his jacket: Morty had no illusions about canvassing in the East End. The mission accomplished, the fruitless hammering on the doors of silent, terrified pensioners, the confrontations with sullen black youths having duly taken place, back in the Lagonda cruising through the dead streets, he grew reflective.

'You know something, Martin? You know something? We've failed these people. All of us. You. Me. All of us. We've failed them.'

'We have?'

'Sure. People have dreams. They want things. They have a *right* to want things. And what happens? People let them down. Society lets them down.'

'It does.'

'I won't let them down, Martin. I promise you that. I won't let them down.'

He lost by 10,000 votes. Back at the loft in Dean Street, as the faces thronged around a television blaring election results, Morty got drunk on the champagne purchased in anticipation of his victory. Rocking unsteadily on splayed feet, plump, knuckleless hands clamped round the endlessly fisted glasses, he looked alone, vulnerable, purposeless. It was then, perhaps, that I realised Morty's chronic unsuitability to his environment, his apparent inability to perform the exacting role in which he had cast himself. Whereas other actors in this noisy drama played their parts with conviction – Terry Chimes with his pantomime leer, Crazy Rodney's guard-dog eyes – the impresario, the actor-manager for whose delight the play had been convened, seemed sadly ill at ease.

It was a salient defeat. Years later I came across the election result in an old Whitaker's Almanack, but the twinge of recognition was unconvincing. Reinvented, unpicked and restitched in stronger, brighter colours, the fabric of Morty's past could not accommodate these frail outlines.


A week now from the last chat with Morty. Early in the evening there is a mild diversion when Kev Jackson telephones. Kev Jackson: quite a well-known name these days, at any rate in the rarified circles in which I once moved. Thirty-one or thirty-two, but a ten-year veteran of the industry, the first staff reporter on *Adult Video World* and in this capacity escorted by a deferential Morty Kronenburg around many a crowded Leisurevision set and through many a thronged Dean Street cutting room. At this time Kev's interviewing style was that of the respectful ingénue. 'Basically, Kev,' Morty would say, propelling him into the armchair and proffering the half litre of brandy, 'I see *Plasma Party* as the first attempt to bring American hard-core slash to British screens in a form acceptable to the British censor.' 'Basically,' Kev's report would begin a week later, 'top UK director Morty Kronenburg sees *Plasma Party* as the first attempt to bring American hard-core slash to British screens in a form acceptable to the British censor.' Such reliability was comforting to Morty in a world characterised by fickle friendships and savaged reputations. 'That Kev Jackson,' he would say, 'that Kev Jackson, he's *all right*.' Later when he moved to Los Angeles as *Adult Video World*'s resident stringer, returning subsequently to work as a showbiz reporter on one of the London dailies, the connection was sustained. I haven't seen him in three years.

'Martin. Kev Jackson. How are you?'

'I'm fine, Kev. What can I do for you?'

In fact I know exactly what it is that I can do for Kev Jackson, Kev having told me copiously on each of the two previous occasions on which he telephoned. However, as old comrades-in-arms we eschew this sort of directness.

'I saw Terry Chimes the other day, Martin. He said to say hi.'

'Terry Chimes,' I say. 'What about that? Say hi from me as well next time you see him.'

'Sure . . . Look, I'll get to the point, Martin. I need to know if you'll help me with the project.'

'The project . . . Look just run that one in front of me again, would you, Kev?'

Kev Jackson's project. The news that Kev Jackson, hitherto considered barely able to hold a pen and to subsist merely by transcribing the press releases sent to him by eager publicists, was writing a book had sent a steely dart winging into the carapace of the adult film world. Even Morty had condescended to telephone me late one night and tell me about it.

'That Kev Jackson,' he had explained. 'Yes, well the word is he's pulling some exposé stunt. "My life in the skin trade", that sort of thing. Some Sunday supplement did a piece on him last week. I wouldn't worry about it, but I thought you ought to know.'

'Who's talking to him?'

'Beats me. *I'm* not talking to him. Terry isn't talking to him. Nobody's talking to him. Somebody told me he flew over to see Scazz Fogelburg though.'

'What did Scazz say?'

'Scazz drove him back to the airport – you know those fancy cars Scazz has – and told him if he ever saw him again he'd kill him.'

'That won't look very good in the book.'

'Aw, Scazz was only joking. You know Scazz. Anyway, like I said, I shouldn't worry about it, but I thought you ought to know.'

Now I listen again as Kev Jackson goes through his list of valiant objectives. 'Basically, Martin, what I have in mind is a serious study – I should say that the *Observer* have already expressed an interest in the serial rights – something that will set the industry in context, re-open the censorship debate, examine, you know, the human consequences of it all.'

'That sounds good, Kev. Could I ask who you're talking to?'

An ominous question. There is a pause down the line. I can imagine Kev Jackson, hunched over the phone in his cramped writer's flat somewhere in London, wondering how much to tell me, wondering in fact if this is a suitable enterprise for Kev Jackson to have involved himself in in the first place.

'You'd be surprised, Martin. For instance, I've recorded interviews with Sheri La Grange and Corona d'Amour.'

Starlets, both of them. Worse, ageing starlets. Sheri La Grange, the younger of the two, hadn't worked since 1976 to the best of my recollection. Corona d'Amour might have appeared in three photomontages in as many years. Collectively useless.

'On the business side I've talked to Ernie Mackay and Rufus Stokes.'

Dim, know-nothing wholesalers in the north of England. No trouble there.

Another pause down the line. I am visited by the sudden, pleasing sensation that Kev Jackson, haughty Kev Jackson with his leather jacket and his sideboards, is waiting for me to respond.

'Well, with that sort of help, Kev, I can't see you needing any assistance from me.'

'Listen, Martin,' Kev Jackson sounds mildly distraught now. 'I'll be frank with you. I got a ten-thousand-pound advance for this – I don't know how much you know about publishing, but take it from me that's a lot of money. That was six months ago. Since then I've got a dozen sides of notes and taped three interviews with people Morty Kronenburg might have slept with in 1970. No one's talking. Morty won't talk. Terry Chimes won't. That psycho who used to drive the van . . .'

'Crazy Rodney.'

'Crazy Rodney. He won't talk. I spent a thousand pounds going out to see Scazz Fogelburg.'

'What did Scazz say?'

'He said if he ever saw me again he'd kill me.'

'He was only joking. You know Scazz.'

'Listen, Martin. You have to give me a break. Talk to me, please. No names, no dates if you like, just talk to me. I won't mention you as a source and I won't tell anyone else you spoke to me. I promise.'

'Why me, Kev?'

'Christ, Martin. You spent eight, nine years working with

Morty Kronenburg. That's longer than Terry Chimes, longer than anyone. Right from the start. *Capital Pick-up, On Heat.* Right the way through you're down on the credits. Writer. Sound man. Executive producer. If I'm going to finish this, you have to give me a break.'

It strikes me that I need to think about this. I need time to balance the manifest disadvantages (Morty finding out) with the definite benefits such an association with Kev Jackson would confer. Outside there are raised voices in the street, the squeal of car brakes. Lights flick on and off.

'Look, Kev,' I say, 'it's seven o'clock. Ring me back in a couple of hours when I've had time to think about it and we'll see.'

'Tomorrow if you like.'

'No, nine o'clock and we'll see.'

'Okay, okay.' He is chirpy now, chirpy and deferential. 'Hey. You remember the last time we met? Back in Suffolk, early '81?'

'No,' I tell him, making sure it's the last thing I say before I put down the phone. 'I don't remember.'

Subsequently a more major diversion, its outlines emerging rapidly from the closing moments of the conversation with Kev Jackson, rises up to claim my attention, as outside the window, enacted in a queer slow-motion manner reminiscent of primordial cinema, a genuine domestic drama is noisily and patiently unravelled.

Drenched as it is in bar-table bonhomie, roadside conversation and late-evening confidence, the neighbourhood harbours several continuing domestic dramas, each of them exposed, discussed and monitored by a circle of avid observers. This is live soap-opera, its allure markedly more concrete than the nightly stake-out around the television set, in which my chief informant is Fat Eric. It is Fat Eric who keeps me up to the minute on these single-parent tragedies, these child-batterings, these chronicles of intrigue and violence, whose conclusions appear so tardily in the columns of the *Eastern Evening News*. 'Those two kids at Number 16 got put on remand,' he will say as he loiters into the City Gates of an evening, or 'Little Angie at Number 27's up the spout again, so her dad told me'. Divorces, pilfered virginities, minor rumbles – these are the street's stock-in-trade, a bush telegraph transmitting widely and effectually at the smallest provocation.

Lately our attention – my attention, Fat Eric's, the attention, in fact, of people residing several streets away – has been largely focused on the Ferguson family seven doors down on the other side of the road. In a world of stylised humanity, the fat fathers with their six-packs, the tired housewives proceeding in Indian file to Friday-night bingo at the Norwich Mecca Rooms, the Fergusons are giant, comic-book caricatures: Mrs, occasionally encountered in the grocer's, a mass of stunning and unsatisfied female flesh; Mr, a harrassed, sat-upon taxi driver; each astounded and embarrassed by a brood of delinquent children. Mrs Ferguson's paramours were legion, so numerous for it to be safely assumed that Mr Ferguson no longer cared, no longer troubled himself about the file of hulking labourers, the besuited salesmen, the easy despoilers of his marital bed. Certainly it must be owned that Mrs Ferguson sometimes looked a little strained, a little more *distraite* in her afternoon saunter from shop to bus-stop to compromised hearth, that Mr Ferguson's pained self-absorption knew no bounds, that his cheerfulness, when encountered in pub or by roadside, became almost tragic, that he grew nearly desperate in his chatter about football, or the vagaries of the city council hackney-carriage licensing depart-ment, but bless you, these were queer people, queer people indeed, and Mr Ferguson's return home at this unexpected hour in these unexpected circumstances was the queerest thing of all.

Objects. Movement. Sound. Black taxi-cab slewing to a halt at right-angles across the street. Slam of car doors. Mr Ferguson, a grim, remorseless figure, seen in hurried transit from driver's seat to front door. A loud hammering. Lights flicked on, then off. A sash opening at an upstairs window, a head staring out and then withdrawn. More hammering. A silence which Mr Ferguson abets by stumbling back from the door and then exting-uishes by seizing a flower pot from an adjacent hedge and hurling it through the glass of his own vestibule. Then a sudden issue of figures out of the gaping doorway: Mrs Ferguson, hair tum-bling down her back, arms upraised in supplication; a pale, middle-aged man, shoeless, in shirt sleeves and carrying, incon-gruously, a briefcase, who trips over the raised step and sprawls for a moment on the concrete with his limbs beating in several directions. Shouting: Mr Ferguson, Mrs Ferguson, the middle-aged man. Then a complicated game of hide-and-seek: the middle-aged man crawling to a refuge beneath the meagre hedge while Mr and Mrs Ferguson bicker, being found and chivvied out again by Mr Ferguson into the doorway; Mrs Ferguson skipping nimbly out into the street, where she flutters anxiously beside the taxi before being dragged back by the hair. More shouting: the middle-aged man, Mrs Ferguson, Mr Ferguson. A grey cat, which has sat until now on the gatepost of a neighbouring house observing the proceedings, streaking fearfully off into distant gardens and alleyways. A sudden flight of all three parties back through the open door, a vicious slamming of the door behind them, a certain amount of interior scuffling, and then silence. The black taxi lies drunkenly across the pavement. A few people come and stare over the hedge, where all that remains is the briefcase discarded by the middle-aged man and a fragment torn from Mrs Ferguson's dressing gown. The grey cat prowls carefully back and resumes its position atop the gate post. Within, the house is dead and quiet, the light still shining from an upstairs room.

Later, as the dusk extends over the slate rooftops, as the groups of children assembled on the pavement fragment and melt away into the dark, as the streetlamps go on and curtains slither into place, I go out to the front gate and smoke a cigarette. Fat Eric lumbers by in a tracksuit and scuffed trainers, pauses, catches the second cigarette in his giant paw, lights up.

'Out jogging, Fat Eric?'

'Doing it for my health, aren't I? That keep-fit lark, isn't it?' says Fat Eric contemptuously. He hunkers down on his knees for a moment, chest heaving, hawks into the gutter. 'You hear about them Fergusons, then?'

'There was a lot of noise. Earlier on.'

'That's right. A lot of noise. Never heard anything like it. *Fuck* of a lot of noise. Kay reckoned I ought to go and do something about it. Didn't reckon on that though.'

'Why not?'

'Domestic disputes,' says Fat Eric grandly. 'Not a good idea, sticking your nose into domestic disputes. Bad news they are.

Know what happened? Someone tipped old man Ferguson the nod that he might learn something to his advantage if he comes home early. What's he find? Old woman in bed with that little bloke the council send round to see people about home improvements.'

'What did he do?'

'Ferguson? Kicked him around a bit. I mean, who wouldn't? A week in hospital, I mean he's fucking lucky really, isn't he? Old Ferguson being soft the way he is. After all,' says Fat Eric with surprising seriousness, 'it's something you can't ignore, isn't it? I mean, a couple of months ago we was in this pub over West Earlham way and this bloke starts giving Kay the eye, offering her drinks and that. Some cunt in a suit. Some rich cunt.'

'What did you do?'

'Punched him in the throat,' says Fat Eric. 'Told him it was lucky for him I wasn't a violent man. But you can't, you can't ignore something like that, can you?'

'You're right, Fat Eric,' I tell him. 'You're right. It's just something you can't ignore.'

Back inside the phone rings. I let it ring seven or eight times, then pick it up.

'Martin. Kev Jackson. Did you have a chance to think things over?'

'Maybe, Kev. Maybe.'

'Come on, Martin. Don't play games with me. A couple of conversations, that's all it would take. I'll even come down and see you if you want . . .'

Obscurely there is fear in this, the hint of a threat.

'Kev. You remember a girl called Elaine?'

'Elaine? Was she the one in *Shameless*? The one who gets out of the pool and . . .'

'That was Elaine Le Brun. Elaine Keenan. You must remember her.'

'Got it. Tall girl with dark hair. With Frank Fellatio in *Girlschool Janitor*. Supporting roles in *Obsession, Heartburn* . . . You think she could tell me anything about Morty Kronenburg? You think I ought to talk to her?'

'I think you ought to find her.'

Encouraged by Kev Jackson's eager silence, I explain the plan.

He finds me Elaine, where she is, what she does, who she's with. I tell him whatever he wants to know about Morty Kronenburg, Terry Chimes, about Leisurevision, about the millions of feet of shiny celluloid, about the glossy secrets of the cutting room floor. Anything he wants.

'Okay, I'll buy it,' he says. 'Elaine. Elaine Keenan. I've got some numbers I can call. Give you a progress report in a week. Now . . . you mind if I ask you some questions straightaway. Tell me about Morty and those Americans.'

'Anything in particular?'

'Where they got the money for a start.'

I tell him a bit about Morty and Scazz and the little men in suits. Faint noises of static crackle down the line. 'They did *that*?' Kev asks at one point.

'If you think I'm lying, Kev, we can stop right here.'

'No,' Kev Jackson says with gratifying humility, 'I don't think you're lying, but . . .' I talk some more. He listens.


The late Seventies: my tornado years. An interview Elaine and I granted to *Adult Video World* circa 1978 gauges the febrile tenor of the times. Beneath the caption 'THE ADULT FILM WORLD'S HOTTEST COUPLE' the two of us are pictured seated in the front room of the Queensway flat, the shot taken from the doorway to give an impression of endless rolling carpet. Elaine – languid, wearing a see-through, peach-coloured camisole – confides that she is negotiating for a 'major' Hollywood project; I announce sternly that I am poised to enter a collaboration with 'Harry' Pinter. It was the sort of thing you said to *Adult Video World* in those days, back when Morty really was having discussions with Ken Russell and Roger Vadim about a script of mine with the working title of *God: The Movie*. I forget who was to play the starring role, but John Belushi had certainly been marked down for a cameo appearance as the Pope.

The money, of course, came from abroad. The English market lay dead, snuffed out by censorship and timid investors, Soho was in retreat as the council cracked down on the film theatres and the bookshops and the rents flew up. Morty made a few low-budget features for the home market around this time under the general title of *Adventures* (*Adventures Of A Teenage Girl, Adventures Of A Travelling Salesman*): in their decorous flashes of breast and thigh lurked only a scintilla of lubricity. But if England slumbered, the Continent was waking up. By 1977 Franco had been dead for two years and you could smuggle film canisters in through the border run to Spain, where six months later they were shown in Madrid art cinemas while armies of mantilla-clad matriarchs protested noisily in the foyer. *Academia Spanko!* was showing in Torremolinos when Elaine and I spent a week there in 1980. The French, of course, took everything they could buy. Where Morty nosed radically ahead of his time was in forging connections with the Eastern bloc. He had a Hungarian distributor as early as 1976 and there was even an implausible exchange scheme, fixed up through the Russian embassy, whereby Morty, masquerading as a fellow-travelling educational publisher, supplied sealed parcels of 'textbooks' in exchange for propaganda histories of the Second World War and enormous subsidies.

I came across the *Adult Video World* interview only the other day. It seems so obviously fraudulent, so self-evidently self-deluding, that one can only marvel at the lame, pitiable intelligence that shepherded it into print. Nevertheless, it is an authentic document.

'So, Martin, tell us how you went about scripting *Imbroglio*?'

'How does a script get written? Some words. Some tinkering. Some more words. Some more tinkering. How long is a piece of string?'

'And now the word on the street is there's a chance of an American deal?'

'Well, we're not counting any chickens, but let's just say that it's next stop Sunset Strip.'

Subsequently the adult film world's hottest couple were photographed holding hands, staring out of the window at the wilds of Kensington Gardens, examining a framed copy of the screen-writing award presented to me by *Adult Video World* for my work on *Manhunter*. My chief memory, though, is of Elaine picking a quarrel with the interviewer, an inoffensive, toupee'd thirty-year-old named Harold Dakin.

'If you don't mind, Martin, I'd like to ask you a few – uh –

personal questions which our readers are keen to know the answers to. Now, your lady Elaine . . . I take it this is a very special relationship in your life?'

At this juncture Elaine slid off the sofa on to the floor and enquired, 'Do you want me to get my tits out?'

'I don't quite . . .'

'No, for the interview, I mean. I mean, why don't I get my tits out and you could take some pictures? There's him as well. He could get out his cock.'

'I'm not . . .'

'I mean, we could do it right here on the rug if it would help the interview.'

They loved it, of course. Elaine was described in the piece as 'smouldering' and 'temperamental'. After Dakin had gone, I said, 'He was only asking questions.'

'Yes, well there are questions and questions. I can just about take stuff about sex scenes and *exposing your baddy*, but special relationships? Forget it, I quit.'

'You needn't take it personally.'

'I needn't? How the fuck else am I supposed to take it? Oh baby, Harold Dakin with that bloody wig falling over his ear and having to write everything down in capitals and that drooling photographer. It could all be an enormous joke, only then it isn't a joke at all.'

For some reason this exchange sticks in my memory.


We move on now: history comes tumbling randomly out of the opened locker. I sell the place in Queensway, dull now and cheerless, buy another one in West Kensington. I sell the other place in Newbury – I never went there anyway – and buy another in Salisbury. I sell the Aston Martin and buy a Lagonda. I lose heavily on all these transactions, but it doesn't seem to matter. 'The money's all there, Martin,' Morty breathes whenever that vulgar subject is mentioned, 'the money's all there.' And the money *is* all there, all of it. Morty and Terry Chimes, by this stage, are grandly opulent beings, weekend in the Seychelles, think about buying Scottish castles, Irish salmon farms, Welsh mountains. The first Mrs Kronenburg gives way to the second, the second Mrs Kronenburg to the third. There are accountants, lawyers, estate agents, stockbrokers, telling us to spend money, to maximise assets, to upgrade our investments. Not to be out-done, I give Elaine a cheque book and a Peter Jones expense account, come home one day to find the flat strewn with gift-wrapped parcels: stereo systems, cookers, fridges, clothes, and Elaine sitting amid them like a child in a toyshop. 'What did you buy all this for?' I ask, not unkindly. 'I don't know,' she says, 'I just wanted to. Do you mind?' 'Of course not,' I tell her. Later I haul the collection up to the loft, inventory it and calcu-late the bill. It comes to £11,000. It sits there for a year until I instruct Crazy Rodney to take it away and sell it.

I do other things. I bring home travel-agents' brochures and instruct Elaine in the catechism of the high-powered inter-national tourist.

'Mykonos?' 'No.' 'Madagascar?' 'No.' 'Java?' 'If you like.' I do like, I like very much. Overcoming this initial reluctance, we go on long, aimless, sun-drenched excursions. We traverse Samarkand, we sidle beneath avenues of lamp-post-high rhodo-dendrons in the foothills of the Himalayas, take pot-shots at wildebeest from the back of a jeep scuttling through the veldt. It is all very expensive, all very odd. Back home I razor pictures out of the *National Geographic* with a Stanley knife, plot new forays, establish fresh locations. Sometimes in these vagrant trawls through distant continents I explore the business angle. I go to Hamburg and check out the porn *kinos* and the latest sex hardware in the Beate Uhse shops. I traipse through the stacked warehouses of Amsterdam, piled high with technicolor pudenda. I attend lavish promo launches in Munich preview cinemas, nod my head sadly over the on-screen thrash and regret that it won't do for the British market. They all know Morty, these serious German pornographers with their designer suits, these fresh-faced Dutch sex traders with their university degrees and their MBAs. 'Herr Kronenburg,' one tells me at a trade convention in West Berlin, '*ist ein grosse* libertarian.' I listen to the chatter about the latest victory in the censorship war, the latest feminist assault, shake my head, collect my plane ticket, fly back to an older, prohibitive world.

I do more things, different things. I give parties, grand parties, expensive parties. At the place in Fulham, sometimes, or at Tramp's, Xenon, Stringfellows, whatever the latest fashionable hotspot is. Everybody comes. Morty comes, Terry Chimes comes, and their impossible women. The industry is there, of course (it's called an industry now: it has trade papers in which Morty, Terry and I are occasionally profiled), the grizzled veterans from Fifties Soho, the starlets, the moneymen up for the night from their Essex hideaways, but also other people. Pop people. Morty's East End frighteners. The odd footballer, page three girl, darts player, snooker ace. And still, mysteriously, it is affordable, still it is there. It is at this point in my life that, for the first time, I am unable to comprehend how much money I am earning. This fact is visited on me one Sunday morning in 1977 when I attempt to open the top drawer of the bedside table, in which I am accustomed to store loose change, credit-card counterfoils and the like. The drawer is wedged shut with fifty-pound notes. Taken out and counted – a surprisingly laborious task – it realises £1700. 'What do I do with this?' I demand of Elaine, marching into the bathroom where she sits amid ski-runs of lather examining her toenails, and depositing a fan of notes on the mat. 'Take it round to the bank.' 'No, you have it.' 'No, I don't want it. You have it.' We compromise by spending half of it. On lunch. In Paris.

Raging, restless years. *Intimate Strangers* and *Love in a Void*. *Thrash*, *Splash* and *Confessions of a Sex Maniac*. Years of change, both in Dean Street and Tin Pan Alley. Punk rock arrives and suddenly Terry Chimes and I are spending three nights a week in clamorous holes in the ground off Oxford Street listening to the Clash, the Jam, the Damned, Buzzcocks. Bobby Dazz and the Sugarlumps are jettisoned from the Grunt Records roster in favour of the Crabs, the Cut-throat Razors and the Bicycles from Space. Briefly we are punk prophets, New Wave impresarios. Morty thinks about making *The Great Rock 'n' Roll Swindle* with Malcolm McLaren, turns the idea down; the Sex Pistols do, however, get to play a couple of tracks on *Oh Bondage Up Yours*, a short that Morty made around this time, and Sid, always hard up for a bob or two, had a cameo in *Leather Rat*.

Raging, restless years. I sell the place in West Kensington, dull now and cheerless; buy another one in Bishop's Park. I sell the place in Salisbury – I never went there anyway – and buy another in Winterbourne. I sell the Lagonda and buy a Ferrari. Morty and Terry Chimes, by this stage, are even more grandly opulent beings, weekend on Martha's Vineyard, think about buying French chateaux, Greek islands. Where is the money coming from? Sometimes, during the course of modest, day-long lunches and drinking sessions, Terry Chimes and I ask ourselves this question. There seems no ready solution. We make *Blood Feud, Slash, Trash* and *Organ-grinder*. And in the intervals of this restless, rackety existence there is Elaine.

I do mad things with Elaine. I recall a conversation from around this time. Early summer. Late morning. The day gapes before us.

'So what do you want to do? Sex?'

'No.'

'Food?'

'No.'

'There's five hundred quid in the drawer. We could go and blow it at the races.'

'*No.*'

Try again, more circumspectly.

'There's a new outfit in Paris Morty got a letter from, asking about the export situation. We could fly over there, check them out, stay the night and come back in the morning.'

'No.'

'Terry Chimes is making a video with some new band he's found, halfway up a mountain in Scotland. We could fly up *there*, check *that* out, stay the night and come back in the morning.'

'No.'

'We could get Crazy Rodney to take us to Hackney dog track . . .'

'No, for fuck's sake.'

Try again, more cravenly.

'So, tell me what you'd like to do. Tell me what you'd like to do and we'll do it. Anything. Anywhere. Think about it.'

She thinks. I wait. Rio de Janeiro? Some new, unprocurable drug? Nothing? Eventually she says, 'I'd like to get in the car and go to Oxford for the day. I'd like to have afternoon tea somewhere in the country. With scones and jam. And I'd like to go in a punt. You can take me.'

Incredibly, we pursue this unprecedented course. We take the Ferrari and proceed at a gentle pace down the A40. Unflustered, I negotiate the complex local traffic system. We examine the cool greenery of college lawns, silent in the afternoon shade, nimbly evade the skidding cyclists in the Broad, peer into the windows of Blackwell's bookshop, mingle with loud, confident under-graduates on the riverbank. Later, as we cruise back along the Westway to help Morty entertain a couple of East End money men the expedition takes on otherworldly shapes and pro-portions, becomes wreathed in mystical trappings, an Alice-in-Wonderland trip deep into some wholly fantastic bolt hole. The incident is never referred to again.


Sometimes, early in the morning when the haggard light spilled out over the eaves of Dean Street, Morty grew serious.

'I mean, what do you think about all this, Martin?'

'All this?'

'The books. The films. The mail order shots. The chicks who'll sit there at the other end of a phone and tell you they'll eat you for five quid an hour.'

'It's a living.'

'Sure, it's a living. Did I ever tell you about my mother, Martin? Lives in a retirement home now at Ponders End. I go see her on Saturday afternoons. She thinks I'm a chartered accountant. Well, I *am* a chartered accountant, but that's not the point. You remember my kid? I brought him to Terry's barbecue that time. He thinks I run a toy company. He's four-teen. I found a copy of *Bouncers* in his room the other day. How do you think I felt about that?'

'I imagine you felt pleased and proud, Morty. I hope you did.'

'Did I *fuck*? I tore it up and threw it away. Plus I stopped his allowance for a month . . . What I'm trying to say, I suppose, is . . . What I mean is, do you believe in God, Martin?'

The question arose periodically in our line of business. Terry Chimes had once asked it of me immediately prior to his departure inside a massage parlour in Wardour Street. Cindy Lu Win had once asked it between takes on a film called *Jungle Frenzy*.

'It's best not to think about it.'

'Uh huh. I think about it *all the time*. I do. When we're on a shoot. When we're tying up a deal. Night times. That time last week when we were trying to get Katy, er Julie, . . . that time we were trying to get Julie to go down on the guy who was . . . I was thinking about it all the while, thinking, what does God think about this? What will God do to me because of this?'

'God's tolerant, Morty.'

'Jesus, don't give me that, Martin, don't give me that liberal crap. Ever. You ever read the Bible, Martin? *Our* Bible. Have you any idea what God does to people who don't shape up? Even to people who're just minding their own business. You ever read about Job?'

'He was the man who scratched himself with a piece of pot?'

'Sure, Job. Job was just sitting there one day looking out over his vineyard and suddenly God comes along and really fucks him up. I mean really screws him. And he wasn't even doing anything. "The unmerited suffering of the good man." That's what the books call it. Now if God can do that to Job, what can he do to me?'

'Perhaps Job had done things the Bible never revealed. Perhaps it was simply reparation?'

'Listen, Martin, you don't get my point. Job was just an ordinary guy. Okay, maybe he fooled around a little, maybe he coveted his neighbour's ox – we don't even know if he had a neighbour. We're none of us perfect. Job's sins must have been, well, *marginal*. But that doesn't save him. God just comes along and walks all over him.'

'It was a long time ago.'

'Jesus, Martin, don't you understand about religion? As far as God's concerned it was last week, yesterday. The rules don't change. Nobody ever renegotiated the commandments. Now, take a look at me. I make dirty films. I print dirty magazines. I got a barracks full of flats down in the East End – shit-heaps, most of the tenants are pensioners – and I never do any repairs and I raise the rent three times a year. I have half-a-dozen, a dozen people owe me money and if the interest doesn't come in on the first of the month I send Crazy Rodney round with a sledgehammer. I had a guy's arm busted last week. Do you think that's bad?'

'Pretty bad.'

'I'm unfaithful to my wife and I'm ashamed to tell my kids what I do for a living. I'm telling you, Martin, sometimes I lie awake at night just imagining what's it going to be like up there, just wondering what it is that God's going to do to me.'

Morty's guilt. At the time Morty's guilt seemed merely fanciful, a half-humorous gloss, the buccaneer's momentary regret at the pall of smoke rising over the burned-out port, the ravished doxy and the jemmied casket, as the Jolly Roger flaps in the breeze and the pirate galleon sweeps on into the sunset. But what about my guilt? The guilt of the accessory, I suppose, the bosun's diminutive mate who creeps up to the strongbox after everyone else has taken their share and is last in the line for the ravishing. Guilt nevertheless, and just as fit for retribution. Sometimes I lie awake too, just imagining what it's going to be like up there, just wondering what it is that God's going to do to me.

The thing of horror sits four feet away on top of the video. It came first thing this morning. So far I've played it through three times, with breaks for coffee, cigarettes and restless, edgy stares out of the window. Provenance London, typewritten name and address, postmark scuffed into anonymity. At first I thought it was one of Morty's showreels, a negligent secretary using an old mailing list, but it wasn't, *Christ* no, it wasn't at all.

Shot in colour, with good lighting and deft camerawork, which is to say that the close-ups don't waver and there is accurate panning to and from the action. Unlike the photographs, somebody subscribed for a lavish set: acres of bedroom, fluffy carpets. A brief trawl past an open window discloses neat, rolling gardens. The film is a standard surprised-by-a-stranger short. It begins with a few establishing shots: the room, landscaped from the doorway, the bed with its casually ruffled sheets, dressing table. After perhaps ten seconds spent straining to hear the soundtrack I realise that there isn't one. This is one of those jokey, money-saving ones they made in the mid-Seventies using captions. Sure enough, just as the saucy, fur-coated blonde steps in through the door the first of them slots into focus. HOME EARLY FOR A CHANGE. The girl smirks into the camera, jinks the fun-fur inch by inch off her shoulders and drops it on to the carpet to reveal – a touch improbably – a scarlet camisole and stockings. Removing the camisole takes a good two minutes (TIME TO RELAX) and there is an interesting diversion with a hairbrush. I take a good look at the girl's face as she does this: the standard minor actress's grin, off-centre, stultified, masking layers of unconquerable resentment. Naked, finally, monster breasts cradled in pudgy dairymaid's hands, she plumps herself down on a chair by the dressing table.

There the camera leaves her, angling off to the window where, sure enough, a burly oaf in white overalls is leering away through the rungs of a stepladder (NOT ALONE!). After this I could write the shooting script myself: the anguished gesticulations, the feigned surprise, the scrabbling at the glass (I HAVE TO TALK TO YOU), the meticulous coupling. Whoever shot it was a stylist in his or possibly her way, a subtle user of props (the bedside candlestick over which the camera lingers, the light bulb which detonates at a crucial moment). The conclusion, in which the couple lie spent and exhausted on the bed while the camera tracks over discarded rose petals on the white carpet, released an odd, elegiac note.

You will have anticipated the conclusion. The window cleaner was me. Worse, I remember nothing. For a moment I cast around in my memory for an odd fragment or two, those tiny pieces of rubble which might somehow be fashioned to authenticate this vast, appalling edifice, but there is only bare, level terrain. Tearfully I wind back the last minute or so of the tape and watch it again, see myself roaming effortlessly and with Herculean attack through this past which I never knew existed, this unimagined secret life. Afterwards I curl up on the sofa in a tight, foetal ball. Outside the rain falls endlessly.

# Part 2

EXTRAORDINARY THINGS CONTINUE to happen. This lunchtime in the City Gates Fat Eric, after various achingly polite preliminaries, asked me to lend him three hundred pounds. I declined. This afternoon as I sat anxiously rewinding the window-cleaner tape for the umpteenth time I discovered a second and yet more indirect request, specifically a copy of *Brides* magazine wedged down the side of the sofa. I took this away and hid it. Later on Suzi says, 'Have you seen a magazine I left in the lounge?'

'What sort of magazine?'

'It's called *Brides*,' Suzi says without apparent self-consciousness. 'Have you seen it?'

'No. I haven't seen it.'

Later on, looking up from her marking, Suzi says, 'Do you know how old I am, Martin?'

'Thirty. Thirty-one.'

'Thirty-two. Do you know what that means?'

'Tell me.'

'It means I have to start deciding about things. It means I have to start deciding about my *career*, whether I ought to carry on what I'm doing, whether I ought to do something else.'

Such utterances are readily decoded.

Suzi goes on, 'About my career. About *babies*. Do you know what it's like to be thirty-two and not be married? I saw a girl I used to be at school with today in the city. Three children and the eldest is twelve. Do you know how I felt about that?'

'Tell me.'

'No,' says Suzi, 'you tell me. You're the one who's so bloody clever. What do you think I've spent the last two years doing? Why do you think I've stayed here?'

Oddly there is no rancour in this. Suzi says reminiscently, 'Do you know why I went into teaching? Because I liked children. I mean, *liked* children. Not just didn't mind having them around, or wanted to form their characters. That's what a lot of teachers want to do: they want to form kids' characters. I don't. I just *like* children. Do you know when I was sixteen, when I was going out with Adrian, all I could think about was getting married and having children. Live in a house like this and see Adrian off to the Norwich Union every morning and have children. There'd be three of them . . .'

'Suzi . . .'

'Three of them,' Suzi says firmly, 'two girls and a boy. And I'd call them Tom and Ceridwen and Natasha . . .'

'Suzi, will you just . . .'

'Tom because of that children's book *Tom's Midnight Garden* . . . Did you ever read that when you were a kid? Ceridwen because mother came from Wales and that was her grandmother's name. And they'd all be terribly clever and do well at school and I'd be terribly proud of them. And you, you just . . .'

'Suzi,' I say, 'Suzi. You don't even like me.'

'No,' she says, 'I don't, do I? I've been living here for two years and I must have been to bed with you two hundred times and I don't even like you.'

'What about the others? What about Bob and Marcus and Justin? Did you like them?'

'I don't know. I haven't a clue. You don't know what it's like, do you? Being a girl. Having tits and blonde hair. Suddenly there are all these men wanting to go to bed with you, and you . . . well, it's just something you do. You have a boyfriend and he takes you places. Do you understand?'

'I understand.'

'No, you don't,' Suzi says patiently. 'You don't understand at all. I'm thirty-two and I want to have a baby and I've been wasting my time here for two years and you don't understand at all.'

Later, after she has gone out, the telephone rings on endlessly in the hall. I stand there in the darkness for a moment cradling my hand over the receiver, think better of it, turn away.


'Do you want to stay for the second half?'

'I ought to make that phone call.'

'It would be a pity to miss the violin piece.'

'I suppose it would.'

'In any case I just went and looked at the telephone kiosk and there's a queue.'

'Yes.'

Somewhere in the recesses of panelling above our heads a bell rang shrilly. Nearer at hand two men in evening suits who had been speaking to each other with disagreeable emphasis raised their heads and then lowered them abruptly. The smell of cigar smoke hung heavily on stagnant air. Elaine stood examining me with the air of a child convinced that some treat, long unreasonably denied, might still be won through sheer persistence. 'Make sure you're still here when I get back,' she said finally.

Returning to the Wigmore Hall after a ten-year absence brought back older memories, of a kind not usually associated with such places. Happily, they were not those of familiarity – the decor changed now and anonymous, the framed portraits scarcely remembered – but of past association, the whole conveying an air of threatened gentility, liable to sink at any moment beneath an encroaching, vulgar tide, but until that time still capable of keeping its head narrowly above water. Dark panelling, the raised dais strewn with chairs, the glimpse here and there of piled programmes and fussing officialdom – all these suggested a school prize-giving, hedged about with all manner of pleasurable anticipation and incidental spectacle. But there were older memories too, accumulated in childhood, prompted now by the discarded instruments propped up against chairs, sheet music flapping against its wire supports, harsh concert-hall light: memories of my father commenting with his usual asperity on an amateur performance in St Andrew's Hall, or seen himself on the edge of a remote and crowded chorus. Rehearsed and brought out again in this way, these associations had the effect of undermining present reality. The hall with its cavernous ceiling, the Wigmore habitués in Dickensian subfusc, the conductor with his white tie – all this was an insubstantial pageant wheeled out to impress case-hardened tourists. It was my father in his shabby dinner-jacket, showing his teeth as he sang, who was real.

Standing at the entrance to the foyer, the crowd first thickening and then falling away into a succession of tightly ordered queues, one could establish a perspective on the apparent chaos. Seen at this remove the throng of concert-goers was no longer random, but instead took on recognisable shapes and divisions, was transformed into tightly knit centres of conversation, each grimly maintained against knots of turbulence, or single figures, armed with cigarettes and wine glasses, staking out a patch of personal territory. Beyond, a darkened corridor hung with photographs led to the street. Here, deaf to the clamour, a commissionaire sat drinking tea out of a mug.

Elaine came back carrying two glasses of wine. She said, 'I was the only person in the ladies who wasn't speaking Polish.'

'Did you try them in Russian?'

'That's not even funny.'

Leaflets, scattered here and there over the seating area, piled up in foot-high bundles at the door, bore out this remark. Their tone was unambiguously menacing, the images they evoked — workers massing behind shipyard gates, tanks crawling over the white country — uncomfortably out of place amid the genteel furnishings, as if I had discovered one of Morty's magazines in a nursery. On this dark November evening the concert preliminaries had been solemn. Two Poles, uncomfortable in hand-me-down English clothes, spoke hastily of the situation in Gdansk. An academic from the University of London discussed possible government responses. The dull English faces watched impassively. Afterwards Elaine had heard a woman say, 'It's all very sad, but I don't see that there's anything we can do.'

Convened at short notice, for the Polish crisis had risen suddenly to claim the attention of the public, the night's audience was appropriately polyglot. Shabby expatriates, their arms queerly folded high up their chests, lingered in ones and twos near their seats. A few Polish aristocratic ladies of elderly vintage sat in state on cane chairs near the foyer, attended by a woman who claimed to be secretary to the government in exile. It was to this group and its paraphernalia that the eye returned: a vista of raised, beaky faces, silent gravity, the lorgnettes archaic even for the Wigmore Hall, the effect at once alien and historical, a Cracow drawing room of the last century mysteriously transported into the present day. An elderly man, previously half obscured as he disposed of a coffee cup, shuffled hesitantly forward, his eyes straining in recognition.

Elaine said, 'It's Mr Tovacs.'

I had not at this point met Mr Tovacs, or even seen his picture, yet there was about him a disconcerting air of familiarity, as if one knew all that it was convenient to know and that a common ground conducive to dialogue already existed. Mr Tovacs was at this stage in his long career quite a well-known man. He conducted intermittently a small, cosmopolitan literary annual, seldom seen in bookshops, but mentioned favourably in newspaper arts pages, but he was better known as an obituarist, the chronicler of hectic artistic lives lived out in pre-war Central Europe. There was about these memorials a tangible glamour, deriving not so much from the choice of subject – mostly minor surrealist or expressionist painters – as from the strong scent of Mr Tovacs' own personality. Without being stated in so many words, his past affiliations were sharply apparent. You could not read a page of his billowing, un-English prose without deducing that its author had known Firbank, watched Brancusi at work, or devilled for Picasso. Obscurely, these hints had the effect of diminishing the importance of his subjects: it was Mr Tovacs who had survived, you felt, rather than the acquaintances of his youth.

Seen at close range he seemed a curiously generalised figure: the shock of white hair, stained yellow at the fringes with nicotine, rising so stiffly that it might have been suspended by invisible wires, brooding features, an oddly pained expression suggesting much inner disquiet. Fattish, giving the impression of a once sturdy frame run to seed, dressed almost wholly in black, he looked every inch an émigré, uncomfortable, absorbed, the thirty years or so spent in a foreign country clearly of no account when set against the sharper outlines of the past. Examining him, you thought, inevitably, of fictionalised portrayals of an English exile, of seedy legations in the Bayswater Road, World Service broadcasts and carefully nurtured, impotent resentment. There was something quaint, too, about his demeanour, something trammelled, the apparent vitality of his gestures – his first action was to kiss Elaine soundly on both cheeks – rebuffed by small, shuffling movements, the sense of innate feebleness.

He said, 'This is a memorable evening, a memorable evening. I was dining with Professor Sikorski – he is connected with the London University – and he told me about it, so of course I came straightaway. A memorable evening. Perhaps, who knows, I shall write something about it if I am allowed, if I am permitted? Of course, a great many people are interested in my poor country, a great many, and that is to be applauded. But there is also great ignorance. There is also that English habit of making a judgement not necessarily connected with the facts.'

Deconstructed, its key fragments detached from more superfluous materials, this speech, as I was later to discover, provided several clues to Mr Tovacs' character. It conveyed the assumption of his own centrality while hinting at his connection with people of more formal influence and importance (Professor Sikorski was a well-known Polish expert). It advertised his literary credentials while canvassing the possibility of exclusion and even censorship, an intrigue that neither of his listeners could be expected to fathom. Above all it placed his own position beyond doubt: that of a guest, caught up in a family crisis, who knows what ought to be done, but is uncertain of the ability of his hosts – well-meaning but ignorant people – to take the necessary steps.

Mr Tovacs went on, 'This Walesa, this trade-unionist. You will not think it possible, perhaps, but I knew his father. This was before the war, of course. Everything in Poland is before the war. The man was a shoemaker, a village shoemaker. I offered to go to the BBC, to go on television and tell this story, but no, they were not interested. They did not think it *newsworthy*.'

Elaine said, 'I remembered the pianist who played in the first half. Isn't he your protégé?'

'The young man who performed the Schumann study? He is a friend, nothing more. His mother is a friend of my wife. It may be that you met him at the studio.'

A faint shiftiness came over Mr Tovacs as he made these observations, as if he feared that in revealing the existence of a wife, a studio and his connection with Elaine he had somehow given himself away, disclosed some part of his personality that were better concealed.

Elaine said, 'Is Jerry here?'

Mr Tovacs said with an effort, 'She is here. That is, I am expecting her to be here.'

It was not a tactful question. Mr Tovacs made one or two more shuffling motions with his feet and then relapsed into silence. I reflected on the information which the previous few moments had yielded up. I was not at all surprised to find that Elaine knew Mr Tovacs. Elaine knew a great many people from the social category in which Mr Tovacs and his kind reposed, the category of minor poets, impresarios, failed street actors. Invited to parties at the loft, where they stood awkwardly in groups maintaining a morose, silent solidarity, they annoyed Morty beyond measure. 'Fucking *artists*,' he would say. 'Just a load of read-my-poems, pay-my-bills, fucking *artists*.'

The bell rang a second time, now with greater effect. A musician or two began to wander intently across the dais. Away behind us beyond the foyer a door slammed and there was a sudden blare of traffic. I thought of Morty's pinched, eager face, the light spilling out over the desk-tops in Dean Street, of restless days and telephone calls. A tall girl in a scarlet mackintosh came into the foyer and began to pick her way slowly through the crowd towards us.

Elaine said, 'Jerry's here.'

The girl said brusquely, but with an air of having rehearsed the words, 'I had to take a fucking taxi all the way from Finsbury Park. Six pounds and twenty pee. You could have told me where the place was and not had me screeching round like some fucking tourist.'

Mr Tovacs did not seem put out by this assault. He said, 'That was very extravagant. You could have taken a bus. I am always telling you to take a bus. You cannot expect me to give you the money, you know that.' He turned to us. 'Jerry is an American. You will have noticed how Americans always pretend that they do not know where places are in London.'

There was an unmistakeable air of authority in this, the hint of some contract unfulfilled. Jerry shrugged. 'You could have told me anyway. You knew I was going to be there all afternoon.' Nearer at hand she seemed older than when moving towards us: creased in concentration, her face lost its youthful lines and grew indeterminate, caught somewhere between girlhood and middle age. She said, 'Anyway, it all worked out. You could at least give me the money for the fucking cab.'

By now there were only a few people moving back from the foyer; seated heads stretched before us back to the stage. Mr Tovacs said sharply, 'I shall do no such thing. And I will not permit you to talk in this way.' He gave Elaine a stiff little bow. 'I must apologise for this. It has spoiled a most interesting conversation.'

'Interesting, asshole,' Jerry said, by now thoroughly ill-humoured. Mr Tovacs ignored her. 'We shall meet again,' he said, 'and in more agreeable circumstances.' As he moved off towards his seat, not looking behind him, the girl following unwillingly in the rear, I caught the first brief hint of exclusion that was to dog my dealings with Mr Tovacs, the thought that I had intruded into an atmosphere, at once tense yet containing its own rules and ordinances, in which it was better not to linger. There was something unusual about the way in which he dealt with the American girl, although at this stage I knew nothing of their relationship, a deep-rooted irritation untempered by conventional courtesies, something which rose now through the cigar smoke and the declining hum of conversation and suggested deeper antagonisms. Obscurely it established Mr Tovacs in my mind as somehow a figure of power, buttressed by inner resources which it was impossible to fathom, bland and emollient, but ready to turn nasty if provoked.

I said to Elaine, 'Let's get out of here.'

'I thought you wanted to stay.'

'Just do it,' I said. There was a sudden burst of random, unfocused applause from beneath the stage. 'Just do it.'

Outside the streets were dark and empty. Light blazed out of the silent shopfronts. In the odd hour before the pubs closed and the theatre crowds departed the city lay dead, a few buses chugging in mid-lane, taxis shunted up at the roadside, sleeping traffic. Often at these times, late at night in the loft at Dean Street, cruising with Morty through the grim dawns, I played tricks on this silent, inanimate world, took the houses in the grey squares back a century and a half and populated them with East India nabobs and John Company merchants, put powdered footmen at the door, rearranged the road beyond. Altering them in this way, clearing the weeds out of rank, jungly gardens and sending nursemaids and gentlemanly children scurrying around them, somehow gave character to these buildings, a sense of proper function. The thought that where Arab banks and carpet showrooms now fought for space, infants had skirmished and Regency bucks hobnobbed brought comfort of a sort.

Lolling in the taxi, resentment yielding now to an easier exhaustion, Elaine fitted snugly into this reinvented landscape, took her own place in the charade. Given flowing skirt, bonnet, parasol, she resembled the subject of a painting by Fragonard, displayed a naivety that was already compromised, an experienced eye that, amid the innocent trappings of swings and summer lawns, knew very well what it was about.

I said, 'Where did you come across him?'

'Tovacs? Oh, he knows everyone.' She pronounced it in the Irish way, 'uvryone'. 'He knows Morty. He probably came to a party at the loft. I don't remember.'

This in itself was not surprising. Plenty of queer people came to Morty's parties: advertising men, soap-opera queens, disc-jockeys. I had once seen a minor member of the Royal Family peering uncertainly through the throng. Mr Tovacs, the translator of Cocteau, Joyce's amanuensis if the accounts were true, must have been the queerest fish to swim into that dense and populous pool.

'What about the girl?'

'Jerry? Oh, just someone of Tovacs'. One of Tovacs' women. There's a bunch of them. They put his book together for him so they can go round saying they slept with a man who slept with Colette.'

'He sounds quite a guy.'

'You don't want to believe all that stuff,' Elaine said.

Later I was to hear similar estimates of Mr Tovacs, the hint that these widely advertised affiliations were largely bogus, that his motives as an editor in a publication given over to famous names were no more than those of the autograph hunter. For the moment he seemed a person of infinite resource, an impresario who had wandered on to some meagre, poorly lit stage to invest it suddenly with a cascade of light and sound. And, though there were other more urgent questions to be resolved, questions about my dealings with Morty, my relationship with Elaine, it was the image of Mr Tovacs which persisted as the taxi sped westward towards Kensington and Fulham and Elaine slept, an image at once precise and oddly suggestive. The conjuror had arrived, I realised, taken out his magic box and released a flight of exotic wildlife; older memories, taking in my father, self-absorbed and aloof among the distant chorus, moving nearer at hand to include Morty's face beneath the flaring light, resting evenly on an earlier life, long forgotten but now sharply in focus, in a landscape to which, after long exile, I had returned.


More photographs. I found them quite by chance in a steel tin, wedged shut with elastic bands, in the shed at the bottom of the garden. Not vivid genitalia, but family photographs, old sepia shots from the Twenties and Thirties, muddy greys and browns, placed there I suppose by my father at some remote point in time and then forgotten. Stylised, formal attitudes. My father in his early teens, hair scraped back and parted in the middle, standing self-consciously with his hand resting on a chair back. A middle-aged woman in a cloche hat holding a baby. A holiday party arranged awkwardly in a charabanc: none of the figures is recognisable.

With the photographs came other memorabilia: a folded sheet of newspaper, unfurled to reveal the front page of the *Daily Herald* of 6 June 1944; a caricature of a small, eager mannikin perched athwart a stack of boxes the better to wield a snooker cue and captioned 'Jack Benson plays a cunning shot', a joke on my father's comparative slightness; a programme from a football match between a Celebrity XI and RAF Fighter Command Europe, printed along the edge in my father's handwriting the words 'Lawton did not play'; a closely written sheet headed 'Films seen in 1941'. I looked at them for a while. They revealed a side to my father's life of which he had rarely spoken and of which, as a consequence, I was altogether ignorant. Marrying in middle age, uprooting himself from early environments, cutting himself adrift from the ties of family, he had managed without obvious effort to detach himself entirely from this former existence, had grown up, moved on, ignored whatever memories of these early days might have risen to disturb him. Rather than bringing him closer to view the effect, oddly enough, was to distance him yet further. There was a sense of exclusion about this carefully hidden treasure trove, the air of secrets, however innocent, kept purposely out of sight, aspects of my father's life which he wished quite deliberately to conceal. There was no place for me, I realised, here among these shabby mementoes, these evocations of a life lived out in my absence. The way was barred; the door shut firmly across the path that led back to my father's early life could not be re-opened.

Later I show Suzi the photographs. She looks at them with faint interest, as usual making comments that draw herself, however narrowly, into the subject at hand.

'Father used to wear his hair like that.'

'When did he stop?'

'He didn't. He says he's the last man in England who still has his hair parted in the middle.'

There is a faint, suspicious brightness about Suzi. She says eventually, 'Christopher rang today.'

'Christopher?'

'Christopher I used to go out with. You remember.'

'What did he want?'

'Just to have a chat. You know, catch up on old times. He's at the Norwich Union now. He's a *manager*.'

'Is that good?'

'He's got a *secretary*,' Suzi says.

Christopher telephones several times over the next three days, Christopher with his manager's job and his secretary. Hearing his voice I experience a faint twinge of phoney terror, like ghostly knocking heard a long way off.

A wet October here in Norfolk. Grey clouds drift in westward from the sea to hang low over the city, alternate with fierce, unexpected sunshine. Even here, twenty miles distant from the coast, the air harbours a faint tang of salt. With the clouds come the gulls: razorbills and sandpipers blown south from Jutland to perch on telephone wires and scavenge outside the fish-and-chip shops. Characteristic tokens of the Norwich autumn: overbright buses trawling the rainy streets, the scent of burning leaves, knots of blue-uniformed schoolboys. From nearer at hand come more specific signs of a changing season, an irrevocable shift in the pivot of the year: Suzi engrossed in her marking; Fat Eric and Kay back from an autumn holiday in Majorca, Torremolinos, Ithaca, wherever, the former plumper, sun-drenched, content, instigator and victor of a memorable wine-bar upset, the latter thinner, paler, more terrified. Norwich play a smattering of early-season games, canter over a set of newly promoted mediocrities, go down heavily at home to Liverpool, and the papers buzz with rumours that Kevin Flack is unhappy, won't sign a new contract and wants a transfer. Intrigued by Fat Eric's restless ventilation of these issues I agree to accompany him to the big pre-Christmas game against Manchester United. In Heigham Park the bowls and the tennis are over now, the old gentlemen and the bouncing housewives gone elsewhere and the gates locked at six. The streetlamps go on earlier. Early in the morning along The Avenues there are conkers all over the road, blown down from the big horse-chestnut trees during the night. I walk down there sometimes and pick them up, carry them back home and store them in jam-jars above the sink, get an odd, indulgent smile from Suzi.

Kev Jackson telephones once or twice: stray fragments of intelligence creeping down the wires. He says the publishers are paying for the calls. He thinks he might have known someone who might have known Elaine in the six months or so after the crash, thinks he might be able to find a phone number for one of her ex-flatmates. In return I convey scraps of speculation about Morty's private life, I advance a theory of Terry Chimes' bisexuality, I suggest that Crazy Rodney was 'misunderstood'. The hint, the pregnant deflection, the eventual compromise, 'integrity' lurking shyly in the background. He believes it all, a limitless, effortless gullibility.

In the afternoons I amble out into the countryside, through Trowse, Keswick, Intwood, Caistor-by-Norwich, along narrow roads hazily recalled from childhood where the hedgerows rear up on either side and ploughed fields stretch away as far as the eye can see, where there are quaintly overgrown pathways leading to forgotten churches smelling of damp and mildew, where the touch of a hand on the door sends woodpigeons panicking from their roosts above the stained-glass windows. Stoke Holy Cross, Hempnall, Brooke – small straggling villages, their origins proudly displayed in Pevsner and Ekwall, their forefathers asleep in the mouldering churchyards, full of reedy meres and rotting elm trees, sluggish tributaries veering off from the Wensum over the South Norfolk flat. Neatly tended village greens, blowsy shopfronts and decomposing thatch. Across country, out towards Brooke, the landscape turns bare and motionless, the silence broken only by a solitary tractor, a train heard a long way off, space peopled suddenly by an ancient on a bicycle, a loitering farmworker. Like a Thomas Hardy poem. Back along the Ipswich Road in the fading light the illusion is debunked: stretched traffic, the first neon signs of hotels and guest houses. Not like a Thomas Hardy poem. Autumn moves rapidly on now. The beech leaves lie piled up in Jessopp Road. Norwich beat Chelsea, lose to Southampton. Kevin Flack, dropped for the Southampton game, tells the *Eastern Evening News* that he is 'thinking seriously' about his career. I have long conversations with Fat Eric about money and opportunity (my money, his opportunity). I have longer conversations with Kay about violence and resignation (Fat Eric's violence, her resignation). I make long, unsatisfactory phone calls to Morty, most of which consist of me listening into a dead receiver while the wind whistles down the wire and Morty, prised eventually from some high-octane business roundtable, arrives to offer consolation. I watch Suzi, a fleeting, marginal presence now, down there on the edge of consciousness, arrive and then depart, depart and then arrive. It all feels very stretched, very thinly spread, this dim, low-key season, somehow exhausted and furtive. I lie awake at nights on my back, Suzi a slumbering, stertorous hump beside me, trying to bite the head off the twisting darkness. Fear, like a flashing blue light, its reflection ricocheting off the walls, rises effortlessly up to join me.

Snow fell overnight. Waking in the small hours I watched it floating gently down over the shrubberies and tiny gardens beyond the mansion block. By morning a level off-white blanket lay over the grass and the paths of asphalt.

At breakfast Elaine was fractious. She sat in the kitchen, hunched in a dressing gown, her hair untended, and drank tea resignedly. At length she said, 'Are you going in this morning?'

'Not unless Morty wants me.'

'He won't want you. He told me. You know how Morty is when he's after a deal, when he's after money.' She gave the word an unusual emphasis. 'Besides, he thinks you're losing interest.'

'Why should Morty think I was losing interest?'

Nearly four years had passed since Elaine and I had met in the studios at Dean Street. In that time I had grown used to her bewildering variety of moods. At first I had assumed that these proceeded out of an extreme sensitivity to circumstance: an ambiguous remark, a momentary diversion from some standard pattern of behaviour would be enough to infuriate her for hours or days. But there was something else, I saw, a part of her character which I had never been able to appease. Elated or downcast, confidential or remote, she still displayed an inner intransigence – varying in degree from ironic sympathy to out-right contempt – which was beyond the power of conciliation. Morty, curiously, possessed original views on this topic. 'Seen a lot of chicks like that one,' he said once, amid much crapulous bonhomie. 'Think about it, Mart. You spend the first fifteen years of your life growing up in some refuse heap and being shat on by your mum and dad. And then suddenly, wham, you look like a million dollars, you're five feet ten with torpedo tits and guys are literally begging you to sleep with them. So what hap-pens? You're pretty pleased with yourself – after all, you might not like all the guys, but at least you can pick and choose – but not *that* pleased. Ten to one says you spend the next fifteen years in a permanent sulk because you're not omnipotent.'

'And then what happens?'

'After you're thirty? That's when it gets really bad. Your tits cave in, your bum splays out, all the guys are just fucking you for old times' sake and you hate yourself for not having all the things you hated having when you had them.'

Pertinent though Morty's observations were, they had no prac-tical bearing on my feelings towards Elaine. These had long ago been frozen into sharp relief. I was, I assured myself, obsessed with her, while finding her – now more than ever before – intolerable.

Not looking up from the table she went on, 'He thinks you're lacking in *commitment*. He thinks the scripts you put in are too bloody boring for words. He thinks you laugh at him.'

It was not a new accusation. 'Morty knows where I stand.'

'Flat on your back. That's what Terry Chimes says.'

And so we bickered on, as the pale early sunlight diffusing over the snow gave it an egg-yolk sheen, as the central heating switched itself off and the room grew cold: a long, intimate disagreement at whose core lay not malice, but a gross unfamiliarity with temperament. Four years spent living hugger-mugger in West London flats, four years spent in Dean Street, or on location in odd parts of England and Europe had imposed, I thought, a false, effortless solidarity, disguising all manner of failed connections.

'Anyway,' Elaine said finally, 'at least I still seem to be working for my living.'

In these later days Elaine worked for a promotions agency in Newman Street. The job was not onerous, requiring her only to don exotic costumes and decorate merchandising stands, but she resented it inordinately. Like Faulkner in Hollywood, or Eliot in his bank, she was determined to give value for money while admitting the mundane nature of the task.

'What is it today?'

'God knows. Last week it was some new type of mineral water and I had to wear a headdress with a sort of lemon attachment. This week it's probably sanitary towels.'

She left shortly afterwards, gathering up her things in sharp, angry rushes, throwing on coat, scarf and hat without ceremony. After she had gone I wandered absently around the flat, examining the havoc of her departure: in the bedroom a tussock of spent tissues and a heap of underclothes, in the hallway half-empty coffee cups and a clutter of video cassettes. There were other discoveries. On the top shelf of the bookcase in the study I found one of Mr Tovacs' novels – *Incandescence*, an early one – and put it aside for future study. Then, as the pale winter morning wore on, I went into the front room and stood looking out over the empty tennis courts and the file of trees in the street below.

Alone in the flat, without occupation or interest, I had one infallible resource. It amused me to think of the other places I had inhabited in London, to subject them to an endless process of comparison in which there were no finite answers, but merely shifting points of view, an elaborate decor now surfacing to dislodge the memory of an inconvenient location, a leaky top-flat roof safely anaesthetising, in terms of awfulness, the remembrance of a musty basement. At thirty I was a veteran of London flatland. I had lived all over the western city, at first in Ealing, Acton Town, in queer maisonettes hunched in the shadow of the Westway, over takeaway restaurants in Hanger Lane. Later, as Leisurevision's activities had expanded, I had embarked on a remorseless process of betterment: moving steadily eastward, taking in Gunnersbury, Shepherds Bush and Hammersmith, before settling on Fulham, later more fashionable still, now designated simply an up-and-coming area. At present we lived in a sidestreet off the Fulham Palace Road, Bishop's Park not far away, the river dimly discernible through distant tree tops. I was immune to such places, the raw feeling of impermanence never quite dislodged by redecoration or long tenancy, always liable to be knocked back to the surface by a phone call for a bygone resident, the stack of unidentifiable post in the hall. Even here in a Fulham mansion block, where the flats changed hands at relatively long intervals, we still received three or four phone calls a week for people of whom we had no knowledge. Joe. Anne. Samantha. A Mr Perrick who had lived here in the 1960s. Someone called Karas. I used to wonder about this file of former tenants. Were their lives so chaotic, their homes so impermanent, I thought, that their friends had simply lost track of them, moved in a slow, vain pursuit forever two or three addresses behind? I imagined long, serpentine trails spread out all over London, a vast, spreading plant of fractured alliances and vain enquiry, letters piling up in abandoned hallways, telephones ringing on in silence. A few callers rang repeatedly, unconvinced by explanation or denial. Sometimes late at night a call came from overseas, crackling away on a fading international line. The request, conveyed by a halting African voice, was always the same: a Mr Solomon with whom the caller needed urgently to speak. We knew of no Mr Solomon, but the calls continued, sometimes pacific, resigned, at other times voluble and excited. Elaine had an uncanny ability to predict them. 'For Mr Solomon,' she would say sometimes if the phone rang around midnight. She was rarely wrong.

At about half-past ten Morty rang. He seemed subdued.

'How are you getting on with that script?'

'Which one? The one set in the girls' school? It's not above half finished.'

'Yeah, well, don't bother finishing it. Terry's backer's gone back to the States. And between you and me the only people he's likely to be paying money to in the next few months are lawyers.'

'I see.'

'We ought to talk,' Morty went on. 'There's things happening, things you ought to know about. You want to come and have lunch?'

'I should like to have lunch,' I said.

'Great. Well, be at my club about quarter to one.'

'Which club would that be?'

Morty named an address north of Oxford Street. 'It's a proper club,' he went on. 'Waiters and all that. Make sure you wear a tie.'

Morty seemed unabashed by these instructions. After he had rung off I went back into the lounge and sat leafing regretfully through a folder which contained the fragments of *Girls' School Party*: it seemed a pity to waste it. Later I put on a tie and set off through the heavy slush of Bishop's Park to the underground station.

Morty had not prospered since his bid for parliament a year and a half before. In the months after the General Election a Sunday newspaper had run a four-part exposé of his career to date, police had called at the studio in Dean Street, and there had been talk of an Inland Revenue investigation. These were minor problems, nimbly evaded, but they were the symptoms of a deeper malaise. Whether it was that older associates had run scared of this newfound notoriety, that unlooked-for commercial pressures had come to disrupt Leisurevision's easy ascent, or that in his search for fresh spheres of influence he had simply overreached himself, the Morty who emerged from this hectic, indiscriminate period in his life was a reduced and chastened figure. Two years before there had been a string of blonde receptionists at the loft, a party a month and a procession of transatlantic visitors. Now there was only Crazy Rodney to man the row of telephones and placate the printers' representatives, and the American businessman who called at Dean Street was a rare migrant, like some bizarre, brightly plumaged bird blown off course by high winds and disappointed by this small, arid garden. Morty did little overseas business now. There were still familiar callers. The northern cinema owners and the tape salesmen who had supported him in his early days continued to arrive, but there was about them a hesitancy, an unwillingness to commit themselves to long-term agreements and future projects. They thought Morty a risk, that, in the business jargon of the day, he sailed too close to the wind. Meanwhile the reels of unused celluloid tape lay piled up in the storeroom. There had not been a film made at Dean Street for a month and a half.

Morty's club reflected something of these reduced circumstances. It lay in a tiny mews off Portman Square. Its membership, drawn from the ranks of minor actors and obscure journalists, was undistinguished. Gloomy portals gave way to a glass cage where a porter sat smoking a cigarette, and a small, windowless cell lined with shabby armchairs. Here I found Morty conducting some transaction with a bald, elderly man.

'Paying my sub,' he explained, 'they like you to be regular here.'

We ate in a narrow first-floor dining room, looking out over the traffic. There were half-a-dozen other diners, wary middle-aged men occupied with newspapers or each other, a single resentful waitress. Morty, however, was unreasonably absorbed in his surroundings. 'You meet some pretty interesting people here,' he said at one point. 'You see that bloke over there? Used to read the news if I'm not mistaken.' Later he said, 'There's an MP comes sometimes. If he turns up today I'll introduce you to him.'

After lunch we went upstairs to a cramped, deserted smoking room filled with camera portraits of thirty or forty years previously. Morty's face brightened. 'Former members,' he said, tapping one of the glass frames. 'Know any of them, do you?' I looked for a while down the lines of heavy, dissatisfied faces.

None was recognisable. Eventually, high up on the right-hand side, I discovered the face of a minor novelist of the 1930s.

There was a small silver bell on the occasional table. Morty shook it confidently. Nothing happened. This seemed to depress him and he sank down heavily into an armchair. I looked at him for a moment. In his leather jacket and canvas trousers he seemed out of place amid the solidity of this faded world.

'How are things?'

Morty shook his head. 'Things are bad. Look, I know I haven't called you for a week or two, Martin, but it's because . . . I got a letter from the bank this morning. That's okay, I can handle that. But what about the next letter and the one after that? But it's not that, it's the . . .' Some weightier grievance floated before his eye for a moment and I watched him grasp at it. 'I went down the video mart this morning, you know, the one in Shaftesbury Avenue. Used to do a lot of business there. They used to take *Thrash* and stuff like that in fifties in the old days. Now it's all foreign stuff. Color Climax stuff that somebody's been through and wiped all the hard-ons off. In German and *not even any sub-titles*! And you know those import videos used to be expensive. Ten, fifteen quid. Well, they're selling them at six now.'

'What does Terry say?'

'Terry?' Morty waved his hand ambiguously in front of his face. 'Terry's . . . Look, Grunt are strapped for cash right now. That comeback album they did with the Express last month. Well, it was a complete turkey. They paid twenty grand to have it plugged on every radio station in the UK and it sold two thousand copies. That tartan gimmick just doesn't cut it any more. Plus Bobby Dazz wants to buy Lucille or whoever some more cosmetic surgery and he's sueing them for five years' unpaid royalties. So you can forget about Terry for the moment.'

Outside the window grey clouds were moving in from the west. The sky was dull and opaque. It was barely three o'clock, but already the streetlamps were going on.

'So what happens? What is it that's happening that I ought to know about?'

'Yeah, well, I'll tell you about that. Terry says that, well, never mind about Terry. You know Terry's got the clap again?'

'I didn't.'

'Straight up. Reckons it's that girl he brought to the party, the one who . . . Anyway, the thing is, you remember *Resurrection*?'

I nodded. A florid, elaborate screenplay, conceived two years previously at the height of our prosperity, it had seemed extravagant even then. The plot I remembered intimately: I had devised it myself. A notorious Victorian roué takes a young wife to satisfy his ever-more-libidinous urges. Inexplicably they fall in love. He is then struck by acute paralysis and dies. His wife, at first consoling herself with a succession of young men, mourns him earnestly. He then returns to earth as a ghost to confront her. They discuss the nice theological point as to whether one can have sex with a ghost. 'Only your love,' the spectre of wicked Sir George finally informs his bride, 'can make me rise again.'

'What about it?'

'Got a backer,' Morty said unexpectedly. 'At least I think I have. Or at least if he can't find all the money, then he knows people who can.' He shook his head doubtfully. 'How much do you reckon it would take to make *Resurrection*, Martin?'

I thought. In its original form *Resurrection* had been lavishly framed: a cast of twenty, multiple locations (including an implausible scene in which Sir George and his wife attend a *levée* at Windsor), myriad period costumes. At the very least, a fortnight's shooting time.

'Half a million.'

'I told him three-quarters. To be on the safe side,' Morty explained. 'But we'd have to trim it. Take out some of the fancy stuff.'

'The scene in the hot air balloon?'

'And that other bit, the bit at the court ball. We could trim that if it came to it . . .'

And so for twenty minutes we plotted happily. We made Sir George a country squire rather than a minor peer, we reduced the number of his wife's lovers from six to three, shifted the scene of their reconciliation from a felucca on the Nile to a punt on the Cam. We made the grand ball at which he had his fatal stroke a select dinner party, altered Sir George's passion for stag-hunting to a mania for stamp-collecting. It was easy work and we relished it. When we had finished, Morty said, 'I like that. The client'll buy it. Sex. History. Cutaways while the heroine takes off her crinoline, I like that. Maybe bring in some big names. Gladstone. Disraeli. That sort of thing. Find some place in the country to film it.' He looked at his watch. 'Jesus, Martin, I've got to go. Promised Terry I'd meet him at four. You feel like coming along?'

I shook my head.

'Uh huh. Right then, I'll catch you later.'

We wandered back along the narrow, linoleumed corridors, down the rickety staircase to the hall. Here in the glass cage the same porter still sat, still smoking a cigarette. A spirit of mild curiosity, which had lain dormant during the truncations and realignments of the previous half-hour, flared briefly into life once more.

'Who's the backer, Morty? Who's giving us the three-quarters of a million?'

Morty shrugged. 'Oh, some guy of Terry's. Some guy Terry picked up somewhere. An old guy, edits some book nobody's ever heard of. Foreign name. Tomas. Tovacs. Something like that. You ever heard of him?'

Once more the ratchet clicked slowly into place. 'Yes,' I said, 'I've heard of him.'

And for some reason I secreted this information inside me, not yet wanting to impart it to Elaine, and added it to my old worry about Morty and my new worry about Elaine, added it to the inklings of subterfuge and dissimulation which I had already detected and carried within me for a long time, seeing in these unexceptionable signs the certainty of some future reckoning, like faint trails of smoke seen across the horizon, a tiny crackle of distant thunder.

I came back to the flat to find that Elaine had preceded me. A dazzling metal-blue cape hung over a chair back. From along the hall came the sound of rushing water. Elaine lay in the bath reading a copy of the *Evening Standard*.

'What was it today? More mineral water?'

'Worse. Condoms. I had to wear this blue costume and be Captain Condom and stand in the middle of a room full of schoolkids telling them that sex was a healthy and meaningful experience.'

'Did they look as if they believed you?'

'They just looked spotty. Embarrassed and spotty. One of them tried to ask me out.'

'What did you say?'

'I was very naughty. I told him I liked it rough. I told him sex was about pain, not healthy and meaningful experiences. And then I gave him the supervisor's home number and told him that if he still wanted to go through with it he should ring in the evening and ask for Madame Domina.'

'Then what happened?'

'Oh, he just started apologising, you know how they do. But he was very sweet. He called me "Miss".'

I wandered back into the hall and to the telephone, where a series of messages had accumulated on the answer machine: messages from out-of-work actors who thought I could put in a word, casting agencies who wanted to ask me to lunch. Clearly the news of Morty's backer was out. As I bent down over the receiver it rang again.

'Martin? Morty. Something else I wanted to talk to you about.'

A great blare of noise washed over Morty's voice and faded away again.

'Where are you calling from?'

'Jesus, someplace Terry took me. The Bazooka Club. But listen . . . The thing about *Resurrection* is that we've got to move fast on this one, right? Development costs, site hire. It's going to need money up front. So basically I'm doing a debt recall. Everything that's gone out in the last two years has got to come back in. All of it.'

It was the ancient language of Dean Street. In times of plenty, distribute your surpluses in the hope that in times of hardship you might be able to call them back.

'Where do I come in, Morty?'

'It's . . .' There was another remote, clangorous eruption, as if somebody had dropped a tray a long way off. 'The thing is I want you to take tomorrow off and go and see Frank Fellatio.'

'I didn't know Frank still worked for you.'

'He doesn't. Not since *The Sword Swallower* back in '78. But he owes me two grand. I want you to take tomorrow off and go and get it.'

'Look, Morty . . .'

'Jesus, Martin. You know what I expect at a time like this? I expect a little loyalty. That's right, a little loyalty. Nobody's asking you to smuggle drugs, or beat up some old lady. Just go and see Frank and collect the two grand. Crazy Rodney'll come with you. A child of six could do it.'

'Look, Morty, I have things to do . . .'

'You know something, Martin? You disappoint me. You disappoint me a lot. Do I make myself clear?'

'You do, Morty. You make yourself perfectly clear.'

The voice blared on like some great implacable dog straining at the end of the leash. Eventually I put the phone down.

Elaine provided no comfort. Throughout her time at Leisure-vision she had maintained an air of grim nonchalance about Morty's activities which allowed little compromise.

'You know what Morty's like? If somebody owes him two thousand pounds, do you expect him to put an invoice in the post? You knew what Morty was like when you got into this. Do you really expect him to turn round and act like Mr Nice Guy?'

'But why me?'

'Jesus Christ, Martin. Sometimes you make me so angry. You do. You don't realise it, but you do. I mean, what do you think these people are? I've watched you with Morty. You treat him as if he was some sort of loveable East End rogue with a heart of gold. Something off the television.'

'That's not true.'

'It fucking *is*. I've watched you. I know. You practically snigger every time he speaks to you. Him and Terry Chimes. He's a *pornographer*. He makes money out of sex. What sort of person does that? Those contact magazines he publishes, the ones where blokes send in pictures of their wives turning their vaginas inside out, what sort of a man do you think does that? A philanthropist? And where does that leave you with those bloody clever scripts you write about schoolgirls entertaining the rugby team in the shower?'

'You wouldn't understand.'

'You poor baby,' Elaine said pityingly. 'You never had a chance, did you?'

Later, when Elaine had gone to bed, I sat by the gas-fire and read Mr Tovacs' novel. I had done so once before, but could remember nothing of it. It was a small, slim volume which, while printed in English, had been published on the Continent in the late 1940s. There were recommendations on the jacket from Connolly, Spender and Eliot. As I read, phrases from some ghostly unwritten review ran through my head: 'The spirit of Norman Douglas and the politics of Joseph Roth'; 'a Bohemian Sitwell'; 'Firbank in *Mitteleuropa*'. It was a queer, recondite work of a kind unfashionable even then: florid, overwritten, decked out with classical quotation, the atmosphere that of a hothouse, the prose orchidaceous. Its plot was picaresque: a young man's wanderings in an unfallen, pre-war Europe, his dalliance with the women he meets in hotels along the way, a long bravura passage retailing his impressions of a cornfield in summer. And everywhere the hint of approaching doom: aeroplanes hanging in the autumn sky, lines of marching men, crowded railway stations; a potent symbolism, honed by a key scene in which the hero, making love to his mistress in the open air, raises his head to greet a swirl of descending propaganda leaflets, each marked with a swastika.

When I had finished I turned back to the title page. Here there was a dedication: *A mon ami Jean Cocteau*. I put the book back on the shelf in the study and went to bed.

It snowed again that night and I stood for a long time at the window watching the pale, even flakes falling over last summer's rose bushes, turning the outstation of dustbins and refuse bags into angular hummocks like ancient burial chambers. Snow coming in from the west and falling over the suburbs of outer London, over Ealing, Hammersmith and the Fulham Road. As ever I thought of other snow, falling long ago, on Eaton Park where I had gone as a child with my father, of snow falling over the level East Anglian plain, over remote landscapes that existed only in the imagination. Elaine slept on, her face turned slightly to one side, and I watched her too, until other faces, other memories, emerged to fill this dense, penumbral frame: my father, other girls to whom in this silent, half-waking state I could no longer put names, a virgin field of snow seen once in the countryside outside Norwich which I had not dared to despoil. Random images, suggesting both extinction and renewal, concealment, the transformation of old, familiar things into shapes that were new and unrecognisable, the whole coalescing into unreality, dominated by colour, by whites, greys, blue-black shadow, dead, submarine faces.

In the small hours the phone rang once more. I listened into the crackling receiver for a while, silent, but appreciative of the spirit which ordained this fruitless quest, this search across thousands of miles for this person of whom nobody knew and of whom there was now no trace. The voice, for once uninterrupted, seemed appeased, content to ramble slowly on, digressive, uneasy, always returning to its unanswerable question, its puzzled disbelief, a litany given shape by recurring phrases and quirks of diction. At dawn, the snow gone now to fall over other gardens, cerise streaks of sunlight moving into the western sky, I went to bed.

I woke late to find that Elaine had already disappeared. A sheet of notepaper lay propped up against a milk bottle on the kitchen table. It read, 'Back later, just do it.' There was post on the mat: bank statements, a rent cheque from the Norwich solicitors, an early Christmas card with a scrawled, anonymous signature. I took the letters into the living room and read them staring out over the tennis courts, where two elderly men were stepping warily over the frozen surface, patting the ball dextrously back and forth. Pictures of Elaine hung everywhere: Elaine, wide-eyed and obdurate in a promo shot Morty had had taken around the time of *Girlschool Janitor*, Elaine in loincloth and warpaint for the Leisurevision remake of *Tarzan*, Elaine among a group of partygoers, an ellipse of bland, disinterested faces that included Mike and Bernie Winters and Barbara Windsor. It was then, curiously, that I became aware of what had happened. Something had gone wrong, I realised. The machine had broken down, some vital part of its mechanism had become impaired, torn adrift in a grinding of gears and blunt edges, the whole lying useless and irreparable.

There had been similar moments before in my life: moments with women, with my father, with ambitions, long tended and stoked up, whose promise had finally ebbed away. Such situations, I knew, required a decisive gesture, an uncancellable tug at solid but untenable moorings. Once in my early twenties during the time with Roger Garfitt I had seized on the first half of a novel I had written, a manuscript on which I had expended two years' patient labour, and burned it page by page. It would never be published and that realisation, at that age and at that time, was enough. The present, I realised, demanded an identical course, a slewing away from the slaughterer's embrace back to familiar certainties. And so I stood for a moment amid the pictures of Elaine, as the old men continued to play tennis and the green tennis balls rose every so often into view, wondering what I might do with myself and in whose hands the solution lay.

Time dragged.

The negotiations for the funding of *Resurrection* proved more irksome than Morty had imagined. Two years before he might have found a distribution chain, or even a bank to underwrite Mr Tovacs' promised thousands, to provide down payments for equipment and venues. Now such days were over. Influential connections, made in the boom years of the Seventies, patiently maintained thereafter, proved unhelpful. The American owner of an adult cinema chain passing through London and enticed into Dean Street shook his head. It would not do, he thought. The days of costume drama and all its attendant exoticism had passed. What the American public wanted was straight sex and no messing. Casting sessions, planned in anticipation of his agreement, were hastily cancelled. Later Morty tested older and more durable affiliations in Europe, wires stretching out beyond the censorship laws of the United Kingdom; they were to no avail. Finally, with affected reluctance, Morty decided to sell several of his freeholds in the East End. 'I'll get a hundred grand maybe,' he explained, 'and it's a bad time for property, but what can you do?' In the event the houses in the Bow Road realised seventy thousand pounds. It was a bad time for property. But the money proved narrowly sufficient. A second group of actresses arrived at the loft to take off their clothes and parrot the lines of dialogue I had written for them. The proceedings were enlivened by the presence of Mr Tovacs himself. He sat in a deckchair at the back of the room and seemed flattered by the deference paid to him. 'You would not perhaps think it possible,' he explained, 'but I have some small experience of these matters. In Berlin, before the war. I must say that this seems very tame by comparison.' Mr Tovacs brought another girl with him, not American, who spoke no English. At intervals during the auditions they conversed in an odd, unidentifiable language.

The image of Mr Tovacs hung heavily over these weeks of preparation: interested, amused, inscrutable. He came into Morty's office and sat poring over books he had brought with him, or chatted affably with the cameramen. At other times he was gone, off to attend meetings about the Polish crisis, meetings at which toasts were drunk to the Gdansk shipyards and Jaruzelski burned in effigy. He returned from these gatherings subdued, a little fretful, bored by Morty's talk and the Dean Street chatter. It was Elaine, characteristically, who put this change in temperament into focus.

'They don't like him you know at those *Solidarność* rallies. I went to one once. Very cool. Lots of old ladies looking down their lorgnettes at him. They wish he wouldn't come.'

'Why?'

I saw little of Elaine at these times. It was a routine to which we had become habituated: a routine of snatched conversations, information gathered in the course of day-long absences carefully stored up for future use.

'Tovacs. Not a Polish name. Hungarian. A vicarious attachment, don't you think. And then there's the question of the money.'

'Plenty of wealthy Hungarian émigrés in London, surely?'

'Not like Tovacs. Tovacs is properly rich. I went to a party at his flat once. Expressionist paintings all over the walls. Real expressionist paintings, not copies. Sideboards full of silver. They don't like that, the Poles. You talk to them about how they got here and you hear about abandoned castles, all the stuff the Nazis took. "My father was a prince and I live in a bedsit on the Bayswater Road." You saw the ones at the Wigmore Hall. They might look like royalty in exile – some of them are – but they're as poor as churchmice really. Moth holes all over the court dresses. Tovacs brought all his with him. No commissars to get rich on what he left behind.'

'When did he get out?'

'Nobody knows. Nobody says. I'll tell you another thing. Get Tovacs to talk about the Jews. Tovacs is good on the Jews. Tovacs lived in Germany. Don't ask me how I know. It just came out once. Not what you'd expect.'

So I had another pastime in these days of waiting and desultory preparation. As Morty fretted over cashflows and storyboards, as negotiations were set in hand to hire a country house where *Resurrection* might be filmed, and as Elaine retired yet further into herself, I set about investigating Mr Tovacs.

Even at this early stage I found Mr Tovacs a figure of consuming interest. The literary affiliations, the hint – conveyed in the story about Walesa – of exalted connections in quite another sphere, what Elaine had said about the Jews, an overwhelming appropriateness to his environment. Each of these factors, unremarkable in themselves, combined to provide a purposeful air of mystery, a series of minor conundrums brought together in a single acrostic of intricate design. Though the specific enquiries which arose about Mr Tovacs – his relationship with Morty, his interest in Morty's operations – might receive satisfactory answers, a greater puzzle remained, one whose bearing on our own lives could not be ignored, whose capacity to threaten a far from impregnable position promised future disturbance. Absorbed, engrossed, giving the impression of being caught up in a dozen careless intrigues, there was something about Mr Tovacs which set one's teeth on edge: a tiny intimation of disquiet rising up to disturb the expressions of amity, which only constant surveillance might keep in check.

The trail led in many directions. From an antiquarian bookseller in Cecil Court I purchased, at exorbitant cost, an early volume of *Pages*, Mr Tovacs' literary annual. Printed in the late 1940s, a Picasso nude on the frontispiece, the endpapers a design by Henry Moore, its theme was the reconstitution of European culture. There were poems by Tambimuttu, Spender and Maurice Sachs, none at their best. Mr Tovacs contributed a queer, billowing editorial, extending to several pages, in whose resonant periods and lapidary phrasing I detected the mark of the polyglot. There were winsome marginalia, messages of support from Shaw, Sartre and Edith Sitwell. It was a wholly exotic production, un-English, a whiff of high European culture blowing across the straitened domestic landscape. There was an air of cultivated modesty about the introductory notes, with their references to 'Mr Eliot' and 'M. Proust', as if the writer were determined to demonstrate that he was merely an impresario, one who had assembled this august company, but was scarcely fit for inclusion within their ranks; here and there an odd tart remark suggestive of some long-dead literary controversy. At no point did the writer reveal anything of a personal nature.

The catalogue in the London Library listed a dozen items: books, pamphlets, a Proust symposium printed in Paris on the thirtieth anniversary of the writer's death. Many of these had now disappeared from the shelves, but after persistent searching I secured a further three novels – *Columbine, Harlequin* and *Pierrot*. Published in the 1950s by an obscure English firm, these were handsome productions, finely bound and with engravings by Augustus John and Felicien Rops. *Columbine*, in particular, attracted my attention. A long short story, scarcely more than a hundred pages in length, it concerned a woman known only as 'C' at large in a fantastic world of ancient castles and perilous mountains, and her efforts to avoid 'the enemy'. The model, clearly enough, was Kafka, but the incidental descriptions of landscape and scene had all the glamour of the fairy tale. The book's conclusion, too, suggested fable, a fable gone horribly wrong, perverted out of its original course: C, imprisoned by the enemy – sinister, black-coated men – becomes their willing ally, betrays her family and lover and is fêted by her pursuers.

Mr Tovacs himself was a more elusive quarry. There were several references in the more gossipy memoirs of the period, many of them contradictory. His age was variously estimated as 72, 65 and – bizarrely – 90. He was supposed to have been Matisse's pupil, to have collaborated with Moholy-Nagy and been the friend of Sylvia Beach. I suspected immediately that such descriptions had an apocryphal quality, that Mr Tovacs was no more than one of those busy minor figures who attach themselves to any cultural landscape, moving on from city to city, from salon to salon, steadily accumulating their rows of footnotes in the cultural gazetteers. I found him everywhere, in Stravinsky's *Collected Letters*, in the correspondence columns of *Horizon*, even – impressively – in the *Fontana Dictionary of*

*Modern Thought*, polite, knowledgeable, suggestive. But still amid this wealth of allusion, resplendent among these exalted connections, there was no trace of his essential nature. In the company of men and women whose lives now lay documented to an infinite degree, he had somehow managed to evade the biographer's grasp.

And then, quite by chance, I discovered a work by various hands, published in London in the 1950s under the title of *Émigrés*. Compared to the elevated productions to which Mr Tovacs customarily put his hand, this seemed every inch a commercial undertaking: a series of essays in which foreigners now resident in the United Kingdom reflected on the circumstances of their arrival. Their tenor – ambassadorial, Anglophile – was not wholly dispirited. Mr Tovacs' essay was the exception. In contrast to optimistic titles such as 'Why I came to London' and 'Land of opportunity', his own was headed simply 'Exile'. It began, conventionally enough, with a résumé of the theme of exile in literature: Adam and Eve, the Exodus, the Greek myths, Viking sagas, moving on to medieval themes of loss and estrangement. A short coda seemed to strike an autobiographical note.

The exile [Mr Tovacs had written] takes with him to his new life not only a sense of dispossession, of removal from a land that is rightfully his, but the sense of grievance. This grievance takes many forms. It is directed, most obviously, at whichever agency ordained his departure, at a social or economic force, at an ideology, at an individual, but it is also directed at himself. For the exile views himself as one cast out from some roseate, primordial garden, as one who has fallen from grace. And like those expelled from an original Eden, he is conscious that in a large measure the blame lies with himself rather than with those who expelled him. Looking back he can only reproach himself for his failure to compromise, to conciliate, to become as one with those who dismissed him. We are all, in a certain sense, born in exile, spend long ages working our passage back over uncharted seas. But the true exile is one who lives with his anxieties, to whom the older world, with its sense of infinite promise, is now more real than that which has taken its place.

KAY SAYS, 'I thought you come from London at first. I thought you were really strange. But you're from round here, aren't you? I can tell it sometimes when you talk to him.'

Early afternoon in Fat Eric and Kay's cluttered lounge. Bobby Dazz on the record player, the sheen of sunlight reflected off the abandoned lager cans. Shuffling in from the kitchen, tray balanced precariously on one hand, Kay stops to look at me, a momentary shrewdness suffusing the peasant features.

'I'm a Norwich boy, Kay. Always will be. Colman Road Primary and the Grammar. You know, the boys in the blue blazers.'

'I know. The Spuds, we used to call them. King Edward potatoes, you know. Now Eric, he used to *hate* the Spuds.'

It's a private school now, gentrified by the Labour government. Kay reminisces on, 'Used to hate them. When he was fifteen, you know how it is with those grammar-school boys, he hit this kid in the mouth with a hockey stick. You never saw anything like it.'

Kay. For some reason I get to see a great deal of Kay these days. I see her sidling past in the gloomy forenoons on her way back from the shops in Unthank Road, I glimpse her staggering back from the off-licence under the weight of Fat Eric's carry-outs. We meet in the newsagent's, in pubs, takeaways. Skulking back from long, cross-city trawls in the late afternoon there comes, inevitably, a time when I stop and register the identity of the figure under the tree, smoking the cigarette. There are, it should be said, very good reasons for these encounters, splendid reasons. Why, Kay is buying a newspaper, a drink or a takeaway, or simply 'out for a walk'.

Fat Eric's impedimenta lie nearby: over the sofa and across the floor, giant spoor left by some gross, untidy beast. Duty-free

Marlboros, still in their cellophane, videos, a sheet torn from the *Eastern Evening News*, bearing the legend 'Kevin Flack signs new contract'.

Kay goes on, 'I used to think you were making it up at first, all that stuff about Bobby Dazz and the Glasgow Express. But you're not, are you? Making it up, I mean?'

'No, Kay, I'm not making it up.'

'When I was a kid,' Kay says absently, 'I used to like the Express. I mean, *really* like them. This girl and me, right, we used to dress ourselves up in the gear. Sew tartan flares into our jeans and that. I often wondered what happened to them.'

Died. Went mad. Vanished. 'Show business is a funny thing, Kay. People come into it and then they leave it, and sometimes nobody knows why.'

'Uh huh.' Kay opens one of Fat Eric's cigarette packets and scoops a Marlboro into her mouth. She smokes with peculiar intensity, in bitter, angry puffs. Looking at her as she sits there on the sofa, legs drawn up beneath her teeming haunches, pudgy forearms dangling, I realise that this is what is known in local terms as 'letting yourself go'. Suzi uses this expression sometimes. For her it means not washing your hair three times a week and drinking too much on your birthday. For Kay, alas, it means not washing your hair at all and drinking too much all the time.

Outside a skateboard clatters on the concrete. The wind lifts. All day it has been blowing in from the coast, from Yarmouth and Cromer and Sheringham, bringing the gulls and that odd smell of salt. Later, as the unprompted monologues grow longer and the cigarette smoke rises, Kay grows confidential. She says, 'Oh, he's a wrong 'un, Eric is, a right bastard. I don't mean he'd do anything really bad – he wouldn't break into people's houses, he wouldn't hurt them or nothing – but he's a wrong 'un just the same. Where do you think he gets the videos he sells in the pub and the cigarettes? And that stall on the market. Him and that Ron. You didn't ever meet Ron, did you? Proper pair *they* are.

'. . . I suppose I should have told him to go away. Can always do that, can't you? Tell them to go away. I don't know. I was seventeen. I didn't know anything. And then I'm in this pub in Earlham and this bloke comes up, and he's got the money and he's got the chat and reckons he can get me a job. Got this place we can live in, I didn't think about it. Eric weren't like anyone I'd ever met before, not in Fram. After I came down here this boy used to ring me up, just friendly like, you know. I honestly don't think he were interested. Anyway, Eric smashed him with a glass one night in the Gates . . .

'. . . He don't do that so much now. I mean fighting's for kids, isn't it? That lot you see on the park, the Steins. Eric isn't one of them real nutters, you know, the ones you see at the match, the ones who'll hit anyone just to see what happens. Not like that.' Using the cigarette like a magnet to draw the room towards her, Kay smiles for a moment, like the terrorists' mothers one sees on the television, the relicts of the brave boys in Long Kesh, still doling out their foolish charity, and the certainties of life with Fat Eric, of life with this terrible shiny beast, painfully unroll.

'You're tough, Kay. You can take it.'

'That's what Eric says. "You can take it," he says, when we're in the pub with Woody and that lot, making me drinking that Pernod. The fucker,' Kay says.

Later, when I get up to go, she says, 'I meant to tell you: it don't mean anything, you know. Oh, I know you and Eric're mates, and he buys you drinks and goes after your money, but it don't mean anything. He's sly, Eric is. I can see the way he looks at you in the pub. He'll have Ron round to talk to you next, that's what he'll do, and then you'll have Ron ringing you up, wanting you to do things. Just little things at first. You know, twenty quid for repairing the van because you're mates and they're hard up. Once that starts you won't hear the last of it. It'll be bigger things after that. You know, two hundred quid for a trailer and "You got any contacts?" and getting asked round Ron's for meals. Big house up Thorpe way he's got; I been round there once and it's full of stuff you'd want to ask questions about. And then you're one of Ron's mates and where are you? Got Ron sitting on your neck, asking you to do things.'

'So long, Kay. Thanks for the coffee.'

Kay shakes her head. 'You don't know anything about it,' she pronounces. 'Eric now, he's a hard case. He doesn't care about people and he doesn't care about me, but he don't mean any harm. Ron, he's something else. Eric's scared of Ron. Says he isn't, but he is. I can see it. Eric, he might talk big now and again, but Ron, he's a real *villain*.

'I reckon Ron's really hurt people,' Kay says.

Outside the street is grey and sad. The privet hedges are covered with a watery film. I go back to the house – no Suzi and the flies scuttling over the unwashed plates – and think about some other *villains*, about Morty and Terry Chimes, Crazy Rodney and Charlie Scaduto. Did Morty ever really hurt anyone? I don't know. Like many another small-timer on the way up Morty was skilled in the art of frightening people – the well-intentioned word that, obscurely, prompted some rival to start another business in another town – but I don't think he ever really hurt anyone. I go to the hidey-hole beneath the staircase, take out the video from its sleek box and juggle it from hand to hand, wonder about the person who sent it. Did he ever really hurt anyone? The light fades and the dark moves in through the uncurtained windows. Eventually Suzi arrives, lets herself in, and finds me half asleep on the sofa.

'Nice dreams?' she asks, scarlet-faced and wearing her tennis gear.

'No,' I tell her, 'not nice dreams. Not nice dreams at all.'

Later in the evening Kev Jackson telephones, a pleased, proud Kev Jackson, whose voice tingles with self-importance. He says, 'I have that information you wanted. Like to hear it?'

'Where did you get it from?'

'Been asking around,' Kev says affably. 'You remember Tony Winder, that guy Morty used to hang out with in the early days? Well, I took him out to lunch and . . .'

'Fine,' I say, cutting short this recitation of source material. 'Just fine, Kev. What did you find out?'

'It's all on file,' Kev says. 'Just listen a minute, will you? Okay: Elaine Keenan. Born County Kerry, Eire, 1953. Around in London late '75, early '76. First starring role was in *Girlschool Janitor* with Frank Fellatio. Played the governess in *Stately Lust . . .*'

'I know all that.'

'This is just background,' Kev concedes. 'Ten or fifteen films with Morty. You can still pick them up in Soho. I watched a couple the other week at some video store in Brewer. Quite hot, even now. An inspired performance in *Mother Superior* . . .'

'I know all that too. What about later on? After *Resurrection*, all that early Eighties stuff. What about then?'

There is a pause. Paper rustles faintly down the wire. 'Yeah, well that's when things start getting confused. Terry Chimes – I talked to him last week, he says to say hi again – reckoned she went to Berlin, starred in that Color Climax series, *Chambermaids*. You ever see any of those?'

'No.'

'Well, take it from me, Martin, it would make your hair curl. Show that on a screen anywhere in the UK and you'd have the Vice Squad round to breakfast, dinner and tea. Hard-core and then some. Couldn't see if it was her or not, though. All the girls were blondes and they didn't have a castlist . . .'

He prattles on and I look away out of the window at the dark hump of the park rising up above the hill, back to the desk where there is a photograph of Suzi, a very young Suzi with half-formed, snowball breasts swelling out of a halter-top bathing costume, a memento of God knows what teenage saturnalia.

'. . . Then I talked to this other guy I met at the *Adult Video World* party, used to work at one of the model agencies, reckoned she was in Manchester working for some PR outfit.'

Suzi's face in the bathing costume picture looks absurdly flat, like dough rolled up into a slab, features stuck on as an afterthought.

'Look, Kev,' I interject, 'this is great. I mean, I appreciate what you've done and everything, but you have to get me an address.'

'An address?' He considers this for a moment, wide-eyed Kev in his writer's flat, somewhere in teeming London. 'That could be difficult.'

'A phone number then. Just a phone number and I'll tell you everything. Morty. Terry Chimes. The money. All of it.'

He rings off after this. I pad down to the lounge where Suzi is marking essays in a vague, bovine way.

'Who was that?' she enquires.

'Just a friend.'

We look at each other for a while reflectively. Eventually Suzi turns on the television and I sit down with the *Eastern Evening*

*News* to relish again its cheering quota of tree-bound cats, confectionery shop break-ins and Kevin Flack's groin strain, and there is harmony of a sort.


It happens on the way back from the Manchester United game. Woody and the others have disappeared somewhere, vanished into the early evening maelstrom of the city, peeled away to fish and chip shops, to pubs and pizza joints. Just Fat Eric and I plodding away on our homeward route, through the boarded-up walkways of the market, up past the City Hall, over the dark expanse of Chapel Field Gardens. It happens there in a dense patch of shadow, the street lamps buzzing away imperfectly above us, where the path descends towards the subway. Fat Eric, subdued by the excitements of the previous three hours, Norwich having miraculously contrived a 2–1 victory, is discoursing soberly on the topic of Kay. 'A real *alki*,' he deposes courteously, 'a real *boozer*. I come back from the stall the other day – Ron and me, we'd put in a good twelve hours – and there she is on the sofa, pissed out of her head . . .' It happens when the four boys, all curiously resembling each other – vee-neck pullovers, short hair, trainers, white, moon faces – ease out of their lair somewhere in the murk beside us and come galloping on. It happens so fast that I don't even appreciate what it is. I even apologise as the first one stumbles into me, say 'Excuse me' in a mildly puzzled way as he veers round and shuffles into me again. Even at this point, as numbers two and three cannon purposefully into Fat Eric's *embonpoint* stomach, the feeling is less that of fear than slightly aggrieved bewilderment, the thought that somebody will shortly explain what this is about, that there is some perfectly convincing reason for this odd circuitous sequence of push and shove, pantomime blind man's buff, like a children's game I used to play at primary school where you stand on one leg, fold your arms and try to barge your opponent into oblivion.

Fat Eric? Fat Eric is magnificent. I once saw a television nature programme in which a solitary, determined moose fought off the onslaught of a pack of starving timber wolves, tossed them on his antlers, ground them remorselessly into the dirt with his hooves, stamped viciously on their pinioned skulls, until the wounded remnant slunk miserably away. This is a fair approximation of Fat Eric's fighting technique. Grim, resourceful, steeleyed, he wheels backwards, comes down hard with his foot on a rashly extended instep, takes out a second assailant with a flailing forearm, goes to corner a third up against the subway wall. The pale boys look worried now. This wasn't what they expected, wasn't what they wanted at all. The fourth one, who has been scuffling with me in a half-hearted way, thinks better of it and sets off at a run, disappears into the silence of the park. Fat Eric, by this time, has got his quarry in an arm-lock, whips a massive knee up into his face and sends him sprawling on to the tarmac. 'Bastard,' Fat Eric is muttering in a detached monotone. 'Bastard, bastard, bastard.'

It stops soon after this. The first two of Fat Eric's victims limp away. The third lies in an untidy heap propped up against the subway wall. Fat Eric kicks him a couple of times for good measure and then strides on. 'Them kids,' he says, 'ought to be more careful who they have a go at.' Later he says, 'Fucking Steins. You can tell it from what they wear. Them purple veenecks. Dead giveaway they are.'

We plod on through the subway, emerge on to silent, empty streets. The incident is never referred to again.


In addition to his flat in Kensington, Mr Tovacs had premises in Red Lion Street: a set of rooms above an émigré bookshop which sold newspapers in a variety of languages and displayed portraits of exiled Eastern European royalty. It was here that Mr Tovacs conducted the editorial business of *Pages*, from here that he addressed his contributions to the correspondence columns of weekly magazines. A Polish relief organisation, supported by several MPs and prominent *literati*, operated from offices on its upper floor. It was here too that, one evening late in November, the various collaborators in *Resurrection* were bidden to assemble.

Rain, sweeping in sharply from the direction of High Holborn, gave a menacing aspect to a landscape with which I was already familiar. The old *Spectator* offices, where I had peddled articles six or seven years ago, were a stone's throw away in Gower Street. Here too Roger Garfitt and I had once come in search of vacation jobs with a news agency in Red Lion Square. The glamour model, I remembered, had rented a flat in Coram Street, handy for the *Daily Mirror* building in Holborn Circus. Each of these associations bore its own fatal quota of distress: memories of overlong waits in gloomy reception halls, fruitless self-adver-tisement – the news agency found to be bogus and offering only unpaid 'experience' – silent recrimination. Turning northwards from High Holborn, the lines of traffic immediately diminishing into a single vehicle twenty yards ahead of us, apparently pro-ceeding under some constraint, this sense of unease became almost tangible: a pressing reminder of past uncertainty and enduring hurt. The rain continued to fall. Elaine said, 'Did anyone tell you to expect a party?'

'No. Did they tell you?'

'I found out,' Elaine said inscrutably. 'Nobody told Morty or Terry either.'

'Will that make a difference?'

'I shouldn't think so. But it might cramp Morty's style.'

'Who'll be there?'

'Writers. The Polish lot. Tovacs' women.'

'Tovacs' wife?'

'No. Definitely not Tovacs' wife.'

I was used to this compartmentalising of professional and private lives. Morty's wives, their number now settled at three, were brought out annually at parties held on New Year's Eve. There was supposedly a Mrs Chimes living somewhere on the Suffolk border. Nobody I knew had ever seen her. Looking at Elaine as she stood in the reflected glare of the streetlamp, I realised that this revelation explained various peculiarities in her get-up: it explained the beret, worn rakishly at an angle on one corner of her head, and it explained the gleaming definition of her features. She seemed nervously expectant, I thought, the possessor of a store of secret information which might be doled out during the course of the evening.

'Have you been to these things before?'

'Once. About a year ago. That time you were in Amsterdam with Morty.'

'What happened then?'

'Not much. There was a string quartet playing mazurkas, and Tovacs talked a lot about Picasso.'

The bookshop stood halfway along Red Lion Street, between a silent restaurant and a boarded-up newsagent's. Its frontage, previously reserved for a display of unpromising-looking titles, was now dominated by a huge *Solidarność* banner, extending across almost the entire width of the room. Noise – music, indistinguishable voices – drifted down from an upstairs window. The car which had slowly preceded us along the street stopped abruptly and a brooding, bulky figure emerged.

'That you, Martin?'

'Over here.'

Terry Chimes said, 'Thought it was you when I turned into the road. Couple of cunts holding hands under a streetlamp. Thought it was you.' He cast an eye briefly over the window display. 'Fucking awful place to have a party, don't you reckon?'

I turned and looked at him. Boisterous and unimpressed, Terry Chimes seemed an incongruous visitor to Mr Tovacs' lair. He was wearing what he sometimes called his 'cunt-hunting' suit, a garment in outsize red-check, its trousers flared to the point where they resembled Oxford Bags, a white shirt with wide, drooping collars. He carried a bottle of whisky, lodged stiffly under his elbow like a swagger stick.

'Any sign of Morty?'

'Left him at Dean Street. Still fixing up that place in Suffolk for the shoot.'

'Suffolk, is it now?'

'Sure. Aldeburgh, or Southwold, or somewhere. Some country house somebody told him about. In the middle of a field of sugar beet and five miles to the nearest boozer.'

He seemed disinclined to talk. By now it had begun to rain even harder and we clustered beneath the overhang of a small porch to the right of the shop. Here, beyond an illuminated glass door, steps rose sharply into darkness. Elaine pressed the buzzer. On the far side of the glass, legs, weirdly truncated by the angle of the staircase, slowly descended. A voice said indistinctly, 'Welcome to the bat-cave.'

It was the American girl, Jerry. She gave no sign of recognising any of us, or being particularly interested in our identities. Dressed in a black body-stocking, the general air of gloom brightened by a scarlet sash tethered around her waist, her attitude suggested someone constrained by higher authority into a role she considered entirely beneath her.

'The party's upstairs,' she said.

As we filed past she lay back against the banisters and examined us critically. Elaine and I seemed to pass muster. As Terry Chimes drew level with her on the stair I heard her mutter, '*Not fancy dress.*'

Beyond, a dark corridor opened out to reveal a long, angular chamber, high-ceilinged and brightly lit, the further end widening into a recess dominated by a broad trestle table on which lay wine bottles and plates of sandwiches. That this was a place of business recently converted along lines thought suitable for entertainment seemed clear from a general air of untidiness. There were cardboard boxes all over the floor, bookshelves pushed back to the walls and draped over with cloths, a pile of stamped envelopes pressed into service as a doorstop. Thin, unidentifiable music, apparently coming from some fixed point high above us, was finally located in a wind-up gramophone placed on an occasional table by the door. As Elaine and I stood uncertainly by this humming relic Mr Tovacs, previously unseen behind a knot of guests, detached himself and moved hastily towards us. Showing by the alignment of his body that he spoke to Elaine, he said, 'I am delighted to see you again. It was good of you to come. No doubt you have brought Mr Kronenburg with you?'

'Still at Dean Street,' Elaine said. 'He'll be along later, I shouldn't wonder.'

Mr Tovacs nodded. The transformation in his appearance was, I realised, complete. Seen in the unfamiliar setting of the Wigmore Hall a month before he had seemed uncertain, ill at ease, unable for the most part to defend himself from unwelcome questions and chance insinuations. Here, on what was presumably his home territory, he looked entirely in his element, a creature of infinite resource, concealing reservoirs of expertise that would enable him to deal with the unlikeliest contingency. He wore predominantly the clothes that I remembered from our first meeting, but there were quaint and somehow wholly appropriate additions – a spotted foulard scarf, a buttonhole, odd, parti-coloured shoes, the whole adding an extra, resonant dimension to the earlier portrait. It was a dandy's get-up, I thought, not many miles distant from the music hall comedian. In fact, if Mr Tovacs suggested a prototype it was Archie Rice in *The Entertainer*.

There was a sudden press of new arrivals: two girls of about Elaine's age, a venerable Pole in a greatcoat whom Mr Tovacs kissed decorously on both cheeks and then directed toward the drinks table.

I said, 'Are all these people connected with the Solidarity campaign?'

'A number. They are also artistic people, literary people.' Mr Tovacs looked cautious as he said this, as if he would have preferred an explanation of my interest in the Polish situation before going any further. 'After all, we are in Bloomsbury, are we not? A very suitable place for a *salon*?'

'A very suitable place. I suppose you must have entertained many celebrated people here?'

It was obviously the right thing to have said. Whatever doubts Mr Tovacs might have had about my interest in him were immediately dispelled. He said, 'You are kind enough to say so. There was a man here last week from a newspaper asking the same question. He wanted to know about Eliot,' Mr Tovacs went on, a shade petulantly. 'An ignorant man. It is no use talking to such people. What is it to them that Cocteau sat in that chair, or that in this room I took dictation from Maurice Sachs?' He paused. 'And yet today I find that I have achieved distinction in quite another sphere.'

'What sort of distinction?'

Mr Tovacs fished carefully in the inner pocket of his jacket, at length emerging with a crumpled press cutting. Taken from the 'Pseud's Corner' column of *Private Eye*, it was an extract from an obituary Mr Tovacs had written of a recently deceased Bulgarian poet. I ran my eye over the quaint, orotund phrases: 'An embodiment of the *Zeitgeist* . . . The inhabitant now, alas, of that remote, nether pantheon . . . Plangent, crystalline verses . . .' To the casual reader it was a pretentious enough piece, certainly, but there was something oddly authentic about Mr Tovacs' eloquent memorials. Overstated and absurdly phrased, the motivation that lay beneath them seemed more or less genuine.

'It's a bit unfair.'

For some reason I supposed Mr Tovacs to require consolation for this indignity. Paradoxically he seemed delighted by this exposé of his literary style. 'No, you misunderstand me. It is the English sense of humour. Always, it has never ceased to amuse me. Art. Literature. Always, I have thought, these are closed doors to the English mind. But the English sense of humour? It endures. It is a constant. Somehow it is a compensation for these deficiencies . . .'

A mounting babble of noise from the far end of the room now exploded into crescendo. 'You must excuse me,' Mr Tovacs said, 'we will talk later.' I watched him ease his way off through the throng until he disappeared into the press of bodies, then turned – Elaine nowhere to be seen by this stage – to consider the room at large.

Looking at the scene of Mr Tovacs' party, some fifty people now, crammed into a space adequate for perhaps half that number, it was possible to locate echoes of an older age. The literary odds and ends, the boxes of magazines, 'artistic'-looking women with untidy fringes – all this suggested a Connolly/ *Horizon* gathering along lines parodied by Evelyn Waugh. But there were other, decidedly unliterary, parallels. The sound of upraised, foreign voices, the gesticulating elderly men, the sense of angry, embittered exile: this seemed to belong to a yet more distant past, to evoke images of clandestine plotting, the secret police waiting at the door, frustrated hope – like a painting of the Paris Commune. The presence of so many women – young women dressed in black like Jerry, slightly older women in evening gowns with their hair scraped back across their foreheads, a few elderly gorgons of the type seen at the Wigmore Hall – all without exception attendant upon and observant of Mr Tovacs, introduced a third element, that of the seraglio.

Amid this throng, a gathering in which no one age or nationality predominated, a single figure stood out. Terry Chimes sat on a chair in the middle of the room cradling the bottle of whisky in his lap. He seemed hopelessly out of place, someone not up to the demands placed on him by his milieu, his appearance – the bizarre suit somehow appropriate – suggesting inner resources which he did not actually possess, like a Christy minstrel brought on to play Othello. As I stood watching him, Jerry came up. Mysteriously, all trace of her previous neutrality had vanished. She said, 'You were the guy who turned up at the Wigmore, right?'

'Right.'

'Uh huh. I heard you giving Tovacs all that soft soap about the fucking magazine.'

The note of aggression, trailed faintly in the first question, deepened in the second. She went on, 'All that stuff about Eliot. I heard. And taking dictation from Maurice Sachs. Has he told you about Picasso yet?'

'Not yet.'

'Uh huh. Look up there.'

At eye level on the wall beside us there were innumerable framed photographs, sketches, drawings in sepia and pencil, caricatures: Eliot seated on a footstool, one knee hoisted over the other, staring gloomily into space, a tall curly-haired man who might have been Stephen Spender standing beside him. Above, figures from an older, foreign era predominated: the Countess de Noailles, de Max in Pierrot costume. Among this profusion of portraits, theatrical scenes, aggressively posed literary groupings, was a framed drawing, notionally sketched in black ink, of a single, unidentifiable face, executed on what appeared to be a paper napkin. Beneath it ran a line of type: 'A gift from Pablo Picasso, Paris 1958.'

'Picasso drew this?'

'Uh huh. Do you know what he did it on?'

'No.'

'It's a piece of toilet roll. Straight up. Tovacs followed him into a public lavatory one time and asked him for a contribution to *Pages*. Caught him with his pants down. Literally. Picasso was so surprised that he just tore off another sheet and scribbled on it.'

'Did he get a lot of contributions like that?'

'Tovacs? Tovacs would dig up somebody's grave – some

Nobel prizewinner's grave, that is – if he reckoned there was an unpublished short story buried along with the corpse.'

I had heard hints of this before. A recent volume of *Pages* had contained a *Times* crossword allegedly completed by Graham Greene at a public dinner in the 1960s and detached by Mr Tovacs while his fellow guest was out of the room. Though it was good to hear these stories corroborated they did not detract from Mr Tovacs' allure as a personality. There was something ridiculous, certainly, about his pursuit of Picasso into the public lavatory – what exactly had he said, I wondered? How had he introduced himself to the startled artist? – but also something dogged, a persistent unwillingness to settle for second best.

Jerry said, 'Looks like your friend could do with some help.'

'Which friend?'

'Medallion man. The guy you came with.'

In the centre of the room Terry Chimes stood talking to one of the girls in black, a younger and more appetising version of Jerry herself. The contrast in their attitudes was marked: the one cheery, confidential, insinuating, the other puzzled, laconic, suspicious. The conversation – animated on one side, reluctant on the other – stopped when Terry Chimes put a hand on the girl's shoulder and whispered something in her ear. The girl raised her eyebrows and marched off. I moved across.

'Chat-up lines not working?'

Terry Chimes prodded the carpet resentfully with his foot. He said, 'Thought I was on to something there. Right little prick-teaser if you ask me.' His manner changed abruptly and he raised his head. 'I can't stand those arty girls. Always wanting to talk about fucking music.'

'I should have thought that would be right up your street.'

'*Classical* music. Mozart and Wagner and all that crap.'

'What did you say to her?'

'I told her,' said Terry Chimes mournfully, 'that she ought to take a look at the size of my oboe.'

At close quarters, the bottle of whisky brought with him now, I noted, a third empty, he seemed unusually gloomy. It could not, I thought, be on account of the rebuff – after all, Terry Chimes was used to accumulating five or six of these in the course of an evening. I guessed that there was some deeper malaise.

'Some of these girls,' he went on, 'just can't take a joke.'

Simultaneously we found ourselves caught up in one of those periodic, wide-scale displacements of people that characterise large parties held in small rooms. A line of women who had been grouped around the trestle table suddenly detached themselves and moved resolutely forward. Two men, one of them the elderly Pole in the greatcoat, who had been innocently grouped in front of us were now spun out at right angles by the force of this assault. In the confusion I caught sight of Elaine standing in the doorway talking to Mr Tovacs. Then, inexplicably, the movement stopped, the lines re-formed and Terry Chimes and I found ourselves together again.

'How's business, Terry?'

I had never known how to talk to Terry Chimes, what way in which to address him, which subjects might be likely to amuse him. Sex, usually a reliable standby, might only depress him further. Business seemed a suitably anodyne topic.

'Business is bad. Bloody bad I'd call it.'

'The Express anniversary tour wasn't a success?'

'Fucking disaster area.' He made a small, menacing movement with the bottle. 'Nobody's interested in a load of thirty-year-olds wearing tartan trousers. Not even the Glasgow Apollo. Plus the LP didn't sell.'

'*Songs from Auchtermuchty?*'

'That's the one. We've tried giving it away with soap powder, but that didn't work either.'

'What about Bobby Dazz?'

'Fucking his secretary, last I heard.'

'And those new young groups you were going to sign up?'

'No good. No good at all. Do you know what worries me about pop music now, Martin?' There was another abrupt change of gear; Terry Chimes' tone became declamatory. 'It's that I just can't keep up with it any more. With the changes, I mean. Ten years ago you knew where you were. Girl groups. Guitar groups. Kids from America. Novelty records. You knew what the fucking categories were. Find some bunch of Irishmen singing in a pub in Romford, put them in matching suits, give them a flash name, buy lunch for a tame DJ and Bob's your uncle. But it's not like that now. The styles used to change every year or so. Now it's every three months. Take New Wave . . .'

I could see Elaine signalling to me through the crowd. There was no way of knowing how long this monologue might continue. Terry Chimes hastened on, '. . . Take New Wave. I could cope with New Wave. Chug-a-chug guitars and kids in leather jackets singing flat. Might smash the place up once in a while, but you could sell stories to the papers about how they were good boys really and went home every weekend to their old mums in Lewisham. Trouble was it didn't last. And then there was this Two-Tone thing. Pork-pie hats and sunglasses. Uncle Rastus and his Swinging Six, that sort of thing. Trouble was that didn't last either. You remember that nigger saxophone player I signed? Fucking disaster. Now it's all New Romantics. I had this geezer in my office last month wearing a fucking *ruff*. Course I turned him down flat. Next week he signs to CBS for a quarter of a million.'

He paused to brood for a moment on this ripe fruit that had evaded his grasp. Then he said, 'Morty here yet?'

'I haven't seen him.'

'I need to talk to Morty.'

'What about?'

'Money.' Terry Chimes gave me a faintly exasperated glance, as if this was an obvious answer. He looked across to where Mr Tovacs, supported by two or three of the black-clad girls, had begun a monologue involving elaborate gestures and tossings of the head. 'Arty parties I can just about put up with, so long as the money's there. Put up with anything,' Terry Chimes went on, 'so long as there's some folding stuff at the end of it. The question is: is there?'

'Morty said he'd had a cheque.'

'Development costs,' Terry Chimes said contemptuously. 'Rehearsal rooms. Camera-hire. Getting those cunts at Starfinder off their arses for a bit. Mr fucking Teasy-weasy to do the hairstyles. Isn't anything else. I dunno what Morty's up to. Off hiring actresses, booking the site – this place in Suffolk is costing the fucking earth – like there was no tomorrow. Question is: who's going to pay for it? The old pantomime dame over there?'

Something in the corner of the room caught his eye and he drew himself up to attention, like a drunken NCO upbraided by a superior officer. 'I'll catch you later, Martin.'

The faint air of unease that had characterised Leisurevision's dealings with Mr Tovacs had not until now been given such coherent shape. Left abruptly to my own devices I thought for a moment, as I had thought several times before, about the impulse that had driven Morty, usually the model of circumspection, into this unlikely partnership. Awareness of artistic potential (Morty had a naive admiration for what he called 'real artists')? Desperation?

There was a small case of books directly in front of me, from which the cloth had slipped away. A half-filled wine glass, balanced precariously in a delta formed by two of the larger volumes, looked as if it was about to topple over. Having rescued it, I stood looking at the books. They were volumes of Ezra Pound's speeches, the broadcasts made on Rome radio in the early 1940s. I flicked through the first of these for a moment in the same half-intrigued, half-disgusted way that I occasionally examined the hard-core magazines Morty brought back from the Continent. Odd sentences stood out from the lines of solid, leaded type: '. . . The Jew must realise, if he is to realise anything at all, the consequences of his actions . . . The fate of the Jews of Eastern Europe we already know about. The Jews of America we can only warn . . .'

A voice beside me said, 'Pound was a very great writer, you know.'

I turned and discovered Mr Tovacs looking at me with an expression in which pride and embarrassment were uncomfortably mingled, rather as if, I thought, I was a schoolmaster who had chanced upon an exercise book full of his adolescent poetry. Several plausible enough replies suggested themselves.

'You knew Pound?'

Mr Tovacs looked pleased. There was, as I had realised by now, an immediate, fail-safe way of appeasing him whenever the conversation turned to literature. This was to suggest that he had known personally, or at any rate had some lesser connection with the writer being discussed.

He said, 'Only a little. Towards the end of his life, and then only a little. He was not,' Mr Tovacs paused, as if weighing the words carefully, 'he was not, what is the word you would use, a *sympathetic* man. And he had made that fatal mistake for the intellectual, for the artist, in Anglo-Saxon countries, of engaging himself in politics. An interesting phenomenon: the artist as man of action. It is not something which is . . . encouraged, perhaps?'

'I suppose not.'

I remembered what Elaine had said: 'You should hear Tovacs on the Jews.' It seemed safer to change the subject.

'Do you know Suffolk?'

'Suffolk?'

'Suffolk. *Resurrection* may be filmed there, I think?'

Mr Tovacs' eyes, which had narrowed markedly during the conversation about Pound, now resumed a blander look. 'There is a place on the coast, is there not, where musical festivals are held? Aldeburgh or some such name? I went there once as a guest of Ben's.'

It was typical, I reflected, of Mr Tovacs to have known Britten. He looked as if he might be about to say something else about the Aldeburgh festival, but then, raising his hand in an odd sort of benediction, thought better of it and began to shuffle away. His figure receded, was caught up again in a knot of elderly women, and then disappeared. I looked about the room for Elaine, last seen in the area of the trestle table, but there was no sign of her. As I watched, Morty appeared in the doorway, wavered slightly as he caught sight of the press of people and then moved determinedly on. There was, I saw, something peculiar about Morty's appearance: beads of moisture on his forehead; the left side of his face seemed violently contorted. I guessed that this late arrival was the result of an unscheduled visit to the dentist. He had come only a yard or so into the room when Terry Chimes bore down on him; they stood talking animatedly. I strained to hear what was being said – from the look on Terry Chimes' face these were not ordinary pleasantries – but another burst of music, this time identifiable as a Schumann *lied* played very loud, drowned out the words. Elaine materialised, apparently from nowhere, at my elbow.

'I want to talk to you.'

'Go on then.'

'No. Not here. Somewhere you can hear what I'm saying.'

I looked at her. The beret hung at an even more rakish angle, so much so that I wondered whether she had secured it there with hair pins. Her hair, previously coiled up and tamed beneath it, had begun to stray outwards; an entire hank cascaded down one cheek. She looked prodigiously bored.

'There's a room upstairs at the back we can go to.'

Reflecting that Elaine seemed to know her way about Mr Tovacs' premises, I followed her out into the corridor, past Terry Chimes who, glancing over his shoulder, winked in a marked manner, and towards a second staircase set at an angle to the one by which we had first entered the building. Here the press of people had lessened, although there were one or two couples – European-looking girls, men in parodies of evening dress – arranged on the lower steps. Elaine pushed past these onlookers with the air of someone intimately concerned with the management of the party who might at some not very distant point turn dictatorial and start to evict people. At the top of the staircase there was a single door which at first sight appeared to be locked. Elaine twisted the handle a couple of times, put her shoulder to it and finally succeeded in wrenching it open.

'In here.'

We found ourselves in a small, sparsely furnished attic – the single window looking out into blackness – which seemed to be used as a storeroom. A few chairs stood at right angles to one another next to a battered sideboard along whose surface ran a line of carved South American figurines – parrots, crocodiles, squat grinning homunculi with wildly overproportioned eyes. Beneath, in decaying cardboard boxes, reposed elderly copies of *Pages*, some of them as much as thirty years old. I inspected the title pages: 'A Laforgue Tribute; Ginsberg at 50.' Elaine, who had been staring angrily at a further display of photographs and framed memorabilia, turned back from the wall and said with an effort, 'I wanted to tell you that I'm clearing out.'

'Clearing out?'

'Clearing out,' Elaine said. She lit a cigarette, something she rarely did except at moments of personal distress, and drew nervously on it once or twice. 'Leaving.'

'Leaving here? Leaving Leisurevision? Leaving me?'

'All of them, probably. I can't stand it any more and I just wanted to tell you.'

There had been declarations like this before. The trick, I had learned, was to accept them matter-of-factly, as the prelude to a neutral discussion of logistics, contingencies and obligations.

'Any particular reason?'

Elaine gave me a look which suggested that it might be unwise simply to humour her. 'The usual ones. What am I doing with my life? What am I doing with you? And don't think any explanation you can come up with now is going to be especially satisfying. It's quite simple, Martin. I just don't like what I'm doing any more. Not now. And you don't help, Martin. You just sit there and you don't ask the right questions.'

'Which questions?'

'Oh . . . I don't know. Hasn't it ever struck you, Martin, just how weird all this is? I mean, *what are Morty and Terry up to?* What is Tovacs up to? This isn't Tovacs' usual thing. Not his usual thing at all. Why does he want to put money into one of Morty's dodgy films? What does he think he's going to get out of it?'

'Have you asked any of them?'

'That's another thing. Morty and Terry are up to something. I don't know what it is, but I don't like it at all and I want out.'

'Now?'

'Maybe not now. Maybe not until *Resurrection*'s over and we get paid. But I want out.'

There was a silence. From below came the hum of conversation, the sound of something – a glass? a bottle? – smashing on the floor, somebody's voice – I guessed it to be Terry Chimes' – raised in protest.

'Look,' said Elaine, 'don't take it personally, okay? We can talk about it some more when we get home.'

It was impossible not to take it personally. Looking at Elaine now as she leant back against the sideboard, one arm apparently about to detach a large, stylised representation of a panther, I realised how unfathomable I had always found her, that this realisation, for which I could not be said to be unprepared, was simply the culmination of a great deal of wayside incomprehension in the years we had known each other. That common ground which authenticates a relationship, so often hinted at in a gesture or apparent understanding, had simply failed to materialise. I continued to stare at her, thinking of all this, until the silence became intolerable.

'Come on,' Elaine said, 'let's go downstairs.'

As we descended the narrow staircase, the loitering couples now mysteriously disappeared, it became clear that some sort of minor crisis had arisen to disturb the even tenor of the party. The music had stopped. From beyond the doorway came the clamour of raised voices. Moving into the room, several clues as to what had happened swiftly presented themselves, the whole suggesting a tableau that might have been captioned 'Wounded Dignity' or 'Honour Spurned', a tumult of activity frozen suddenly into sharp relief by our own arrival on to the scene. Terry Chimes stood in the centre of a group of people which included Morty and Jerry, nursing his right hand and glaring stonily at a second group made up of several other guests, whose leader seemed to be the girl whom Terry Chimes had previously tried to pick up. In the middle of this assembly sat, or rather half-stood, supported by the girl, a man whom I had not seen before, clutching his fingers over the upper part of his face. Fragments of a bottle, Terry Chimes' bottle of whisky judging by the label, formed an odd symbolic barrier on the floor between these apparently opposed forces. At once everyone began to talk again very loudly, the girl in black giving out two or three piercing screams before being silenced by one of the older women. I moved over to where Morty stood with his arms clasped protectively around Terry Chimes' waist.

'What happened?'

Morty shrugged. He was obviously extremely annoyed, though whether with Terry Chimes, or the man now sitting on the floor was difficult to tell. 'Christ, I don't know. I only just got here and my teeth hurt like fuck. Boy meets girl. Girl isn't interested. Somebody interferes. Terry takes a swing at them. Don't ask me.'

Mr Tovacs stood a little way off. He seemed not so much disapproving as nervous, fearful perhaps that what appeared to be no more than a minor scuffle might yet inspire more alarming conflict. He said to no one in particular, 'I really do not know what to say. It is all most regrettable. But perhaps Mr Chimes was provoked in some way?'

Whatever might have been the cause of the fight, it was a signal for dispersal. The two participants were helped away. Two girls who had been helping to serve drinks came and swept up the broken glass and conferred in undertones with Mr Tovacs about a chair which Terry Chimes might or might not have broken. There was a slow but remorseless drift of people towards the staircase, down to the lower floor in search of coats and handbags. Elaine had disappeared, either in the company of Morty and Terry Chimes, or off on some errand of her own. As I stood uncertainly by the door, wondering if I should say something on behalf of Terry and Morty to Mr Tovacs, wondering whether if I went home immediately I should find Elaine, wondering even if it were worth going home to resume that conversation, Jerry moved purposefully towards me.

'Still here? What happened to your girlfriend?'

'Gone already, I think.'

'With medallion man, huh? Boy, that was a scene.' Jerry looked animated, I thought, as if the events of the last ten minutes had somehow provided the high point of the evening. She was holding a half-empty glass which she now put down on a side table. 'Jesus. After that I could do with a drink.'

'Plenty of wine left.'

'*Not* wine. A real drink. Tovacs doesn't keep spirits on the premises. Have to go someplace else. You want to come?'

I considered. It was barely ten o'clock. The probability was that Morty, Terry and Elaine had gone back to Dean Street. There would be no one at the flat until eleven.

'All right.'

'Attaboy. Why don't you wait downstairs while I go fetch some things?'

At the bottom of the staircase a kind of *mêlée* was in progress in which various guests, enraged by the smallness of the cubbyhole in which they found themselves and the inaccessibility of the coats – piled up on a distant ledge – were arguing with each other. I stood and watched this for a moment until Jerry reappeared. She was wearing a long, shapeless dufflecoat and had exchanged her ballet slippers for a pair of fur bootees, this suggesting a store of clothing kept on the premises from which suitable items could be extracted when necessary. Together we stepped out into the street.

'Do you live here?'

'Sometimes.' Jerry set off at a rapid pace. Used to Elaine's notoriously laggard saunter I had trouble in keeping up. 'There's a camp bed upstairs I use when I'm hanging out with Tovacs. Otherwise I go back to Kentish Town. Jesus,' she said, 'Tovacs' parties never work. Always something like that happens.'

'Tovacs seems to enjoy them.'

'Tovacs is an egomaniac. Tovacs would enjoy a party on a desert island with a couple of cannibals so long as it was him doing the inviting. First time we've had a fight though.'

'What happened?'

'The usual thing that happens. You were upstairs, right? Well, medallion man started sniffing round that girl in the black, the one who gave him the brush-off before, and the guy she was with told him to cool it. Next thing you know medallion man goes for him with a bottle of bourbon. Does he always act like that?'

'Sometimes.'

'Uh huh. I figured him for a meathead. You get that in the States. I was at a book launch once in Madison Avenue when Norman Mailer loafed this guy with a wine cooler. I never saw that sort of thing happen here before.'

I considered this information. As well as demonstrating Jerry's familiarity with literary society on both sides of the Atlantic, it suggested that she thought the British way of doing things feeble by comparison, and that a certain degree of violence might actually be necessary in promoting a suitable atmosphere. We pressed on rapidly towards High Holborn.

'Where are we going?'

'A little place I know about just along the street. American beer too; I can't stand that English stuff. Don't worry,' she added, as if these attractions might not have been sufficient. 'It's not far.'

She continued to talk in a desultory way as we crossed the main thoroughfare – deserted now except for taxis – and walked on towards Southampton Row: about Mr Tovacs, about her landlord in Kentish Town, about difficulties with a work permit. I had the impression of a hard, sharp intelligence, oppressed by its dealings with the people it ran up against, but allowed insufficient room for any manoeuvre which might have turned the tables on them.

In Southampton Row she turned sharp left into an alley connected in some way with the shops in Sicilian Avenue. Whatever illusions I might have had about our ultimate destination – I had envisioned a drinking club along the lines of an American gangster film, a speakeasy peopled by burly, hard-faced men in suits – vanished abruptly.

'This way,' Jerry said.

A single outer door, painted in black and white stripes, gave way to a flight of stairs descending into a small, hollowed-out cavern strewn with bar-stools. Here a few people sat individually and in twos and threes drinking in a subdued way. The atmosphere was determinedly American. A sign on the wall, the neon beneath it barely flickering, read 'Sam's bar and diner'. Uncle Sam himself glowered from the wall in facsimile. Curiously the decor reminded me of Morty's club: an air of seediness narrowly kept at bay, the suspicion of people with nothing better to do. Jerry, however, seemed very much at home.

'Ah,' she said. 'Simpatico. You want a drink?'

'Do you come here a lot?'

'Now and again. I get tired of Red Lion Street. Everybody working their asses off just because Tovacs has some French poet coming to tea that no one's ever heard of.'

'How did you get to meet Tovacs?'

Jerry frowned, as if the question was an unwelcome one, reminding of some part of her life that was better forgotten. 'Back home. Some bunfight to launch a book. I used to work for Scribner's in New York. Tovacs gave me his card. A bit later I started sending poems in to *Pages*. Then when I came over here I got in touch again.'

'Did the poems get printed?'

Jerry frowned again, a yet rawer nerve obviously exposed. 'A few. Anyone can get printed in a book like that, you just have to know the editor. Jesus, I was so green in those days. Coming to England. Thinking Tovacs was the big time.'

'Which he wasn't?'

She lit a cigarette and stared at it irritably. 'There are two types of hangers-on: little hangers-on and big hangers-on. Little hangers-on are people like me: people who write poems and hand out the wine at parties. Tovacs is a big hanger-on. Hasn't got any particular talent – not now, at any rate – but he knows people. People like that can make major nuisances of themselves.'

'How do you mean?'

'Tovacs is a real bloodsucker, a real manipulator. You let him into your life, even professionally, and you can spend all your time letting him out again. I'll give you an example. That guy who won the Nobel last month, Milosz. He's a Pole, so of course *The Times* rang up and asked Tovacs to do a piece. Naturally Tovacs jumped at the chance. And then he started asking for things: a plane ticket to Stockholm; someone to help him with the typing. Got hold of *The Times* guy's number and started ringing him up at home. There are easier ways of filling a newspaper.'

'They could cancel the commission.'

'An old man of seventy-five with a heart complaint who knew James Joyce? No, Tovacs doesn't lose spats like that. Once you've got him in your address book he stays there.'

There was a minor diversion as a man wearing overalls and carrying a guitar emerged from a side door and seated himself on a stool by the bar. Having looked rather nervously around the room once or twice and struck a few preliminary chords he began to sing in a put-upon, doleful voice:

In a one-horse town I know so well to the west of Abilene
There's a little girl who waits for me, the best I've ever seen.

Jerry brightened. 'That's Chet,' she said approvingly. 'He plays here most nights.'

We sat in silence for a moment listening to the tale of Mary Lou who had sent a steely dart into the bottom of this poor cowboy's heart. I realised with a kind of belated intuition, that Jerry was drunk. She gazed raptly at Chet for a while longer and then without warning grew sulky once more.

'I expect you just want to sleep with me, isn't that right?'

'No. What gave you that idea?'

'Uh huh. Most of the guys you meet at Tovacs' do. "I read your poems" just means "Flap your tits in my face".'

It seemed a good time to revert to an older topic.

'Tell me about Tovacs.'

'Uh huh.' Jerry considered this for a moment. Chet, having finished his account of the girl from Abilene, looked expectantly around the room: there was a very faint scattering of applause. 'What do you want to know?'

'For a start, how did he get involved with Morty and Terry Chimes?'

'I told you. Tovacs collects people. People who might be useful for Tovacs.'

'But why does he want to put money into one of Morty's films?'

'Actually,' Jerry said, giving the impression that the topic was best approached obliquely, 'Tovacs has had quite a career already in films.'

'He has?'

'Sure. You know all that stuff about *mon ami Jean Cocteau*? All the stuff about the references to him in *Le Passé défini*? Well, practically the only thing Tovacs did do with Uncle Jean, so far as I can make out, was to help him make his films.'

'*Les Enfants terribles*?'

'Not that sort of film. A bit more specialised than that. Hunky *matelots* and that sort of thing.'

I thought about this. The picture of Mr Tovacs which it conjured up seemed, in the light of all that I had so far assembled about him, perfectly credible. Somehow each of Jerry's remarks had the ring of authenticity. The way she conducted this exposé, implying that I could take it or leave it and that she herself could not be bothered either way, seemed to confirm this. Something of what I was thinking must have passed through Jerry's mind for she said quite quickly, 'Sure, I could spill some beans about Tovacs. Maybe I will before I clear out.'

'When will that be?'

'Who knows? This month. Next month. Between you and me I've had just about as much of Tovacs as I can stand. Washing up wine glasses and fending off old roués with bad breath who reckon you might be impressed because they once met André Gide. Not my idea of a great night out.'

Here the conversation stuck. Jerry looked sulkier than ever, eventually announcing that she had to go to the 'bathroom'. While I waited for her I thought about Elaine, whose own plans had been stated in curiously similar terms. It was nearly eleven. Perhaps, after all, she would have gone back to the flat? Perhaps, on the other hand, I could collect her from Dean Street? While I weighed these possibilities against each other, Jerry returned. She seemed faintly surprised to see me, uncertain for a brief moment, I thought, as to my identity. Recovering herself she said, 'Look, don't think me rude, will you, but I want to talk to Chet here.'

I looked over to the bar where the singer, his repertoire apparently complete, sat drinking with his back to us.

'I have to go anyway.'

'Tear your girl away from medallion man? That's the spirit.'

'Yes.'

At the door I turned and waved. Jerry, now seated at the bar, her farouche, pointed features creased into a smile by some remark of Chet's, barely looked up.

In the taxi I pondered on the events of the previous four hours. Oddly, the memory that endured was of Jerry's threatened exposure of Mr Tovacs, the grounds not even guessable, a threat that seemed potent and immediate, hedged about with indications that it would actually take place. Elaine's statement of intent, by contrast, seemed flimsy, uncertain. I had no doubt at this stage that she would once again change her mind. On a broader canvas, the sense of some mystery, involving Morty, Mr Tovacs, the film and all manner of issues scarcely hinted at by Jerry's denunciation, grew stronger. As Kensington gave way to the Fulham Road, the long lines of traffic breaking up now and disappearing, bafflement was replaced by uneasy anticipation.

There was a light on in the flat. Elaine sat in the front room, her feet raised on a stool. She stared at me unblinkingly.

'You were home early?'

'There wasn't anything happening at Dean Street. Terry thought he might have broken a knuckle, so Morty took him to hospital.'

'Had he?'

'No. Terry's such a *jerk*. He wanted to go back there with Crazy Rodney and take out the guy who hit him.'

'What did Morty say?'

'He got tough. You know that way Morty gets when there's money involved and someone's not taking it seriously. It was quite funny in a way. They stood there in the Out-Patients shouting at each other until the security guards thought they were a couple of drunks who'd come in off the street.'

I thought for a moment about this all-too-plausible scene. Then, without warning, two things happened. First, the flood-lights from the adjoining tennis court were switched off: the numinous haze outside the window fell away into darkness. At the same time the phone in the hall rang urgently.

'It'll be for Mr Solomon.'

But it was not for Mr Solomon. At some remote point in the history of the flat it had been owned by a Mr Kreutzner. It was for this man, a vague, shadowy figure to whom bills and circulars were still occasionally addressed, that the call was intended: a woman's voice, high, querulous and resentful. Halfway through the lavish monologue, I put the phone down. Elaine lingered in the hallway.

'You want to know what I think about all this? About all this *filming*?'

'Tell me.'

'I think it sucks. I don't think it'll ever happen. Not really. Tovacs is always going on about putting money into things. Fancy editions of crappy poetry. Paying some publisher to do his memoirs. Wants to be the big impresario, you see, and give parties where people nudge each other when he comes into the room. But it never comes to anything. The crappy poetry just lies around in proof and the publishers, well, the publishers aren't exactly queueing up.'

'Morty seems to think it's okay.'

'Morty's just desperate,' Elaine said with unprecedented hos-tility. 'All these years of doing his arty porn and thinking he's some sort of libertarian into the bargain, and all of a sudden the money isn't there any more and over in Europe they've just discovered real filth for a change and suddenly all this prick-teasing stuff doesn't cut it.'

'And what about you?'

'Oh, I'm desperate too. Incredibly desperate. Do you know what I found the other night when I was cleaning up, Martin? I found that copy of *Ireland's Own*, with that picture of me my dad sent in when I was fifteen. And it just cracked me up. I mean, I haven't got a lot of shame, but I can tell you seeing that was much worse than anything we ever did with Morty Kronenburg. Much worse.'

Often in the ensuing weeks I found myself remembering this conversation; not so much for the warning it conveyed as for the sharp hint of vulnerability. This was not a quality I had previously associated with Elaine. Now, extracted at long last from a mass of unpromising detritus, it became central to my conception of her, something capable of redeeming the indifference and the casual neglect. When I came to reckon up the balance of our relationship – a process I conducted every so often in a phantom ledger – this knowledge acted invariably as a trump card, sweeping away the opposing catalogue of hurt and embarrassment. The air of delusion hung irremovably over my dealings with Elaine, but I knew that it would fatal to acknowledge it. Only this bright, consoling fantasy kept my own desperation at bay.

In the event Elaine's pessimism was unfounded. Slowly but inexorably, like some Heath Robinson contraption always surmounting the apparent certainty of failure, the juggernaut of film production creaked forward. There were further meetings above the shop in Red Lion Street and further lunches at Morty's club. A country house near Southwold on the Suffolk coast was hired for filming and a date set in early February. Morty, alone of all the various people involved in the enterprise, remained unmoved by this evidence of progress. 'I feel like the guy in the story,' he said on more than one occasion, 'the guy in the story who was told that he couldn't marry the girl. So he goes out to drown his sorrows and ends up in the town brothel and gets a dose of the clap. Next week the girl rings him up and tells him that she's changed her mind.'

THIS MORNING SUZI says, 'I'll need the front room tonight. You remember?'

'No. What for?'

Suzi gives me one of those intent, sorrowful looks in which she specialises these days. 'I did tell you. For Terry's coaching.'

'Yes.'

Terry's coaching. Generally in the course of her professional life Suzi concerns herself with nine- and ten-year-old boys, but there is a sideline in after-hours encouragement for exam-chastened adolescents, hulking sixteen-year-olds needing to be dragged through *Dombey and Son*, or helped to devise a plausible account of M. Jambon's *vacances*. Such sessions are a more or less unavoidable consequence of Suzi's job, her school being one of those swindling private establishments aimed at the dullard progeny of the comfortably off. Gross, lymphatic farmers' sons from the Norfolk plain, pallid mannikins whose parents have profound doubts, don't you know, about the value of a comprehensive education, an actual half-wit or two – these are the types who turn up here early on winter evenings with their expensive atlases and shiny calculators, all the hapless paraphernalia of the scholastic loser. I think about this as Suzi chunters on, looking up as she reaches her peroration.

'So if Terry arrives before I get back you'll let him in, won't you, and give him a cup of tea?'

'Sure.'

Terry is the likeliest of several likely lads whom Suzi is trying to coax through their O-levels. Seventeen and a half – already failed them twice – and from the roving, knowing eye he turns on his instructress you get the feeling that he'd rather be doing something else. Poor Terry. He ought to be out there bringing in the hay, or manhandling bags of fertiliser, but no, the horny-handed satrap of some farmhouse out Reepham way has decided that he needs *qualifications* and the result is this shambling, tongue-tied display of ignorance twice weekly in the front room.

'See you later then,' says Suzi. I check the post on the mat, find nothing alarming, look up. 'See you later then,' Suzi says again, 'after rounders.'

After rounders. In recent weeks Suzi has stepped up her schedule to an unprecedented degree: a ceaseless round of marking, administering, conferring with the parents of her delinquent brood. I ask her about it sometimes.

'Why do you do all this?'

'All what?'

'All the stuff nobody pays you to do. Running the PTA ceilidh. Making the punch for the staff party. Helping the dimwits to get a grade seven rather than a grade eight in their CSEs.'

'It's my *job*,' Suzi says with apparent sincerity. 'I mean, that's what I'm there to do, isn't it? Take Terry . . .'

'He's a halfwit.'

'. . . He's just a bit slow, poor kid. And if I can help him to do a bit better than he would have done otherwise, then he'll feel that he's achieved something.'

There is more to it, though, than the marking and the PTA meetings. In the past month or so Suzi's social life has undergone a decisive change in gear, grown suddenly hectic and indiscriminate. I come home sometimes and find her crouched happily over the telephone talking to women with names like Jackie and Debbie, girls she knew at school, it turns out, transformed by the years' caress into bustling mothers of three with bungalows at Cringleford and serious husbands who work in insurance. They come round here occasionally: rosy Norfolk girls with wide hips and solemn offspring already dulled by the weight of parental expectation.

Suzi goes out. The day assumes its characteristic focus. I play the window-cleaner tape through again, marvelling at my pitiless, unremembered dexterity. Outside the familiar processions soldier by: the files of schoolchildren, the old women out shopping, the restless unemployed. Later on, in the afternoon, as the mist rises over Heigham Park, I slip out in search of Fat Eric, find him immersed in the purposeful chaos of his lounge, ponderous and inert, but prepared to discuss business plans and hint at the alleviation of his chronic, plenary indebtedness. There is no sign of Kay. 'Nice to see you, squire,' Fat Eric intones, and the time slips effortlessly away, gone in a spiral of cigarettes and instant coffee, in silent autumnal frowsting. Kay comes back, a brace of carrier bags dragging sadly behind her, and we take tea wedged together on the shiny sofa while Fat Eric stares wordlessly at the blaring TV and I wonder idly, the thought stealing up on me unawares, quite shocking me with its insidiousness, how long this can go on, this quiet burrowing life, here in the corner of this quaint, frozen world.

Later still the light of the streetlamp glimmers through the dark, uncurtained room, as Kay falls asleep on the sofa, one arm twisted awkwardly over her face, jaws unclenched. Fat Eric has disappeared on some unexplained errand: I can hear him upstairs moving ceaselessly from room to room, a giant antediluvian lizard slapping his tail on the floorboards. I wander out into the musty hall where half-full packets of Marlboro are strewn about over the carpet and there lie accumulated on the strip of lino that serves as Fat Eric's doormat a winded football, two Sindy dolls in cellophane wrappers and a pram filled with what looks like cement.

Back at the house Suzi and Terry are already ensconced in the front room, a fact brought home to me when I blunder in to discover them regarding the piled textbooks, hear Terry's voice – that slow, clueless voice – stutter off into embarrassed silence.

'I'm sorry,' I say, 'I didn't think you'd be here.'

Suzi looks up from the pad of paper spread across her lap. 'I did *tell* you,' she says. I look at Terry, over whose pitted, knowing face there is already rising the ghost of a smirk. 'Stay if you like,' Suzi goes on, equably. 'We've nearly finished as it happens. Terry doesn't mind, do you, pet?'

'*I* don't mind,' Terry says negligently. I sit down and affect to study the sports pages of the *Eastern Evening News* with their alarming intelligence about Kevin Flack's depressed cheekbone fracture, and the lesson proceeds, intently fascinating in its intimation of warped communication lines, its chronic bewilderment.

'Terry was just telling me about *The Mayor of Casterbridge*,' Suzi goes on. 'It's his set book.'

'Fine,' I say. 'Don't mind me.'

'Don't mind Martin,' Suzi says. 'Just carry on with what you were saying, Terry.'

Terry makes a few laboured observations about *The Mayor of Casterbridge* that are quite startling in their lack of conviction. I gaze at him as he does this, brow furrowed, forefinger tethered rigidly midway down the page, get a sudden inkling of the epic contempt in which he holds this inexplicable ritual, something devised, apparently, with the express purpose of boring and disconcerting him, his bemusement at whichever fate ordained this monstrous thraldom which he has no power to escape or alter.

Suzi's voice drifts in above the drone, 'You see, Terry, the point about this man is that he's a corn-factor. Now, if you were in his position, how would you feel? How would you feel about all the things you've just been telling me?'

I catch her eye as she says this: there is not a trace of mockery, not a shadow. Terry says something about it all being mechanised anyway these days and Suzi nods at him professorially, worlds away from me in my chair, lost in some elemental world of Honest Effort, Hard Work and Just Rewards. Getting up, sauntering back to the hall, I am struck by the dreadful realisation that her humanity shames me.

And then out in the hall, at the foot of the staircase, drenched in artificial light, something very odd indeed happens: out of the tail of my eye I catch a glimpse of my father staring out over the topmost banister. A late-period incarnation of my father, the hair neatly Brylcreemed back over his scalp, the eyes unfocused but alert, a split-second framing between the strips of wood and the billowing space beyond. Blinking slightly, I repeat the glance. He isn't there. I press on upwards. Down below the voices echo.


I heard the news of Mr Tovacs' death – a month ago, in a Paris nursing home – quite by chance, on a radio news programme sandwiched between fat stock prices and an interview with a government minister about export credit guarantees. Subsequently a number of weekly magazines printed obituaries, Channel Four screened a programme about him made thirty years before and he became for a brief period a subject of interest to the arts sections of Sunday newspapers. There was talk of 'Zeitgeist' and a serious young critic devoted nearly a page of the Daily Telegraph to the suggestion that he represented 'a link between the ferment of early modernism and the less confident art forms of our own age'.

I read these memorials with interest. Many of them, hastily composed and presumably compiled out of reference books, gave the impression of having been written by people with little or no knowledge of Mr Tovacs' personality. He was widely and erroneously spoken of as the friend of Diaghilev (Mr Tovacs' published work showed a marked distaste for the Ballet Russe), the patron of Beckett (he had abominated Godot) and the amanuensis of Joyce. There was the inevitable confusion over his age, variously located in the mid-sixties, early seventies or late eighties. Several newspapers had produced more or less relevant illustrations: a charcoal drawing by Augustus John of a Sitwell dinner (no figure recognisable) which he was thought to have attended, a Horizon frontispiece (his name, on close inspection, not listed among the contributors), a dubious Sutherland caricature. The Times notice, alone among these respectful éloges, appeared to be the work of someone who had known him at an earlier period in his life and had some conception of what it was that he might have been thought to represent. Its tone was quaint, leaving one to suspect that it had been written some years before.

> With his death, [The Times obituarist wrote] the world of European high culture has lost not so much a genuine creative force as a potent impresario. Even more, it has lost a living relic of one of the most turbulent and exciting periods in its recent history. There are few enough men of whom it can be said that they knew Proust or saw Firbank plain, but Tovacs was one of this rare breed. Inevitably, perhaps, his affiliations and his gift for friendship took precedence over his own literary output. His novels are now perhaps no more than period pieces, exotic blooms out of a landscape long barren and fruitlessly retilled, although in such works as

*Harlequin* and *Columbine* we may note an early attempt to link the symbolism of Apollinaire with the brooding introspection of Kafka . . . *Pages* is his enduring memorial. In it he forged a literary vehicle that was truly international in its scope. Gide wrote for it, Moore and Sutherland decorated its covers. In its half-century or so of precarious existence it played host to a galaxy of talent composed of stars as varied as Ginsberg, Creeley and Mishima. And it is in *Pages*, this refuge from the grasp of a less tolerant world, that Tovacs is at his best. His prefatory notes, lush arboreta of hothouse prose, where the shades of the great departed meet and talk, where Rabelais is invoked to examine Baudelaire and Fragonard walks with Rothko, are notable not only for the suggestiveness of their conceits, but for their self-effacement. In the cavalcade of lustre and *éclat* which Tovacs assembled, it was his nature to see himself only as a minor attendant . . .

There was a great deal more of this. Accurate, perhaps, in its assemblage of names, it gave no hint of the knowing, confidential tone with which Mr Tovacs had invested his editorials. He had hobnobbed with his authors, I thought, taken Eliot and Rimbaud out into the compendious, book-lined study of his mind and subtly patronised them. Milton's shade and Rabelais' grosser spectre might have wandered through these brightly lit corridors, but it was for Mr Tovacs' benefit that the diversion had been staged. Reading through this stately summary of his life and achievements I was left with the very faint suspicion that, in defiance of probability, through aliases, perhaps, or complex channels of inducement, Mr Tovacs had written it himself.

Christmas came: a chill and desolate feast. Grey clouds moved west over the bare South Norfolk landscape; the Caistor-by-Norwich road where I walked on Christmas afternoon was aflood with icy water. Within the house at Glebe Road lay equal desolation. A year ago there had been a pine tree, strings of coloured lights and a certain amount of conviviality. Now there was only quiet unease. Stray flames of conciliation which had sprung up unexpectedly in the previous week had been damped down or extinguished. Early on Christmas morning Suzi departed to Bungay to spend the day with her parents. I ate my lunch alone in the dining room.

Over the years I had grown accustomed to these solitary meals. My father regarded Christmas as an institution got up for the exclusive benefit of the retail trade. 'A hundred and fifty years ago,' he used to say, 'Christmas was a civilised festival. But then a lot of shopkeepers, encouraged I regret to say by the Prince Consort, got hold of it and invested it with the vulgarity of commerce. Paper hats,' my father said severely, 'extravagant decoration and over-eating. All quite unnecessary.' But there was a second line of thought commonly brought out at this time to justify the absence of hospitality and excess. 'A lot of people,' my father would say, 'simply make Christmas the excuse for holding a sort of open house to acquaintances they very probably dislike and would certainly avoid at other times of the year. Well, we are a big enough unit as it is.' Such stringency could not be gainsaid. Later on there had been other Christmases – Christmases with Morty and the current Mrs Kronenburg in Essex, Christmases with Elaine in country hotels – yet the tradition remained. It was here, I thought, here in Norwich amid rain and recrimination that the true spirit of the season resided.

Suzi returned late in the afternoon. The present from her parents – a vast bottle-green smock – lay gleaming from the back seat of the car. Looking at her as she stood in the hallway, face crimson from the wind, booted feet moving up and down in an exaggerated military step, I wondered at the impulse that had brought her back. It was, I realised, part of an engrossing ritual. What was it she had said about Nick and Tony and all the others? 'It wasn't working out . . . Thought we'd carry on for a bit and see . . .' I was familiar with the words, their casual evocation of emotional fracture. Each of Suzi's relationships, I saw, had followed this pattern: a build-up of expectation, a year or so of pleasure, a slow fading away. There was, I thought, a predictability about them which she found consoling. It was, for her, how a relationship worked. In a month, or a week, she would leave me. Until that time she was content to hang on, precariously, in the face of ever-diminishing returns.

A single custom survived from former Christmases. Suzi, I had discovered early on in our relationship, was an inveterate player of indoor as well as outdoor games. Cardboard boxes containing Scrabble pieces or Trivial Pursuit cards lay everywhere over the house. There was also in her room a tea-chest filled to the brim with relics of her childhood – spillikins, Cluedo, a complicated pastime which involved spearing small translucent fish with a kind of metal spatula. It was to this treasure trove, late on Christmas night, that we repaired.

Suzi said, 'I'd like to play the memory game, if you don't mind.'

'I don't mind.'

And so we played the memory game, which of all the diversions with which Suzi occupied her leisure hours was the one she favoured most. In essence it was an aural version of Kim's Game, the tray and its random collection of objects replaced by a tape recorder. Each player selected a cassette – Suzi had a vast array of old Light Programme comedies specially recorded for the purpose – and, having listened to it for a certain period, was asked a series of questions.

'*Hancock's Half-Hour?*'

'Too easy.'

'We haven't listened to it for ages.'

'If you like.'

Long years of practice had made Suzi adept at the memory game. She knew by instinct which pieces of information might attract my questions, precisely the level of recall necessary to win points. As the tape recorder played – it was 'The Blood Donor' – she wrote tiny, indecipherable notes on the back of an envelope.

'What does Hancock say when they tell him they want to take a pint?'

'He says, "But that's an armful." '

'Correct. What is the name of the nurse . . . ?'

It was to no avail. Whatever strategies I had thought to confuse her with, whatever technicalities I had dredged up to confound her, none had the slightest effect. She won handsomely.

'It's a question of technique,' Suzi said. She frowned at the scrap of paper. 'There comes a time when you begin to see it in your mind.'

She was generous in victory. Later when we moved on to

other games, to Monopoly and then to a complex re-enactment of the Second World War which I remembered playing with my father, the result was the same. There was something pitiless, I thought, about this absorption, something that lifted it on to a higher level than an exchange of playing cards. Occasionally, when I made some spectacular blunder, or was detected in some flagrant lapse from the rules, I caught her staring at me. It was an odd look, in which righteousness and contempt were neatly blended, as if these were real banknotes being passed across the table, real ships being inveigled across the Atlantic to eventual sabotage. In this, as in so many other things, I had been found out.

After lunch on Boxing Day I walked through the wet streets to Eaton Park. In the pale light of a winter afternoon the place had a gloomy air. The grass had grown wild and untended on the bowling rinks; there were weeds creeping up through the tarmac of the tennis courts. I wandered on through an avenue of moulting trees to the bandstand. Here too there were signs of decay. The boating pond had been drained: strange detritus, lumps of stone and wooden fence posts, lay across the concrete floor. The roof of the bandstand sagged uncomfortably. Beneath, a small area had been cordoned off and there were workmen's tools propped up against the pillars. A few children on bicycles or carrying shiny plastic toys roamed around the gravel pathways.

Beyond the circle of changing rooms and the boarded-up tea-shop with its advertisements for ice-cream and Seven-Up a turfed incline led down to the soccer fields. There the ground was soft and wet; in the distance three small boys were taking desultory shots into an empty goal. I had played on these fields myself as a child. The teams still ran in my head: Buckingham Rovers, Avenue Rovers, South Park Albion; each name taken from a street adjoining the park.

On the western edge of the fields there was a stone gatehouse where, entombed behind barred windows, extravagant model yachts could be glimpsed. As I walked towards it a figure emerged out of the shadow beneath the gate and moved hesitantly forward. I became conscious of a sidelong glance, a faint straining after recognition. A voice said, 'It's Mr Benson, isn't it?'

I turned and found Mr Robey. Removed from the confines of his office and the bar of the Maid's Head he seemed a diminished figure. He wore a flat check cap of the kind affected by middle-aged men in situation comedies and a shiny oilskin jacket. There was a small cigar smoking in the fingers of his left hand (he explained the cigar in the course of the evening by saying, 'I don't usually smoke, but somebody gave me a packet and it seemed a pity to throw them away'). It was two years since I had seen him, but he fell in beside me and began talking in the manner of one who resumes a conversation broken off a day or so previously.

'It is Mr Benson? I never forget a client. It's an advantage, isn't it, for someone in my line of work?'

'I suppose it is.'

'But you'd be surprised how many people do. I've seen solicitors, professional people, walk past clients in the street a day after they've shown them out of their offices. That sort of thing looks very bad.' Something seemed to strike him and he turned towards me. 'That was a good evening we had, wasn't it? I always say you can't beat a good evening with people you've got something in common with, people you've been to school with. Did you go to the old boys' dinner this year?'

'No.'

'No, I don't remember you there, now you come to mention it. It was a good evening, though,' Mr Robey said defiantly, as if I had somehow called the event into question. 'A great success. We had a civil servant who was something high up in the Foreign Office. I can't say I'd ever heard of him, but everybody said it was very good.'

By now we had reached the outermost limit of the park. Here stunted trees lay in clumps, following the curve of South Park Avenue. Behind us a fiery orange sun cast angular shadows across the playing fields. It was growing dark.

At the gate Mr Robey stopped. 'I say. You'll think this awfully forward of me, I know, but what would you say to trying to find a pub somewhere? Somewhere we could have a bit of a drink and a natter?'

I remembered the family portraits on his desk. 'Won't your wife be expecting you back?'

Mr Robey looked uneasy. 'Between you and me, my wife's taken the children round to her mother's in Thorpe this afternoon. So this excursion is rather in the nature of a breather.'

'While the cat's away?'

'*Exactly*,' said Mr Robey, with unexpected fervour. 'That's exactly what it is.'

There was a pub at the very end of South Park Avenue called the University Arms where on rare occasions I had accompanied my father. It was here, driven by some unspoken mutual instinct, that we repaired. Inside, dark wooden beams and a single, flickering striplight combined to produce a sub-aqueous effect. Two elderly men sat playing dominoes by the fire.

Mr Robey brightened. 'Well, this is a find,' he said. 'What will you have?'

'A small whisky.'

'Nonsense. Always drink doubles at Christmas.' Mr Robey advanced on the landlord. 'Two double whiskies if you please.'

This was a new and unexpected version of Mr Robey, a bright, capering figure come to confound the anonymous wraith of the solicitor's office. He came back from the bar carrying the drinks in outstretched hands and laid them with an odd little flourish on the table.

'Actually,' he said, 'I used to come here before. Back in the old days. It was handy for the university, you see.'

'You were a student at the UEA?'

'Not me. Keele,' Mr Robey said sadly, as if this explained any later misfortunes to which he might have been subject. 'No. UEA girls. When I was in the sixth form at school we used to take them here.'

'I don't remember that happening in my day.'

'You'd be surprised,' said Mr Robey sagely. 'You'd be surprised at what went on.'

There was an expression which my father had used with reference to a decayed crony of his from the Norwich masonic club. 'Mr so-and-so,' he would say, with infinite contempt, 'was rather a dog in his day.' Mr Robey, I saw, had been such a dog. I remembered his kind from school: loud, confident teenagers who drove their fathers' cars, who spent summer weekends at beach parties on the coast at Bacton and Cart Gap and could be seen arm-in-arm with busty sixthformers from the Norwich High School for Girls. This early superiority had rankled. Monitoring the reports of their later careers – accountants, estate agents, insurance salesmen – I had always felt a keen sense of reparation.

Something, plainly, was preying on Mr Robey's mind. Presently he said, 'Extraordinary stroke of luck us meeting up like this, wasn't it?'

'I suppose it was.'

'To tell you the truth, it was a bit of a godsend you turning up like this. In fact, if I hadn't seen you when I did there's no knowing what I might not have done with myself.'

Years spent with Morty's entourage had accustomed me to confidences of this sort. 'What on earth is the matter?'

'Christmas,' said Mr Robey bitterly. 'I can't seem to get through it any more like I used to. It was all right in the old days. I could go down to the rugby club, play in the Boxing-Day game with some of the old crowd and we'd have a hell of a time.'

Another piece in the jigsaw puzzle of Mr Robey's dog-days clicked neatly into place. Above our heads the lighting flared suddenly into life and then receded again. 'Couldn't you do that now?'

'Crocked. Dodgy cartilage. If I run more than ten yards my knee gives out. Happens to us all, I suppose,' he went on. 'But it's not the same, you know, just standing on the line and watching the others. You feel you're missing out.'

'What does your wife say?'

'Barbara? She's a grand girl, Barbara, but she doesn't understand. Not about sport. Women never do. I never knew a woman,' said Mr Robey, as if defining some incorrigible sex-wide deficiency, 'who really cared about sport. But she's a grand girl, Barbara. I wouldn't like you to think that I was doing her down.'

It was what men said about women they had grown tired of, or of women they suspected had grown tired of them. Suzi, I realised, was a grand girl. It meant imperfection, resentment, that fatal waning of interest.

Mr Robey's eye, which had been ranging nervously around the bar, now fell on our empty glasses. 'Look,' he said, 'I know it's a terrific cheek, but would you mind just talking to me for a bit? You're a man of the world – you've done some interesting things, I can see that. Solicitors notice things about their clients, you know. I could tell that from the moment you walked into the office. I'd take it as a great favour if you'd just talk to me for a bit.'

An idea which had previously existed only in outline suddenly assumed coherent shape in my head. 'Mr Robey . . .'

'Geoff.'

'Geoff . . . Now you mention it there is something you could give me your professional opinion on. Would that be agreeable?'

'I'm all ears,' said Mr Robey. 'Go right ahead.'

And so I explained about the telephone calls, about the photographs and the video cassettes. And as these people also had their place in the story I explained about Morty, Terry Chimes and Elaine. It was a considerable monologue. Throughout it Mr Robey listened with an expression of rapt interest. When I had finished he said, 'This is way above my head, I don't mind saying. Someone unknown to you has been sending you pictures in which you appear, but you don't remember anything about it?'

'Nothing.'

'Extraordinary,' Mr Robey said. All trace of his depression of spirit had now lifted. 'I think we'd better have another drink and put our heads together about this. You see *technically* nobody has committed any crime, except of course sending obscene materials through the post. Even if you could find out who was responsible there wouldn't necessarily be any means of bringing them to court.'

We had another round of drinks. 'I acted once in an obscene publications case you know,' Mr Robey went on. 'Shocking business it was. Married couple out at Thetford used to sell photographs of themselves by mail order.'

'What happened?'

'Let off with a caution. All to do with freemasonry, if you want my opinion,' said Mr Robey moodily, 'but then it's all a question of knowing the right people, isn't it?' A sudden flash of belligerence lit up his face. 'Between you and me, Barbara's dad is high up in the masons.'

Later, when we were very drunk, we found ourselves outside in the darkness of South Park Avenue. Light gleamed from the surrounding housefronts. Mr Robey said, 'Do you know what we could do? We could get a taxi and go into town. Go to a night-club and have another drink. A proper drink.'

'Do they have many night-clubs in Norwich now?'

'Dozens. Samantha's. CJ's. Danny's Den. We could go to one of those and have a proper drink. Lot of trouble they have in the city these days, fighting and so on – always having people in my office charged with causing an affray – but so what? I'm pretty quick on my feet. I can take it. Let's go to a night-club.'

We wandered unsteadily along South Park Avenue for a while. On the rare occasions when a vehicle passed us Mr Robey leapt into the road behind it and shouted 'Taxi' very loudly. Then abruptly, his mood changed.

'It's no good. Better go home. Wouldn't do, would it? "Respected local solicitor charged with causing affray in night-club." It was good of you to suggest it, but we'd better not.'

'You could come back to my place and have a drink.'

'It's kind of you, but no. I've enjoyed our little chat,' said Mr Robey decisively, 'don't think I haven't, but no.'

And so on the corner of South Park Avenue we separated, he to move purposefully along Colman Road past the grey expanse of the infant school, I to walk less confidently through the succession of alleyways and side roads that led to Glebe Road. There was no sign of Suzi. I threw myself fully clothed on to the bed. Hours later I woke to find the light on and the telephone ringing downstairs in the hall.

A voice said, 'Merry Christmas, Mart.'

It was Morty. He too was drunk.

'Where are you?'

'Christ. At Terry's. Someplace in Essex. Saffron Walden, Great Dunmow, I don't remember. Full of fucking cows and fields of cabbages. You want to speak to Terry?'

'Is he there?'

'Hang on.' There was a flurry of remote, disconnected movement. 'No, he's fucked off somewhere. Went to the off-licence with Rodney or something. Hey, I got something to tell you though. That business of the pictures, those photos you keep getting sent. Terry heard something about it the other day.' There was a silence. 'You still there, Mart?'

'Yes.'

'Where was I . . . ? Yeah, that business of the pictures. Well, somebody Terry was talking to reckoned it's some mad chick that's doing it. Some mad actress that must have got pissed off with you in the past. Wants to get back at you and that sort of thing. You got any ideas?'

'Have you?'

'No. There was that Lynsey Laguna didn't like the way you monkeyed about with her scripts . . . Jesus, she earns two-hundred grand a year in the States now, she wouldn't want to do a thing like that. It beats me, Mart, it beats me. I should just sit tight if I were you, just sit tight and Terry and me'll see what we can find out.'

'Yes.'

There was another long silence. Dimly in the distance I could hear Morty's heavy breath panting down the line. Finally he said, 'Look, it's Christmas, Mart, Christmas, and Terry and me were thinking we ought to see you. Old times' sake and all that. Why don't you, why don't you just come on over?'

'Jesus, Morty, it's seventy, eighty miles away.'

'Yeah, I know that, I know that. But Terry's got some tame mini-cab firm. Reckons they owe him a favour. They could be over in an hour.'

'It's almost midnight, Morty.'

'Yeah, I know that. You know something?' Morty said evenly. 'You disappoint me a lot.'

'I'm sorry.'

'Yeah,' Morty said. 'But I'm still disappointed. Lots. You remember that, Martin. So long.'

The line went dead. I stood for a moment in the hallway considering the vague air of menace with which Morty's words had been attended. Then I went back to bed.

Much later in the small hours I woke to hear the sounds of Suzi moving about below: a faint hum of voices, clicks of dislodged crockery. The television rasped noisily for a few moments and was then switched off. Outside it began to rain. From the distance, beyond the dark rooftops and the scudding clouds, came the sound of thunder.

On New Year's Day Kev Jackson calls again. Coming back from the City Gates, awash with festive bonhomie, I hear the phone ringing outside the house, dash in and pounce on the receiver just before it expires. Kev is brief, businesslike.

'I got that address you wanted.'

He mentions a domicile somewhere in Greater Manchester.

'That's great, Kev.'

'Don't mention it . . . There's a phone number as well.'

I convey the proffered digits to the message pad. Kev Jackson goes on, a touch nervously now. 'Good Christmas, Martin?'

'Can't complain, Kev. What about you?'

'Actually,' Kev Jackson says quickly, 'I got an invitation from Morty Kronenburg. Over to Terry Chimes' place. Near Saffron Walden. That farmhouse he built after RCA bought him out of Grunt.'

Out in the street I can hear Fat Eric making a raucous, vagrant progress back to his front door. 'Glad to hear it, Kev. I thought Morty wasn't talking?'

'Oh well.' Kev Jackson turns nonchalant and unassuming. 'It's not so much about the book . . . Well, I don't want to give too much away at this stage, Martin, but Morty and me, we've got interests in common.'

Interests in common. Morty and I have interests in common. Elaine and I, wherever she is, have interests in common. Whoever it is who's sending me these pictures and I have interests in common.

'Too bad you couldn't make it yourself,' Kev Jackson goes on. 'At Christmas and that. That reminds me, Morty sent you a message.'

'He did?'

'Sure. He said to say, "Wait and see is best." '

'Just that?'

'Just that. "Wait and see is best." Now, I have a few questions here I want to ask you.'

I turn the words over in my head as Kev Jackson chunters on

about a tedious and negligible scandal involving some purloined tapes and the *News of the World*. Outside there is a tumultuous crash which, experience suggests, is something to do with the beery pageant of Fat Eric's return, then silence. I put down the phone, stand by the window looking out in the empty streets.

A bit later I dial the number Kev Jackson gave me. It rings on endlessly. Several times over the ensuing days I try it again. No one ever answers. I wonder about writing to Elaine, I wonder about bombarding her with a torrent of allusive postcards, wonder even about taking a train to Manchester, confronting her on her doorstep. Eventually I do none of these things. Prompted by mounting inner disquiet I do, however, pay a visit to Norwich Central Library and, adrift amongst the pale students and the restless flotsam of the reading room, take a look at a Greater Manchester street directory. There is, as I suspected, no trace of Elaine's address.


Rain, slanting in from the west, came suddenly out of sky the colour of slate. Above, a group of sea gulls, jerked upwards by a gust of wind rising from the head of the dunes, hung motionless for a moment, squawking plaintively, before flapping slowly landward. Becalmed at the point where blocks of charred, unidentifiable wood lay half in and half out of the water they regrouped, heads low down against white pelts, feet balanced uneasily on this precarious perch. To the left choppy, gravy-coloured sea rose and fell inexorably, empty except for one or two low, solid shapes far away on the horizon. Dusk, which had stolen up unawares in the last fifteen minutes, drew nearer.

Elaine said, 'Do you think we ought to turn back?'

'It's only a mile to the town.'

'A mile back to the house if it comes to that.'

'There's four of us,' Jerry said. 'We ought to take a vote, at least.'

Back along the beach at the point where the coast began its slow curve in the direction of Lowestoft, mist was rising in dense, vaporous trails, partly obscuring the woods where we had walked only an hour or so before. I reflected on the inconsistency of the human spirit when presented with even the mildest obstacle of climate. The walk had been Elaine's idea. It was she who had instigated the route, she who had assembled the accompanying party, she, even, who had rummaged around in old cupboards and cloakrooms to procure suitable clothing and footwear. Now, by a strange but compelling twist of logic, it was she who seemed the most anxious to turn back.

Jerry said, 'We could at least walk up to the top and take a look at the place.'

Beyond and to the right, past outcrops of sandstone, shoreline bric-à-brac of rotting spars and plastic containers, a path rose shakily to the cliff-top. Here there was further evidence of human debris: cigarette packets stamped into the sand, discarded fishing nets, salt-encrusted onions – a characteristic piece of east-coast jetsam – beaten into pulp. Looking back, the pattern of the rain increasing now to produce tiny indentations in the sand, I was struck by older associations: M.R. James's ghost stories, invariably set in this part of East Anglia, in which tatterdemalion wraiths rose up unexpectedly out of the sedge and demons capered beneath the sea wall; a painting by Wilson Steer of fog hanging over a marsh near Walberswick, folk tales of black, phantasmagoric animals said to haunt the coastline. In these circumstances – late afternoon in early January, twilight rapidly descending – it would not have been surprising to see Black Shuck or one or other of the local spirits loping hungrily up the beach.

Something of this feeling seemed to have occurred to Elaine. Pausing at the foot of the steps, where the overhang of the cliff face combined with encroaching shadow to create an atmosphere of unusual gloom, she said, 'I wouldn't like to come here after dark.'

'No one's asking you to.'

Crazy Rodney said, 'I know what you mean. Gives me the fucking creeps.'

Reaching the summit of the cliff, the wind gusting horizontally against the outcrops of sea grass, it was possible to hear echoes of an older world. Mist rolling away in queer clumps and hillocks over recently tilled fields, now breaking up in wispy, striated patterns, suggested something bordering on the prehistoric: Saxon coastguards, perhaps, staring anxiously out to sea, a vista of archaic battledress, beards, 'noble' expressions, in the manner of one of those fanciful paintings of the pre-Raphaelite school. Obscurely the town, a mile away, its outlying flanks discernible in the grey sea defences, bore out this impression. Church spires, rising out of the fog, a few lights already shining, the distant houses towards Blythburgh disappearing into shadow, it seemed as remote and self-absorbed as any medieval encampment. You imagined gatekeepers, venerable constables of the watch, Shakespearean paraphernalia of curfews and cock-crows.

Remote, dense, engrossed: I had always visualised the East Anglian landscape in these terms. History supported this sharp, austere conception: longboats nosing into the Suffolk creeks, dark sails along the river Wensum, King Edmund, his chest shot full of arrows like a pincushion, dying at Hellesdon, the monks scurrying westward from the sea. This feeling was strengthened by the experiences of the past week: fog, a constant feature of the terrain, rolling up at a moment's notice to obscure harsh views of sedge, bracken and scrubby pasture; rushing wind; cattle seen dimly through the mist like ghostly monsters out of a primeval landscape. We had descended into an older world, I thought, regressed into some elemental amphitheatre presided over by remote, clangorous gods.

On the cliff top serpentine pathways rose and fell: up to distant, vapour-shrouded fields, down to the low walls of shale and concrete. Ahead lines of tangled fencing, torn paper flapping heavily on the wire, enclosed nondescript pasturage. Sheep, huddled up against the posts, stirred anxiously at the intrusion. Here we lingered for a moment, stamping our feet against the cold, lighting cigarettes, in silence broken only by the wind and the skirl of the gulls.

Crazy Rodney said, 'So what happens there?'

'What happens where?'

'Down there. Sarfwold or wherever. What happens?'

'It's a town, Crazy Rodney. People live there.'

Hunched in his greatcoat, looking neither to right nor left, tendrils of cigarette smoke obscuring his pinched, watchful face, Crazy Rodney cut an incongruous figure. Massive inner resentment, narrowly kept at bay over the past week, now welled up uncontrollably.

'But what the fuck do they do?'

'Watch television. Look at the sea. Make money out of the tourists.'

Crazy Rodney shook his head. 'Carrot crunchers,' he said. 'Fucking carrot crunchers.'

'We'd better go back,' Elaine said. 'See whether Morty wants to retake that last scene.'

Jerry said, 'I never came any place like this before. Never.'

Another gust of wind whipping up from beyond the face of the cliff set the issue beyond doubt. It was now raining very hard indeed. Two-by-two, Jerry leading with Crazy Rodney, Elaine and I following close behind, we set off cautiously along the coast path.

Kessingland Manor dated from the early nineteenth century. Here at around the time of the Napoleonic wars some newly married Suffolk squire had built for himself a capacious family dwelling: two long vault-like reception halls, a low, draughty kitchen, a warren of bedrooms and servants' quarters. Later inhabitants had added on billiard rooms, gun rooms and out-houses; the whole constructed in greying limestone, taking on the character of an impregnable and faintly Gothic-looking fortress.

Terry Chimes proved to be unexpectedly knowledgeable about bygone domestic arrangements. He said, 'A hundred years ago there'd have been three, four, half-a-dozen horses, probably a coach as well. Kept them in the barn next to the courtyard, I shouldn't wonder.'

'What makes you think that?'

'Nearly bought a place like it myself once. Fucking estate agent – bright bloke he was, been to Oxford and that – told me what to look for.' Later he said, 'Bloody great barrack and all. Wouldn't surprise me if we had to do all the shooting outside.'

However the interior had proved surprisingly amenable to Morty's design. Arc-lights had been rigged up in the second reception hall towards the back of the house; one of the gun rooms was a mass of electrical equipment. Actresses, parcelled out three or four to a bedroom, had so far voiced only minor complaint.

'In any case,' Morty had said, 'if they don't like it, they know what they can do. Plenty of other girls ready to flap their tits about and they know it.'

Returning to the house, one proceeded by a complicated series of landmarks. Paths through coils of dense, wet bracken gave way eventually to a precarious back road, bordered by ravines of mud, finally a dirt-track overhung by sere, dripping elms. By now darkness had fallen. In the drive, where cars and vans lay drawn up in a haphazard semi-circle, a flashlight hovered for a moment and then moved haltingly towards us. A voice said, 'Who's that?'

We identified ourselves. Morty's face loomed up suddenly out of the murk.

'Sorry, Martin. I thought you were those American girls.'

'Which American girls?'

'The two the agency were supposed to be sending. I've been expecting them since lunch-time. I suppose the fucking trains are out again.'

There was a railway station at Halesworth, ten miles away. At intervals over the past five days it had disgorged a succession of new arrivals: exotic, gaudily dressed girls, bewildered by the unpromising terrain in which they now found themselves; sharp-faced men in suits, old allies of Morty's from distribution agencies and cinema chains, come to check on progress. In this ceaseless shambling to and fro across the level East Anglian countryside there had been casualties: actresses stranded in anonymous Suffolk towns where there were neither buses nor taxis; one of Terry Chimes' Grunt Records understrappers finally run to earth in Dunwich some miles down the coast. It was impossible to predict what might have happened to the American girls.

'I'd better go and have a look,' Morty said.

We left him standing uncertainly in the beam of torchlight and moved on towards the house. Here there were signs of recent activity. Packing cases, their tops prised open, their contents – pieces of unfamiliar lighting equipment – strewn about, lay in the vestibule. Two members of the film crew, vague anonymous men who had not been heard to speak during the course of the shoot, straightened up as they saw us, as if expecting some rebuke, them resumed their work. Mr Tovacs sat alone in the hall, his legs angled towards an electric heater, reading intently. Seeing us he rose noisily to his feet and gave a mock salute.

'You came upon me unawares,' he said, 'wholly given up to literature. Is that not always the case?'

In the interval since the Red Lion Street party Mr Tovacs' character had undergone a decisive shift in orientation. Previously he had given the impression of being no more than an interested spectator in the plans for filming *Resurrection*. Now, gradually, yet with increasingly confidence, he had emerged into the role of patron, someone intimately involved with each twist of a complicated piece of machinery, fearful lest his own interests should be ignored. Taken round the building by Morty, made party to various technicalities, he had the intent but slightly suspicious look of a tourist, conscious amid much communal diversion that responsibility for settling the bill lay with him alone. There was something ominous, I thought, about his continual presence on the edge of scene and conversation, his quaintly phrased questions: the scent of trouble.

The girls disappeared to their rooms, Crazy Rodney to the kitchen where, fires kept burning throughout the day, there was a promise of warmth. Mr Tovacs seemed disposed to talk. I examined the book he had just put aside. It was a paperback of *The Spoils of Poynton*, an appropriate choice in the circumstances. Much of Kessingland Manor's furniture and ornaments had survived the house's transformation into an upmarket holiday home. There were a number of superior knick-knacks lying about on tables, stout sideboards, a profusion of oil paintings dominated by a large, square portrait of an elderly patriarch in stock and side-whiskers. Mr Tovacs surveyed all these benevolently, his gaze finally resting on the portrait.

'He is a splendid fellow, is he not? A fine old *bourgeois*? One could make an interesting study of the social attitudes of Victorian portraiture. Art as the handmaiden of imperialism. I expect he gave people a terrible time in his day.'

This remark, unexceptionable in itself, gave another clue to the change in Mr Tovacs' character. He had, so to speak, moved up a gear, ascended to a new level of self-absorption and invulnerability, what the Victorian novelist – James himself, if it came to that – would have called a 'high demeanour'.

'Have you been here all afternoon?'

Mr Tovacs frowned at the painting, as if finally deciding that it did not match up to the exacting standards he required of portraiture. In one way or another he seemed extremely pleased with himself.

'Very little has happened. I believe there is some problem about transport. Earlier on your Mr Kronenburg made an attempt to film some scene in the barn behind the house. It grew very cold so I ventured indoors.

'It is none of my business,' Mr Tovacs went on. 'The technicalities that form a part of this project. Though naturally one has one's opinions.'

'There has been an *argument*,' Mr Tovacs said.


Snow fell later that night. I watched it, sitting up in bed, the curtain undrawn: a grey expanse of parkland, darker clumps of trees and shrubbery, all steadily obliterated by a pale, relentless tide. Snow falling over the wide East Anglian plain, descending to swell the mutinous sea, confirmed the impression of antiquity. I thought of wolves roaming through the frozen thickets, horses' hooves scraping the ice, old, unsanitised fairy tales of cheerless hearths and evil visitants. Beside me Elaine slept noiselessly, one arm flung out over the white sheet, hair spilled out across the pillow, so that she too seemed somehow a part of these unreal landscapes, lost and transient, like the wolves ripe for dissolution when the storyteller snapped his fingers and brought an end to his tale.

When I woke at dawn the room was empty. Outside the landscape had taken on sharp, unfamiliar outlines: fence posts running across snowy fields like the piping on a dress; a line of rooks rising suddenly from the woods and moving in formation away inland. I was dressed and sitting on the bed by the time Elaine returned.

'You poor baby,' she said. 'You were supposed to be asleep.'

'Where have you been?'

'Where do you think I've been? Out for a walk? Playing strip-poker with Terry Chimes – there's no point by the way, he always cheats. Jesus, Martin, I suppose you'll start talking about *loyalty* in a minute and mature relationships.'

'Who is it then? Is it Morty?'

'No.'

'Terry?'

'It doesn't matter who it is. What matters is that you shut up about it.'

'Or is it Crazy Rodney? He always has to have at least one actress a shoot. He told me once.'

'You poor baby,' Elaine said again. Mockery and faint, derisive sympathy could not be disentangled. 'I treat you so badly, don't I?'

'No worse than you always did.'

'I treat you so badly,' Elaine went on. 'So badly. And do you know what the joke is? The real joke is that you never do anything about it.'


The American girls emerged for the first time at breakfast. Sullen and fractious, they spoke only to each other.

'Too fucking cold to work. If Kronenburg wants me to work he'd better lay on some heating.'

'But honey, you got a contract.'

'Yeah and I got a weak chest as well. No heaters, no nude scenes.'

Later in the kitchen Cindy, the second American girl, said, 'You have to excuse Mary-Beth. She's had a lot of disappointments lately.'

'What sort of disappointments?'

'The usual sort of thing. I mean, you wouldn't believe it to look at her, but she used to be a serious actress. Her pa used to be head of East Coast production at Universal: she got a lot of parts that way. Supporting roles, nothing you could write home and tell your folks about, but, well, serious. She got to screw Rod Steiger once in a motel scene. Can you imagine that? Screwing Rod Steiger in a motel scene and it's the high point of your career. But then her pa died and she ended up in the skin trade. It just goes to show, I suppose.'

Traces of Mary-Beth's earlier respectability remained. She pronounced the few lines that the script allowed her in an odd, strangulated parody of an English accent. Cindy shook her head. 'All on account of when she was a kid,' she explained, 'and her pa used to show her these tapes of Edith Evans playing Lady Bracknell. Right from the start, right from when she was in high school drama proms, she thought that was the way actresses were supposed to speak.'

In the intervals of filming, members of Morty's cast emerged on to the meagre terrain of the surrounding countryside. Here they loitered unhappily in the snowbound lanes or took buses to Lowestoft, ten miles along the coast, in search of amusement. Numbers of them descended on Southwold where they could be seen staring moodily from the windows of teashops, or pondering the newspapers in the sailors' reading room. An undercurrent of mutiny, never quite allowed to rise to the surface, was narrowly kept in check by these relaxations.

Meanwhile I had plenty with which to occupy myself. Even in its revised and attenuated form, *Resurrection* had proved unmanageable for the limited resources with which Morty now found himself provided. Substantial cuts would be needed. I made Sir George a housebound invalid, his dissipation confined to voyeuristic eavesdropping on kitchen maids innocently exploring each other in the hayloft. I invented a makeweight subplot in which two of Sir George's grooms competed for the attentions of a buxom cook.

Though Morty approved these alterations, his mood remained grim. He said, 'You're doing your best, Martin, I can see that. It's just that . . . Christ, we've got to lose that scene at the wedding breakfast.'

'The one where they drink the bride's health and it turns into an orgy?'

'That's the one. We haven't got the costumes. Well, not enough of them. Didn't have enough money to hire them.'

'Well, shoot the whole thing nude then. As a sort of joke. You know, Sir George starting where he means to go on. Or have them all wrapped in blankets. I don't know.'

'Christ, Martin, sometimes I don't think you're taking me seriously. Sometimes I . . . Look, I'm sorry, Martin, I'm not getting at you. It's just that . . . Look, Martin, I've got problems like you wouldn't believe.'

'Tovacs?'

'No, not Tovacs. I can handle Tovacs, specially as he's come up with most of the money now. Keeps putting his nose in, keeps asking for things. Always asking for things. When he got here he wanted a phone put in his room. Yesterday he wanted a car to take him back to London for the night. I soon told him to fuck off about *that*. But it's not Tovacs, it's his girl.'

'I hadn't noticed anything.'

'You wouldn't. Glued to the fucking typewriter, aren't you? Well, there's something going on there. You just take a look and tell me if you don't agree with me. And fix the fucking wedding breakfast. I need to get it on tape.'

In the intervals of fixing the wedding breakfast – reduced eventually to a sober foursome involving Sir George, his bride, the best man and the head bridesmaid, a horde of imaginary guests continually spoken of as being 'in the other room' – I monitored the relationship between Jerry and Mr Tovacs. Outwardly all was as it had been before. They appeared together in public, sat next to one another at meal times, retired at night to a bedroom on the upper floor. But Morty's surmise was, I realised, correct. There was a sharp flavour of animosity about their dealings, the hint of Jerry's deep reservoir of resentment only now being allowed to seep out into the clear water around it. Once, passing their room late at night, I heard the sound of voices raised in recrimination: sharp, unmistakeable voices in which Jerry's predominated. I dismissed them as of little account: a diversion, perhaps, running in parallel to my own greater disquiet, faint echoes of a wider and more personal anguish.


In retrospect I recall this period as a series of potent but scarcely reconstitutable images: smudged portraits on the crackling tape, random, blaring soundtrack. Crazy Rodney on the cliff top; Morty, serious, aggrieved, casting his eye over a tableau of naked actresses; the American girls bickering in their dressing room; a memory of Terry Chimes met unexpectedly on a walk in the lanes and flashing me a smile whose significance I was not then able to appreciate; Mr Tovacs ambling pointedly from room to room in search of an electric heater; playing card games with Jerry in the dull forenoons. Later these pictures fade away, replaced eventually by the single figure of Elaine: Elaine in her role as *ingénue* bride, swooning on a sofa when faced with the first unignorable evidence of her husband's designs; Elaine cavorting with whoops of bogus lust over Sir George's recumbent body; Elaine backstage, wrapped in a towel, staring fiercely into space.

Time dragged.

Weather conditions, which had improved with the disappearance of the snow, rapidly worsened. Thin rain falling steadily across the barren fields alternated with winds rushing in from the coast. Crazy Rodney, who penetrated as far as Southwold harbour, reported waves as much as twenty feet high and the threat of flooding. At night absolute blackness descended, a blanket of cloud and mist impenetrable even by torchlight. It was in these conditions that Terry Chimes, returning late one evening from a pub in Kessingland village, tumbled into a roadside ditch and broke his ankle.

In the evenings Jerry and I played Scrabble.

' "Yapok". Five letters. That's seventy-eight points.'

' "Yapok"?'

'It's a South American water opossum,' Jerry explained. 'Your go.'

When I had taken my turn she said, 'We ought to take a look at the score. Go ahead and add it up, will you?'

'Two hundred and seventeen against sixty-five.'

'I like a close game,' Jerry said, without apparent irony. 'Now, where'd we get to? "Zydeco". That's twenty-two points, plus the triple word score which makes sixty-six.'

'Don't you mean "zodyco"? A type of Afro-American dance music played in the southern states. With an "o"?'

'Not in Alabama.'

Mr Tovacs hove into view, hoisting his way carefully around the long kitchen table as if he doubted his ability to walk unaided. He said, 'I have just been reading the scene in which

Owen and Feeda are interrupted by Mrs Brigstock. I recommend it to you.'

'For Christ's sake,' Jerry said, without looking up from the board. 'Go away.'

Unexpectedly Mr Tovacs' attitude changed. He seemed suddenly detached, quite unable to cope with this dismissal. He said, a shade peevishly, 'I am not feeling at all well. It is probably the cold. I wish you would come and talk to me.'

After he had gone I said, 'Shouldn't you go and see him if he isn't feeling well?'

'Later,' Jerry said, 'later I will, maybe, if I feel like it. Maybe I won't, who knows? . . . "Xylitol".'

' "Xylitol"?'

'There's a dictionary if you don't believe me.'

I read: 'A sweet, crystalline, pentahydric alcohol derived from xylose and present in some plant tissues.'

Upstairs in the master bedroom Morty was hard at work.

'Okay. When it comes to the bit where you take your clothes off I want you to take your time over it. I know it's fucking cold, but Rodney here'll make sure the heater's turned up. Then when you come out from behind the screen you get the feeling there's somebody there. Stare around a bit, look under the bed if you like. Then scream.'

Mary-Beth, got up in a passable imitation of a Victorian parlourmaid, stood with her hands on her hips. Sir George, a mustachioed figure with terrific check trousers, lingered unhappily in the corner of the room. She said suspiciously, 'Let's get this straight. You want me to take my clothes off behind the screen while he hangs around looking like an old man in a park? I never did a strip show where I stayed out of sight before.'

'You wouldn't understand.'

'What wouldn't I understand? I happen to be a fucking *actress* and don't you forget it.'

'Just do it,' Morty said wearily.

Silence descended, broken only by the whirr of the camera. Eventually Mary-Beth said, 'Listen, Rodney or whatever your name is, you can take your fucking hand *off*, okay?'

Even in these later days, harassed by inadequate resources, supported by inferior talents, Morty's sense of irony had not

wholly deserted him. Two or three years back a screenplay such as *Resurrection* would have produced a range of extravagant responses, stirred him to contrive a number of delicate conceits, each somehow capable of assimilation into the flamboyant over-all design. Actors in punctilious period costume would have found themselves weaving rare and subtle patterns in a remote and inchoate tapestry, cameramen resigned themselves to picking out individual threads in a grander mosaic kept for the most part out of reach by its creator. This desire to exclude collaborators in his films from all but the most cursory knowledge of their aims and intentions was an essential part of Morty's temperament. He maintained that his employees – actors, cameramen, tech-nicians – gave their best performances when set to work in isolation, wholly ignorant of the wider mechanisms whose com-ponent parts they were instructed to engineer. Allied to this characteristic was a second Kronenburg trait: an element of surprise, introduced at the most improbable moment, with the connivance of a bare minimum of those involved. There is a moment in *Stately Lust* which perfectly encapsulates this tend-ency. An early Leisurevision effort, notionally derived from *Lady Chatterley's Lover*, the film depended for its apogee on the tumultuous coming together of Lady Maud (played by Lila St Claire) and her manservant Hodges. This liaison took place in a potting shed, featured a wide range of Edwardian corsetry – a subject on which Morty claimed to possess specialised know-ledge – and relied for its incidental effects on views of a garden party taking place outside the window, the absence of Lady Maud and her lackey becoming steadily more flagrant. At a crucial moment in the proceedings, and without warning, Morty introduced a live ferret into the shed. He continued to film throughout the resulting confusion: Lady Maud snatching up her garments and fleeing into the garden; Hodges, puzzled, alarmed, finally seizing a pitchfork and preparing to do battle; the ferret, predatory and beady-eyed, eventually attaching itself to his leg; bolder guests clustering round the doorway; the result a bizarre mixture of flailing limbs, rapid, unsynchronised movement, the vague hint – amid much ancillary humour – of menace.

Later Kronenburg productions refined this technique to a start-ling degree: the moment in *Frenzy* when Sheri La Grange and

Frank Fellatio, frozen in mid-coitus, are suddenly entombed beneath a falling roof, emerging amid clouds of rising dust and fractured plaster; the scene in *Scuba Girl Dive Dive Yes* when Corona d'Amour and Barry La Boeuf, wrapped in an underwater clinch, are suddenly prised apart by the sight of a barbed black fin coursing through the water towards them. Chance, random contingency: it amused Morty to direct these gusts of sharp, realistic air throughout the stylised, hothouse landscape of his art. 'Basically, Martin,' he would remark, 'basically what your average punter doesn't understand is that pornography is funny. A girl and a guy pretending to fuck each other. It's a scream. Might be a turn-on for a bit, but how do you take it seriously? That bit in *Night Nurse* where Mitzi says to the guy, "Okay, big boy, let's see if you can rise to the occasion." You'd have to be pretty stupid not to laugh at that.'

'Some people are pretty stupid, Morty.'

'They'd have to be pretty stupid to take *me* seriously.'

Despite these disavowals there was much in the Leisurevision *oeuvre* to delight the cineaste. Self-aware, reflexive, ceaselessly turning in on themselves in frequently alarming ways, Morty's productions displayed a healthy awareness of their own artifice. Generally this emerged as a minor twist on the cinematic thread – a sudden cutting away from the main action to a window or a polished surface, a split-second reflection in which the eye of the camera was briefly revealed, a mirror hung at an oblique angle behind the set – but there were hints of a grander subterfuge: *Casting Couch*, for instance, shot in 1976, a film about the making of a pornographic film, the deceit only disclosed in the final moments when actors, cameramen, onlookers mingle unexpectedly in the centre of the stage.

In contrast *Resurrection* ploughed a humbler furrow. Odd juxtapositions of the family portraits in the opening sequences; a queer moment in which the camera moves from a shot of Sir George grappling with his bride to linger on a vase shaking perilously on the edge of a nearby sideboard, its final collapse, descent and explosion into fragments coinciding with a dramatic off-stage moan. Its highlight, perhaps, was Mary-Beth's protracted striptease, a divestiture prolonged with the aid of screens, decorousness and protruding furniture, to six or seven minutes of camera time. Even here though, there were signs of approaching dissolution: Mary-Beth, bewildered, uncertain as to what was required of her, struggling with her unfamiliar armature; Sir George, embarrassed and unhappy; Morty preoccupied, offhand in his directions. Watching a rough cut some time later I was struck only by the gap between design and execution, a proud glamour irretrievably compromised.

Elaine said, 'Tomorrow, the next day, whenever Morty finishes filming, then I quit.'

'Where to?'

'I don't know. London. Somewhere in the country. Somewhere I can have a rest.'

'You,' I said, 'have the greatest capacity for self-deception of anyone I have ever met.'

'Fine. If that's the way you want to remember me, then just go ahead. Fine.'

'Look, Elaine, it's not a question of wanting to remember you. It's a question of . . .'

'Listen, Martin,' Elaine said wearily, 'four years I've spent doing this, doing these films and being with you and watching you being so superior about the *irony* of what you do for a living, and that's it, forget it. While we're at it, I'll tell you another thing. In case you're wondering where I was last night and the night before and the night before that, it was with Terry.'

'Terry Chimes?'

'Why not? Terry's pathetic really. He wants to do things Morty wouldn't even dream of filming and that's only when he stops talking about his mother, but I can understand Terry Chimes. I've known a lot of Terry Chimeses. But I can't understand you.'

'I can tell you if you want.'

'It's a bit late for that,' Elaine said. 'About three years too late. Now, why don't you go and do something useful? You could go and find out who's making all that noise for a start.'

Screams, dimly discernible from somewhere in the lower region of the house, now rose in crescendo. Footsteps, audible a long way off, could be heard drawing nearer, mixed with other, less insistent, voices. At the foot of the staircase, Mr Tovacs cowering in a pained and resentful way before her, Jerry was shouting, 'Nazi, Nazi, Nazi,' each repetition increasing in volume and causing Mr Tovacs to shrink further back against the banister. Morty, emerging from a side door, moved swiftly towards them and grabbed her arm.

'Look, if you're going to have a fucking row, there are places where . . .'

'He's a Nazi,' Jerry said, 'he's a fucking Nazi. Go on, ask him. You're a Jew. You ought to be interested, of all people. Go on, ask him what he did in the fucking war.'

Mr Tovacs spoke for the first time. 'This is all most unnecessary. I will not allow you to speak to me in this way.'

Jerry said, 'I'll tell you what he did in the war. He was a fucking collaborator. Don't ask me how I know, but he was a fucking asshole collaborator. Stuck in Poland after the Occupation . . .'

'You are making a very great mistake . . .'

'Loading Jews into railway carriages . . .'

'You had better stop this now . . .'

'In the fucking ghettoes . . .'

'*Stop it now . . .*'

Simultaneously three things happened with astonishing rapidity. Mr Tovacs, who had been opening and closing his mouth noiselessly, suddenly began to topple down on to his knees. Jerry burst into tears. Onlookers – Crazy Rodney, the two American girls – now came forward to attend to Mr Tovacs' collapsing form.

'And another thing,' Jerry said to Morty as these actions continued, 'you shouldn't believe anything he tells you about money. Not a word.'

Mr Tovacs was helped to a sofa in the hall where he lay without speaking, his face in repose an odd compound of bewilderment and fatuous content. Later ambulancemen, diagnosing a mild heart attack, came and took him away to Lowestoft hospital. Morty went off to telephone. Jerry, who had declined an invitation to accompany the ambulance, sat on a chair in the kitchen smoking furiously. She said, 'You know how you get intuitions about people? Well, I used to get them about Tovacs.

Little things. He'd talk a lot about what he did in the Thirties and he'd talk a lot about being in Paris after the war. Never about anything in between. So I thought, never mind, perhaps he doesn't want to talk about it, perhaps it was all too harrowing. My dad was like that. He was a fighter pilot in Germany in 1944, but he didn't want to talk about it. Wouldn't ever say. But Tovacs couldn't stop dropping hints. Going on about the Jews. Going on about Ezra Pound being misunderstood. In the end I wormed it out of him.'

'What did he do?'

'Nothing you could put your finger on. Nothing you could even say was a war-crime, not now, not forty years later. From what I can make out he was some sort of Nazi stooge, some-where in occupied Poland. You know, pretended to be sympath-etic to the resistance and all the time he's supplying information to the other side.'

I remembered the plot of *Columbine* with its hints of divided loyalties, eventual betrayal. 'Then what happened?'

'Who knows? Nobody knows. Poland gets liberated. Tovacs disappears. Turns up again in Paris with a literary magazine and a nice line in introductions to Eliot and Stravinsky. People die. People forget. People move on. I don't suppose anybody knows what really happened.'

'People could find out.'

'Maybe people did. I remember once Tovacs being terrified when some old Polish guy he hadn't seen in decades turned up at Red Lion Street. I don't know what they said to each other, but it was like something out of a Victorian novel. You know, when the brother everybody thinks died thirty years ago comes back to claim his inheritance. Old, grim faces and the dread hand of the past. That sort of thing.'

'What about the money?'

'I don't know,' Jerry said. 'Who knows? Who can tell what the old buzzard's done about the money?'

Later I walked down through narrow, uneven pathways to the beach. Storms had blown up the previous evening, persisted long into the night, and left queer relics on the greying sand: more strings of onions, a fraying mauve jersey wreathed with seaweed, spongy accretions of cotton wool. Along the horizon, grey sea rising to meet the scarcely less grey expanse of sky, long ships – four or five of them, almost amounting to a flotilla – moved in a slow, inch-by-inch progress. In the distance, at the point where the beach curved into a promontory of dunes, odd formations of rock and sandstone jutting out almost to the limit of the shoreline, there were figures moving hastily in and out of vision, the effect resembling a complex game of concealment and revelation, oddly enticing. There were footprints in the sand, two sets, the second hemmed in by furrows and pockmarks, suggesting a walking stick, impeded movement. I followed them for a while, head down against the wind, until they veered hard left towards the dunes, the trail lost in softer, shifting sand, clumps of sea grass. Simultaneously it began to rain. I gave the beach a last, fleeting inspection – gathering clouds, the dark shape of a dog or some other animal nosing far away amid the strewn jetsam – and turned back towards the house.

Morty stood disconsolately in the driveway. He said, 'You seen Terry?'

'There were people down on the beach. It might have been him.'

'Trust Terry to piss off at a time like this. I just phoned the bank and we're seriously fucked.'

'How seriously?'

'Seriously seriously. That last big cheque of Tovacs' – the one that covered the letting fees, the one that was going to pay for the promotion – well, you can take it from me that it never got through.'

'What are you going to do?'

'What can I do? There's two or three scenes left to film – we can cut that last bit in the hayloft. If I finish shooting at least there's a product at the end of it.'

'How long will it take?'

'Four, five hours. Terry said he was going to organise some sort of piss-up. At least we can all get drunk after I wrap.'

The rain came in more fiercely now, plastering the strands of sandy hair over Morty's forehead. He looked doleful, enraged, uncomprehending.

'What did you tell the girls?'

'The girls?' Morty stared wonderingly. 'Fuck the girls, Martin. Just fuck them.'

Twelve hours later at 4 a.m., bright arc-lights burning furiously into the night, the wind blowing noisily against the uncurtained windows, the actresses red-eyed and exhausted from lack of sleep, Morty wrapped.

'**Y**OU COULDN'T POSSIBLY understand,' Suzi says.
'No?'

'You couldn't possibly understand what it's like. When you're about fourteen. First you have to have been kissed. Not just on the mouth: everywhere. And if you haven't, then you have to say you have. A bit later you have to sleep with somebody. Properly, so you can tell the other girls about it. A bit later you don't have to just sleep with somebody, you have to sleep with them a *lot*.'

'You do?'

'*You have to have a boyfriend*,' Suzi says fiercely. 'You just have to.' She recites the prurient enquiries of long ago, like some easily remembered catechism. ' "What did you do last night?" "Oh, I did my homework and then Barry rang." "What did you do at the weekend?" "Oh, I watched television and then I went round to Barry's." "How many times did you do it?" "Three or four times, I don't remember." And the thing was,' Suzi says, 'that the boys didn't really want to do it at all. They'd have sooner been mending their bikes, or playing football. It was just something they had to do so they could go and talk to their mates about it as well.'

Early evening in Glebe Road, warm mellow light diffusing through the room and another discussion of the vexed question of Suzi's past. Suzi, it has to be said, is behaving oddly these days: no longer irritable, distant, combative, but watchful, conciliatory, solicitous. She makes a habit now of cooking me dinner when she comes home, standing over me as I eat it. But there are signs, tell-tale signs . . . Last night, for example, she was up in the loft, the repository, among other bulky items too large to be stored in her bedroom, of her suitcases. This evening comes another cautious hint of what lies in store.

'I went and saw Christopher after work today,' she says.

'How was he?'

'He was all right. He lives in this bungalow up Eaton way. Very posh,' Suzi pronounces.

'I suppose he would. Being a manager.' The irony rises up, is considered, rejected and goes away again.

'We had a long talk,' Suzi says. 'A long talk. And we agreed that it would be nice to see each other again. Just as friends.'

There is a silence.

'It's funny,' Suzi says. 'But all the time I was sitting there on the sofa – he's got this new sofa, he's ever so proud of it, he bought it at Debenham's – all the time that I was sitting there I couldn't think for the life of me what it was that I used to see in him.'

We have a mild, complicit laugh over this that extends, unusually enough, to a short-lived necking session on our own sofa, before the telephone rings and Suzi clambers up to answer it. I add this to the other bizarre portents that the last week has yielded up. Two days ago I lent Fat Eric three hundred pounds, three hundred pounds in five-pound notes extracted from the building society and conveyed to him by way of a brown-paper envelope at lunch-time in the City Gates. Oddly, this was received not with wild and fulsome gratitude, as one might have expected, but with what amounted to indifference, Fat Eric merely looking rather glum and stowing the envelope hurriedly away in the pocket of his jeans.

Yesterday, having devised further enticing bait on the subject of Morty and Terry Chimes, I rang Kev Jackson. The phone rang for a long time before he picked it up.

'Kev. Martin Benson.'

'Yes.'

'I was thinking . . . about what we were talking about the other day. I've got some more information that might interest you.'

'You have?'

'About Morty and Terry Chimes. The stuff you wanted for your book.'

I could hear Kev Jackson breathing heavily down the line for a moment. Then he said, 'Look, Martin, let's forget about it, shall we?'

'About Morty and Terry Chimes. About that girl you were interested in.'

'Let's just forget about it, shall we?'

'But what about your book? What about your ten thousand from the publishers?'

'Let's forget about that too. I'm sorry, Martin, but it's all finished. It's *all over*.'

After that he rang off. When I redialled, the phone rang on endlessly, was picked up and then sharply replaced.

Meanwhile Suzi comes back into the room. She looks thoughtful, preoccupied.

'Who was that?'

'Just a friend,' I say. 'Just a friend.' She goes upstairs after this. There are more shiftings and scuttlings in the loft.

And then one day I come home and find her gone. Five o'clock on a steely January afternoon, four hours back on the road from Brooke, I return to discover that certain aspects of my life are irrevocably changed, altered out of recognition, fallen lamentably away. The harbingers follow an odd, cumulative pattern: the shoes gone from inside the door, a queer emptiness from inside the hall finally revealing itself as the absence of the occasional table. The telephone lies on the carpet, message pad stuffed haphazardly underneath it. The note on the top is a day old: 'A man rang. Said he'd ring back later.' I press on upstairs into Suzi's bedroom, bed stripped and vacant, wardrobe thrown open and gaping, stop for a moment on the landing – a white untarnished square where the Monet poster used to hang – head downwards again into a kitchen where the miniature bottles of herbs are gone, the cupboards ransacked and some pitiless intelligence has gone through the cutlery, removed its own and left the rest in a shiny pile on the draining board. There is a peculiar angriness to the chaos, I note: cups lie shattered in the sink, chairs skewed over on to their sides, the contents of a bag of flour rises like ghostly dust from beneath my wary feet.

Another prowl through the upper regions of the house, in the hope of finding some faint departing trail. The bathroom has been cleaned out, only a box of aspirins and a packet of disposable razors left to decorate the top of the cabinet. In a drawer of the bedside table I find a heap of tampons and a copy of *The Friendship Book of Frances Gay*, nothing more. I go to the lounge last of all. Here the absences are more fundamental: the row of glass animals on the mantelpiece gone capering off to some lusher resting place, snooker videos gathered up and taken away. Still no note, still no explanation. Even here, amongst all the unpromising evidence of emotional fracture, the potent symbols of accumulated resentment, one would like it in writing.

The photographs lie on the carpet beneath the TV. I don't notice them at first, so preoccupied am I with the reproach of the empty shelves and the vanished invitation cards. When I do, I sidle up gingerly, as if it might be possible to take them by surprise, catch them unawares, somehow anaesthetise the hurt that they undoubtedly contain. For a long time, seated there with these celluloid rectangles on the floor beneath me, I notice only incidentals: the white envelope they came in ('Miss S. Richards' firmly typed on the front), the tiny imperfections of shade, shadow and misalignment, the fuzz of unexpected movement confusing the camera's eye. Blurred, dog-eared snaps. As the inspection proceeds, this air of remote detachment hypertrophies. Finally, when I come upon myself, note the painful activities I appear to be engaged in, it seems nothing more than an embarrassing memento from childhood, brought out twenty years later by indulgent grandparents. This is not real. Real life disintegrated some time back, went away beyond recall, and in a moment or two the Queen of Brobdingnag will saunter airily by with a sabre-toothed tiger straining at its leash. I snap out of my trance, switch on the TV, move over to the drinks cabinet, find a bottle, bring it back.

Later on when I wake up from this wretched, drink-fuelled sleep there is still no sign of Suzi; the television blares wordlessly on. I scoop up the pictures from the carpet where they lie undisturbed and look at them again. They could be fakes, of course, just about. The one in which the girl stares up anxiously at her brooding pursuer, the one in which the dreadful implications of what is going on are so neatly apparent, it could just be a masterly contrivance, stills blended expertly together, only the faint, blurred foreground suggesting artifice, a tiny unevenness in the way the whole is constructed trailing the thought that perhaps it didn't happen, that perhaps somebody made it up. And the ones shot in shadow, in which the faces disappear into a background of jittery limbs and sharp, reflexive movements, it might have been anyone. At any rate, it might not have been me.

Eight o'clock. Three doors down Kay will probably be waiting, hoping I'll be round. And all of a sudden I want very much to be sitting in Fat Eric's front room amid the sprawl of lager cans and discarded trainers, beneath the watchful gaze of *Norwich City: The Division One Story*, I want very much to sit there listening to Kay impart more homely details of life with Fat Eric, about how he hits her and won't let her go out in the evenings. I want very much to tell her some more gilded lies about Bobby Dazz and Barbie. Outside it's dark, the street lamps loom up and I have this nasty habit of bumping into things – the gatepost, the hedge, a skateboard which some conniving infant has left in the road – but in the end I find myself trembling by the fence that adjoins Fat Eric's porch.

The house is dark, just a faint glow deep in the shadow of the upstairs window, but I press on. I ring the bell emphatically a couple of times and then, for good measure, I slam my fist against the wide expanse of the door. I shout, 'Kay,' once or twice fairly loudly. I wonder about flinging some gravel up at the window. People wander past, dim outlines caught in the tail of my eye, but, bless you, they don't notice, they don't care. Round here you don't interfere in such circumstances. Finally there are minor, reluctant noises from within, uncertain footsteps that start and stop, go away and come back again, and Kay opens the door.

'I was upstairs,' she says, 'I didn't think you were coming.'

'Kay . . .'

She doesn't look well, Kay doesn't, or happy, or particularly pleased to see me. What with the bruised temple, the slow, animal stare and the nightdress clutched absently around her, I get the impression that Kay would rather be somewhere else, somewhere miles away from myself and Fat Eric and all these other cunning tormentors.

'I can explain, Kay,' I tell her, 'I can explain everything. I only want to talk to you.'

'You'd better come in,' Kay says.

Inside, the chaos is more random, more purposeful than ever. Pictures hang drunkenly in their frames. One of the ducks has disappeared from the wall, leaving a gout of dislodged plaster, and the contents of the video shelf have been upended over the floor where they lie like scattered dominoes. A broken bottle. Smashed ashtrays.

Kay says, 'Eric done that. He come home at dinner-time and done it. Him and that Ron. Well, not Ron. Ron just stood there and looked as if he was somewhere else. I've been sitting here since then wondering why he did it.'

'Why did he do it?'

'I don't know. Come home at dinner-time, and tells me I'm a tart and he isn't going to stand for it. You want to see the kitchen,' Kay says. 'He put a chair through the window in there.'

'Kay . . .'

'It was that Ron. Ron put him up to it. Just at the end, before they went, Ron takes me to one side and says, "Eric's very upset. You want to remember that next time, remember how upset Eric can get." The fucker!'

In the kitchen smashed glass gleams palely from the floor. A pool of something white and viscous glistens from the table. I arch a finger over it and taste: milk. At once I realise that I've been here before, back in the old days, in the East End, when I once went to examine a house Crazy Rodney had smashed up at Morty's behest. Crazy Rodney had done a thorough enough job – fire irons through the patio window, television set lobbed out into the back garden, electrical fittings dangling brokenly from the ceiling – but what had struck me was how unconcerned the family had been. Perhaps, having had long-term dealings with Morty, they were used to having their home smashed up? Perhaps when they went to switch on the television and instead found it lying in the garden with its entrails spilled out on to the grass, they simply shrugged their shoulders and opted for some other diversion? Perhaps it really didn't matter any more? As I remember it they ended up making me a cup of tea while Crazy Rodney stood with his hands behind his back looking guilty and eventually unbent sufficiently to replace one of the light bulbs.

No such nonchalance here, though. I look at Kay: a fat girl in a nightdress crying in a wrecked kitchen. Kay looks at me. Outside in the distance I can hear the cars on the ring road, cars heading off to Dereham, or Wymondham, or away over the Suffolk border to Ipswich. Smoke drifts in from somewhere near the park and suddenly it feels very autumnal here in the kitchen, very played out and dying.

I say, 'Leave it. Get up and go away.'

Kay flops her head down on my shoulder. 'I wish I could,' she whispers. 'Tell me how.'

There is a swirl of movement behind the door, the sudden hint of an intent, purposeful passage, the light goes on and, 'What the *fuck*?' Fat Eric says.


A tradition of post-filming parties went back to the early days of Leisurevision, back to the time of *Capital Pick-up* and *Stately Lust*, films shot in single rooms in a matter of hours with tiny budgets and minuscule casts. Later the celebrations had expanded to the point where they became recognised marker flags on the social calendar, eagerly anticipated by people with only scant connection with Morty Kronenburg, prolonged to almost unprecedented periods of time and only reluctantly allowed to reach any sort of point of dispersal, their main incidents kept alive in any case by an endless process of orgiastic reminiscence. These were lavish entertainments. Two hundred people had assembled once at Dean Street after the completion of *Sex Riot* in the late 1970s. A squadron of American investors had flown in from Cannes on a Lear jet to witness Morty putting the finishing touches to a film called *Girl Hunt*. Such conspicuous expenditure was painfully absent from the present scene, where crates of supermarket wine, brought back by Terry Chimes from an expedition to Lowestoft and lying about on chairs and tables in the main hall provided a single point of focus.

*Bright, scary light. Cigarette smoke rises in dense, vertical clouds to the ceiling so that we shoo them away with our hands. The people stand around in small, discontented groups warming themselves at the big storage heaters. Morty prowls aimlessly among them, stops for a moment at the foot of the staircase to look at them, moves on upstairs on some mission of his own.*

In the corner Terry Chimes, propped up against the wall with his crutches jammed under his arms, says to Crazy Rodney, 'Of course, with the dogs you're not talking big money, not at all. Catford. White City. Romford. Used to go there five, six years ago when I'd got a good tip, try and put thousand-pound bets on. Bookies wouldn't look at you. Thought you were up to something.'

Crazy Rodney says, 'I used to go to Romford with my dad. Late Sixties when I was a kid. Had a dog as well, Satan's Pride. You ever hear of that? But dad reckoned it was all fixed. Used to stand by the side of the enclosure, the other trainers did, trying to stamp on the dogs' legs.'

Terry Chimes says, 'But you're not talking big money, not these days. Me and me mates set up this queer bookie once, for a laugh. Queer bookies. Had these runners called Cedric and Quentin, right? We set him up. Had this other mate who was in the know. All of us went and put five-, six-hundred-quid bets on this 50–1 outsider. Course, after a while he realises there's something going on, starts dropping the price, but by then it's too late. It won by a length. We cleaned him up for twenty or thirty grand. Last queer bookie ever turned up at Catford.'

Mary-Beth says, 'Yeah, I hung out with the best of them in my time. Belushi. Ackroyd. Billy Murray. All that *Saturday Night* crowd. They'd see me sometimes in the street and they'd say, "Hi, you doing anything?" and I'd just smile, you know, the way you do. Or we'd go off and have breakfast someplace and they'd tell me how screwed up they were. But, yeah, I hung out with the best of them in my time.'

Cindy says, 'Don't worry yourself, hon. You had a good career ahead of you and then you fucked up. What's so bad about that?'

Terry Chimes hobbles back from the kitchen, a champagne bottle wedged tightly under each arm. Still grasping his crutches he lets the bottles bounce down heavily on to the table. He says, 'First bankruptcy party I ever came to. Make sure you don't leave anything.'

There is a smattering of polite, nervous laughter.

Morty stands in the centre of a crowd of wary spectators. His mad eyes swivel crazily in his gopher's forehead. He says, 'What beats me is why he did it. I mean, did I ever show the guy any disrespect? Did I ever tell him to get the fuck out of my studio?' He takes another swig from the bottle. 'I spend two-hundred grand making a film and then they turn round and tell me the money isn't there.'

*In the bright light the room swells to gigantic proportions. The walk back to the table is a hike past grim, swaying giants, through intense searing heat. I look for Elaine amid the vast untidy throng – so many sad, gaping faces – fail to find her. Only the violent contending voices.*

Mary-Beth says, 'You wouldn't think it, would you, but I was very strictly brought up. My pa was a Baptist before he got into Hollywood. I remember when I was seventeen, going to an audition for the first time, and this director puts his hand on my tits. Boy, did I give him something to remember me by.'

Cindy says, 'I just lay down and opened my legs, honey, I didn't have your strength of character.'

Everybody seems very drunk now, very boisterous and unhappy and mad. I go and stand in the corner of the room, beneath the brooding portraits, and listen to Morty and Terry Chimes bawling at each other. Terry Chimes says, 'The thing about music now is that you don't even have to pretend to be talented. That's why it's changed. When I signed the Express, right, everybody knew – well, everybody in the industry knew – that they couldn't play, but it didn't matter. They just *pretended* they could. That's all over. The gimmick now is that you don't even pretend. I got this band Grunt's going to launch in the summer. They're going to go on *Top of the Pops* and just fuck about, play football and smash up their instruments. And the thing is, the record's going to be like that too. Just three and a half minutes of fucking about . . .'

Morty says, 'What annoys me, what really pisses me off, is all the pictures I never got to make. That remake of *Ben Hur*, the film about the World Cup. All the pictures I never got to make.'

Terry Chimes says without interest, 'You'll survive. You'll make it.'

Mary-Beth says, 'And then you hit thirty-one, thirty-two, your tits start to sag and your face looks like a crocodile-skin handbag and what the fuck are you supposed to do with the rest of your life?'

Cindy says, 'I had this girlfriend saved up enough money for a silicon implant. But then the stuff solidified or something, and they reckoned if you could have cut the tit off you could have gone bowling with it.'

*Everything seems very played-out and dead now, very dead and played-out. I notice small things: Morty's neck as he bends over to whip the cork out of another bottle, glistening like red tyre rubber, Terry Chimes' blackened toes sticking out of the plaster cast, Crazy Rodney's eyes narrowing as he tracks the path of the American girls. Terry Chimes wrestles with the wire cage of another champagne bottle and then gives up, smashes the neck against the fireplace. I monitor the expressions of the family portraits, note how they seem to change, one moment remote, the next interested and companionable. Elaine arrives suddenly in the room, looks severely around her once or twice and then marches over.*

I say, 'Where have you been?'

'Packing my things. Packing my things to leave in the morning. To get out of here,' Elaine says angrily.

'Do Morty and Terry know?'

'They know enough. Jesus,' Elaine says, 'none of you three *owns* me. I don't have to ask anyone's *permission* before I clear out.'

Bright, scary light. There is something very wrong here, some irrevocable fracture shot through the burnished glaze. I remember odd things: I remember Elaine spreadeagled beneath Frank Fellatio – game Frank, swept away now in the clutter of time – that vanished morning in the loft; Crazy Rodney on the tower block stairs. Those conversations with Morty upstairs at Dean Street, burrowing on into the grim dawn. A blinding summer's afternoon in Glebe Road with my father seated in a deckchair under the tree and the sun beating in from over the park. Low flat fields under the pale East Anglian sky. I wave my arms from side to side and it seems for an instant that I am on the ocean floor, blundering on through thousands of cubic feet of water, bemused by the ghostly light high above me.

Elaine says, 'Are you okay?'

'Perfect. Fine. I need to talk to you. *I need to tell you things.*'

'What things? What do you need to tell me about?'

*The people in the pictures look as if they're about to walk out of their frames, skip out and come tumbling into the room. The voices, retreating now, flying up to the ceiling where they buzz and hang, are coming from a long way off. Elaine paces towards the far door and the corridor and I follow shakily, uncertainly, losing my way on the shortest of journeys, off through the low, flat fields.*

Morty says, 'I could have been an *artist*, that's what it is. But it's a class thing, isn't it? That Tovacs, knowing Picasso and everyone, what would he want to be doing with someone who makes dirty films for a living?'

Terry Chimes says, 'Couple of working-class tossers, you and me, that's what we are. Couple of working-class tossers, and proud of it.'

Crazy Rodney says, 'Never worried me. Not with girls and that. Get some flash piece, pearls and daddy's got an estate somewhere. Me, I'm a breath of fresh air to a girl like that. Eat out of your fucking hand they will if you ask them.'

Mary-Beth says, 'That East Coast thing, it works against you, you know. I had a good education. I could have gone to Ivy League, married a lawyer, or somebody in real estate.'

Cindy says, 'You once got to screw Rod Steiger in a motel scene. How many people can say that much?'

*Bright, scary light. The room somehow rolling off its hinges, shaking from side to side, lurching out of kilter. Remembering the first time I slept with Elaine. The narrow bed in the room in Hammersmith? That grim resolve. The faint slipperiness of yielding skin. Elaine rising above me, fading away again. We wander off through the sparse, empty rooms, into the kitchen where one of the sound men lies fast asleep in a chair with his tongue hanging out, fat and lumpy like a mollusc, on through pantries and gaping corridors.*

Elaine says, 'I used to wonder about you, what it was that made you so different from everybody else. At first I thought it was just detachment. There are people like that. You don't come across them very often, but there are people like that. Then I thought it was fear, I thought it was just that you were frightened of people, Terry and Rodney and people like that. But I was wrong about that too. Now I think it's just superiority. I think it's just that we're all really beneath your contempt. Something Terry said, "All the time he looks at me it's as if he's surprised I can actually talk." '

*Vague, distant noises. Scuttlings and shufflings. Sharp, intrusive movements. Somewhere away in another room the sound of breaking glass. Elaine stands in front of me, pale and indignant. Carefully, doggedly, patiently negotiating the obstacles, the heavy shifting air, the monstrous furniture of this cartoon world, I move towards her. I watch her expression change, from anger, to consternation, to wide-eyed incredulity. The room lists, shudders, explodes.*

When I wake up, daylight, bright intense daylight, is streaming through the high windows. The room is cold, empty. Terry Chimes, a grotesque, staring figure, stands at the foot of the bed.

'Elaine . . .' I say.

'Gone,' Terry Chimes says. 'Packed up and gone away.'

'Where?'

'Not where you'll find her,' Terry Chimes intones. 'Not where you'll find her.'


What happens? Amazingly, perhaps, he doesn't hit me. In fact he doesn't touch me at all, merely stands to one side in the wrecked kitchen as Kay and I awkwardly disengage, looking anguished and formal. It is, I realise, a *feudal* look, the look that the ancient family retainer gives his lordship's scapegrace brother over the pilfered silver, the look that the gamekeeper lavishes on the squire's son discovered in bed with his wife, a gaze of shattered illusions, old confidence pitilessly fractured.

'Fat Eric,' I say, 'Fat Eric, I can explain. I can explain everything.'

All of a sudden everything is quiet, very undramatic. Kay, seated now on one of the tiny, elfin chairs, snivels silently to herself. The moon shines in through the uncurtained window,

254

is lost immediately in the coruscating light. Fat Eric broods solicitously above me for a while and finally says, 'It don't matter. Just get out, that's all.'

'But I can explain.'

'Just go away, will you?' Fat Eric says thickly. 'Don't want you round here no more.' He shuffles towards Kay, fists raised, and I think, oh God this is where we see some real violence, this is where we see some proper action; but no, Fat Eric merely places one arm protectively around his weeping doxy, swivels round to face me again.

'Don't want you round here no more,' he repeats with surprising dignity. 'Just go away, will you?'

I leave them there amid the wreckage, steal out as guiltily as any adulterer into the pale streets, back to the silent house.

Half an hour later a small package lists gently through the letterbox. I turn the contents out on to the kitchen table, shrink back in incredulity. Sixty five-pound notes.

Slipping upstairs at midnight, drunk, fearful, shot by both sides, I come across Suzi's departing gesture. Sauntering into the bedroom, twitching back the coverlet, I discover Elaine staring up at me from the white sheet, Elaine reclining in the white rose backdrop of the *Virgin Bride* poster. There are other pictures there too, burnt and curling at the edges: Morty and Terry Chimes arm-in-arm, Crazy Rodney in his lank frightener's overcoat. Lila St Claire and Talia Silk and Corona d'Amour in all their pneumatic glory, a glistening sea of bogus smiles and eerily juxtaposed flesh. I breathe heavily, shaken by the familiar scent. Pornography has a smell all of its own: that shiny, heavy odour of expensive art paper put to nefarious use. Morty used to claim that he could identify a copy of *Upfront* concealed in a pile of *Radio Times* with his eyes closed. I scoop up a handful of torn pages and the paper coverlet shifts and lists, breaks up and flutters limply to the ground. Skeleton leaves on the forest floor, dark, ocean-floor eyes.

The tape comes at 9 am. I knew it would. I sat waiting for the postman's knock. I take it to the video, slam it into the sleek, accommodating holder.

Filmed on an eight-reel. Monochrome. Grainy, with smudges on the tape: a crackling soundtrack. There are initial establishing shots: a long, low coastline, surf crashing down on grey sand, a high aerial view of distant woods, before the camera moves down, burrows inward through trees, fantastic traceries of foliage, dense scrollworks of fern, to the house. Potent rural symbolism: a weathercock swinging idly on a vane, a horse sweeping away through rising meadows, cut short by sharp detonations of static, thin black lines that veer across the screen, weave together and break apart. The camera moves in on a wide, featureless room, without windows. Seated on a chair, dead centre, knees pulled up to her chin, is a mournful-looking girl with abundant dark hair who, without further preliminaries, begins to take off her clothes, garment after garment, folding them neatly over the chair and then sitting down beside them. The tape crackles. A silent expressionless man – early thirties, perhaps, with receding hair – approaches, also naked. What follows is standard hard-core, something you could see at any hour of the day in one of the Triple X shops at Frankfurt airport, except that, except that at the height of this passionless frenzy the man brings both his hands up sharply from the carpet, as if performing a complicated piece of physical jerks, and clamps them purposefully around the girl's throat. The last thing you see before the screen goes blank is that rictus of glaring agony.

Elaine. Myself. What more to say?

When the telephone rings I pick it up instinctively. An unknown man's voice: subdued, apologetic.

'Martin? I take it you got the tape?'

'Who are you?'

'Never mind. I take it you got the tape?'

'I got the tape. What do you want me to do?'

'Nothing. Just sit there and wait is best.'

There are other voices away in the distance. I strain to catch them.

'Who are you? What do you want?'

'Wait and see, Martin,' the voice says. There is the first faint hint of mockery. 'Just wait and see is best.'

Ten o'clock on a January morning. Outside, real life is grinding remorselessly into gear. A milk float rattles into view. Fat Eric's Hillman surges past up the hill in a cloud of exhaust fumes. Infant voices blown back on the wind. Last night's photographs still lie accusingly on the carpet. I fetch a brush and dustpan from the kitchen and, wondering a little at the nature of the task, start to sweep them up.

Later I will remember. Somehow, in the end, you always remember. They fall down when you hit them. Somehow I never envisaged this, that they might fall down, sprawl headlong across the floor, prove incapable of revival . . . Although Morty distrusted such elementary techniques of crowd pleasing, from time to time a Leisurevision production would climax in a fight sequence. These were elaborately staged: Frank Fellatio in *Stately Lust* picking up an antique cuirass the better to engage his wife's seducer in combat; a fight between Lila St Claire and Cindy Lu Win in *Man-eater*, set in a kitchen, in which volleys of crockery were hurled unceasingly across the narrow valley of a table. To these stylised incidents could be added more straightforward bouts of fisticuffs: an epic punch-up at the conclusion of *Roadhouse Stud*, the episode in *Furore* where Barry La Boeuf, shirt torn across his chest, arms flailing, standing triumphantly athwart the prostrate body of his paramour, sees off the pack of bicycle-chain-wielding hoodlums. Such scenarios allowed Morty to indulge his pronounced taste for parody, engage in a wholescale mockery of the conventions of the on-screen rough house. He examined typical episodes of cinematic violence with something amounting to disdain. 'Ridiculous,' he would say. 'One guy punches another guy in the mouth. It's the sort of punch that would knock out Mohammad Ali. I mean, have you ever been hit in the mouth, Martin, really hard? Take it from me, you don't get up. But no, the other guy just rolls over, shakes his head, picks up a table and throws it back. Just popcorn.' Leisurevision fight scenes reproduced these conventions to an improbable degree: fountains of gore spurting from mute, uncomplaining orifices, incidental scenery – chairs, tables, bicycles – pressed into service as weapons. There is a bizarre twenty-minute sequence at the end of *Satan's Slaves*, shot in distinct imitation of Kubrick, where whole limbs are torn away, but the protagonists – their faces, torsos, arms gouged out of recognition – still fight invincibly on. More characteristic than this – Shakespearean even in its mockery – was Morty's unwillingness to allow any sort of natural termination to these scenes.

Thus in *Stately Lust* the villain, stabbed, pounded, lies inert in a pool of blood while Frank Fellatio and his wife embark on a passage of tender reconciliation, only to be interrupted, moments later, by a yet more ferocious onslaught, ending when Frank entombs his attacker beneath an up-turned grandfather clock. The film's conclusion, cutting away from the final, remorseless coupling, depicts a bloodied hand twisting inexorably from beneath the splintered wreckage.

But in real life they fall down when you hit them, they fall down and don't get up. The head jerking back against the too-solid floor, the pained expression – half annoyance, half bewilderment, the arms drawn up protectively around the sagging, lumpy torso, eyes aslant. And afterwards: no movement, no straining after revenge, no laboured return to the war zone, no resolute picking-up of teeth from the carpet, just silence, the odd, awkward arrangement of limbs beneath the bright, merciless light.


And afterwards, after the crash. What happened then?

We move on now: history comes loitering out of the rest-room, idles at a snail's pace through the long, trackless days. I sell the place in Bishop's Park, dull now and expensive, buy another one in Cricklewood. I sell the other place in Winterbourne – I wish I could afford to stay there – and don't replace it. I sell the Ferrari and buy a Ford Escort. I lose heavily on all these transactions and it matters, it matters a great deal. 'Go easy on the money, Martin,' Morty breathes, whenever that increasingly vital subject is mentioned, 'the money ... the money's a bit tight at the moment.' And the money *is* a bit tight. Morty and Terry Chimes, by this stage, are sadly straitened beings, weekend in Suffolk cottages, think about selling their timeshare apartments, sports stadium executive boxes, Wimbledon concessions. The third Mrs Kronenburg sits tight in Ongar and nags Morty about her allowance. There are accountants, lawyers, estate agents, stockbrokers, telling us to save money, cut back on expenditure, minimise our investments. Not to be outdone I take away the cheque book and the Peter Jones expense account I gave to Emma, Elaine's replacement, but come home twenty-four hours too late to find the flat strewn with gift-wrapped parcels – CD players, microwaves, freezers, clothes – and Emma sitting amid them like a child in a toyshop. 'What did you buy all this for?' I ask angrily. 'I don't know,' she says. 'I just wanted to. Do you mind?' 'Of course I bloody well do,' I tell her. Later I haul the collection into the meagre hallway, inventory it and calculate the bill. It comes to £18,000. Two days later I take it away and sell it.

I do other things. I bring home travel-agents' brochures and instruct Emma – a resentful, tight-lipped Emma – in the catechism of the low-powered domestic weekend-awayer. 'Scarborough?' 'No.' 'Great Yarmouth?' '*No.*' 'Isle of Wight?' 'If you like.' I don't like, I don't like *at all.* Overcoming this initial reluctance we go on short, purposeful, rain-swept excursions. We traverse the North Yorkshire moors, we sidle through the clotted streets of out-of-season Blackpool, stare at the smoky industrial towns from the gangway of a coach speeding back down the M6. It is all very expensive, all very odd. Sometimes in these anxious trawls through flyblown English cities I explore the business angle. I go to Liverpool and check out the black-windowed cinemas and the Private Shops in Shaw Street. I traipse through the street markets in Manchester where you can buy old Leisurevision videos from the Seventies at three quid a time. I attend cheapskate promo launches in Midlands drinking clubs, nod my head sadly over the on-screen thrash and regret that it won't do for the foreign market. They all know Morty, these amateurish Brummie pornographers with their C&A suits, these wrecked Glasgow filth merchants with their thick accents and their fetid breath. 'Morty Kronenburg,' one of them tells me at a trade convention in Macclesfield, 'is fucking bad news just at the moment.' I listen to the chatter about the latest council closure, the latest firebombed rubber shop, nod my head, collect my rail ticket, slink back to a newer, scarier world.

I do fewer things, the same things. I give parties, cheap parties, *cost-conscious* parties. At the place in Cricklewood, mostly. Hardly anybody comes. Morty, Terry Chimes and their predictable women – the corkscrew curls, the ravaged complexions – they don't come. Other people come: friends of Emma's, hard-faced girls who work for PR agencies in the West End, broken-down cameramen, Crazy Rodney. They are subdued, reflective little gatherings. And suddenly it is all hardly affordable, suddenly it is hardly there. It is at this point in my life that, for the first time, I am unable to comprehend just how little I am earning. This fact is visited upon me one Friday evening in November 1981 when I open the top drawer of the bedside table, in which I am accustomed to store loose change, IOUs, red-stamped electricity bills. Down beneath the swirl of incriminating paper there is a handful of five-pound notes and silver. Taken out and counted – a surprisingly easy task – it realises £37.50. 'What do I do with this?' I demand of Emma, marching into the lounge where she sits staring vacantly at the television and depositing the coil of notes on a sofa cushion. 'You can give it to me.' 'No, I'd better keep it.' 'No, you don't want it. I'll have it.' We compromise by spending all of it. On dinner. In the Kilburn High Road.

Quiet, trammelled months. I sell the place in Cricklewood – I couldn't meet the mortgage payments – rent another in West Hampstead. I sell the Ford Escort and don't buy anything at all. Morty and Terry Chimes, by this stage, are fabulously reduced beings, weekend at home, think about selling their domestic appliances, their gardening equipment. Where has the money gone to? Sometimes, during the course of snatched, ten-minute breaks Morty, Terry Chimes and I ask ourselves this question. There seems no ready solution. We fail to make *Housewives' Party*, *Schoolgirl Affair* and *Frenzy*, projects of Morty's from way back, as no one will give us any money. And in the intervals of this tense, low-key existence, there is Emma.

I do mad things with Emma. I recall a conversation from about this time. Late autumn. Early evening. The night gapes before us.

'So what do you want to do? Stay in and watch a film?'

'No.'

'Go and see what there is in the video shop?'

'*No*.'

'There's fifteen quid in the drawer. I could go down to the Indian takeaway.'

'*No*.'

Try again, more circumspectly.

'There's a new nightclub in Harlesden Crazy Rodney got me

membership of. We could take a bus over there and check it out.'

'No.'

'We could go and see your mum and dad in Ealing.'

'*No*, for fuck's sake.'

Try again, more cravenly.

'So, tell me what you'd like to do. Tell me what you'd like to do and we'll do it. Anything. Anywhere. Think about it.'

She thinks. I wait. Eventually she says, 'I'd like to get a cab, go into town and have dinner at Boulestin's. Four courses. I'd like to go to Paris for the weekend and stay in a decent hotel. You can take me.'

Incredibly, we try to pursue this, of late, unprecedented course. We take a cab and proceed at a gentle pace down the dark, noisy streets towards Covent Garden. Unflustered, we march past welcoming doormen, negotiate the complex Boulestin menu. We order champagne cocktails, smoked salmon, Dover sole and fresh English strawberries. The fantasy of wealth, opulence and abandon persists until the end of the meal when my Masterclub card is returned to me, grimly, on a plate with the news that I am no longer creditworthy. Eventually, with the maximum display of resentment and outraged female propriety, Emma pays. Later we take a bus back up the Kilburn High Road to attend a cramped bedsitter party held by two of Emma's venomous attendants; the excursion takes on otherworldly shapes and contours, becomes wreathed in mystical trappings, an Alice-in-Wonderland trip deep into some wholly fantastic bolt-hole. Another time. Another world. The incident is never referred to again, largely owing to the fact that, shortly after this, Emma left me. Two days later I came breezily back to the flat, after a crate of lager taken incontinently in the company of Crazy Rodney, and simply found her gone. There was no note – there seldom is in such circumstances – merely the evidence of a precise, tidy mind in retreat: the bedside drawer plundered of its stock, the stack of clothes cleared from the wardrobe, the electric heater even. Two days later there came a postcard which claimed that 'I gave you the best of me and what did you give me in return? Anyway, you never had any fucking money.'

What did I do? I remember standing uncertainly in the lounge for a while before swaying off to search for fresh signs of Emma's departing spoor. I even remember crying a bit, not for Emma, certainly not for Emma, but for the sense of passing time which loomed up briefly in front of me and then slowly receded. In the bedroom I found at last a tangible reminder of her going: carrier bags of mementoes from the Dean Street days spilled out randomly over the bedspread. There were rows of videos in their black plastic boxes, the odd copy of *Bouncers, Flesh*, that sort of thing, scuffed black-and-white photographs, a few of Morty's old business cards. Surmounting it all, curiously enough, was a photograph of Elaine. I looked at it for a while – it was an early one, the gesture unconvincing, the abandon suspiciously feigned, the general effect not in the least erotic, simply a bored and not particularly happy girl taking her clothes off in front of a camera – before settling down to gather up the sprawling detritus.

A week later, the rent unpaid and the furniture sold off, the threatening bills lying piled up in the hall, the stray messages from Morty and Terry Chimes unanswered, I left London for good.


Nearly dark. Outside in Glebe Road the streetlamps are going on, singly and in twos and threes, up the hill to the distant horizon of bunched cars and clustered rooftops. Rain coming in over the dun East Anglian sky. Below there is dense, uneasy silence.

*Wait and see is best.* The car arrived about an hour ago. It sits there still, ten yards down the street, wedged up against Fat Eric's day-glo Hillman. I wouldn't have noticed it were it not for the two figures in the front, narrowly outlined in the lamp-light glare. Occasionally they light cigarettes and I can see the tiny orange glimmers rise and fall. What else? Earlier on Fat Eric and Kay went past arm-in-arm, the former clutching a stupendous carry-out from the off-licence: I don't think they saw me. Twice in the last hour the telephone has rung. I haven't answered it. The second time it rang on uncontrollably for three or four minutes until at the end, just before it stopped, it was like a drill boring into my ear canal, a circular saw biting into the blameless trees.

I pad across to the window, steal another look at the car. Shadows obscure the watchful faces. Two hours back I had a mad idea. Pack a suitcase, head off to the city centre and find a bus. A bus to anywhere. To one of those gaunt, windswept villages on the coast: Bacton, Sea Palling, Mundesley. Winter out in a fisherman's cottage behind the dunes, walk along the empty beaches, watch the glistening sea and think about it all. But then a queer, paralysing inertia set in. What if there wasn't a bus? What if there wasn't a cottage? By the time the car arrived it had reached the status of a pleasant daydream, something to occupy the mind in the face of more pressing contingencies, nothing you would actually do.

I have always dreaded a deliberate step.

Morty had strong views about how a piece of cinema should end. He disapproved, instinctively, of films which erupted into a single, mighty conclusion – the couple, after much incidental tribulation, ecstatically reunited, the flaming car disappearing over the cliff top, the sudden remorseless shifting of circumstance This is not to say that he distrusted the working out of inexorable fate, merely that he had a dislike of finality imposed for its own sake, of lines drawn randomly at the foot of a page when the interior logic of what had gone before suggested endless turnings over and re-evaluation. His own films occasionally ended with a single potent image: a figure fixed unalterably in the camera's eye; a tangle of moving limbs; a face transfixed suddenly by exultation or despair. More often they suggested a process that was destined to continue, the camera apparently removing itself at some quite arbitrary point, interrupting a scene whose climax might reasonably appear to take place at some time in the future. So a Leisurevision production might end in the middle of a conversation – the following remarks tantalisingly absent – with two lovers taking off their clothes, with a couple, enigmatic, their intentions by no means clear, striding hesitantly towards one another.

Just as Morty believed that there was no such thing as a finite beginning, so he believed that there was no such thing as a finite end. It suited him to allege uncertainty, to leave his audience at a crossroads of plausible exit routes, each somehow hinted at, or at any rate not discounted by what had gone before. This characteristic invested even his most trivial productions. An example of this was a short early film erected around a girl's inability to decide between the contending attractions of twin brothers. A plot of exquisite tergiversation, each shift in allegiance swiftly cancelled out or overthrown, it ended with the girl confronted simultaneously by both men and compelled to make a last, irrevocable choice. As she opens her mouth and begins to speak, silence descends: the credits roll. Each of her attendants remains impassive. Or there was the use of telephone calls, in Morty's hands transformed into a device of unparalleled complexity and confusion. Numbers of Morty's films ended with telephone calls: with buxom women crouched anxiously over cradled receivers, sudden intimations of emotional fracture or despair. I remember in particular a film called *Embracing the Slaughterer* – the Brechtian title chosen by myself – in which the technique received its most systematic application. An erotic thriller, a genre in which Morty excelled, its motif was the reparation exacted upon a venal anti-hero by his former associates. Invested with every kind of deception, involving complicated snares and ruses from which the stooge was quite unable to extricate himself, it concluded with the man entombed in a silent house with a single sinister familiar. Quietly, with only the briefest flurries of Kafkaesque dialogue, an air of desperate menace was built up: references to 'them', a message which 'they' will ultimately deliver, a destiny which is in 'their' hands. Finally, a state of maximal anxiety having been sustained almost to breaking point, the telephone rings. The familiar answers it, his expression ambiguous, remote. As he puts down the receiver and turns to his companion, the film ends.

But I digress . . . Outside there is movement in the street, car doors slamming, footfalls on the pavement, a muffled undercurrent of conversation. And thinking about it, I would have liked to be in Bacton or Mundesley, staring out across the mutinous sea, in a world without redress or retribution. The rain gusts against the window, the mad, unappeasable rain. Beyond, a blanket of cloud hangs across the line of the park and the naphtha glow of the far-off streets. I look out of the window: the car is empty now, the figures are gone and the wind surges up through the road's dead corridor, uncurls itself and taps its fingers against the pane. Somewhere in the distance glass shatters, and I remember other glass breaking long ago, Terry Chimes standing over the broken bottle in Mr Tovacs' studio, the bulbs exploding in the Dean Street loft. There is pandemonium in my head, the telephone begins to ring again in the hall but I pay it no heed, sit here tensed and expectant, waiting for whatever will happen to happen.